ECHOES
ON THE
WIND

A Maggie O'Shea

Romantic Suspense

Dear Jimmy —
Welcome to
Maggie's World —
Music Tells our Stories
xo
Helaine Mario

Helaine Mario

Suncoast
Publishing

Echoes on the Wind / Helaine Mario

Hardcover ISBN:978-1-7351849-7-5

Paperback ISBN: 978-1-7351849-6-8

SUNCOAST PUBLISHING

Sarasota, FL

Cover Design by Madeira James

Author Photo by Ron Mario

DEDICATION

For my beautiful Family – Jessie and Brad, Sean and Jenny,
my brother Rod and his dear wife Dori,
You are always there for me.

For the Dear Friends who know (almost) all my secrets –
My Sisters of the Heart, Barbara, Deborah and Pat
& 'Mes Gloires' – my Glories – Sheila, Bonnie, Kathy and Snookie

For my five beautiful Grands, who fill my world with magic –
Ellie and Tyler Danaceau, and Clair, Declan and Ian Mario
Always love what you do. Don't let others define you.
If you can help someone, help them.
Try to leave the world a better place.
And, darlings, always know that I love you unconditionally.

And for Ron, my blue-eyed vagabond
For 57 years you made me think, feel and laugh.
I miss you like crazy, I love you still.
More than you can imagine…

TITLES FROM

HELAINE MARIO

Firebird

The Maggie O'Shea Series:

The Lost Concerto

Dark Rhapsody

Shadow Music

Echoes on the Wind

PRAISE FOR HELAINE MARIO
and
The Maggie O'Shea
Romantic Suspense Series

"Mario has once again hit all the right notes with Shadow Music, drawing the reader into a landscape of art and music... using a tuning fork of spine-tingling suspense."
—Sandra Brown, *New York Times* best-selling author

"Gripping, intense, and lyrical, [Shadow Music] is a heartbreaking journey wrapped in a page-turning mystery. Ruthless greed, devastating courage, long-lost secrets—and a riveting ending that's a crescendo of emotional realization, deep understanding, and haunting inspiration."
—Hank Phillippi Ryan, *USA Today* best-selling author

"Music is not just backdrop here but also a character that permeates Maggie's life... bolstered by the transformative power of classical music, Maggie finds what has been lost, including herself. Brava!"
—*Library Journal* (Starred Review)

"From Manhattan and Washington to Vienna and Salzburg, *Dark Rhapsody* by Helaine Mario takes the reader on a suspense-rich journey into a violent collision of the worlds of lost art, famous musicians, and international politics. Mario writes with the soul of a poet, painting her characters and scenes with deft touches of insight and wit. Her heroine, Maggie O'Shea, will burrow into your heart. *Dark Rhapsody* is that rare novel—a story that's a page-turner and a deeply felt character study."
—Gayle Lynds, *New York Times* best-selling author

BRITTANY

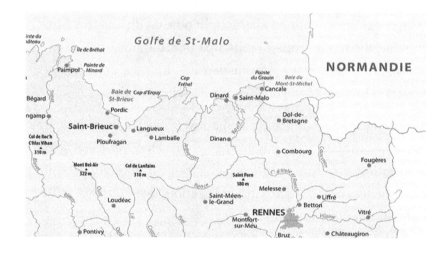

Brittany plays an important role in *Echoes on the Wind*. I have included this close-up map of northeastern Brittany to help readers envision key locations in the story. If you were to sail north by ferry, you would reach London in approximately 2¾ hours. If you were to take the train east from Saint Malo, you would reach Paris in approximately 2¾ hours. Brittany's closest neighbor to the north is Normandy, a crucial location in turning the position of power from the Axis to Allied troops. The Allied invasion on 6 June 1944, became known as D-Day. Allied troops landed on the coast of Normandy, marking the start of the campaign to liberate Europe and defeat Germany.

Cancale is the location of Clair Rousseau's cottage on the north coast of Brittany, France.

OVERTURE

"Like so many things that matter, it began with an accident."
David Ignatius, 12/28/98

NOVEMBER, 1943. THE NIGHT TRAIN TO PARIS

Light and dark.

The bleak November landscape rushed past the train's window. Black tree branches against the dark night sky, then a sudden flash of light. Then blackness again.

The blackout had claimed the streetlamps and cottage windows. Clair Rousseau stared out the rain-streaked glass, waiting for the next glimpse of light. A lone lantern. Car headlights tilted down, a sliver of gold beyond a cracked curtain. Sheet lightning over distant hills, a glimmer of light on water. But all she saw was the blurred, pale oval of her reflection staring back at her. Dark hair scraped back, framing huge eyes beneath winged brows, sharp cheekbones, the too-wide mouth.

No hint of the emotions flowing through her, except for the deep purple shadows beneath her eyes.

The dim, four-person compartment was cold, and she pulled her coat more tightly around her body. The seat beside her was still empty, thank God. Across from her, two German officers. One asleep, snoring loudly, his hands slack between thick gray-green uniformed knees. The other awake, a *Gauloises* cigarette clamped between thin lips, a jagged line of white scars marring his left cheek. The narrow, fox-like face stared at her through thick round glasses and wreathes of curling blue smoke. His jacket was heavy with insignia, oak leaves, medals. Military Intelligence, she thought with a sudden chill. A high rank, SD or Abwehr. What was he thinking?

The watchful, unblinking eyes made her afraid. Like a snake's eyes, waiting to strike. She looked away, forcing herself not to reach for her satchel, touch her identity papers for reassurance.

The carriage's glassed door slid back and forth with an unnerving rattle as the train rocked around a bend. From the hallway came the sharp scent of burning coal, wafting back from the old steam engine several cars ahead. A cloud of steam billowed past the window like sudden fog.

She could feel the vibration beneath her, hear the rumble of the train's wheels speeding along the tracks. The lonely call of a train whistle, echoing in the night. A quick flare of light, illuminating the rain like silver threads streaming down the window.

Light and dark. Light and dark.

Movement at the edge of her vision. A tall figure appeared in the hallway, beyond the door. Her chest tightened. Would she ever feel safe again?

A sharp crack of thunder, a sudden bright flash lighting her face.

"Mademoiselle Clair?"

Startled, her head came up. The stranger had stopped, was staring into the compartment. Across from her, the watchful German stiffened and slid pale eyes toward the voice.

Be careful.

There was something familiar about the gaunt face, the faint, questioning smile just visible above a thick woolen scarf. She stood quickly, stepping between the German and the carriage door to block the officer's view.

"Oui," she said softly, peering into the dim hallway. The man nodded and moved closer. Something about those gentle eyes, the arch of silver brows. Memory surged. *Father Jean-Luc.*

She flashed him a warning glance for silence and stepped into the train's narrow corridor, closing the door firmly behind her. *"Mon Père,* is it really you?"

"Oui, ma petite, c'est moi." The priest pulled the scarf down to offer a glimpse of his white Roman collar, then lost his smile as he gazed over her shoulder and saw the Germans. "But we cannot talk here. Come with me."

He slipped a hand beneath her elbow and guided her to the end of the dark passageway, where an open exit door led across shifting metal plates to the train's next car. She felt the sudden bite of night wind on her face, cold and wet with mist. Here the clatter of the train wheels was loud enough to hide their conversation.

They sheltered just inside the doorway, in the shadows, away from the rain. Outside, the countryside of France rushed by, then disappeared in a billow of black smoke. In the dim corridor, the planes of the priest's face were lit by a tiny, flickering overhead bulb.

Light and dark. Light and dark.

The priest looked down at her, shook his head. "Little Clair Rousseau," he murmured. "Now such a beautiful young woman. It's been–what?–four years since we met? You were just thirteen, I think. Playing the piano in your parents' apartment. Bach, yes? It was so beautiful, so stirring. I hope you are still playing?"

She shook her head. "You need hope to create music, *Père."* She looked back toward her carriage compartment. The hallway was empty. "But I remember that day. The war was coming. You asked us to help you remove the stained-glass windows from Sainte-Chapelle. To save them from the bombing."

"You were fearless, Clair. I remember watching you, swaying at the top of that impossibly high ladder. The morning light was coming through the stained glass, spilling over you like shimmering jewels. I'll never forget it. I told myself, Clair means light, she is perfectly named."

He leaned down. "And I can still see your sister, Elle—too young to help us, *bien sûr*—dancing around the altar."

Her expression softened. "Elle loved to dance. It was the last happy day I can remember." She lifted her eyes to his, took a breath. "Paris was another lifetime, *Père*."

"You cannot lose hope," he told her. "The glass pieces are in a safe place. Beauty and goodness cannot be destroyed. You will see the stained-glass windows back in Sainte-Chapelle when the war is over. I know it."

She shook her head. "I wish I had your faith."

"God has his plans. There is a reason we've met by chance on the night train to Paris." Concern flashed in his eyes. "But you've been in Brittany? Dangerous times for a young woman to be traveling alone, Clair."

She looked out at the black trees rushing past the doorway, and felt the blackness deep in her heart. "I am alone now, *Père*."

"*Mon Dieu*. What happened?"

"My father knew that war was inevitable. Not long after we saved the glass my parents moved us from Paris to the coast near Saint-Malo to be safe. Such irony. They had no idea how dangerous Brittany would become. And then..."

She could not stop the sudden rush of tears that filled her eyes. "The Gestapo shot my father last year, in a retaliation roundup for an act of sabotage by the Resistance. He was with the Liberty Network, they had bombed a train track. He stepped forward, admitted it, hoping to save the others. But still they took thirty innocent people from our village, murdered them in the square."

"Oh no, Clair." The priest made a quick sign of the cross. "I am so sorry. And your mother, your sister?"

"I don't know, *Père*. I was studying in Paris, I begged them to come stay with me. But *Maman* refused. When I returned last month to see them, the house was empty. They were just… gone. The neighbors said the Germans took them, in the night. The mayor was told they were being relocated to Poland."

The priest paled. "*Désolé*. I will pray for their souls."

Anger erupted, spilled out. "Prayers did not help my family! I have no time for prayer now. Or sorrow. Even avenging my father will have to wait. I need all my energy now to find my mother and my sister."

He bent toward her. "I am afraid you are still too fearless for your own good. Tell me what you're doing, little one."

She turned once more to scan the dark hallway, then leaned closer. "I excelled in languages in my *lycée* studies these last years," she whispered. "I am fluent in several languages, including German and English. I hope to find a new job, in the Hotel Majestic in Paris, where the German High Command is quartered. Then I will join the Resistance, find a way to get news of *Maman* and Elle. I must find them!"

He gazed down at her for a long moment, then put a hand on her shoulder.

"Perhaps I know of another way," he murmured.

The sound of a door opening. Wavering shadows spilled into the train's corridor. Then the red glow of a cigarette, a spiral of smoke. She froze as the German officer turned toward them.

"Find me at Èglise Saint-Gervais, in the Marais," the priest whispered quickly. "I am with the Resistance there. You could work with me, we need someone like you to –."

A sudden terrifying screech of metal wheels. Clair felt herself thrown to the floor as the train braked, slammed to a shuddering stop. Stunned, Clair reached out, felt the still body of the priest beside her. "*Mon Père...*"

Shouts in German in the darkness, the clatter of heavy boots. When she raised her head she saw flashing blue lights against the night sky.

Light and dark. Light and dark.

PART 1

"An echo of the past…"

Victor Hugo

"There are four things in this life that will change you:
Love, Music, Art, and Loss.
The first three will keep you wild and full of passion.
May you allow the last to make you brave."

—Erin van Vuren, Poet

CHAPTER 1

THE PRESENT
PERFORMING ARTS CENTER, MARTHA'S VINEYARD

Light and dark.

The stage was shadowed, lit only by a handful of overhead lights. One of the lights began to flicker, a bright flash illuminating Maggie O'Shea's face for a brief moment, then casting her into darkness.

Maggie sat at the Bechstein grand piano, marveling at the power, the responsive touch, the unique tone of the beautiful instrument. Prokofiev deserves no less, she thought.

The score propped above the keyboard was marked by penciled notations, heavy lines, arrows and slashes. Prokofiev's Piano Concerto No. 2 was the ultimate challenge for a pianist, but Maggie had chosen it because it was so emotional, so personal. So incredibly beautiful.

It has the most to say, she thought.

And, oh, she had so much she wanted to say. Always, since she'd been a young child whose bare feet did not yet reach the pedals, she had spoken through her music. Told the piano her secrets long before she told anyone else.

Her earliest memory was of being curled beneath the grand piano, listening to her mother play, surrounded–cradled–by music. Then later sitting on the piano bench by her mother's side. The smoothness of the keys beneath tiny fingers, the sound that seemed to magically flow from her shoulders to her fingertips. Seeing the colors, making the piano sing. Making the rest of the world disappear.

But this piece – face it, *every* piece lately – was giving her trouble. Something, some emotion, was just out of reach. Her mentor, the legendary pianist Gigi Donati, would say she was taking the easy way out by mastering technique but not the emotion. She could hear Gigi's smoky, exasperated voice in the shadows. *No, no, no! You are not growing, Maggie, your music is lifeless. Imagine you are kissing your lover goodbye for the last time. What do you feel? Now, again!*

Maggie sighed. She had been playing the first movement for an hour, with nary a lover in sight. Without *Espressivo*, as Gigi would demand. She would say, *You don't know the music yet. Take the time. Grow with the music. Illuminate its secrets. Make it yours.*

The light high above the stage flickered again, slipping her out of the light into darkness.

Light and dark, thought Maggie. The story of my music. The story of my life.

She closed her eyes, took a deep, shaky breath, and began to play the next phrase of music.

Look into the heart of the music, whispered Gigi from behind her. *Find its light. Find its soul.*

A few more chords, and suddenly Maggie's fingers stiffened, locked, slipped off the keys. Shaking her head, she gathered the sheet music and dropped it to the bench.

I just can't, Gigi. I know what's wrong, why I can't play. I just don't know how to fix it.

But deep down, she did know. What she needed was to *feel*. But once again, part of her was frozen.

You will not give up, she told herself. *You have so much joy waiting for you.* Raising her left hand to stretch tensed tendons, the engagement ring on her finger flashed emerald in the theater lights.

The flash of emerald green in a shadowed cabin. The memory washed over her and once again she was back in the moment.

She saw Michael's face, as craggy and strong as the mountains he loved, his granite eyes locked on hers.

What are you doing, Michael?

It's called offering you a ring, Maggie. The color of your eyes, the color of the mountains. It's been hidden in my sock drawer for months.

I know it's a ring. I mean…what are you doing?

Jumping off a cliff, it seems. Don't make me get down on one knee, darlin'. I'll never get back up.

Silver eyes blazing like a torch. *Marry me, Maggie.*

I…You…Oh, Love.

I'll take that as a yes, ma'am.

She smiled. Colonel Michael Jefferson Beckett. A man who had fallen in love with her when he didn't want to, a man she hadn't wanted to love back.

And yet.

It just *was*. Like music. And right this minute he was back in those beloved mountains of his, at his cabin in Virginia's Blue Ridge. Working on a secret project, he'd told her, with Dov, the Russian teenager in his care.

She pictured the battered, rugged face she knew so well. The quirk of his mouth, the spiky silver brows, eyes like river stones lockeds on her. His stillness, as if he was carved from mountains he loved. The way he listened…

Michael standing behind her, wrapping her naked body in a woven blanket.

Michael beneath her in the shadowed bedroom, whispering her name against her lips while her hair fell like dark rain around his face.

She breathed out in a long sigh. It had been an emotional several months but now, finally she was letting go of the past. Moving on. Ready to marry again. To spend the rest of her life with the Colonel, Dov and their rescue Golden, Shiloh. She had never expected this gift, this second chance at love.

She shook her head, barely recognizing the woman she'd become. For so long she'd thought of herself as a city girl. But the small cabin in the Blue Ridge Mountains was becoming her center. Her home. She heard music differently in the quiet of the mountains. Listened better.

Suddenly wanting to hear Michael's voice, she dialed his cell. Message.

"Hey you, it's me," she whispered. "Call me tonight, I'll wait up. I have so much to tell you."

If only...

If only she didn't have to tell Michael the secret she'd been keeping from him these past few weeks. That once again, a vicious murderer was threatening all she held dear. Dane, with his scarred, wolf-like face and mirrored sunglasses hiding his eyes. The one nightmare she could not put behind her.

Because now Dane was back in her life.

Over 4,500 miles to the east, the man who called himself Dane could not sleep. Still hours before dawn, shadows lay sharp across the tiles of the villa's bedroom, angling from the terrace doors. Dane sat in a cushioned chair, crutches propped beside him, staring out the glass at the black Aegean far below — waiting for the sun's light to spill over the horizon and fill the dark water with gold.

A sudden shift of the moon, and he caught his breath at his reflection in the window, All the mirrors in the villa had been shattered years ago, by his own hand. As shattered as his life. Now, caught off guard, he stared at the disfigured face of the stranger wavering in the glass.

Without warning his mind flung him back several years. He had been standing in the Kennedy Center's Grand Foyer, his French knife secure under his tuxedo jacket, when he had caught a glimpse of himself in the floor-to-ceiling mirrors. Tall and god-like, he'd had muscles that rippled beneath the silk, a strong carved face, flowing hair the color of wheat, streaked by the Provençal sun. A diamond in his left ear, mirrored aviator glasses that hid tiger-colored eyes. His stride had been long, fast and as powerful as the Jaguar he drove.

And then he had crossed paths with Magdalena O'Shea.

First, the badly burned hand, thanks to an encounter with Magdalena's colonel at a Provençal abbey. He held up his right hand, now encased in a tight black glove. Then the botched plastic surgery in Italy after being forced into hiding. The scarred, distorted face, the loss of an eye. And then, months later...he looked down at his withered legs. The fall. The sickening feeling of spinning into the void. The excruciating pain that followed. The months of unbearable physical therapy.

All because of one woman, Magdalena O'Shea.

He glanced at his Rolex. Early evening in the States. Firas should have arrived in Martha's Vineyard by now. He smiled. Until the time came, Firas would be his legs.

The image in the glass wavered, dissolved, and Dane turned away. "For death remembered should be like a mirror," he whispered. "Who tells us life's but a breath, to trust it, error."

CHAPTER 2

PERFORMING ARTS CENTER, MARTHA'S VINEYARD

The theater was quiet.

Maggie sat very still in the flickering shadows, trying to slow her hammering heart. One day at a time, she told herself. One *thing* at a time. She would not give up because of fear. She would tell Michael about Dane, they would deal with him together. She would find her way back to music again.

Tonight, she needed to focus on the reason she was here, in the Vineyard. She thought of the document in her purse. So many questions about the past needed answers.

Just four days earlier, she'd been at The Piano Cat, her music shop in Boston, suitcase packed and ready to spend a weekend celebrating her grandson Ben's second birthday in Cape Cod. The postman caught her just as she was locking the shop's bright blue door and handed her the thick envelope covered in airmail stamps, forwarded from Martha's Vineyard. "All the way from France," he smiled.

Years earlier, Maggie had arranged for all mail sent to the Vineyard cottage to be forwarded to her in Boston. Usually, the package consisted of gas and electric bills, property maintenance, the Vineyard Gazette and requests for money. But this time, only the official-looking envelope from France. She did not recognize the return address. It was addressed to her mother, Lily A. Rousseau, in elegant black script. But her mother had been dead for decades.

Maggie shook her head, pushing the thought of the document – and all the questions it raised – away until she got to her mother's cottage in Menemsha.

By serendipity, she'd caught the early ferry to the Vineyard. So she'd decided to stop here, at the theater. Spend a few hours with Prokofiev, center herself with music before stepping into the past. The Performing Arts Center here in Oak Bluffs was just a thirty-minute drive from her mother's cottage at the western end of the Vineyard. She still could be there before dark.

A phone call to the manager, an old friend, had resulted in the key to the stage door. Her gaze swept the theater, empty and dark now, with only the tiny aisle lights winking. But she knew how beautiful it was. Just a bit bigger than a Broadway theater, the Vineyard's Arts Center was modern and intimate, with its paneled wood ceiling, contemporary lighting, rich plum colors, and those stark white panels for excellent acoustics. She'd given a concert on this stage almost every summer for many years, to help raise funds for the community she loved.

The stage – any stage – was home for her. She could *feel* the history, the ghosts, all around her. The stage was her safe place. All the familiar sounds and scents and memories, the place where she belonged. All the infinitesimal fragments of herself and her music that she'd left behind wherever she'd played the piano over the years, like all the musicians who had come before her. She was in the scuffed wood of the stage, the motes dancing in stage lights, the swish of heavy velvet curtains. The long tuning note of the "A" string. The place where she could fall into her own private world of beauty and music.

Maggie looked down at her engagement ring once more and took a deep, healing breath. She had never expected to be this happy again.

If only…

She checked her watch, forced the anxiety to the back of her mind. It was time to head to Menemsha. Time to deal with the documents from France, and the letter, so shocking and unexpected, addressed to her mother. Hopefully the answers were here, somewhere in her mother's old cottage.

And after that? She would go to the mountains, tell Michael about the danger that had come back into her life.

One thing at a time.

A sound, somewhere high above her. A scrape. A footstep?

A thrum of ice along her spine. She glanced up at the narrow catwalk, some thirty feet above her head. Placed high above the stage, the elevated platform housed much of the stage lighting and sound equipment for the technicians. This afternoon, the catwalk was hidden in deep shadow.

She'd locked the stage door behind her; thought she was the only one in the theater today. She lifted her head to listen. Nothing. Imagination.

The backstage and wings were quiet, clothed in darkness. Just the few lights left on, for safety, and to illuminate the Bechstein. Her thoughts flew back to another darkened stage, months earlier. Carnegie Hall. She'd thought she was alone there, too. But someone had been watching her. Waiting for her. Someone who had sent her hundreds of blooded-red roses.

Dane.

Another sound, the scrape of a shoe.

Not imagination. "Who's there?" she called.

The lights went out.

Maggie rose from the piano bench, fear clutching her chest as she stood in total darkness. *Don't panic. You know the way to the exit. You know self-defense.* "SING," she whispered, hearing her instructor's voice. "Stomach, Instep, Nose, Groin."

A rush of air, just to her left.

And then the crash, loud as an explosion, metal on metal, glass shattering across the stage. The sharp sting, like slivers of ice, against her leg.

Good God! She ducked, sheltered behind the Bechstein.

High above her, the thud of running feet.

Oh no you don't. You don't get to threaten me on my stage, damn you! Not again.

She found her iPhone, clicked on the flashlight. Ran toward the metal ladder that led up to the catwalk. Shoving the phone into the pocket of her shirt, she reached out, grasped the rungs, began to climb.

Hold on, don't look down. Damn, damn, how many rungs were there? Hand over hand. Just do it.

Somehow, she reached the top.

High above the stage, the catwalk disappeared into the darkness. She stepped onto the platform slowly, gripped the railing with her left hand, and aimed the flashlight toward the far end of the catwalk.

A profile of a man, pale and narrow, caught in the light. He stopped, turned to look directly at her, and smiled. Then he vanished into the shadows.

Light and dark.

Her breath rushed out. A stranger. *Not Dane.*

Footsteps on metal stairs, the slam of a distant door.

But there was something left behind on the metal catwalk.

A single blood-red rose.

CHAPTER 3

BECKETT'S CABIN
THE BLUE RIDGE MOUNTAINS, VA

The cabin was set among towering pines in the foothills of Virginia's Blue Ridge Mountains. Colonel Michael Beckett stood on the redwood deck that cantilevered out over the mountainside, listening to his messages, his eyes on the deep blue lake below him.

"Hey you, it's me." Maggie's voice, low and fluid. He smiled, pressed the phone closer to his ear. "I miss you, Michael. I miss Dov and Shiloh. I miss your mountains." A breath. "I'll wait up. I have so much to tell you."

Something in her voice. It made him think of a swan gliding smoothly over the surface of the water—but paddling furiously underneath. Yeah, something was wrong. He dialed her cell, but it went straight to voicemail. "Call me, darlin'."

She'd be here this time tomorrow. About time; he'd missed her like crazy. Missed the wildflower scent of her hair, the electric shock of her touch. The way her hand reached for his when they sat in front of the fire. The music that spilled from her heart.

He pictured her standing alone on the deck, in the quiet of a day's end, gazing out at the mountains she'd come to love. Her beautiful face lifted to the deepening sky, huge emerald eyes framed by a dark cloud of hair. Speaking eyes, he always called them.

She was complex, intense, funny, crazy talented. Infuriating. Brave as hell. Wore her heart on her sleeve, loved fiercely. Music was so deep in her; she could make the most beautiful music he'd ever heard out of thin air. Yet somehow, she'd chosen him, a man who couldn't find a piano in a music store. He still wasn't sure why a woman used to stage lights and the world of international music wanted to live with him deep in the mountains.

All he knew was that she gave him the deepest sense of peace he had ever known.

She also was a woman on a first name basis with trouble.

"Maggie's gonna love this, Dov." Beckett held the newly sanded birdhouse up to the light.

The boy, who rarely smiled, just lifted his chin and shrugged too-sharp shoulders. The "v" of the bird wing scar on his cheek was stark on his pale skin.

Man and boy stood in Beckett's old garage, just behind the cabin. Beckett's black Jeep was parked on the right side of the garage, beside one ancient bike and a newer, used three-speed. He had remodeled the left half of the space into a wood workshop. The air smelled of motor oil, varnish, fresh woodchips, and pinesap.

"I dunno," said the boy. "You're sure she'll like it? It's a *birdhouse*, for crissakes, not a jewelry box."

"You kidding me? Maggie O'Shea lives and breathes *outside* the box." Beckett grinned as he ran a hand over the smooth, graceful angles. "It's beautiful work, kid, you should be proud. And no one loves birds more than Maggie. She worries about them every fall when they fly south and then stands on the deck for hours, watching the sky, waiting for their return. Heck, she's even named our cardinals. Barack and Michelle, Wolfgang and Constanze."

This won a faint smile. "Yeah, that sounds like Maggie."

"She'll be back here tomorrow night. You can surprise her." Beckett set the birdhouse down carefully and turned to boy. "So, you want to take a bike ride before dinner?"

At the mention of dinner, Shiloh, Beckett's aging, three-legged Golden Retriever, raised his head, eyes bright with expectation. Rescued years earlier from an Afghan village, after losing his front right leg in a firefight, the dog had found his forever home here in the mountains.

The boy squatted down to rub a gentle hand from the Golden's silken head down his scarred back to his tail. The dog fluffed with pleasure and pushed a wet nose against Dov's cheek.

Late day sun angled in through the garage windows, streaking the boy's shaggy pale hair with gold, glinting deep in the impossibly blue eyes. Beckett felt the familiar stirring. Dov had been with him now for some six months, a lanky Russian foster kid from Brooklyn. Distrustful and haunted, the almost-sixteen-year-old still suffered from PTSD following his mother's brutal murder and his own confrontation with his mother's killer. Even with the unconditional love of Shiloh and a beautiful, scarred mare named Lady in Black, the angry dark moods and night terrors continued to strike.

Beckett shook his head, knowing he was out of his depth. The kid was all jagged edges, with loneliness, aggression and fear warring in the distant blue eyes. And yet—there were brief glimpses of the man still forming his hopes and dreams. Moments of quiet dignity. Beckett knew he had to be patient and give the boy the time he needed to heal. To trust life again.

We're all scarred in one way or another, thought Beckett, his eyes on the boy and the dog. Kid liked working with wood, was good at it. Today was a good day.

So far.

"So," said Beckett, "any idea what you'd like to build next? Skis, maybe, with the winter snows coming—"

The boy's fierce low voice stopped him in his tracks. "You're not my damned social worker, man! I don't need your keep-the-poor-street-kid-busy therapy."

Whoa. Beckett turned slowly. "You really think that's what I'm doing?"

Twin blue flames returned his stare. "Aren't you?"

What the hell? Beckett hesitated, his eyes on the five-foot high oblong shape against the far wall that was covered by an old sheet. Then he spoke to Shiloh. "Guess it's time to show this kid what we've been working on late at night."

With a look that said, *"About time,"* Shiloh lumbered to his feet.

"Go for it," said Beckett, gesturing at the draped structure in the corner. "It's not quite finished, but I guess it won't hurt for you to take a look."

The boy was beside the covered shape in three long strides and yanked off the sheet to expose a bookcase fashioned from glowing cherrywood.

"Jeez, Colonel…"

"Nice work, right? Guess you're not the only one who knows his way around a saw and a piece of wood."

The boy ran a reverent hand over the smooth shelves. "It's beautiful. These last few days, I just thought you were giving me Busy-Hands-Rehab. But this…"

"Working with your hands – with wood – is an art, kid. Hard, honest work, a skill you can be proud of. Maybe even use some day. Some of my best times as a kid were in my dad's workshop." He smiled at the memory. "Although you might be right on about the therapy. Late nights with the wood have sure helped me and Shiloh get through some bad times, right, boy?"

The Golden did not disagree.

His eyes locked on the bookcase, Dov said, "Where are you gonna put this?"

"Where do you think? Your *room*, kid. You're the guy with all those books."

The boy's eyes darkened. "I'm staying in the *guest* room, Beckett."

"Not any more, Dov. Haven't you been paying attention?" Beckett glanced at the Golden and wagged his spikey silver brows. "It's *your* room now. You *live here*. With us."

The boy stared at him, his face registering doubt, disbelief— and something more. His fingers fastened on the black leather cord he always wore around his left wrist.

Watching the expressions race like storm clouds across Dov's eyes, Beckett felt his chest tighten once more. Uh oh. Too soon? Kid needed to know he belonged. To not be afraid. But damn, why did he mention those times with his own father?

At that moment Shiloh stiffened and shifted to attention, ears flat back as a low growl rolled from his throat.

Man and boy turned. A breath, and then they heard it, too. The sound of wheels crunching on gravel. The cough of an engine. Silence.

Dov froze, his face the color of ashes. "It's him," he whispered, panic icing through his words. "He's come back for me."

"Like hell he has," muttered Beckett, reaching for the jagged-toothed ripsaw on the workbench.

A shadow crossed the window. Beckett and the Golden moved at the same time to stand between the boy and the slowly opening door.

CHAPTER 4

MENEMSHA, MARTHA'S VINEYARD

Maggie stood on the weathered cottage porch looking out over Menemsha Pond, waiting for the beauty to calm her racing heart. In the pale November sunlight, the water shimmered like a tarnished pewter shield. She inhaled deeply, the air sharp with the familiar low-tide scents of shells and seaweed, fish and damp sand.

The shingled gray cottage, left to her so long ago by her mother, Lily, was set in the pines just above the tiny fishing village of Menemsha, on the southwest corner of the Vineyard. Maggie gazed out past the harbor to the sea. How often had she stood here as a child, wondering what life held for her?

Over the years, she had run across these beaches and moors in good times and bad. She had played Chopin on the beloved old upright under the skylight in the living room, given birth to her son Brian in the ancient brass bed upstairs during a raging storm. She had married her husband, Johnny O'Shea, on the windswept cliffs of Aquinnah, watched for his sails to appear on the horizon every day at sunset, and screamed into the roaring dark when he disappeared so tragically from her life.

Now, standing here at this moment, she felt she'd come full circle. She was taking her life back, beginning a new one. It was time to bring Michael here, share with him this side of her life. Her past. Time to come to terms with the memories, both joyful and heartbreaking. She knew who she was now, where she was going.

Unless…Her heart hammered painfully against her ribs as the images flooded into her head—the crashing spotlight at the theater, the crimson rose left on a dark catwalk high above the stage. The frightening face staring back at her. Who was it? She closed her eyes, her body taut as piano wire. This story isn't over, she told herself.

What if Dane came back into her life? What if all the happiness she was finding again was taken from her? The past rushed at her, dark and bone-crushing.

Dane, the disfigured and vengeful man with the terrifying yellow wolf's eyes and whispery voice. The man who, for over a year, had stalked her and tried to take her life. The man who had threatened her and the lives of those she loved, who had filled her rehearsal room last year with hundreds of blood red roses –and later, a single red rose on her pillow, perhaps the most terrifying moment of all.

Maggie shuddered at the memory. "I am so over those damned roses," she said aloud.

For months, she'd thought Dane was dead. She'd been with him that fateful night last spring in New York, seen him take his last breath. But there was no record of his death. The woman he had loved, Beatrice, had returned to Greece—to the Aegean island where Dane had gone to ground once before, after almost killing Maggie and the people she loved. Could he still be there, hiding in the sharp Aegean shadows? Like a wolf, lying in wait…

Maggie gazed into the dark woods beyond the cabin, overwhelmed by an inexplicable sense of dread. Evening light slanted through bare branches that shifted and whispered in the shadows. Was that brief glimmer a face, staring back at her? God, was someone watching her, right this minute?

Stop it Stop it Stop it! No one was out there. Don't panic, don't give him that power over you. Push Dane to the back of your mind.

Her engagement ring winked green in the slanted light. Maggie shivered, as if touched by a sudden cold wind, and gathered her jacket more closely around her. The crashing light, the rose, the music just beyond her reach. Her mother's unsettling legal documents, threatening to thrust her into the past.

Maggie closed her eyes. For more than two years she'd lived with loss and grief, violence and terror. But finally, these last months since the engagement, her life had turned the corner. She'd been strong, happy. Moving on. She'd played the Rach Two at the Kennedy Center as if inspired, as if Rachmaninoff himself had guided her hands, until she no longer knew where her arms ended and the piano keys began. And the hours spent with Michael at his cabin in the mountains were filled with laughter and love. Everything had felt hopeful. Right.

Until two weeks ago. First, the late night calls, with only rasped breathing when she answered. Then the mail, with no return address, sent to her music shop in Boston. A photograph of a piano, its keys covered in blood. A newspaper clipping featuring a recent article about her, ripped into pieces. And, arriving just before she left Boston, a rare edition of Shakespeare's *Hamlet*.

Now, the shattered stage light. She needed to look into Michael's eyes when she told him. No way that conversation would end well.

Tonight, for the first time since her engagement, she found herself unsure, uneasy, with a sudden and inexplicable sense of foreboding that her happiness was not going to last. Her breath caught in her throat. For the first time, she had the stomach-plummeting feeling that her wedding wasn't going to happen.

But, oh, she yearned for the new life they planned—the cabin in the mountains, sleeping every night in Michael's arms, building a new family together with Dov and Shiloh, surrounded by her beloved music. All her hopes and dreams for the future.

If there is a future for us, she thought darkly.

Maggie lifted her chin, squared her shoulders, set her gaze on the sun spiraling toward the silvered sea. Everything is going to be *fine*, she told herself. You are going to have a beautiful wedding, a calm and happy life. For a brief moment, she almost believed it.

Her phone buzzed. Michael? No, an unknown number. She squinted down at the unsigned string of words.

Hello Magdalena. Are you enjoying the sunset?

Spiders skittered up her spine. She stared into the black tangle of trees, their tips catching the last orange glow of the setting sun. Off to the left, the sudden shiver of dark branches, the sharp snap of a branch. *No. I won't let you frighten me, damn you.*

Taking a deep breath, she focused on the words inscribed on the tee shirt she was wearing. *Never Underestimate a Woman with a Piano.* "Big mistake," she muttered. Very deliberately, she turned her back on the darkening woods, entered the cottage and, with a decisive snap, locked the door against the shadows of the night.

CHAPTER 5

BECKETT'S CABIN

"Sugar! Christ, man. A warning would have been nice," said Beckett, carefully setting the saw back on the table.

The tall, dark figure wandering around the workshop moved into a pool of lamplight and stopped, his eyes on the serrated saw. "Yo, Mike. Is that any way to greet an old pal?"

"You do what you gotta do," said Beckett. "Isn't that what you always say?"

"Mama's Rule *Numero Uno.*" Department of Justice Agent Simon Sugarman grinned as he squatted and held out a hand the size of a catcher's mitt toward the Golden. "Hey, my man Shiloh, gimme five."

Shiloh just stared at him.

"Hard to high-five with only one front leg, Sugar," muttered Beckett. His old friend still looked more like a Black rock star than an agent, with those brooding dark eyes, jet hair buzzed close, the sheen of a beard on his ebony jaw – and the single brilliant diamond earring catching the light.

Sugarman rose to his feet, flashed a broad smile as he ruffled the dog's golden coat. "Just an expression, right, Shiloh, my man?" He turned to Dov. "Howya doing, kid. Keeping Beckett out of trouble?"

Dov flashed a look at Beckett and cocked his chin. "The colonel says there's bad trouble and there's good trouble."

"He's right," said Sugarman. He turned to Beckett. "We've got to talk."

Beckett frowned at Dov. "Talk is code for *bad* trouble," he murmured. "Why don't you take Shiloh for a walk and I'll catch up with –"

"No way in hell, Beckett," said the boy, stepping closer. "I'm not going anywhere. I've got a right to know if this is about me." He glared at Sugarman. "Are you here because of Yuri Belankov? Have you found my mother's killer?"

"Why don't we all go into the cabin?" said Sugarman. "I sure could use a cold brew."

When they were settled in front of the fireplace, Sugarman turned to the boy. "No word on Yuri Belankov," he said quietly. "But he's high priority. My Justice team has been searching for him since he disappeared back in April. And I've called in favors from all my pals—guys at the CIA, Interpol, Customs, Homeland Security. Even the Feebs. These guys are good, they owe me. No way Yuri's getting back into the States without me knowing."

"He told me we weren't done," said Dov, his voice cracking with strain. "Swore he would come back for me. For Lady in Black."

"Not gonna happen," said Beckett. "Shiloh and I, we won't let him near you. Or your mare. *Capiche?*"

"I thought the flash drive my mom left for me would help find him," murmured the boy.

Sugarman pressed his lips together. "About that…"

Beckett scowled. "About *what?* The kid did good. There's enough info on that drive to call a Grand Jury, send Belankov away for a very long time."

"The thing is," Sugarman said slowly, "there was a fire in the evidence room two days ago. Hundreds of files and boxes lost. Including your mother's flash drive."

The boy paled, his "v"scar blazing. "Are you fucking kidding me, Agent?"

Sugarman held up a hand. "You like crossword puzzles, kid? Gimme an eight letter word for 'Capacity to accept delay or trouble without getting upset. Or angry.'"

Dov looked at the Golden as if to say, *what is with this guy?* Finally he said, "Patience." He stared at Sugarman for a long moment, his eyes old beyond his years. "But patience eventually runs out, Agent, and then I've got a special nine letter word for you – 'open, armed defiance.'"

"You've sure got some *cojones*, kid, but I suggest you save your *rebellion* for the Sunday Times." Sugarman shook his head. "We're going to find Belankov. That's a promise."

Dov gestured to Shiloh. "Whatever. I won't hold my breath. The Brigadier and I are out of here."

"Brigadier?" said Sugarman, looking around the room.

"Military dogs are one rank higher than their human," said Dov. "It's a sign of respect. And since Beckett is a colonel..."

"Got it," grinned Sugarman, saluting. "Brigadier Shiloh." Then his expression grew serious as he stepped closer to the boy. "Trust me, Dov, we won't stop looking for Belankov. With or without that evidence, he is gonna pay for what he did to you and your mom. And your mare."

Beckett and Sugarman watched the boy and dog disappear down the hallway. Then Beckett's eyes locked on Sugarman. "What the hell, Sugar? The flash drive just went up in smoke? FUBAR, man. You fucked up beyond all repair."

"Not beyond repair. I'm working on it, Mike. Trust me."

"Heard that one before. Find Belankov, Sugar. Because that kid has a huge target painted on his back. He knows it. And Dov has a way of taking things into his own hands. You and I both know Belankov's coming back for him. When we least expect it."

"Yeah. He's coming back. But not soon. His game of Russian Roulette went wrong, he's wanted for some very serious charges. He needs to wait for the heat to cool down."

"He won't wait for long. Belankov believes he lost everything because of Dov. He has a score to settle." Beckett leaned closer, locked eyes with his old friend. "You could have called us about the lost flash drive, Sugar. So how about you tell me why you're really here?"

The sun was just rising over the chimneyed rooftops of Paris when the man entered the Northwest gate of the Jardin du Luxembourg. He was dressed in a laborer's clothing—baggy pants, heavy dark jacket with the collar up, scuffed work boots. A black cap, pulled low, covered most of his hair and shaded his dark eyes against the setting sun.

He walked through the rose garden—nothing more than sad twisted stems on this cold November morning—toward the dozen chess tables and metal chairs set on gravel beneath a row of plane trees. Large brown leaves drifted and swirled across his path. Even at this hour, several aging men and one woman sat in the chairs, wrapped in their coats and scarves, absorbed in their games. At the far end of the row, only one seat remained open. An aging Frenchman was dragging the small metal table into a patch of weak sunlight.

Ah. Emil was here today. Half hidden by the cloud of smoke from his ever-lit *Gitanes*, he was a good player, smart and quick. A worthy opponent. Perhaps he would begin with the Queen's Gambit today. A favorite Russian opening, *da?*

Chess was proving to be a useful way to pass the time. To challenge his mind. To teach his dark Russian soul patience until he could return to the States. He'd set his plan in motion. Soon, he would take back the life that was stolen from him.

He shuffled toward the table. "Eh, Emil, I had dinner last night with a chess grandmaster. But the tablecloth was checked in black-and-white squares. It took him two hours to pass the salt. Ha!"

The man seated at the table stared at him without comprehension.

Yuri Belankov sighed. "You need to get a sense of humor, my friend." He pulled the empty chair toward him, sat. *"Allons-nous jouer?"*

Shall we play?

CHAPTER 6

MENEMSHA, MARTHA'S VINEYARD

All the cottage doors and windows were locked and protected by a state-of-the-art security system. Thanks to Maggie's childhood friend Rick, now a Vineyard detective, a Menemsha Sheriff's SUV was parked in the front driveway. And although she still refused to own a gun—one of the few up-all-night-but-still-unresolved arguments with Michael—she had her father's old hickory baseball bat beside her.

Maggie sat cross-legged on the faded carpet in her mother Lily's old bedroom. Her own bedroom was just down the hall. She hadn't been in this room for at least a year.

It was a beautiful room, with high windows overlooking the pond. A cluster of silver-framed family photographs graced the bureau. An ancient turntable, her mother's prized vinyl records, a desk piled with sheet music. The soft blue woolen throw, still draped like a shawl over the reading chair. The walls, bedding, and curtains, diaphanous with dusk, were the color of pearls. Being in the room was like being inside a seashell, the only color coming from a large landscape on the far wall.

Now flames crackled in the iron stove in the corner, the glass of wine beside her sparked with ruby light. The old brass-trimmed leather trunk at the foot of the bed was open in front of her, surrounding her with her mother's scents of sandalwood and Guerlain.

The ancient trunk had belonged to her French grandmother – her mother's mother, Clair Rousseau, the woman Lily had always referred to as *Maman*. The initials *CR* were carved into the ornate lid. Maggie had been raised by her father's mother, in Boston, after her mother had died. She'd never met this French grandmother, knew very little about her. Her own mother Lily had died too soon, before she was able to share all the stories of her past. Before they were able to travel to France together, as a promised birthday gift, to introduce Maggie to her French grandmother.

Her gaze moved to the bureau, found the photograph of her mother's parents – a faded, formal sepia portrait of a fair-haired man in a U.S. Army uniform, cap in hand, and her slender, twenty-something grandmother, staring straight ahead, in an ivory satin gown that pooled at her feet. A lace veil fell like a gossamer curtain over her eyes, but Maggie could see her expression – wistful, with just a hint of sadness. What had she been thinking?

So many questions I wish I had asked.

Maggie gazed down at the letter in her hands, the one she'd brought from Boston. The reason she was sitting here now with the open trunk before her.

It was a legal document, written in French on heavy cream vellum, addressed to her mother. Her French was rusty at best, but there was her mother's maiden name, Lily A. Rousseau, and the name of a French law firm, Saint-Malo Avocats, on the embossed letterhead. It appeared to be a decades-old deed to a property in Brittany, near the village of Cancale, somewhere on the northwest coast of France.

La Maison des Échos.

The House of Echoes.

Somewhere, in the far reaches of a child's memory, she heard the soft lilt of her mother's voice. *"We will go to Brittany, Maggie darling, to La Maison des Échos. You will see where I was born, you will finally meet your Grand-mère Clair. See her world. Hear her music."*

Maggie closed her eyes, chin lifted, listening. The words disappeared like smoke into the shadows of time, but – she had been with her mother right here, in this room. Her mother had gestured toward the lumoinous oil painting on the wall.

Maggie rose to her feet, drawn across the room by an invisible thread.

The landscape, painted in glowing oils, was as beautiful as she remembered. A whitewashed cottage with a dark, pitched roof stood against a sky that reflected a sea the color of old pewter coins. The ancient house, set on the edge of a low, rocky promontory, faced the water. Seawater foamed and swirled against stone and gorse in autumn shades of amber and gold and deep emerald.

Maggie stepped closer but could not read the artist's single scrawled name. *G? C?* Lifting the painting from the wall, she turned it around. Written across the crackling brown paper backing were the words: *Bretagne en Automne. La Maison des Échos.*

Brittany in Autumn. The House of Echoes. Where her grandmother had lived, where her mother Lily was born.

Her grandmother Clair had left her daughter a house in France. This house.

The House of Echoes.

Blinking back sudden tears, Maggie replaced the painting and once again sat on the floor beside the old trunk. I want to know you, *Grand-mère.* Tell me who you were.

One by one, she lifted the contents. Over the years, her mother had added her own keepsakes and treasures. Fading albums, letters and cards tied in a blue ribbon, a small cloth doll wearing a faded pink tutu. Her mother's? Her grandmother's? What was the doll's story? We always think we'll have more time, she thought.

Shifting several small boxes aside, she searched for anything related to her Grandmother's past, her life in Brittany. Maggie lifted a crumbling bouquet of dried flowers that smelled of lavender. Beneath, a thin sheaf of music.

Ah. Her six-year-old son Brian's first piano scores, tucked into the trunk for safe-keeping long-ago. The *March of the Middle C Twins* was on top. Her fingers brushed the hard-earned gold stars pasted at the top of sheet music yellowed with age. She pictured her young son seated on the old piano bench, short legs dangling far above the pedals, scuffed red sneaker laces untied.

Maggie smiled. And now she had just spent a perfect long weekend in Cape Cod with her son, his wife Laura, and her grandson, to celebrate Ben's second birthday. Brian was a jazz pianist, and she had watched him holding his own precious son on his lap while he played Ellington and Monk, Bach and Mozart. The child as charming as his father, even more so with that single devastating dimple in his left cheek. I want to know Ben when he's fifteen, she thought.

In the blink of an eye. Her son's first scores of music would be the perfect gift for her grandson.

She gathered the music, set the pages aside, and continued to search through the keepsakes so carefully stored in the trunk. A pink satin photograph album caught her eye, and she hesitated. Then her breath came out on a soft sigh as she lifted her mother's album.

Maggie's mother Lily had died tragically when Maggie was just thirteen. The heartbreaking loss so early on had changed her life in ways she was still discovering. The love was always there, but guilt and sorrow still hovered as well, like an echo in a distant valley.

Maggie opened the album slowly, prepared for the familiar stab of loss. But the old photographs, showing her mother as a young, vibrant woman, were quite stirring and beautiful. Lily, slight and dark-haired, her startling emerald-green eyes caught forever by the camera. On a park swing. In jeans and boots, on horseback. Seated at the old Steinway, her head thrown back.

Maggie ran a gentle finger over a photo of her mother standing alone on a shadowed, empty theater stage, head lifted as if listening to some far-away music. What was she thinking?

Turning the last page, she caught her breath. It was an old photograph, one she had never seen before. A young teenaged girl in a red coat stood alone before a whitewashed cottage perched on the edge of a low, rock-strewn bluff, with the sea frothing white over the stones.

A jolt of recognition. Maggie turned to gaze at the single painting on the bedroom wall. The cottage in the photo was the house in the painting. *La Maison des Échos.*

The words of a long-forgotten conversation with her mother spun into her head. *Your grandmother moved with her family from Paris to Brittany when she was thirteen, just as World War II began. It was so cold there, right on the sea. Her father bought her a red coat, the color of cherries…*

Staring at the girl in the old photograph was like looking into a decades-old mirror. This is my Grandmother Clair, she thought.

Maggie removed the photo and set it aside. Setting the album back into the trunk, her hand brushed the fabric that lined the sides. A whisper, a soft, papery crackle.

Curious, she bent closer. A zippered pocket, almost invisible against the patterned-silk lining.

She tugged at the zipper, reached inside, withdrew a thick sheaf of folded pages yellowed with age. Unfolding them slowly, she held her breath.

There were a dozen sheets of paper. The first several pages were music scores for three Chopin preludes—well-worn, pencil-marked and creased. Each was dated December, 1943, seemingly written in her grandmother's hand, followed by a personal note. Maggie held the music to the light. *Chopin.* Her grandmother, too, had played Chopin.

The first score was Chopin's Prelude No. 13 in F-sharp Major. Maggie hummed the opening nocturne-like notes. The music was aching, saturated with sorrow. Across the top of the page, next to the date, her grandmother had written, *The loss is unbearable.*

Loss. Chopin had refused to title his pieces, she knew. But two musicologists who studied Chopin had named his preludes— pianists Alfred Cortot and Hans van Bülow. Cortot had named this piece *Under a Night of Stars, Thinking of my Beloved Faraway.* It was van Bülow who had named this prelude, simply, *Loss.*

My grandmother knew loss, she thought. A lover? A child? A friend? *Her music?*

Maggie's chest tightened as she remembered the agonizing year she had been unable to play her own music. The hollowness, the desperation. The *loss.* She was struck by a powerful sense of connection, as if the preludes were an unbreakable thread linking her to her grandmother over the decades.

She lifted the second score. Beneath the title for the Prelude No. 22, also dated December, 1943, her grandmother had written *I have been asked to join the Rebellion.* On the last score, Chopin's Prelude No. 15, her grandmother had written, simply, *Avril's Prelude.* Who was Avril?

Maggie sat very still, staring down at the music, jolted by a sudden lightning bolt of realization. Loss. Rebellion. A French woman's name. All dated 1943. My grandmother is telling me what happened to her during the war, she thought. She is telling me her story.

Setting the scores aside for a moment, she opened the few remaining pages of the packet she'd found. It was a letter, written in French in flowing script, on fine parchment. One by one, Maggie unfolded the thin pages of the letter, searching first for the signature on the last page. *Reste en sécurité, ma chère. Clair.* Stay safe, my dear one.

Clair. Her grandmother. A faded blue train ticket, caught in the folds, fell into her lap. *Saint-Malo to Paris. 9 PM. First Class Carriage.* It was dated November, 1943.

Maggie smiled, grateful for the French her mother had taught her. She returned to the first page. It was dated December, 1943, just one month after the ticket for the night train to Paris. The letter began, *My dearest.*

Her grandmother Clair had written to someone she had loved. *Stay safe, my dear one.* Who was he? Or she? How had it come to be hidden in the trunk? Had the letter ever been sent, delivered to the mysterious 'dear one'?

Only one way to find out.

Maggie tilted the paper toward the flickering firelight, and began, slowly, to read.

> *My dearest,*
>
> *I pray this reaches you, finds you safe. So much has happened since we said goodbye for the last time. I have no idea if you are still alive. I miss you so much, my heart is full of sorrow…*

Sorrow. Loss. The heartbreaking notes of Chopin's Prelude No. 13 echoed around Maggie. She closed her eyes and saw a young woman with dark hair beneath a night of stars, her body bent in grief.

Clair

"Loss"

CHAPTER 7

PARIS. DECEMBER, 1943

> *My dearest,*
>
> *I pray this reaches you, finds you safe. So much has happened since we said goodbye for the last time. I have no idea if you are still alive. I miss you so much, my heart is full of sorrow.*
>
> *The war has stolen everything, everyone I loved, from me.*
>
> *But if you are out there somewhere, ma choupette, I will find you, I promise. I finally have found a way. And like so many things that matter, it began with an accidental meeting. Not long ago I was on the night train to Paris…*

In the drafty attic room above the tiny bistro on Place Saint-Michel, Clair Rousseau sat by a frozen dormer window, thinking of her beloved. Beyond the glass, the vast night sky glimmered, the stars like ice crystals. The final chords of Chopin's Prelude No. 13 trembled on the old Victrola, then echoed into silence around her.

She set down her fountain pen to swipe the hot tears from her cheeks. She had been writing for over an hour, pouring out her heart to her baby sister.

Elle. Three years younger. The last time she had seen her sister, Elle was standing by their father's grave in Brittany, wearing a too-big coat the color of a morning sky, holding a white daisy in her hand.

Now, Clair saw Elle everywhere. Always in motion. Weaving her bicycle through the Marais. Riding the carousel in the

Luxembourg Gardens, her face smeared in chocolate icing. Skipping after a wild kitten on rue du Mars. And later, in Brittany – a blur of blue, dancing on wet cobblestones in a soft December snowfall, her small arms thrust high in the air. Elle, with her heart-shaped, freckled face, her hair the color of summer wheat. Their father's deep blue eyes.

Elle.

Her nickname ever since she was a toddler unable to pronounce her given name, Elodie.

I see you everywhere I look, Elle.

Where was she? Where had the German soldiers taken her sister and their mother?

The pain was unbearable. Grief is the price we pay for love, she thought. Her mother's words, whispered after their father was murdered, floated in her mind. *You must always take care of your baby sister, Clair.*

And then, just when she'd thought all hope was lost, there had been the chance meeting with the priest on the night train to Paris. The unforgettable scarred, fox-like face of the Nazi who stared at her through the smoke of his *Gauloises* and followed her into the corridor. The train, shrieking to a halt. The terrifying questioning until he was called away. Finally, her identity papers were accepted and the train was allowed to proceed. Two days later, the visit to *Père* Jean-Luc at the old church of Saint-Gervais in the Marais.

Clair could still smell the incense and the dampness of ancient stones. She closed her eyes and fell into the memory.

She pulls back the heavy curtains of the confessional, kneels in the shadows.

The wooden grate slides back. The familiar silhouette of the priest, head bowed. "Bless me, Père, for I have sinned…"

"Clair! Praise God you're okay. That terrible night on the train, I thought you were hurt, ma chère. I searched for you for hours."

"I looked for you, too, Père. I wasn't hurt, just frightened. I couldn't find you. Then the Germans took me aside for questioning. Thankfully my papers were in order. But by the time I was released you were gone."

"I have been so worried, child. I'm glad you've come."

"I had to come. I need to know, Père, how I can help you fight the Nazis. So you will help me find my mother and my sister."

In a soft whisper, he had told her that his brother ran a Resistance network that operated in Saint-Malo. That he'd been charged with forming a new Resistance group here, in Paris. The Ghost Network—*Les Fantômes*—named in honor of the Holy Ghost, the third spirit of the Holy Trinity, whose gifts were wisdom, understanding, knowledge, fortitude. The secret meetings in the basements of local churches. She could help them fight the Nazis. And in turn they would try to help her find out what happened to her mother and her sister.

The words spilled and tumbled from her pen, ink splashing across the fine parchment.

Père gave me absolution, Elle. And then—I can still hear his final words, whispered through the wooden grate. "Will you join us, Clair?"

I can promise you this. Whatever I decide, I will never stop searching for you.

Reste en sécurité, ma chère. Clair

CHAPTER 8

Simon Sugarman turned away from Beckett, looked toward the night-filled window that framed the mountains. "Okay, so Yuri Belankov is not the real reason I'm here."

"Can't you just show up one day with some good news, Sugar?"

"Maybe someday, pal. But right now I'm here because of you – and La Maggie."

Beckett lunged to his feet. "Maggie? Christ, Sugar, why didn't you say so! Is she okay? What the devil has happened now?"

Sugarman held up his hands. "She's fine, Mike. Far as I know. But Interpol called from Greece. A body was found floating in the sea off Mykonos."

"Dane had a villa on one of the Greek islands. Was it Dane?"

"We're not that lucky. It was the Italian woman who lived with him. Beatrice."

"Drowned?"

"Nada. She was dead before she hit the water. She was stabbed in the heart, Mike. By a dagger. Bastard must have looked her right in the eyes when he did it."

"Is this a dagger which I see before me?"

It was another sleepless night. Dane sat in the shadows of his bedroom, staring at the French Laguiole knife glinting on the wooden table and remembering a night many years earlier. The stage at London's Shakespeare Theatre. *Macbeth*, Act 2, Scene 1. His favorite soliloquy, from one of Shakespeare's bloodiest plays.

He had worn a frayed purple velvet robe, so heavy and hot under the stage lights. Dust motes swirled in the air every time he moved across the stage.

Dane closed his eyes, seeing the stage once more. At the start of his speech, Macbeth imagines that he sees a dagger floating in the air, and wonders if it is real or if his guilty conscience has imagined it.

"The handle toward my hand? Come, let me clutch thee," Dane whispered into the shadows. Once more he felt himself become Macbeth, the Scottish king who murdered his brother-in-law, King Duncan, so that he could accede to the throne. Now, slowly, slowly, he felt the guilt fill his head, begin to haunt him. Felt Macbeth's fear that the dagger was real.

Dane saw the knife handle turned toward him, the blade flashing in the stage lights, and once again felt the temptation to grasp the blade in his fingers.

He flung his hand into the darkness, just as Macbeth, doubting himself, had reached for the dagger. But the dagger wasn't there.

"Or art thou but a dagger of the mind?" Dane quoted in his low, intimate voice, once more blurring the boundaries between the real and the imaginary.

Dane blinked. Real or imaginary? Because Beatrice, the woman he had loved, had held a dagger to his neck in this very room. Beatrice, the woman who, in the end, had chosen to betray him. *I wanted her to suffer*, he thought. He saw her floating, face up, in the warm Aegean Sea, her long dark hair wavering like ribbons of seaweed around her still face. As dead as Lady Macbeth.

"I have thee not, and yet I see thee still," he whispered.

But then Beatrice's face dissolved, as if a stone had been dropped into the sea, and the pale still face beneath the water became the face of Magdalena O'Shea.

CHAPTER 9

MENEMSHA, MARTHA'S VINEYARD

Maggie sat on the cottage bedroom carpet, her grandmother's open trunk before her, her fingers gripping the papers in her lap.

Her grandmother Clair had lost her baby sister, Elle, in a wartime tragedy. Grieving, filled with rage and hopelessness, she had taken the night train to Paris—and by a stroke of fate had reconnected with a priest who asked her to join the Resistance.

Had she said yes? What had happened to her in the months that followed? What had happened to her sister?

A grief-stricken letter, a ticket on the night train to Paris, Chopin's emotional music—all messages from her grandmother that somehow held the answers.

Searching the zippered pocket once more, her fingers closed around one last item, a fine link chain. Maggie withdrew a tarnished gold locket, held it so that it spun in the air, catching the firelight. She released the small latch, caught her breath. The photos were old, sepia-toned, with a very 1940s feel. Set in the left disc, a man's face—handsome, narrow and bony. Intense eyes, too-long dark hair, silvered at the temples, curling around his neck. On the right disc, a beautiful, high-cheek-boned face with huge luminous eyes framed by waves of black hair stared back at her.

A face exactly like her mother's. Exactly like her own.

It was the woman in the album photograph. Her grandmother. Intrigued, Maggie turned the locket over. A brief message and a date, etched in script.

Toujours se Rappeler. 1943

"Toujours se Rappeler," murmured Maggie. Always Remember.

Slipping the chain and heavy disc over her head, she felt the circle of gold settle between her breasts. Warm. Close.

"You have a story to tell me, *Grand-mère,*" she whispered. "I will find those memories for you, I won't let them be forgotten." She gazed down at the music scores in her lap and smiled. "And your friend Chopin is going to help us."

"Okay, Father, yes, sounds good. Symphony Hall. I'll see you there tomorrow, eleven a.m. I have news, and so many questions I want to ask you."

The cottage living room was lit only by the red glow of embers in the old stone hearth. Maggie clicked off her phone, picturing her father as she'd last seen him. Maestro Finn Stewart, tall and lanky, with his beaked nose and brows like birds' wings, standing on the Carnegie Hall stage. Conducting his beloved Beethoven, long white hair flying around his face, arms thrusting, carving through the air.

He was coming to Boston to discuss guest-conducting the Boston Symphony Orchestra in the new year. She wanted to see him again. *And she didn't.*

Her feelings for her father were still so… complicated. He had disappeared from her life just as he had vanished from the stage in the middle of a performance of Beethoven's *Eroica,* so many years before. They had found each other again just a year ago, after decades apart.

Decades filled with lies and secrets, sorrow and loss.

But he loves you, Maggie told herself. He always has. He believed he had no choice when he left you. *And yet.*

Some wounds never quite heal, she thought. We just get better at hiding them.

She gazed around her mother's cottage. The main room was full of shadows and memories tonight. She thought about the long-ago times here with her parents, before her mother's death, those wonderful rare weekends when all three of them had been together on the Vineyard.

Hot chocolate, the smell of fresh-baked cookies. Music under a skylight full of stars. Her mother sitting at the piano, gold firelight flickering over her face. A pre-teen Maggie dancing and leaping around the room, wrapped in one of her mother's long silken scarves. And her father, larger than life, waving his arms in his wild, theatrical motions, laughing down at them.

Warm, happy memories.

Until it all shattered with her mother's death, and her father's disappearance not long after. After that, she had been raised by her father's mother, Gran Stewart, in Boston. Never, after all, meeting her other grandmother. Her French *Grand-mère*.

And that brought her thoughts full circle. Pouring a second glass of Pinot, Maggie sat on the old piano bench and touched her grandmother's locket, warm and close between her breasts.

What was your story, Clair?

Her eyes settled on the three preludes she had found in her grandmother's trunk. In late 1943, her grandmother had suffered heart-shattering loss, which she shared in the letter to her sister and in Chopin's aching Prelude No. 13. The second prelude was the No. 22. As the bars of music spun into her head, Maggie caught her breath as she recognized the piece – Chopin's Prelude No. 22 in G Minor. The musicologist Cortot had titled this piece *Révolte*. Rebellion.

Rebellion. The word tingled across her mind. Across the top of the page, her grandmother had written, *December, 1943. I have been asked to join the Rebellion.*

Somehow, she knew, Clair's answer to the priest had been yes.

Would I have been so brave? she asked herself. What would I have done?

The answers were in the music. Through the preludes, she would learn her grandmother's story, find the connection to her grandmother and those vanished years.

She began to play.

CHAPTER 10

SYMPHONY HALL, BOSTON

The next morning was cold, the breeze sending brown November leaves swirling and clouds racing across the gray dome of sky.

Maggie hurried across Massachusetts Avenue, her eyes on the century-old Boston Symphony Hall rising gracefully from the street. The white-columned Renaissance building glowed in the morning light, reminding her of a Greek temple. The beautiful hall was a second home to her. She had given her first performance on that stage just after her eighteenth birthday.

No reason to be anxious, and yet –

A man sat hunched on the shallow marble steps, gazing at the traffic, a Starbucks container clutched in his hand. Long wisps of white hair lifted in the breeze, dark slacks fluttered against sharp-angled legs.

Maggie climbed the steps and sat down next to him.

"Hello, Finn." It was still easier to call him Finn than Father. Or Dad.

Finn Stewart turned to her and raised wispy bird-wing brows. "Hello, sprite," he said in the low bass-like voice from her childhood.

No awkward hug, just the tentative half-smile.

He'd been on tour, and she hadn't seen him since the spring. He was thinner than she remembered, and the lines in his face had deepened into ravines. But the sharp falcon face, and those fierce sapphire eyes, as blue as the wool scarf knotted around his neck, were the same.

He leaned closer, and she caught the old familiar scent of tall pines and winter forests.

"You look so much like your mother," he said softly, raising a frail, brown-spotted hand to touch her hair. "It's good to see you."

"And you," said Maggie. She realized with shock that it was true. She and her father had been estranged for so long, and were still finding their way back to each other. Slowly. One conversation at a time. It wasn't about forgiveness. For her, that was the easy part. The child had never stopped loving her father. But the woman—the woman needed time to find the trust again.

Maggie took a deep breath. "Welcome to Boston," was all she said.

Finn glanced at the glowing emerald on her left hand. "I see you are still engaged to Colonel White Hat."

"I'm happy, Finn." She tilted her head at him. "How was the tour?"

"We made some good music in Paris. And it's always fun to glare at the horns, isn't it? But –" Finn Stewart looked down at his gnarled, veined hands. "I'm tired of impersonal hotel rooms, Maggie-girl. Tables for one in strange restaurants where I can't speak the language. It's a lonely life."

His words took her by surprise. "But you're a rock star. All the photographs in the magazines show you surrounded by celebrities and beautiful women."

He scowled at her. "I don't get those girls anymore," he muttered. "Just the grandmas now."

She laughed. "Ouch. Well, maybe it's time to settle down for a bit. Find a place to call home. Plant some roots again?"

Her father bent toward her, concentrating on her words. A beat of silence, and then he nodded slowly. "I've been thinking about finding a condo near Carnegie Hall. Or maybe something here, in Boston, near you, and closer to my grandson and his family." He gave her a faint, wistful smile.

"We all would like more time with you, Finn." Dangerous ground. "Boston is a good place to live. You could come to the music shop, hang out, play chess. And I'm going to need major help with Chopin."

"He's always been your favorite. But you have moved far beyond what I can teach you, Maggie."

"Never." She leaned in, as if pulled by an invisible wire. "The Philadelphia Orchestra called, Finn, they want me to solo with them in the spring." She watched his face light up. "Something, right? One of the preeminent orchestras in the world. It's not too far from Michael's cabin, so I would be close to home. But…" She took a deep, shuddery breath.

"But what, sprite? Spill."

Midnight phone calls, frightening texts, a play by Shakespeare. A crashing stage light. A single rose left on a catwalk.

"It's nothing. I'd rather talk about you. How did your meeting go with the BSO?"

It was as if a gray curtain came down over his eyes. Her father frowned, the mirth disappearing as the crevasses around his mouth deepened into rivers. "They want me to teach this summer at Tanglewood. Visiting Artist, Master classes and such."

"That's a wonderful opportunity for you." She watched his expression change. "Isn't it?"

"I'm a city boy, sprite. Too many trees in the Berkshires, too much fresh air."

"Give me a break, Maestro. You love outdoor concerts, hanging out in the backstage tents and schmoozing music with all the other musicians. What's the real reason?"

He lifted his eyes to the sky. "Those who can, do. Those who can't, teach."

Maggie touched his arm. "You're kidding, right? Teaching is hardwired into your soul. I remember how fascinated you were to learn something new, how you would immediately share it with me. Those crazy exercises for the rapid jumps spanning two octaves…"

"Ah, Stravinsky's Three Movements. Not for the fainthearted." His voice was low, rusty. "You remember that?"

"Of course I do. And I remember how it was when you were composing. You looked as if you were taking a nap – eyes closed, still as a statue – and then all of a sudden you would jump up and run to the piano."

The old smile lit his eyes. "Your mother always said I did my best composing on my back, on that lumpy sofa on the porch."

"You are made of music, Finn, we both know it. You live and breathe every chord, you love it all. Conducting, composing, teaching. Listening. This is your world."

He remained silent, staring at the traffic. "Nothing lasts forever, Maggie."

Something in his voice. "When I found you in Austria last year, you hadn't been able to conduct in a very long time. But you still chose to work in a music shop! Music is in your bones, dad."

"Yours, too, sprite. Nadia Boulanger was right. 'Do not take up music unless you would rather die than not do so.'" He locked his eyes on hers. "So, maybe you are ready now to tell me what you don't want to talk about?"

You still see right through me, Dad. "It's just... well, that invitation to join the Philadelphia orchestra?" A breath. "They want the Études."

Finn's eyes widened. "Chopin's *Studies?* Jesus, not the Six! Those damnable double thirds..."

Maggie nodded slowly. "Afraid so. The Six. And the Ten. And—just shoot me now—the Eleven."

Her father dropped his head, sharp shoulders began to shake. "Finn? Dad?"

He threw back his head with a sharp bark of laughter. "Holy *fuck*, sprite, no one can play those pieces. Your mother wouldn't go near them. They terrified Ashkenazy, Horowitz. Hell, even Chopin! Those Études are at the top of every 'Most Impossible

Piano Pieces' list." Finn shook his head back and forth in disbelief. "Twenty-seven Chopin studies to choose from and they ask for the three most wildly difficult Études in the world," he murmured. "And you said *yes*."

"Don't remind me, damn you. It's not funny, Finn."

"Oh, but Maggie-girl. It *is*." He stopped, tilted his head in thought. "The only pianist I ever knew who had the audacity to take on the Études was your grandmother Clair – when she was a teenager, no less! She once told me that her secret was talking to Chopin before she played his scores. She was a piece of work, all right." He grinned. "A real badass."

Maggie stared at him. "*Grand-mère* played Chopin. She talked to him…" The Chopin preludes she'd found in the trunk slipped into her mind. "I've been thinking so much about my French grandmother. There's news, Finn. About my mother and grandmother Clair. It's time I learn about my French grandmother's life."

"It's not an easy story to tell, sprite." Shrugging sharp shoulders as if suddenly unsure, her father struggled slowly to his feet, clearly in pain, and held out his hand to her. "Too cold out here. Let's talk inside, shall we?"

Conversation over. Maggie stared at her father's gaunt face, the hooded eyes. Something was off, a wrong note played. She took his hand. His fingers were icy, trembling. Shaky. The strong grip, the edgy, aggressive energy were missing. The ferocity.

Resisting the urge to take his arm to steady him, she stood and followed her father up the steps toward the high glassed doors.

CHAPTER 11

SUNRISE RANCH. HUME, VA

Michael Beckett parked his Jeep next to the barn by the far paddock, feeling, as always, a sense of peace when he saw the mares grazing in the meadow.

Just a short ride from the cabin, he'd found the property nestled in a light-filled valley not long after he'd met Maggie, knew it would be perfect for his Shelter to Service program. His gaze took in the paddocks, bunkhouses, barn and stables. The gym, pool and basketball courts, all wheelchair accessible. Now, Sunrise Ranch was fully operational, dogs working and training alongside Vets to help Wounded Warriors, and an animal rescue program inspired by Shiloh.

And where *was* Shiloh this morning? Probably with Dov and Lady, his chosen "pack."

Smiling, Beckett entered the barn and stopped in the doorway, unexpectedly stirred by the sight of the boy and his horse. Dov had his face pressed against the mare's neck. Lady in Black stood calm and still, her single liquid eye – the other lost to abuse before Beckett had rescued her – on the boy's bent head. Sunlight from a high window sparked on her black coat, lighting Dov's shaggy golden hair. It was a still life of vulnerability – and trust.

Beckett stepped into the stable, and the moment passed. He watched the boy begin to brush the gleaming flanks, slow and easy, across old, jagged white scars – and the more recent black stitches from the gunshot wound, courtesy of Yuri Belankov.

Shiloh lay sprawled on the stable floor between the kid and the mare, dozing, his gold fur pressed against the mare's front hoof like a giant fuzzy slipper.

Stopping safely outside the stall, Beckett grinned. "You and Shiloh are still the only ones she'll let near her. But she seems to be healing well."

"Stronger every day," said Dov, stopping to run his hand over her velvet-soft muzzle. "Lady has a brave heart, Colonel." He grinned. "And I think, deep down, she knows you're the one who rescued her."

"Deep *deep* down, maybe. Because that's not what that look in her eye says when she sees me. So I'll keep my distance, kid."

The boy nodded, turned away.

"What?" said Beckett. "No biting wise-guy comeback? You feeling okay?"

"I'm fucking okay, dammit. Let it go, Beckett!"

"Whoa. Lose the attitude, kid. I get that you have to test me if you're ever going to trust me. But pretending you're okay isn't being strong. Acting is just that—an act."

"I've asked you a zillion times. What part of 'Leave me alone' don't you get?"

"Everyone else has left you alone. I won't."

Dov turned back, his eyes flashing blue fire. "It's just – I can't get the image out of my head. Seeing Lady shot, right here, just because she tried to protect me. All that blood..." His breath heaved. "One more reason Yuri Belankov has to pay."

"Yes, he does. But vengeance isn't the answer, Dov."

A dark scowl. "Maggie would say you're too noble to understand vengeance."

Beckett's silver brows spiked. "Sounds like her, but she'd be wrong. You don't want to go through life with a dead body on your back, kid."

"Says who? What've I got to lose, Beckett?"

Beckett wanted to say, *Us*. But he said, "You don't want to throw away your life for revenge."

"What life, Beckett?" The boy's body vibrated with anger. He held up his left wrist, encircled by the leather cord. "I never take this off because it reminds me that I've never been in one place long enough to matter to anyone! I've bounced around in foster homes with folks who didn't give a crap if I lived or died. *No one* showed up for my fucking fifteenth birthday!"

"Christ, Dov."

Shiloh raised his head, liquid eyes sad and knowing.

Now the boy's words tumbled loud and fast, as if a dam of pain had burst. "I never met my father; hell, I'm not even sure my mom knew who he was. My grandfather was blown up in a war. I found my mother's murdered body in an alley. And then the Russian who killed her shot my horse and disappeared. What kind of life is that, man?" Dov swept an angry hand around the room. "This is just another place for me, Colonel. None of them last."

Beckett stepped closer. "Yeah, you've been dealt a handful of bad cards, seen way too much for a guy your age. No normal family for you. But families are made, not born. Your story's not done, dammit. Look around you, Dov. The mare, she survived, she loves you like crazy. You've got Shiloh. This beautiful ranch we bought, to help other Vets. You've got a bed, and pancakes every morning. Books!" He couldn't resist adding, "And now a place to keep them. Hell, kid, that new learner's permit you just got? Okay, so maybe we're not the Brady Bunch, but it could be a whole lot worse."

"Could be a whole lot *better* if I'd just had the courage to shoot Belankov when I had the chance."

"Now you're out there where the buses don't run. Just think about this, kid. About the consequences of the decisions you make. Decisions that will change the course of your life, Dov.

What if you'd shot Yuri Belankov that day? How would your life be different? There are no pancakes at Rikers, believe me. No beautiful mares. No books, no Goldens."

"But at least Belankov would be gone."

"We all have monsters in our closet, kid. It doesn't work that way."

"No? You ever shot anyone, Beckett?"

Beckett stiffened, ran a hand through his silvered hair. "I know what it's like to take someone's life, kid. To see someone die. It haunts me every damned night. The dead don't just go away, Dov, they sit on your shoulder and whisper in your head."

Beckett leaned close, stone eyes locked on blue.

"When you go to war, Dov, bad things happen. Your grandfather and I watched a young soldier, a brand new dad, step on a mine, his helmet spinning off into a fiery sky. I watched a little kid drown in a lake because I couldn't get to him in time. You come home from war, Dov, but you still have the screams in your head. The helmet spinning into a red sky. The kid in the lake…"

"But sometimes a death is just, right? Deserved. Sometimes the end justifies the means."

Beckett stared at him, chose the lie carefully. "Doesn't work that way."

"But Colonel –"

"Don't you get it? Your mother and your grandfather didn't want that life for you! They wanted you to find the things that make you '*you*.' Discover who you are, not what other people say you are. They wanted you to see the beauty and promise of life, kid. Watch a winter sun set over the Grand Canyon. Photograph Mount Kilimanjaro on a hot dawn morning. Maybe sleep under a desert sky lit by a million shooting stars. Know what the Sistine Chapel smells like. Run on a beach with a dog like Shiloh, while heat lightning turns the sea to silver. Fall in love on a rainy afternoon with a beautiful girl."

They'd want you to know love, to finally take that damned leather cord off your wrist.

"Fall in love? Jeez, man! Time out!" An Olympic eye roll as the boy turned away. "Don't you have to go fishing or something?"

"I have reason to believe the fish have been mocking me lately." Beckett spoke to the boy's back. "I've got a better idea. Get your jacket and some water. Shiloh and I will meet you at the Jeep. Five minutes."

"Okay. But you've got to tell me what a Brady Bunch is."

Beckett looked at the Golden. "Seems to be an eye-roll kind of day." Then he called over his shoulder to the boy. "Just please tell me you've heard of Frank Sinatra, kid."

As Beckett followed Shiloh's shambolic hop toward the Jeep, his earlier words to Dov echoed like tolling bells in his head. *I know what it's like to take someone's life.*

It's never wrong to do the right thing, he told himself. The kid came first. So he would protect Dov, he would deal with Yuri Belankov when he had to. He just had to remember Sugar's Eleventh Commandment: *Thou shalt not get caught.*

Yeah, sometimes the end justified the means.

"The first story is never the last story," he murmured to the Golden. Shiloh gave him a deep, knowing look. They both knew he would do whatever he had to do to protect Dov.

Even if it meant going back down into the darkness.

After checking the lock carefully for any break-ins, Yuri Belankov opened the door and stepped slowly into the dark apartment on rue Palatine in the Latin Quarter. He stood motionless, all senses alive, listening. Waiting for his eyes to adjust to the shadows.

No one was here.

It was an old Russian rule of survival, learned at his babushka's knee – when you are on the run, hide somewhere that doesn't invite suspicion. He'd chosen the busy 6th arrondissement – and surprised himself by liking this small, third floor walk-up apartment. The oldest district in Paris, this quaint neighborhood was so alive. The Sorbonne, the cafes filled with students, the gardens, the bookshops. The chess. And at the heart of it all, Église Saint-Sulpice.

He crossed to the tall windows, parted heavy velvet curtains. Across the quiet courtyard, the twin towers of Saint-Sulpice soared against a sky lit by purple twilight. He was not a religious man, but he found beauty – and solace – in the view.

Da, he'd read *The Da Vinci Code*. Who hadn't? Dan Brown made you famous, he told the graceful old church. But I like you best when all the tourists have departed, and you stand alone, just stone and history, glowing with the light of evening.

Alone.

Well, he'd made a choice, hadn't he? A long time ago. And being lonely was so melancholy, so very Russian. He was no stranger to sadness. And sometimes the price for freedom was loneliness.

Now, he spent the long nights with old friend Dostoevsky. He was almost finished with *Crime and Punishment*, reading it for a second time. Poor, tormented Raskolnikov. Every Russian knows torment, he thought. But all crimes have an underlying cause, eh? However irrational. *Rage does not emerge out of nowhere.*

Paris was beautiful, but he missed the life he'd had. He missed the power, the opportunities, the wealth. His art. His *freedom*.

All because of a Russian teen—Dov Davidov, his hatred for Yuri like blue fire in his eyes. And then there was Magdalena O'Shea. Both had betrayed him.

His eyes found the carved chess set on a small table across the room. Often, to pass the time, he played against the computer.

He was black, his opponent white. Tonight, the White Queen was in danger.

He smiled at the irony.

CHAPTER 12

SYMPHONY HALL, BOSTON

"Mrs. O'Shea! It's so good to see you, we've all missed you." The elderly guard gave Maggie a huge smile as he tipped his hat at her.

"It seems I've been relegated to the status of Magdalena O'Shea's father," murmured Finn.

The guard turned. "I remember that voice. My God, Maestro! Is it really you?"

Finn chuckled. "Hey, Charlie. Still playing the ponies?"

The old guard beamed at him. "Keeps the wife happy, if I do say so." He opened the door into the hall, stepped aside. "Welcome home to Symphony Hall," he said, with a sweep of his arm.

Maggie and Finn entered the hall and stood alone in the quiet, allowing the peace and the history to settle over them. "Spare as a church, isn't it?" said Finn. "But the perfect place to worship music."

The hall was built like a shoebox – long, high and narrow. Modeled after the great music halls of Amsterdam and Vienna, with its inward-sloping walls, shallow balconies and statue-filled niches to allow the sound flow, the acoustics were said to be the best in the United States. "The superiority of angles to curves," murmured Finn.

He gazed up at the clerestory windows high on the walls. Natural light fell through the half-moon-shaped windows in shimmering bars, casting shifting patterns of light and shadow on the floor. "Those windows were nailed shut for years. Glad they were re-opened."

Maggie nodded. "And now, at night, they're filled with the city's glow."

Finn dropped into a leather chair with a tired sigh, gestured to Maggie. She slipped off her coat and sat beside him. He smiled at the words on her tee-shirt: *Talking about music is like dancing about architecture.*

"Damned true," he murmured. Then, "You have questions about your mother?"

"More about *her* mother, really. My grandmother, Clair."

Fastening her gaze on the pipes of the famous organ behind the stage, Maggie told her father about the deed to a property in Brittany. About finding Clair's letter, Chopin's preludes and the locket in the trunk in the Menemsha cottage.

Again he leaned in, watching her face intently as she spoke. "I remember that old trunk," he said suddenly. "Your grandmother shipped it to your mother sometime after you were born. Said she wanted you to have it one day."

Maggie lifted the gold locket from her neck, clicked it open, held it toward him. "Is this my grandmother Clair, Finn? Will you tell me about her?"

Finn Stewart gazed down at the tiny photograph.

"She's the image of your mother, isn't she? And you. A hat trick of beautiful women." Finn closed his eyes for a moment, reaching back into memory. "Lily never talked much about her mother. But I know her name was Clair Rousseau. She was born in Paris in 1926..." His eyes snapped open, twin sapphires finding hers. "I told you Clair was a pianist, too? Like your mother. Like you."

"You said she played the Chopin Études, and his preludes," she said softly. "What else do you remember?"

"What I wish I could forget. It's a terrible, heartbreaking story, Maggie. Are you sure you want to hear it?"

No. She took a breath for courage. "She was my grandmother, Finn. I want to know her story. *Our* story."

He looked up at a marble statue of Apollo on the second balcony. "Clair's father was murdered by the Gestapo for acts of resistance in Brittany. Her mother and her younger sister, Elle – your great-aunt – were sent to one of the camps during the war. Lily said her mother refused to talk about it."

"A *concentration camp*? Dear God, I never knew." Maggie touched her father's arm. "But my grandmother must have survived the war, because Mom was born."

Finn startled at her touch, looked at her blankly. After a long moment, he said, "Yes, she survived. Somehow. I don't know what happened to your grandmother during the war, but I know that Clair eventually married an American Air Force captain from New England – Henry Claymore."

"The soldier in the wedding photograph, at the cottage."

"Yes. Your mother's parents were Henry and Clair Claymore. He was a Yank from Boston. They met in Europe just after the war, I believe. That Vineyard cottage your mom loved so much? It was in Captain Claymore's family, and willed to her."

"But, Finn, the photo of the man in the other half of the locket? He isn't my grandfather Henry."

Her father gazed down at the locket and shook his head. "I have no idea who this man is." He shrugged, handed her the locket. "I know your grandfather and Clair lived in France for years after they were married. Henry came over for our wedding, but he died not long after." Her father gazed down at the pattern of light and shadow on the wooden floor. "Clair couldn't travel. Well, *wouldn't*. She was agoraphobic, terrified to leave the house."

"Oh, no," whispered Maggie, sympathy welling in her heart. "I can't imagine what must have happened to her."

Her father shrugged. "Never knew. But Clair was claustrophobic as well, deathly afraid of small spaces. Wouldn't go near a plane. So your mother went to France for several weeks every year, on her own, to visit her mother. I was always on tour."

"Mom promised to take me to France, to meet my grandmother, for my thirteenth birthday. She was teaching me French, so I'd be ready. But then –" Maggie closed her eyes for a moment, willing away the sudden surge of pain, the searing loss of her mother's unexpected death.

"I know, sprite. Lily died far too soon. For both of us." Her father's eyes were distant, looking into the past. "I remember the first time I ever set eyes on your mother. Her full name was Lily Avril Rousseau Claymore when I met her at Yale. A name as beautiful as she was." He smiled with memory.

"Lily Avril…" Maggie gazed up at her father. "My grandmother wrote the name Avril on a Chopin prelude I found in the trunk. She called it 'Avril's Prelude.' Do you have any idea who Avril was?"

"None. Maybe your grandmother just liked the name."

"Maybe. But I think mom was named after a woman my grandmother knew." Maggie handed him the legal document. "And this deed?"

Finn Stewart glanced at the heavy vellum. "I remember Lily mentioning this," he said suddenly. "A cottage on the coast of Brittany in France, northeast of Saint-Malo, I think, where her mother's family moved before the war. Your mother was born there."

Father and daughter stared at each other. "And now I'm thinking the cottage must be yours," he said into the silence.

"Seems like it."

"Be good to know your history. Maybe where your music comes from." Finn looked at his watch and stood slowly, wincing in pain. "Long day, old bones," he told her.

"I'm leaving for Virginia later this afternoon." She hesitated. "Would you like to come to the cabin for the weekend? See Michael and Dov, the ranch where they work?"

Her father gazed down at her, his expression unreadable. "I'd like that, sprite. But I'll have to let you know." Then he turned and shuffled away from her.

Maggie watched her father make his way toward the exit. Was it her imagination, or was he – less tall, somehow. Stooped. He had changed, in just the few months since she'd seen him. Aged. Yes, he was in his seventies, but he'd been so vibrant when they were last together. Even followed her into the freezing Atlantic Ocean to help a friend.

Now, he seemed suddenly...vulnerable. Where was his usual stride? He moved slowly, his body shaking with tremors. Her father was just not himself. What was going on? Aging? Depression?

Or something more?

One hour later, Maggie set the small blue suitcase by the front door of her Beacon Hill music shop. Her flight to Virginia left at four. By dinnertime, she'd be in Michael's arms.

Smiling, Maggie turned to reach for her briefcase. Her eyes caught a photograph gracing the wall above her Steinway, lingered. It captured a beautiful, intimate moment of a Maestro's hands, against a background of shadows, as he conducted an orchestra. Tuxedoed sleeves, long, graceful fingers cajoling, baton glinting in a bar of light.

She pictured her father's hands now, shaking and gnarled. She felt as if, once again, he was keeping something from her. She wanted to trust him. But she was done with the lies. Why was he still keeping secrets?

Maggie shook her head. We are a family of secrets, she thought. My mother, my father, me. And now apparently her grandmother had kept several secrets as well. Had she ever found her sister? What had made her so claustrophobic, agoraphobic? Who was the man pictured in her grandmother's locket? And who was Avril? Someone who had meant something to her grandmother, someone with a connection to Chopin. A woman whose name needed to be honored – and remembered.

Somehow, Maggie knew that the man, and Avril, were important pieces of her grandmother's puzzle. Will I ever know your secrets, *Grand-mère*? Who is the stranger in the locket? And why did you give my mother the middle name of Avril?

Her cab wasn't due for another twenty minutes. Maggie stared at her briefcase, then at the silent, waiting Steinway set against the shop's bow window. Just do it, she told herself.

Unlocking the brass clasp, she withdrew the sheet music for Chopin's Prelude No. 15 in D-flat Major. "Avril's Prelude", her grandmother had called it. Dark, dramatic and haunting, it was the longest and one of the best known of the twenty-four preludes. Composed by Chopin after a rainstorm, von Bülow had named the prelude *Raindrops*. But Cortot had titled it the far more foreboding *But Death is Here, in the Shadows*.

The first section, Maggie knew, was pensive and beautiful. It was the longer middle section, with its repeating A-flat notes sounding like raindrops, that went deeper, inserting shadows and a haunting tone of death.

Fingers tingling and held above the keys, Maggie closed her eyes and said a silent prayer. Help me find the notes, *Grand-mère*. Tell me who Avril was. Help me hear your story through the music.

Her fingers touched the keys and "Avril's Prelude" came to life.

Clair

"Avril's Prelude"…

Death is here, in the shadows.

CHAPTER 13

PARIS. DECEMBER, 1943

"Stop that infernal banging on my door, you imbecile!"

The cracked wooden door swung open and Clair Rousseau found herself looking into tired red eyes that widened in anger.

"*Merde*! What was *Père* thinking? I ask him for an ugly cow and he sends me a bloody fecking beauty queen!"

The woman was wreathed in smoke, her voice scraping and gravelly from decades of nicotine. Perhaps in her fifties – or older? – her hair, once blond, was cut short and fell in jagged gray wisps around a too-thin face. Hazel eyes were bleary and bloodshot. A *Gitane* cigarette waved in her left hand, its tip burning a red arc through the shadows. Her right hand held a full tumbler of whiskey that sloshed over the rim when she moved.

Clair stared at her network contact in disbelief, listening to the stream of obscenities, certain that if the woman had had a third arm it would be pointing a loaded Luger at her. *What the hell have I gotten myself into,* she asked herself.

"Go back where you came from," muttered the woman finally, turning her back on Clair as she tried to slam the door.

Against all her better instincts, Clair's hand shot out. Pushing the door open, she took a deep breath and stepped across the threshold.

She found herself in a single walk-up room above a butcher shop on rue Mouffetard —*Le Mouffe*— in the medieval maze of the Latin Quarter. Heavy blackout curtains were pulled tight over tall windows, muffling the sound of the hard rain that crashed against the panes. On the wall beside her, a small radiator hissed, no match for air so cold she could see her breath.

Surprisingly, it was not the rasp of Edith Piaf's voice but a Chopin prelude that spilled from an ancient Victrola. It was the dark and dramatic Prelude No. 15, one of Chopin's best-known preludes, often called *Raindrops*.

"You like Chopin?" murmured Clair. "Your music matches the weather today."

A look of pain flashed in empty eyes as the woman glanced at an old upright piano against the far wall. "You know nothing," she muttered.

The irony of fate, thought Clair, gazing around the room. In the dim light, she saw a sink piled with dirty dishes, several empty whiskey bottles, an unmade bed in a dark corner, a thin blanket in a heap on the floor. The piano, half hidden in the shadows. Even with the windows closed, the scent of blood sausage and the high screech of a saw blade drifted from the butcher shop below.

The woman lurched toward her, words tumbling, crude and offensive.

"Oh my good God. Enough!" Clair thrust out her hand, knocking the tumbler of whiskey from the woman's grip so that it shattered on the floor. In the sudden, frozen silence, she said, "We surely agree on one thing. What the hell was *Père* thinking?"

Clair took a step toward the woman. "I am no bloody cow, you crazy ranting bully. I cannot help the way I look, but I assure you, I am no shallow beauty queen. I speak four languages. I work for the German Military High Command, in their headquarters in the Majestic Hotel on Avenue Kleber. They do not know that I speak fluent German. They ignore me, treat me as if I am invisible. They often send me to the Hôtel Lutetia, on Boulevard Raspail. Surely you know it's the home of the Abwehr, the center of Military Intelligence. They focus on counterespionage, sabotage, resistance. I hear information every single day that could help to free the French people and end this terrible war."

Without speaking, the older woman poured another glass of whiskey. Then she swayed toward Clair, stopped and leaned in. Her red-streaked eyes were so close that Clair could smell her cheap perfume and the sharp scent of alcohol on her breath. Clair turned away. "This will never work. I'll find someone else."

"Wait. There is not enough time, we need you tonight. What is your name?"

"Clair. Clair Rousseau."

"*Non!*"

Clair took a step back. "Excuse me?"

"Lesson number one, my fine beauty queen. Never *ever* use your real name. It puts us all in danger. Now. Again. What is your name?"

"I am French, *Madame*, born in Paris. I gave my true identity papers when the Germans hired me. My given name is Clair Rousseau. That is the name the Germans know."

"Then you will need another set of papers, another name. Then maybe, just maybe, you will have a chance at surviving if you are caught."

"And what name do *you* call yourself, *Madame*?"

"My network name is Smoke. But you can call me Avril."

"If I decide to stay."

"You say you are French?"

"*Bien sûr.*"

"*Merde.* I asked for a Yank. The Yanks are well-trained, six months at least in Scotland."

"I'm a quick learner."

A cloud of blue smoke blew into Clair's face, followed by a bark of laughter, like gravel thrown against a wall. "Is that so? Well, we have four hours until we all meet at the church. We shall see." Avril gave her a long, assessing stare and began to mutter to herself. "*Eh bien.* A scarf for your hair. A shapeless black sweater, a pebble in your shoe. Perhaps a cane? Horn-rimmed glasses. Different make-up, of course, purple shadows under those eyes."

With a sudden, decisive movement, Avril stubbed out the cigarette in an overflowing ashtray, tossed her remaining whiskey into the dish-filled sink. "Don't just stand there, Clair Rousseau! Crack the windows, get some air. I think I have eggs, some cheese. Real coffee, from the black market, not that ersatz crap. Let's get to work."

Three hours later, Clair's head was spinning with instructions. *Keep your eyes down. Never let them see nerves, or fear. Memorize your route. Have an escape plan ready. Carry an extra scarf, a sweater, a hat to change your appearance. If you are caught, tell as much of the truth as you can. Hold out for twelve hours if you can, to give the others a chance to escape…*

"They will find out what you love," Avril had said. "They will kill your dog in front of you—your father, your best friend, your lover—to make you talk. Or worse."

A lesson in writing tiny messages, hiding them in a lipstick, the hem of a jacket, a hair ribbon or cigarette case. Another lesson in delivering them. The signals for safety. A loaf of bread in the bicycle basket, just so. A woman's compact, tilted open to catch the sunlight. A blue scarf draped around a neck, reading glasses on a café table. A book of French poets opened to a poem by Baudelaire.

"You will do," said Avril finally, leaning back in the old wooden chair. "Until you won't." Again the steely, assessing stare. "Why are you really here, Clair Rousseau?"

Exhausted, Clair decided that the truth was easier than the lie. "They murdered my father," she said, looking through the smoky shadows at the unmade bed. "They took my mother. And my baby sister."

"To the camps?"

"*Oui.*"

The room was quiet, the brief prelude long ended. The woman named Avril lit another cigarette, watched the smoke spiral like snakes toward the ceiling, then nodded toward the far wall. Her words fell like stones into the silence. "Chopin's Prelude No. 15 has another name, you know. 'Death is here, in the shadows.' That piano over there? It belonged to my son. Before the Nazis murdered him in front of me."

Clair caught her breath, shocked by the naked anguish.

Avril stood abruptly. "Come. It's time to meet the other Ghosts. *Les Fantômes*." She smiled for the first time—a grimace, really, the uneven teeth more brown than white. "Could you kill a man if you had to, my beauty queen?"

CHAPTER 14

GETTYSBURG, PA

"I'm not sure why we're here, Beckett," said Dov. "Bull Run is much closer to your cabin."

They had driven north for two hours, crossing from Virginia into Western Maryland and then through the farmlands of southern Pennsylvania, finally parking near the back entrance of Gettysburg National Battlefield, off Taneytown Road.

"Because your grandfather Yev was my best friend—and he was a Civil War buff," said Beckett. "Manassas, Antietam, Bull Run, Shiloh." He looked down at the Golden who sat quietly, his eyes on the sloping field, as if he understood this was a place of respect. "That's how Shiloh here got his name, he fought his own brave battle." Beckett put a hand on the boy's shoulder. "But this battlefield had the most meaning for your grandfather. He brought me here, to Gettysburg, one time when we were home on leave. Stood right where you're standing. He'd have wanted me to bring you here."

Beckett leaned on the split-rail wooden fencing that crisscrossed the rolling, misted fields. "You're looking at McPherson's Ridge," he said to Dov. "The battle began right here, around eight a.m., on a beautiful early July morning in 1863, just beyond that farmhouse. The fighting lasted over three days. The Union won, but there are no winners when some fifty thousand Americans die."

Beckett's breath came out. "Churchill said, 'History is just one damned thing after another.' But standing here, remembering what happened... I've learned that battles are living things, Dov.

They give, they take. They terrify, they cause unbearable agony. They pulse with blood. They *breathe*. It's one of the rare times I've disagreed with Churchill."

The kid remained silent, staring out across the empty, open field. Imagining?

"This place is hallowed ground, Dov. A field of honor. Yev said you just had to stand quietly and listen. You would hear the stories. Feel the emotions. Of life. And death." He turned to the boy. "I feel close to your grandfather here."

"So do I, Colonel." The words were barely audible.

"There are unspeakable atrocities, unbearable violence and cruelty, in every war. We know that. But your grandfather believed that all soldiers, no matter what side they're on, have a story. A love of family and country in common. Family who miss them, love them, suffer with them. A country they have loved since birth, worth fighting for."

"Sullivan Ballou," said Dov into the silence. Shiloh moved closer to the boy, sensing the story to come. Beckett leaned in, listening. Waiting.

"Learned about him in my American History class," said Dov. "Ballou was a Union soldier who wrote a letter to his young wife, Sarah, just before he went into battle at Bull Run."

"This can't end well," murmured Beckett to Shiloh.

Dov nodded. "Ballou wrote, 'My love for you is deathless. And yet my love of country courses over me like a strong wind.' Like you and my grandfather, Colonel. How you feel about being a soldier."

"A debt we owe to those who came before us," said the colonel quietly. "But any death is a tragedy."

"Ballou died in that battle," said Dov. Shiloh pressed against Dov's leg for comfort, head lifted, listening. "But his last words were for Sarah. 'When my last breath escapes me, it will whisper your name.' He chose love, and his country, too."

"And he wasn't afraid to speak his feelings," said Beckett. "Things don't stay nailed shut, your grandfather knew that. They find a way to come out. You've seen some terrible, fearsome things. But I know your grandfather would have wanted you to be happy, kid, not consumed by anger and pain. Or ghosts. Yev would have wanted you to talk about all those emotions churning inside."

The boy was motionless, silent.

Okay, just keep going. "Look, I know feelings are dangerous for guys like us. Admit just one, and Christ only knows how many more will come shrieking out of the woodwork."

The boy kept his eyes locked on a distant barn. "You first, then, Beckett. What are *you* feeling?"

The Golden shifted, gazing silently at Beckett as if he, too, was waiting for the answer.

Beckett scowled at the boy and dog. "Scared," he said finally. Then, "That's it, that's all I got. Your turn."

"Oh, no, you don't," said Dov. "Scared of what?" Shiloh edged closer, clearly intrigued and enjoying Beckett's discomfort.

Beckett looked out over the flowing, November-brown fields. "Scared that I can't be enough of a family for you, kid. Family is supposed to *protect* you. I didn't do that."

He scowled. "Feels as if I've taken to this fostering thing like a fish to furniture."

"Good one." A heartbeat, and then Dov turned to him, his face a pale mask. Finally he whispered, in a barely audible voice, "Wolves."

"Wolves?"

A shrug. "They howl at me, in the night. In my dreams. We all have our own battlefields, I guess."

Beckett's chest tightened. He looked down at the Golden, nodded. "*Those* wolves," he said softly. "Yeah, kid, we've heard them, too, howling in the dark, haven't we, Shiloh? I think your grandfather heard those wolves, too. He would have told you that before you can move on, you have to move *through*."

"But how do I do that, Colonel?"

"You have us, Dov. Me, Shiloh, Maggie. Lady in Black. We have your back. We have your *six*, remember? Soldiers know that six follows twelve on your watch. You don't have to move through this alone."

Beckett looked down. "And speaking of watches, it's getting late. Maggie arrives in a few hours. Time to get going."

Dov turned. "Wait. I... Thank you, Colonel. For finding out what happened to my mom, like you promised. And for helping me get to know my grandfather."

Shiloh gave a tender woof, eyes soulful. Beckett stopped, smiled his crooked smile. "You're welcome, kid. Did I mention that Yev got his wicked sense of humor from me as well?"

"Don't push your luck," grinned the boy.

"Fair enough." Beckett nodded. "Life is a river, kid. It's going to carry you into the future, no matter what decisions you make." He squinted out across the flowing field. "You ever read *You Can't Go Home Again*? Thomas Wolfe says, 'What was important was not that the beggar was drunk and reeling, but that he was mounted on his horse and, however unsteadily, was going somewhere.'"

Man, boy and dog walked slowly away from McPherson's Ridge, not speaking, each lost in his own thoughts.

CHAPTER 15

BECKETT'S CABIN

Wrapped in a thick robe, Maggie stood at the bedroom's French doors and watched the stars rise like sparks over the dark mountains.

She had arrived at the cabin just as the sun was setting. First, the surprise. Dov and Shiloh had led her out to the deck to discover the beautiful new bird house, its steep roof the color of dark cherries, swaying from a low pine branch. Touched beyond measure, ignoring his wary resistance, she'd hugged the tall, too-thin boy tightly. Celebratory pizza and an action movie had followed. A late night, but one that didn't end when she and Michael had climbed the narrow stairs to the bedroom.

Maggie smiled as she remembered the flickering candlelight, the soft strum of Michael's guitar. He had a low, gravelly, Blake Shelton voice that echoed like a caress in the shadows.

I don't want to live without you, I don't want to love nobody but you.

My home's wherever your heart is, I could be happy anywhere with you.

And then he'd set the guitar down and gathered her against him. And shown her exactly how much he loved her.

God, the way he had kissed her. She just sank into him, arched against him. Lips, neck. Wrist, fingers, breasts, stomach, thighs. Undone by him, the world spiraled, disappeared.

Making love with Michael was like the ocean, she thought. Rolling, surging waves of want. Sparks of light. Deep and infinite.

God, she loved him. The intensity of those eyes on hers, the way his too-long hair curled around his neck. The feel of his skin beneath her fingers. The set of his shoulders, the way he moved, leaned in to listen. The low, intimate sound of his voice. The scent of him, trees and earth and endless sky.

Now he was asleep, snoring softly in the big bed behind her, a path of moonlight folding him in a silver cloak. One bare arm flung over his eyes...

Calm tonight, but she'd been beside him in the bed more than once when the black nightmares invaded his mind. When his body thrashed and shuddered, when he cried out in a language she did not understand. When all she could do was hold on tight.

"Wars change you," was all he would say. But she knew he had gone off to fight for his country as an innocent, idealistic young man and returned as someone else. She'd seen that thousand-yard stare too often, knew he felt responsible for all the lives he hadn't been able to save. Scarred emotionally as well as physically, he was sardonic and cynical, always fighting the darkness. What he called *going to the dark side of the moon*.

He told her she gave him light.

And you give me love, she told him silently, gazing down at him.

"Come back to bed, Maggie." His voice coming from the shadows, as if he'd heard her.

"I thought you were sleeping. It's such a beautiful night and when I couldn't sleep I –"

He reached for her hand, pulled her toward him. "Less talking, more kissing," he murmured.

Later, in the wee hours, they sat together on the big soft bed, eating cold pizza, heads close, watching the sky slowly dissolve from darkness to violet light.

Finally, she put a hand on his chest. "Michael. We have to talk."

"Not my favorite four words, Maggie." But he raised her hand to his lips, then leaned in to listen.

She told him about the deed to the French cottage – *Someone left you a house?* – and finding her grandmother Clair's music and letter in the old trunk in Menemsha. Held out the golden locket, swinging like a tiny pendulum from its long, fine chain.

"I see where your beauty comes from, darlin'," he said softly, his thumb brushing the photo of her grandmother before slipping the locket back around her neck.

He listened without speaking as she described her visit with her father. His memories of her grandmother. His frailty. Her growing concerns.

"I wanted my father back for so long, Michael. But now that he's back, I'm torn. I know that he loves me, but he's keeping secrets, he's not himself. Something is stealing him away from me, bit by bit. All the lies still hurt."

"No one can hurt you like someone you love," Michael said.

"You are talking about Dov now," she told him.

He stared at her for a long moment, a stunned look in his eyes. And then he told her about the boy—the woodshop, the bookcase, going to Gettysburg. Dov's burning anger. The leather bracelet he refused to remove. Sugar's visit, and the ongoing search for Yuri Belankov.

"Dov is isolating himself, Maggie. Talks more to the mare than to me. Hides behind his phone. He knows Belankov will come back for him. The kid is carrying a boat load of hurt, fear and anger. He's a wild card. I don't know what he'll do."

"But you know what you will do to protect him, Michael. What we both will do."

"Whatever it takes, darlin'. But it's on me, not you. Because sometimes the bad guys turn good people into people like them. I won't let that happen to you."

Finally, as the candles flickered out one by one, she told him about the late night phone calls, the photos and book of Shakespeare that came in the mail. Watched his eyes turn to stone as she told him of the intimate text from an unknown number at sunset on the Vineyard. The stage light that crashed so close to her piano in the theater. The single red rose left behind on the catwalk. The stranger's face in the shadows.

"He wanted you to see him," said Michael. "Wanted you to be afraid."

She looked at him. "What are you not telling me?"

His lips tightened as he told her about Beatrice's body floating in the Aegean. The very real possibility that Dane was still alive. Still a threat.

"He may not be physically nearby — yet — but he is pulling the strings, darlin'."

"Oh God, Michael." Gripping his arms. "That sick vicious killer could have my son — my grandson! — in his sights."

"Not gonna happen. Trust me, Maggie, your family is safe. Having a great time at Disney, surrounded by Sugar's team – and thousands of people. Even we couldn't find them."

"But if Dane's still out there, he'll find a way to get to me. To us. It isn't over, Michael. He has taken so much from me, stolen my trust, my confidence. My music. His face slashes like a knife into my dreams. He won't go away. Will I ever be free of him?"

She knew he heard the fear, saw the panic reignite in her eyes.

"Faulkner was right," he muttered. "The past is never dead. It's not even past."

"Hold me," she said.

In one quick move he tossed the pizza aside and pulled her against him. She pressed her body to his, let herself fall into him. *You make me want*, she whispered into his mouth, and he made her forget all about the sound of a shattering stage light and a wolf-like face in the shadows.

Beyond the windows, the rugged mountains guarded them, the night sky was lit by stars. Finally, in his arms, she was not afraid of the dark.

She knew what she was going to do. *What she had to do...*

CHAPTER 16

BECKETT'S CABIN

The sky was already changing, darkness opening into light, when Michael Beckett stopped to lean against the bedroom door, his eyes on Maggie. Wrapped in a thick quilt against the new day's chill, Maggie sat outside, curled in a chair on the narrow redwood deck beyond the French doors.

Shiloh was asleep at her feet, and her face was lifted to the rising sun that tipped the still-dark trees with gold. The sudden flare of bright sparks, deep in his chest. *I wake up in the morning*, he thought, *to see the sun shining on her face*. Dusky hair wild and unrestrained, eyes as deep and green as a mountain lake in the swimming light. Seeing her was like watching a sunrise.

He stepped onto the deck. "Morning, darlin'." Handing her a mug of coffee, he sat down beside her. "This will warm you." He bent closer. "You were surely a million miles away just now, lost in your thoughts. What were you thinking about?"

She smiled at him. "Last night."

"Might have to channel my inner Blake Shelton more often." He wagged his spiky brows at her and gave her the crooked smile she loved. "And resembling Beethoven surely helps."

Choking on her coffee, Maggie dissolved into laughter. "I'm sure Beethoven would be flattered," she sputtered. "But right now…"

Uh oh. "You have that look, darlin'."

"What look?" Amusement glinted in her eyes. Shiloh raised his head, looking like a cat waiting for a flock of pigeons.

"The look you get when you want to talk about something I won't like."

"I was thinking we should talk about our wedding."

His breathing hitched as he looked down at the Golden. "Didn't see that one coming. A warning would have helped."

Shiloh yawned loudly and lurched to his feet. With a "you're on your own" look, he hopped slowly to the edge of the deck and set his gaze on the distant mountains.

"So much for having my back," muttered Beckett. Then, to Maggie, "Can we begin with the honeymoon?"

She grinned. "Don't all grooms love to talk cake and flowers, tuxedos and receptions? Endless lists of guests?"

A feeling that could only be described as panic punched him in the gut. "Right up there with talking about feelings. Okaaaay," he said slowly. "You're a well-known international pianist, the press loves you, maybe you want a big splashy wedding in Boston, or –"

"You goof," she interrupted, reaching for his hand. "I love our quiet world here. I just want to be with you, Dov and Shiloh. My son and his family, my father and godson, our close friends. Your Vets. Right here on the deck downstairs, looking out over the lake. I love these mountains the way I love music."

His breath came out in a long, relieved whoosh. "A ceremony on the deck is perfect." Silver brows spiked, hopeful. "Maybe beers on ice and BBQ?"

"Just as long as there is chocolate cake."

"Even better. When, darlin'?"

"As soon as possible, Michael. I was thinking… next month? Early December?"

"Works for me. I'll set about finding us some heaters for the deck. There'll be snow on the mountains by then."

He looked out toward the distant peaks, gleaming jade against the new sky, and was suddenly quiet.

"What's the matter, Michael?"

"Nothing." A breath. "Everything."

"Talk to me."

"I've been thinking about what you told me last night, Maggie. About your grandmother. I know you, so I know you want to go to France, learn what she was like, discover more about your past. It's a fine idea. Except for the 'only *you* going' part."

A heartbeat of silence. Maggie would know there was much more than he was saying. Always was, thought Beckett. But for now, it was enough.

"I know you don't want me to go on my own, Michael. You want me to stay close, you believe you can keep me safe here. You are the ultimate White Knight."

"More like a Knight Errant. Too tarnished, too dark for valor." Half disconcerted, half amused, he scowled down at her. "For too long it was only me. But now it's *us*, Maggie."

"I want *us*, too. But I want to get to know my French grandmother, Michael, I *need* to know her. My mother died when I was thirteen, my father disappeared from my life for decades. I still need roots, family. I want to know my past, where I came from. *Who* I came from. Where my music comes from. Knowing the past, seeing it, will help me understand the present. Who I am now. And I *know* you want that for me."

"Of course I do. But I'm also a realist. I know Dane is still a danger."

"He is a Master Class in Vengeance, damn him. He's not the 'Quick Death by Ice Pick' type, he wants me to suffer, to be afraid. It's personal, as if he needs to hurt me. He has no more conscience than a wolf, he'll never stop. But the truth is, Michael, Dane could be anywhere. He's proven he can get to me wherever I am. I cannot spend the rest of my life looking over my shoulder, living in fear. Hiding. I can't run forever. I'm done waiting for his footsteps behind me. I won't do it!"

And, we're off. "There are a lot of ways this could go south, Maggie."

"Does he think I won't do anything? Not fight back? He's *wrong*, Michael!"

"Maggie McFierce," he murmured, seeing the resolution in her eyes.

"You always say, 'The only way out is through.' I have to keep going. I want my life back!"

Shiloh raised his head, gave Beckett a warning woof as if to say, *Don't go there!*

Beckett went there. "What the hell, Maggie? Have you been hit by a rock? You are listening to your heart, not your head. Emotions over thinking. Bad idea."

"Is it?" Her voice was icy. Refusing to look at him, she stared instead at his faded "U2 Tour" sweatshirt.

Should have listened to the dog, he thought. *This ship is on its way to the iceberg.*

"I'm taking self-defense classes," said Maggie into the silence. "I'm determined to know how to protect myself. And I know how to be careful."

Beckett met Shiloh's eyes, both knowing that wasn't true. He put his hands on her shoulders, waited until she met his gaze. They were so close he could see his own stony reflection in her eyes.

"Don't look at me like that," she murmured.

"This train is already ten stations past our stop, darlin'. And I'm too old to play Rock Paper Scissors with you."

Her expression flickered with a dozen arguments. Finally she said, "Since I met you, I've been reacting to loss, grief, threats, danger. I'm finally moving on, Michael. With *you*. It's time to take back control of my life. To *act*, not react."

"Acting is fine, Maggie. It's acting *alone* that concerns me. So. New Plan A. I'm going with you."

"And leave Dov alone? We both know Dov is in Yuri Belankov's sights. He needs you here, Michael. Dane is *my* fight, not his. I won't put you all in danger when it's me Dane wants." She held out her hands. "I'm afraid you need a Plan B."

"I have one. Get a better Plan A."

"You are so damned frustrating," she murmured.

"Not sure who is the frustra*tor* and who is the frustra*tee* here," he murmured.

"I just want this to be *over*, Michael! I want to be happy, to concentrate on our wedding."

"We both want the same thing, darlin'."

"Do we?"

"Yes."

"Fine."

"Good."

They stared at each other. Emeralds clashing against granite. A dark silence fell between them.

"Impasse," she said finally. "I need a shower. And time to cool down." She stood, dropped the quilt to the deck. Turning her naked body away from him she walked toward the door.

Beckett stared at her slender form disappearing into the shadows. "What just happened?" he muttered. Shiloh's expression was cryptic as usual. Head versus Rock, thought Beckett. Rock won.

He sure as hell wasn't used to making compromises. Okay, then. Rock, meet Hard Place. Somewhere out there were two violent men who were threatening – *hunting* – the two people he loved the most. So he would find a way to deal with both Belankov and Dane – on his own terms. Whatever he had to do. If someone ended up dead, so be it.

Dealing with Maggie was another matter. Damn the woman. She was complicated, electric, a woman who filled the world with beauty. Smelled like wildflowers. But, Christ, she was willful.

Beckett turned to the Golden. "You think she's waiting for me to come around?" The dog stared back at him. "Yeah, me neither."

CHAPTER 17

MYKYNOS, GREECE

"You did well, Firas."

Dane leaned against the stone balcony of his terrace high above the Aegean Sea. It was hot, the air heavy and shimmering with late-day heat. Far below him, the sunlight from the bright vault of sky reflected in the sea like diamonds trapped under azure water.

Things were moving fast. There was so much to plan.

"The crashing stage light in the theater was just the right message," said Dane in his silky voice. "And the single rose on the catwalk? Inspired! Worthy of my own Machiavellian mind." He listened.

Then, "Yes, you will need to be my eyes and ears – and my legs – until I can take over." He gazed down at the heavy silver cane by his side. "Not too long now, I hope."

More words from across the ocean. Then, "She flew to Virginia last night? Good work. Yes, keep me apprised of her location. I have no doubt that an opportunity will present itself before too long. She travels a great deal, eventually she will come to Europe. Closer to me."

He clicked off his phone and hefted the heavy cane. Five surgeries, long months of vicious pain and physical therapy. Finally, the end was in sight. The wheelchair was the first to go. Then, just days ago, the ugly aluminum elbow crutches – tossed off the cliff into the sea. Soon, he would be ready to travel.

All the suffering because of Magdalena O'Shea. She'd taken his oil paintings, his freedom, his health. *His unborn child.* And now, finally, he would take away something precious to her.

The cane glinted in the white light.

One or two more visits by his therapist, and then… *I will walk again.*

Too bad, really, about the therapist. A miracle worker. But she knew far too much. And she had seen his face. He could not – would not – take any more chances.

She would be back tomorrow. And if he was ready to walk… He gazed out over the balcony at the distant Aegean far below. He would invite her to enjoy the view, one last time. Such a long drop to the road below.

And she would simply disappear into the void, just like the hated crutches he'd tossed off the cliff.

"His virtues will plead like angels," whispered Dane, quoting his beloved Macbeth. He shook his pale silver head, looking down at the diamond-studded sea. Smiling. Shakespeare had invented vengeance.

"And tears shall drown the wind."

Yuri Belankov awoke with a start as his book crashed to the floor.

He stayed motionless on the sofa, staring into the shadows, waiting for his racing heart to slow. He'd been dreaming, again. Almost every night now, the same unsettling nightmare.

There was no sound. He was in a dark alley. The woman's face, so beautiful, but white with death. A necklace of piano wire, blood like red raindrops on her skin. Her body so still on the stones. The boy's face, lit by a streetlamp, staring at him in horror.

Then, out of the darkness, a black mare. Rearing, hooves sharp and shining.

Yuri jolted as if struck, eyes searching the shadows. No alley, no woman. No boy. And no mare, thank God. He was here, in the small apartment on rue Palatine.

Like Koschei the Warrior, he thought suddenly. Another story told at his grandmother's knee. Koschei was an evil monarch, sometimes depicted as a king on horseback. But, although rumored to be immune to death, he could still be killed. In one tale, a stallion brings death to King Koschei.

Yuri swallowed, remembering the dream, the black mare rearing toward him. Have I dreamed of my death?

Like so many Russian folktales, he thought, Koschei's story was a sad one. Once a proud warrior, he was betrayed by his comrades. It would be many years before he could break his chains and take his revenge.

I was once a proud warrior, too, he reminded himself. Until I wasn't. *But do I want to be like Koschei?* All Russian tales end badly, he reminded himself.

He gazed into the shadows, thinking about the mare. She was protecting the boy, he thought suddenly. Doing what I would have done once, if someone I loved was in danger.

Beyond the tall windows, the bells of Saint-Sulpice began to chime.

CHAPTER 18

LOGAN AIRPORT, BOSTON. FIVE DAYS LATER

As soon as Maggie entered the Air France Lounge, she saw him – reading the *New York Times*. With that lion mane of white hair and the eagle profile, he was impossible to miss.

"What are you doing here, Finn?"

The slow, charming smile she remembered. "Waiting for the boarding call for Paris, same as you. Care to wait with me?"

"But –"

He silenced her with a sharp thrust of a gnarled hand, as if he were conducting a troublesome orchestra. "Last time I checked, I still had my faculties, financial means, and my passport. Thought a little change of scenery might be good for me."

And so they sat side by side, father and daughter, in the Air France lounge. She, engrossed in a book on the history of France during World War II. He, cursing a political editorial in the *Times*. Some things never change, she thought.

It had been five days since she'd kissed Michael Beckett goodbye, leaving him, Dov and Shiloh behind in the mountain cabin. Five whirlwind days of planning and phone calls, tickets and packing. Taking an extra self-defense class. Calling her father to say she'd see him in Virginia at the wedding. Or so she'd thought.

Now, here he was, upending her life once again in his inimitable way. And yet – if she were honest, some deep secret part of her was happy he'd chosen to come with her.

Maggie took a small sip of her Pinot. Okay, then. Together, they would pick up the rental car in Paris, make the five-hour drive to Brittany. With the time difference, arriving at their hotel in Saint-Malo late afternoon. And then? Well, then she would finally begin to learn about her grandmother Clair's life. She hoped.

A glance at her watch. Almost time to board. Her eyes found the closed double doors that led to the International Jetway and the jet to France. Michael's words from last night's phone call slipped into her head.

"We all fear what lies behind closed doors," he'd said against her ear. *"Always know what's on the other side of the door before you enter the room, Maggie. Promise me."*

A deep and profound yearning for the colonel washed over her. Within hours of their argument at the cabin earlier in the week, they had talked. Agreed to disagree. "Loving someone means for better or for worse," he'd said. "You don't turn away when it gets hard. You find a way to make it work for both of you."

It had been a very long time since she had left behind a man who loved her, who worried about her. Who accepted her for who she was, even when he didn't agree. *For better or for worse.* I have no idea what's waiting for me beyond those doors, she thought. But I promise I'll be careful, Michael. I just want to learn my grandmother's story.

She was closing her book when the word Resistance caught her eye. She read on.

The French Resistance (French: *La Résistance) was the collection of French movements that fought against the Nazi German occupation of France and the collaborationist Vichy régime during the Second World War, from June 1940 – October 1944.*

When the war broke out in Europe, Paris was a busy cosmopolitan city and the center of business, finance, arts, and culture. When the City of Light fell under German occupation, life became very different for Parisians, especially for the city's Jewish community. Although many Parisians fled, those who remained did not sit back and accept the German authority as it was administered through the Vichy Government…

Maggie closed the book, slipped it into her carry-on. The words in her grandmother's letter, found in the Vineyard cottage trunk, spun into her head. The French priest had asked, *Will you join us, Clair?*

Maggie lifted the golden locket she wore around her neck. Clicking the tiny clasp, she gazed at the two grainy photographs.

On the right disc, her beautiful grandmother, Clair. Had she said yes to the priest? Had her Grandmother joined *La Résistance?* And who was the dark-haired man in the small circle on the left?

Classical music was playing softly in the airport lounge. A pause, and then a Chopin Ballade began to play. Her head came up. It was the No. 3, one of her favorites. Her grandmother must have loved the ballades, too, played them as well.

The image of her grandmother playing the piano drew her thoughts to the music she'd found in the trunk. She closed her eyes, tuned out the airport sounds around her, and focused only on the notes of the Chopin's Prelude No. 22 in G Minor. The *Révolte* prelude, *Rebellion. Molto Agitato.* Very agitated. She sat motionless, listening to the quick, passionate notes in her head, the fierce struggle of will, the dramatic crash of chords at the end – Chopin saying in his music that the ultimate fate of those who resisted was yet to be determined. His emotional, passionate *Révolte.*

Rebellion. She pictured the old blue train ticket. A night train to Paris. And then, Clair's letter – the question asked soon after by a priest in a dark confessional in Paris, echoing in her head. *Will you join us, Clair?*

What had been Clair's response? Had her grandmother joined the Resistance? Surely the music mirrored her grandmother's struggle, the fierce desire to fight back. To find her sister.

The butterfly's wings, she thought suddenly. It was a story her mother had told her – how the fragile beat of a butterfly's wings on one side of the world would stir the air and eventually cause a storm on the other.

Will you join us, Clair?

Somehow, in the deepest part of her, Maggie knew her grandmother had said yes. One long-ago beat of a butterfly's wings… and everything had changed

A voice over the loudspeaker broke into her thoughts, announcing their flight for Paris. Maggie gathered her carry-on and walked with her father toward the double doors that led to the jetway.

The only way out is through.

Michael's words spun into her head. What was waiting for her in France?

The announcement ended, the music resumed. Once more Chopin's chords fell around her. Trying to imagine what choices her seventeen-year-old grandmother had made in Occupied Paris, late in 1943, Maggie took a deep breath and walked through the doorway.

CLAIR

"Rebellion"

CHAPTER 19

The ancient wooden door creaked open. Clair Rousseau took a deep breath and stepped through the doorway into the crypt of Saint-Séverin.

The vaulted space was dark, lit only by a single lantern and a few sputtering candles. Some dozen men and women – mostly women, with just the few men too old or ill to fight remaining in Paris – stood or sat in the flickering circle of light. A heated, whispered argument was in progress. Bomb the supply train coming from the north or wait for instructions from London.

Clair sat on the floor, her back against a thick marble arch, next to Avril. Mercifully, no one was smoking. The air smelled only of candle wax, sweat, and ancient dust. It was cold and damp, and she pulled her coat closer around her body while the words of the argument spun in her head.

Resistance. Explosives. Fire. Bodies. Retribution.

She thought of her father's death, wanted to leap up and shout, *No! Don't do it!* You will only suffer. The people you love will suffer. But then she thought about why she was here. Her mother. Her baby sister, Elle. She saw Elle, aged seven, spinning across their garden, leaping from bench to bench, dancing to the music in her head…

A movement to the left.

Clair glanced over, saw a man shift from shadows into the light. He was tall, gaunt, with a bone-sharp Gallic face and a shock of long, unruly, black hair, silvered at the temples. His eyes found hers. The greenest, most intense eyes she had ever seen.

She felt the sudden flame on her cheeks, hot, as if he had just reached out and touched her. Something shivered, danced along her spine. She turned away just as she heard Avril's rasping voice rise above the whispers.

"Oh, bloody hell, shut up, all of you! You need to hear what this one has to say. Our newest Ghost, eh? You can call her –"

If she calls me Beauty Queen I am out of here.

A sly, wicked glance from Avril. "Call her Buttercup. Tell them what you told me, Buttercup."

Damn the woman.

Clair glared at Avril for a moment, then stood to face the network. A dozen pairs of eyes in too-thin faces stared back at her from the shadows – anxious, fierce, exhausted, distrustful. Hostile.

Holy Mother, help me. She took a deep breath. "There are rumors all over the Abwehr. There is a new Kommandant coming to Paris sometime this winter, to enforce Hitler's orders. I don't know his name yet but his job will be counterespionage. His goal is to wipe out sabotage, the Resistance. His reputation is one of power, abuse and cruelty. He is known as a sadistic interrogator who enjoys inflicting pain, a monster who encourages elimination. There will be no trials, only torture and death in the basement rooms of the Lutetia. This man hates Paris and Parisians, he hates the Jews, he hates our beauty, our art, our culture. He has vowed to destroy our people, our city."

She looked at each person in turn. "I will find out everything I can about him and report back to you. He has to be stopped."

As the questions and discussion flowed around her, Clair felt eyes on her once more. She turned to stare back at the man, now hidden once more by shadows.

Leaning toward Avril, she whispered, "Who is that? Over there, by the statue of St. Theresa."

Avril peered into the darkness. "Ah, my Beauty Queen, you have good taste. He is our fearless leader, the head of Ghost Network. Good luck with that one! His code name is Night."

Night.

Clair turned once more to search the crypt's shadows. The man was gone.

High above her, the bells of Saint-Séverin began to toll, echoing out over the snow-brushed rooftops and chimneypots of occupied Paris.

PART 2

"Music is an echo of the invisible world."

G. Mazzini

CHAPTER 20

BRITTANY, FRANCE

"How much farther, do you think?"

Maggie flashed her father an amused glance. "You sound just like a little kid, Finn."

She was behind the wheel of the rented blue Renault, driving along the old coast road that undulated east from the Breton walled town of Saint-Malo, rebuilt after being bombed to rubble in 1944. Beyond the windows, jagged cliffs fell to a pewter sea. Soon they would reach their destination – a tiny cove just north of the fishing village of Cancale.

Half an hour earlier, they had left the Saint-Malo lawyer's office. She had shown all the required proofs of her identity and signed all the necessary documents for ownership of her grandmother's cottage.

"Mais non, Madame, it was my father who knew your grandmother, I never had the pleasure," said the young French avocat as he gave her the heavy iron keys, the address and directions. *"It was your Grand-mère's friend, Monsieur Jouvert, who contacted us when the cottage became empty."*

According to the lawyer, Maggie's grandmother had arranged for someone to live in the old cottage until it was no longer needed. Apparently, that time had come, and now the empty property legally reverted to Maggie.

"I think the turn is just up ahead," said Finn, staring at his phone and waving a vague hand toward a winding, unpaved road. "Damned French directions are even worse than conducting a Mahler symphony sober."

Maggie smiled as she slowed for the turn. Finn seemed more like his old self today. Yes, he was clearly exhausted, and she could see the tremors in his hands. But there was a new energy in his voice.

The narrow ribbon of road disappeared over a low rise. Ignoring the cold, she opened the window and took a deep breath. "Smell the sea, Finn."

They topped the rise, and she pulled over.

"Oh my God," she whispered, as her father gripped her arm.

Spread before them was a low, rocky headland, falling in waves toward water that swirled silver in the light. Set on the very edge of the promontory, like a small ship ready to set sail, a lone whitewashed cottage faced the wind and sea head-on. Waves foamed and broke against granite that was covered in late autumn plants the color of deep russet and plum and wild jade green.

It was the cottage in her grandmother's photograph, the same cottage painted in the landscape in her mother's bedroom. It looked as if it had been born from the sea.

La Maison des Échos. The House of Echoes.

Maggie drove slowly down the path and pulled up next to the cottage.

Stepping from the car, father and daughter turned as one to gaze out at the remote, misted landscape, carved over centuries by wind and sea. Across the whitecapped bay, Mont-Saint-Michel shimmered like a castle in the distance. Finn reached for Maggie's hand, grasped hard. "I had no idea," he murmured.

"My mother was born here," murmured Maggie. "Oh, Finn, I feel so close to her right now."

The only sounds were the breaking waves, the high cry of the seabirds, and the wind. A sudden gust of air caught her hair, whipping it in ribbons across her face. And suddenly, on the wind, the echoing chords of a piano. Mozart. His Sonata No. 16.

"What the hell?" muttered Finn.

He took her arm and they turned toward the cottage, stopping at the low steps that led to the faded blue door. A low, angled ramp ran along the side of the cottage for easier access to the door. Had her grandmother needed a wheelchair?

The quick bright notes of the Mozart Sonata surrounded them. *Coming from inside the cottage.*

"I thought the cottage was empty," said Finn, reaching for the doorknob.

"Wait, Dad." Maggie and her father stayed by the door, listening until the final chords trembled through the windowpanes, reverberated against the white cottage walls. Then, like a stone thrown into still water, the last notes rippled over tumbled rocks and echoed out over the sea until, finally, they were carried away on the wind.

"The House of Echoes," murmured Maggie.

Moving to the window, she peered through curtains thinned by age into a large, shadowed room. A flash of red, there, by the piano in the corner. A young girl in a jacket the color of cherries sat on the bench, very still, her hair a dark tumble of curls hiding her face.

Her mother's words spun through her head. *My mother Clair had a coat the color of cherries.* Was she imagining her grandmother?

Maggie blinked, shook her head to banish the momentary vision. She knocked softly on the glass, called out. "Hello? Don't be afraid."

A moment of stunned silence. Then the girl jumped up, darted across the room. The slam of a door at the rear of the cottage.

With a glance at her father, Maggie tried the old metal handle, tarnished by years of weather. Locked. Inserting the heavy key, she twisted, and the door swung open with a creak. Finn followed her into the cottage.

Maggie caught her breath. Rubber boots and a thick walking stick stood forgotten against the wall of a tiny foyer. Just beyond, the large main room flickered with dust motes spinning in the light from the windows – windows that were wide enough to frame glimmering vistas of sky and sea.

Hulking, sheet-covered shapes, like animals sleeping under a blanket of snow, filled the room. In one corner, a narrow staircase with shattered wooden steps disappeared into shadows. Against the far wall, the only furniture not covered, stood a scarred baby grand piano. A dust sheet lay crumpled in a white puddle beneath the piano bench.

Through a large arch, an open kitchen, a glimpse of shining copper pots.

"Hello?" called Maggie. "Is anyone here?" Beyond the wide window, another flash of red, disappearing into the tangle of sea pines beyond the rocks.

A soft sound from the hallway. Finn stepped in front of Maggie as they both turned.

A huge cat with fur the color of tangerines leaped into the room, dashed past their ankles to disappear out the still-open front door. They watched the cat run toward the only other house in sight, a steep-roofed home half hidden by the distant pines.

Finn looked at Maggie and grinned. "Well, maybe the cat was playing the Mozart," he said. "Not bad for a cat."

Two hours later, all the windows were open to let in the sharp sea air.

Father and daughter had unpacked and settled their clothing in ancient, cedar-scented armoires in the two bedrooms at the rear of the cottage. Then Finn had insisted on laying the fire in the old stone hearth before disappearing to "take a quick catnap."

Restless, vibrating with energy, Maggie kept working while her father slept. Now the sheets were off the furniture, folded and stored away. Wooden floors swept, groceries unpacked. Cheese softening, wine and sparkling water ready for a toast.

Maggie gazed around the living room, now uncovered. And beautiful, she realized. Beneath dusty sheets she had found a comfortable ivory sofa and easy chairs, a bright patterned carpet from Provence, a huge oak bookcase filled with books, photographs and local pottery – all anchored by the graceful old Ibach baby grand. Now there were fresh autumn flowers from the garden in an earthen jar, diaphanous curtains billowing like sails and filling the room with the scents of the sea.

Finally, as the sun melted into the water and turned it to gold, Maggie sat down at the piano. The Ibach was manufactured by a German company. She had never played one. This one appeared to be very old. Somehow she knew her grandmother had sat on this bench, playing this beautiful piano.

She laid her fingers on the keys, warm to the touch. Played the Middle C. A rich, clear sound. She closed her eyes, and saw an image of a young girl in a coat the color of cherries, sitting alone, playing Mozart in a room full of ghosts.

Like an echo of her grandmother as a child.

Dane gazed out over the Aegean, glinting with the last lights of dusk.

It had been a good day. An excellent day. He was standing now with only the help of the ebony cane, the silver-cuffed crutches already a memory. Good riddance. He looked down at the cane, nodded. Timing was everything. Perhaps, finally, his luck was changing.

Firas had called. Magdalena O'Shea was somewhere in France. Soon, he would know where.

She had come to him. Now, it was only a matter of time.

Dane took a shaky step. Another. Lifted the manila folder that rested on the table, reached for the sheaf of news clippings.

Magdalena O'Shea Performs the Rachmaninoff Piano Concerto No. 2 at the Kennedy Center in Washington, D.C. to Standing-Room-Only crowd.

Classical Pianist Magdalena O'Shea's transcendent Chopin Ballades open Vail Summer Festival.

Magdalena O'Shea to perform Prokofiev's Piano Concerto No. 2 with Boston Symphony in the new year.

Internationally known Pianist Magdalena O'Shea to wed Colonel Michael Jefferson Beckett in a private ceremony this winter.

Dane dropped the clippings to the terrace, watched them scatter in the soft breeze. A plan was slowly taking shape in his mind.

His phone pinged. Firas.

He listened, nodded. "Excellent work. I want you to meet me in Paris tomorrow. I will send the specifics before the night is over."

Dane clicked off his phone and smiled. *So close.* Closing his eyes, he felt Hamlet's words stir in his head.

"Revenge should have no bounds," he whispered into the dusk.

CHAPTER 21

THE HIRSHHORN MUSEUM. WASHINGTON, D.C.

Thousands of miles to the west, in Washington, it was still morning. The sunlight caught the seated couple – the woman's breasts exposed, the man in a crown, his fist clenched – and turned the stiff bronze figures to fire.

Michael Beckett stood with his Golden in front of Henry Moore's contemporary sculpture, titled *King and Queen*. Beckett tilted his head, his chin cupped in his hand, his eyes assessing. The sleek, modern curves of the five-foot-high seated couple reminded him of figures from a Grimm fairy tale, or an Edvard Munch painting.

Nope, not for him. "That crown on the fellow looks more like a top hat. What was Moore thinking?"

Shiloh chose not to offer a comment, but a look of disdain shined in the liquid eyes.

Shaking his head, Beckett gazed around the Hirshhorn Museum's contemporary sculpture garden, set on the National Mall in the heart of D.C. Only a few other visitors wandered in the garden.

No sign of the man he had called. Would he come?

His eyes searched the brightening garden. He had met Maggie on just such a morning, surrounded by emotional stone sculptures, in an old cemetery in Paris. She'd stood in lavender light, looking up at him with eyes the color of a mountain forest. He hadn't known it then but he'd fallen in love with her that very moment.

Loved her more now. Which was why he was standing here surrounded by all these unsettling life-size bronze figures. *He needed to keep her safe.*

Beckett's eyes rested on a huge orange sculpture of a polka-dotted pumpkin, then moved on to a bronze man, headless and missing both arms. And there, an old Chevy Chrysler, crushed beneath a giant basalt stone with painted eyes.

No. No. And, God, No.

He turned away and wandered across the grass, the Golden hopping along beside him. They stopped in front of Rodin's *Burghers of Calais*. "Now *this* I like," said Beckett softly. Six men from Calais, headed to the gallows to save their town, during the Hundred Years' War. He could see the anguish in the men's deeply sunken eyes, the torment as they trudged, feet bare, to their fate. It was emotional, lonely, heroic. He had seen faces like that in Iraq, Afghanistan, Asia.

Dark memories threatened and Beckett reached down to touch Shiloh for solace.

A soft whirring on the stone path behind him, a low voice filling the morning air. "Inspiring, isn't it? Men willing to die for other men, even men they've never met. The original is in the Musée Rodin Sculpture Garden in Paris. I saw it there, in another lifetime."

Beckett turned slowly and looked down at Father Robert Brennan. Currently a visiting professor at Georgetown University, the priest sat, casually dressed in jeans and a leather jacket, in his silver wheelchair. Not a Roman collar in sight. His ascetic, sharp-boned face looked as if it had been carved by one of the garden's sculptors. Wispy hair, the color of wheat, was lit by a halo of hazy light. Beckett suddenly remembered that Maggie always described her old friend as looking like an apostle, and he smiled.

"Father Brennan, thanks for meeting me."

"Call me Robbie. And the Burghers were spared, by the way." The priest reached out to rub long musician-like fingers over Shiloh's smooth head, then gestured toward the round fountain in the center of the garden. "Shall we?"

Men and dog made their way to the fountain. Beckett settled on the broad stone rim and Shiloh chose a patch of grass lit by sunlight.

"Your call surprised me, Colonel Beckett," said Robbie Brennan. "Haven't seen you since April, after that business with the Russians and the Van Gogh. And you don't strike me as a man searching for a confessor." He smiled faintly. "So. Maggie is in Brittany, I believe? I trust she is okay?"

"Far as I know."

"Ah, yes, one never really knows with Maggie."

"She's as unpredictable as a March Madness basketball game," grinned Beckett.

"So, it's the Russian boy, then. The teen you are fostering."

"You're good," murmured Beckett. "Yes, it's mostly about Dov. But I've been wanting to thank you, too," said Beckett, his eyes on the spangles of light glinting on the fountain's surface. "And now, to ask a few favors as well."

Robbie Brennan leaned closer. "I imagine neither is easy for a man like you. Begin where you're most comfortable. You have a captive audience."

Beckett squinted up at the brightening sky and took a deep breath. "I never thanked you for saving Maggie's life in New York."

"Good God, Colonel, she is the one who saved *me*!" The priest looked down at his jean-clad legs, so still and lifeless in the titanium chair, and closed his eyes. "That was over a year ago. As I said, another lifetime."

"Doesn't change what you did. What needs to be said. A man remembers acts of courage."

"Thank you, then. I accept your kind words." He bowed his head, then chuckled. "But you and I both know that Maggs always finds a way to take care of herself. And us as well." His pale gray eyes locked on Beckett's. "She told me about your engagement. You make her very happy. So it seems I owe you a thank you as well."

"I'm the lucky one. Only –" Beckett shook his head, looked away.

"Only, Colonel?"

"The scariest thing on earth is getting everything you've ever wanted…"

"Ah. Because then you have everything to lose."

"I repeat. You're good."

"Thomas Aquinas said, 'Love takes up where knowledge leaves off.' The only tragedy I see, Colonel, would be allowing your fear to push love away."

Beckett nodded, looked down at the Golden. "Guess maybe I needed that confessional after all."

Shiloh raised his head with a look that said, *We knew it all along.*

Beckett said, "I'd like to plan something special for Maggie, Robbie. Was wondering if you would perform the wedding ceremony? She thinks you were born floating in a basket on the shores of the Nile." He grinned. "I know that would make her happy."

The quiet eyes sparked with light. "It would be my honor, Colonel. She has owned my heart for years. But you do know I am a member of the Fallen Priests Club?" He tapped his lifeless legs. "Literally."

"Just makes you as human as the rest of us. You can get all the legal paperwork you need on Google in ten minutes."

"Then you have yourself an officiant."

For several moments, the splash of the fountain's water was the only sound in the garden. "So," the priest said finally, "I know there is more. Tell me about the boy."

Becket pressed his lips together. "You know Dov's mother was murdered last year in New York. Before that she was in prison, so he was in New York's foster care system for almost a year."

"Yes. And I know that his mother's killer tracked Dov to your ranch and tried to kill him. Your boy is quite the survivor."

Beckett nodded. "Yuri Belankov is a brutal murderer. Dov is still trying to get past the horror. The fear. Says he's happy now, at the ranch, but I see the anger still burning in his eyes. And yet, he's a wonder with the horses, and he and Shiloh have become best buds, right, big guy?" The Golden woofed once, a deep sound of pleasure.

"But Dov still has night terrors," said Beckett. "We were doing okay for awhile, but now he seems to be furious with me, keeps shutting me out. I have no idea what I've done." He shook his head back and forth.

"There's a Buddhist nun named Thubten Chodron," said Robbie. "She tells us, 'Don't believe everything you think.'"

Beckett flashed a wry grin. "Look, I'm not good with kids, I don't know how to help him. Maggie told me you used to work with troubled kids in New York. I was wondering…"

"You are exactly what the boy needs," said Robbie Brennan. "I doubt you've done anything to hurt him. But he may not see it that way. I'd be happy to talk with him."

"The thing of it is, I was hoping for a bit more. Spend a few days, maybe, with him at the ranch. I'd like to go to Brittany, surprise Maggie."

"*Surprise* being code for keeping her safe."

"You sure you're just a priest?"

Robbie laughed. "I read a lot of thrillers."

"Then this won't surprise you. Did she tell you that we think Dane is still alive, coming after her? No, of course not. I didn't want her to go to France, thought she'd be safer at home. But the truth is…"

"He could find her anywhere."

"And she knows it. But there's more." Beckett looked up at the clouds scudding across the sky. "Smartest damn woman I know. Beautiful, with music so deep inside her. Only woman I've ever met who could level me with her eyes. But Maggie and Trouble are on a first name basis. Hell, not every great love story starts with a dead body."

"A match made in heaven."

"You know she's a 'leap before you look' woman, chooses heart over head almost every time. Christ, she *invented* fierce. Which means she runs *toward*, not away." Beckett shook his head. "I promised myself I'd protect her. If Dane is alive, she could find herself caught in a Cat Four Hurricane and I'm damned if I'm gonna stand around here just watching the waves roll in."

"Can't imagine that conversation sat well with Maggs."

"Yeah. I got 'The Look' before she left to pack her bags."

"The Look. Ouch."

A scowl. "She plays me like a grand piano."

Robbie Brennan's eyes rested on The Burghers of Calais, their anguish frozen in bronze. "I think your instincts are spot on, Colonel. About Maggie, and about Dane. He is still an extremely dangerous man." The priest leaned closer. "But I can only imagine how hard it is for you to leave Dov. To choose. So, you are trying to figure out how to keep Dov safe but also protect Maggie. 'He that hath wife and children hath given hostages to fortune.'"

Beckett stared at him. "Exactly. I've been to the edge more than once, Robbie. So have you. Not everyone comes back. But you and I, we will always find a way to come back. I trust you."

"And I trust you, Colonel. Okay, then. Maggs talks about the ranch all the time. Do you have a hoops court?"

Beckett's smile quirked. "Yep, tennis courts too. Also a pool, volleyball, cycles, a gym... and the horses. Many of the Vets working there are in chairs. Ramps everywhere, and all the rooms in the bunkhouse are totally accessible."

"A veritable vacation. I should be able to reschedule my classes for a few days, just as long as it's okay with Dov." He reached to rub the Golden's fur. "And Shiloh."

Shiloh's ears twitched, listening.

"Shiloh is a good judge of character. He'll be fine as long as you know he prefers MSNBC to CNN." Beckett grinned. "And something tells me that Dov will be more than happy to put some space between us." Beckett set his eyes on the Burghers sculpture once more, took a breath. "There's just one more thing you should know. It's not only Dane I'm worried about. Yuri Belankov is still out there somewhere, too, Robbie. He has a Russian's long memory, has it in for Dov. And he likes to break precious things."

"Checkmate."

It was late afternoon in Paris, the sun slowly sinking beyond the plane trees in the Luxembourg Gardens. With a sound of disgust, Yuri Belankov's chess opponent, Emil, spat onto the gravel and pushed his metal chair back with a rough movement.

"Don't go away mad," rumbled Belankov. "Once the game is over, the King and Queen go back to the same box, eh? There is always tomorrow."

He watched Emil stalk away, then turned his eyes back to the chessboard.

Very slowly he reached out to stroke the White Queen, his thoughts on Magdalena O'Shea. If she had not betrayed him, he would not be sitting here, alone in a cold November park, missing his work, his travels, his art – the life he had built.

But one thing at a time. First, he had to deal with the boy. His downfall had begun with Dov Davidov. At the end of the day it was all a game of chess, was it not? He already had a strategy in place, should be hearing from his comrades in the States any day now. *Da*. Then he could arrange all the pieces he needed to take back his life.

His eyes fell on the black knight, the chess piece shaped like a horse's head.

I know my next move, he thought.

CHAPTER 22

CANCALE, BRITTANY

The sun was falling toward the sea. Maggie stood on the huge rocks at the edge of the promontory, gazing out over wind-whipped white caps. In the late afternoon light, the sea was the color of polished silver, the air smelled of autumn and salt and wet granite.

She'd given up holding her hair in place. The wind caught it, tossed it behind her in tangled black skeins. She lifted her chin, closed her eyes. It was so elemental here. So wildly beautiful.

At this moment, in this place, she felt her grandmother's presence so strongly. As if Clair's soft voice was whispering to her on the wind, her words echoing from the distant past. It was like holding a shell to her ear, listening to the echoes of the sea.

Maggie imagined a young Clair standing on these very rocks, waiting for... what? *Who?* She felt as if she just turned quickly, she could catch a glimpse of her grandmother, dark hair flying behind her, running across the stones toward a shadowy figure...

Maggie spun around, searching the landscape behind her. But the only thing she saw was the cottage surrounded by swaying grasses and the distant woods. She pulled her leather jacket more tightly around her. Michael would tease her for being so emotional. And yet, she knew this rocky headland would speak to him as well. She smiled, picturing him back home standing on his deck, hands in his pockets, stony eyes on his wild mountains. "I miss you," she whispered. "You would love it here."

If only she could share this place with him. She glanced down at the words on the midnight blue tee shirt he had given her just before she'd left for the airport. *Music Fathoms the Sky.*

His dear face, smiling down at her with that crooked smile she loved. *I'm not quite sure what fathoms means, darlin', but I thought you would like the sound of it. Hell, I'm not sure even Baudelaire knew what it meant. But since you're going to France, I thought some French poetry about music would be just the thing to keep you company.*

Oh, Michael. He always knew how to center her. She'd been so uneasy since the news about Dane. Constantly wondering, where was he? Was he looking for her?

Of course he was.

She raised a hand to catch her whipping hair, and her engagement ring sparked green in the waning light. Once more her chest tightened with foreboding. Why, why did she feel as if there might not be a wedding?

Stop it. You are just missing Michael. Behind her, the lilting chords of Bach floated from the cottage, echoed over the rocks. Maggie smiled, glancing up at the high dome of sky where white clouds raced in feathery ribbons across the vast blue.

Music fathoms the sky, she thought.

Turning her back against the biting wind that bent tall grasses against the rocks, she headed inland, away from the cottage, toward the red-roofed home of their nearest neighbor, just visible through the woods beyond the promontory. Where the girl had disappeared. Someone there had to have known her grandmother.

A rocky path led her through the pines to a small clearing. Not a cottage, she saw, but a contemporary house – two stories, all wood and glass and angles, with a door painted bright blue and decorated with a wreath of autumn leaves. Somewhere inside, *La Bohème* was playing. A black Mercedes was parked in the graveled yard.

Before she could knock, the door swung open and the huge tangerine cat whooshed by her. "Hello there," she grinned. "We meet again."

"Ah, I see you've met Angus," said a low male voice in accented English.

Maggie turned. A broad-shouldered man stood in the doorway, dark hair swept back from a sculpted face, deep brown eyes glinting with humor.

"Angus?" she said with surprise. "Your French cat has a Scots name?"

"Long story, involving a tad too much whiskey, and bagpipes at midnight." The eyes crinkled, a sweep of a long-fingered hand. "You must be Magdalena O'Shea. Please, come in. It's an honor to finally meet you. Welcome to Brittany."

"Yes, I'm Maggie." She took his hand, smiled as she stepped through the door into an open, high-ceilinged room. "Thank you. It's good to finally be here."

He gave a courtly bow. "I am Gerard Jouvert. *Le Docteur.* I run the medical clinic here in Cancale."

Memory stirred. "*Monsieur* Jouvert? My grandmother's lawyer mentioned you. You were a close friend of my *Grand-mère*?"

He smiled sadly. "I'm afraid not. I knew her, of course, but I was just a boy."

"Of course," echoed Maggie. "There is just so much I don't know about my grandmother. It's why I've come. Perhaps you will tell me about –"

A flash of cherry red appeared on the stairs, a clatter of shoes. A young girl of ten or eleven raced into the room, stopped short when she saw Maggie. Slipping shyly behind her father, she peered out, dark eyes huge and wary in the pale heart-shaped face, her expression hidden by a mass of wild tangled curls. A sprinkle of freckles covered her cheeks like brown stars.

"Hello," said Maggie. "I heard you playing the piano at my grandmother's cottage yesterday. It was beautiful. I love Mozart's music."

Gerard Jouvert raised an eyebrow and, setting a gentle hand on the girl's shoulder, he drew her forward. "This is my daughter, Frankie."

"First Angus, now Frankie," murmured Maggie. "Surely not another story of whiskey and bagpipes?" Smiling, she dropped to one knee so that her eyes were level with the child's. "It's so nice to meet another pianist, Frankie. My name is Maggie. I'm here with my father, Finn, from America. My grandmother lived in the cottage a long time ago, so I think the piano might have been hers."

Silence. Dark eyes wide and anxious, her expression grave.

"I hope you will come over to play for us again?"

"Would you like that, *ma chérie*?" said the father into the silence.

The girl blinked, then turned and ran out the door, her long curls flying in dark ribbons behind her.

"Please forgive my daughter's manners." Gerard Jouvert held out his hand to Maggie as she rose. "Frankie's mother died six months ago, after a long illness," he said quietly. "She hasn't spoken since." He gazed toward the window at the distant sea. "I am a doctor but I cannot help my own child."

Maggie felt the sympathy well in her chest. "There's nothing worse than being afraid for our children." She sought his eyes. "My godson was mute for many months after the trauma of being separated from his mother. But time, patience, care and love eventually worked their magic. TJ is fine, now. Just don't give up hope."

Jouvert nodded. "Never." He straightened his shoulders. "I did not know Frankie was at the cottage yesterday. My apologies. We have a piano here, as you can see, but…. my wife was teaching her to play before she got sick."

"I think your daughter must be speaking through the music, then, *Monsieur* Jouvert. Give her time. And, please, I meant what

I said. She is welcome to come play anytime. A piano needs to be played. And I know my father would love to meet her."

"Thank you. I will tell her." He lifted his chin. "This is a strange question, I know, but – well, I suddenly find myself the single father of a preteen girl. Frankie is eleven, and I must confess I am at a total loss." The confusion stirring in his eyes reminded her of Michael.

"A 'Tween' is not an age for the faint of heart. I raised my son alone for many years. How can I help you?"

A sigh of relief. "Would it be possible for you to show me how to braid a girl's hair? It's been so hard on Frankie these last months. My wife always did those things. After she died, Frankie began to go to your cottage every morning before school so that Elle could fix her hair. But now that Elle is no longer there –" He shrugged, suddenly defeated.

Maggie felt the shock of his words hit her. "*Elle*?"

A Gallic eyebrow raised in surprise. "*Bien sûr*. Your grandmother's sister, Elle. She adores Frankie." The doctor bent closer, seeing her confusion. "You did not know? Elle has been living in the cottage all these years, since just after the war. Your grandmother made all the arrangements in her will. But at Elle's request we settled her into an excellent nursing facility nearby, in the village of Saint-Méloir, two months ago…" His voice faded. He set a steadying hand on her arm.

"I see you are shocked, *Madame* O'Shea. But it is true. Your great-aunt Elle is alive."

Clair

"Memories Float Like Perfume

Through the Mind."

CHAPTER 23

"Your sister Elle is alive."

Kneeling in the cold, narrow darkness of the confessional in Église Saint-Gervais, Clair Rousseau froze. "What did you say, *Père?*"

She could hear the smile in the priest's soft voice. "There has been word, finally. I told you not to give up hope, little one."

Clair leaned her forehead against the old wooden slats that separated her from Father Jean-Luc. "How?" she whispered. "Where?" All these months. It was suddenly hard to catch her breath. She began to tremble.

"We believe your sister is in Germany, north of Berlin. A female prisoners' camp called Ravensbrück. Three French women escaped from there not long ago, in a laundry truck. They smuggled out lists of names that they passed on to the Resistance, to the Red Cross. One of the women told a story of a young girl your sister's age whose hair was the color of gold wheat – before it was shaved off."

Clair's stomach turned over. "Oh Holy Mother. And my *maman?*"

"No word on your mother. But the prisoner said the girl is known throughout the camp because she gives secret ballet lessons to the women in her barracks, late at night, to try to keep them strong. To keep them human." Something shook in his voice. "Her name is Elle. They call her *La Ballerine.*"

"Oh, *Père*, could it be true?"

"The age, the hair, the dancing. Her name. It all rings true. I will do everything in my power to find out more, to confirm *La Ballerine's* identity for you. Have faith, little one." The wooden confessional door rattled. "So," said the priest, "I have something for the Ghosts today."

Sliding open the small square door between them, he whispered, "Avril will meet you in half an hour at the Café Matisse on Place Saint-Michel."

A tiny, tightly-rolled paper, smaller than half a cigarette, dropped into her palm. "Peace be with you," said the priest. The wooden door slid closed.

It was snowing when Clair slipped off her bicycle just outside the Café Matisse, on the corner of Place Saint-Michel. The large, awning-covered windows of the old bistro overlooked the Seine, gunmetal-gray in the light, and, beyond, the towers and spire of Notre Dame rose into a sky swirling white with snow.

Just inside the door, Avril sat at a tiny round table sipping a glass of red wine, legs crossed, her book open. *All clear.*

Clair chose a table toward the rear of the café, ordered a coffee, and tried to slow her thundering heart. It was always like this.

I am living a life of lies, thought Clair, not for the first time. Avril's gravelly voice spun into her head. *It is only a matter of time until we get caught, Beauty Queen.*

For a moment, Clair wished Avril was sitting beside her. Against all odds, she and the older, hard-drinking Frenchwoman had proven to be a good team. Together, over these last winter weeks, they had managed to gather and pass on vital information to be sent via radio to "Uncle Bradley," the code-name for the Special Operations British officer in London's SOE who ran their network. Avril had told her he was a major player in the planning of Operation Overlord, the invasion of Fortress Europe.

And so, of course, every bit of information was vital—troop locations and numbers of soldiers, train schedules, ship cargoes, artillery positions, the critical bases for the V1 flying bombs aimed at London. Rumors of rockets at Peenemunde. Rumors of where, and when, the Germans thought the Allies would land—the biggest secret of all.

In her job at the Hotel Metropole, Clair still was considered an attractive piece of furniture. Her seeming invisibility gave her access to many of the private, inner offices and meetings, invitations to small parties on Avenue Hoche. After the second meeting of the network, the leader known as "Night " had given her a Minox Riga miniature camera, easily concealed, so tiny it could fit inside a matchbox. The film was no bigger than the nail on her pinky finger, but it took sharp, focused photographs.

The first time she'd used the camera—"Just open and click," Night had told her—she'd been shaking so hard with fear that she thought the guards would hear the rattle of her bones. But now, she'd lost count of the documents she had secretly photographed in the Nazi offices at the Metropole over the last month.

She smiled when she thought of Night. The silver-streaked temples, the dark, intense green eyes that seemed to burn right through her. Handsome as a Greek God standing in the moonlight. She'd asked Avril about him after that first meeting. What would keep a healthy young Frenchman safely in Paris when every available man was conscripted into the German army or their work details?

Avril had given her familiar bark of laughter and replied, "You will find out when you make your first drop at Café Matisse."

That day had finally come. Today was her first visit, and Clair glanced anxiously around the busy café. Long zinc bar, glassware overhead, tiny round tables scattered around the room, almost all occupied by high-ranking Germans having a late afternoon drink. She lowered her lashes, afraid to call attention to herself.

On the small table in front of her, cigarettes she would never smoke and a small matchbox holding film instead of matches sat next to the ashtray and her almost empty coffee cup.

Real coffee, not ersatz. Clair closed her eyes, took a deep swallow.

When she opened her eyes, she saw a flash of bright blue, just beyond the windows. A young girl with golden hair danced down the sidewalk in front of the café. *Elle?* The images unfurled like a blooming flower. Her little sister twirling in a sea of lavender petals, her hair a banner of gold ribbons. Leaping from bench to bench with a red balloon, singing to a tiny kitten. Riding her favorite pink horse on the carousel in the Luxembourg Gardens. For once the images were sweet, not filled with the sharp ache of longing. *The memories float like perfume through the mind,* thought Clair.

She smiled, hearing the familiar notes of a favorite Chopin Prelude in her head, the No. 7 in A Major, a beautiful piece that reminded her of her sister. The music and memories filled her with hope that she would soon hear more news from *Père*, news confirming that her sister was alive.

The girl beyond the café window turned. A sweet face. But not her sister.

Elle is the real reason you are sitting here, she reminded herself. Every choice, every moment, was about finding Elle. *Focus.* It was almost time.

Her contact was seated two tables away, a beautiful woman in a fitted black dress, real seamed nylon stockings and deep scarlet lipstick, having a drink with three German officers. The nightclubs had remained open for the troops, and she was a popular chanteuse with a voice like Edith Piaf. To Clair she also was known as "Snapdragon," the Ghost Network's best radio operator.

Clair tried not to stare at the stockings, now so impossible to find that most Frenchwomen were forced to draw a seam down their calves with a black pencil.

Snapdragon's compact flashed silver on the table beside her, the all-clear, next to a pack of *Gauloises*. Any moment now she would reach for the cigarettes, excuse herself and make her way past the bar toward *Les Toilettes*, stopping to ask Clair for a match.

The scrape of a chair at the next table.

"Mademoiselle?"

She started, her eyes rising to the Nazi towering over her.

Holy Mother. Her heart began to thunder. She tried to smile. *"Oui?"*

She gripped her coffee cup. *Don't let him see your hands shake.*

Blue eyes staring into hers, then dropping to the matchbox on the table.

If he asks me for a match, I'm a dead woman.

In halting French, the soldier said, "I wonder if I could borrow your –"

Slow footsteps behind her, the soft tap of a cane. The proprietor of the café appeared at her elbow, body bent, smelling of cooking grease and whiskey. "Klaus," he said in perfect German, "I have a case of that French wine you like so much, in the back room."

The German gazed down at her a moment longer, then turned to follow the owner toward the rear of the café.

That low, familiar voice.

Very slowly Clair turned her head to gaze at the owner. Silver-streaked temples, glowing jade eyes. It all fell into place. Night was allowed to stay in Paris and run the café because the Germans believed he was a collaborator.

It was the perfect cover.

Out of the corner of her eye she saw Snapdragon rise from her seat, turn toward her. An unlit cigarette waved in the air. A whiff of Evening in Paris perfume as the woman bent her head.

"*Avez-vous des allumettes, Mademoiselle?*" The words were low, throaty, the voice of a chanteuse.

Shaking uncontrollably, Clair held out the matchbox. Then, suddenly nauseous and unable to finish her coffee, she stood and headed for the door without a backward glance.

CHAPTER 24

Clair had biked the four *kilometres* from the church in the Marais to the 6th arrondissement, crossing the Seine at Pont Notre-Dame, and now she stood, taking deep breaths, in front of the Hôtel Lutetia. In the recent past, the beautiful Art Nouveau hotel on the Left Bank had been home to displaced musicians and artists. But in 1940, when so many citizens evacuated Paris, the Abwehr established its intelligence headquarters there under Kommandant Oskar Reile.

Across the busy avenue, most of the hotel's first floor windows were covered by pine branches and wire fencing, but today polished boots and medals sparked in the spring light as German soldiers hurried in and out of the high main doors and gathered in small groups on the sidewalk to confer. All eyes were on the Boulevard Raspail. The new Abwehr Kommandant was supposed to arrive any moment, with orders, she had heard, to end sabotage and espionage. To concentrate on finding and interrogating suspected Resistance fighters.

The word interrogation caused a sharp knife of ice to slide down her spine. She had been working for the Resistance now for more than three months, but it never became easier. The bone-crunching fear was always with her. And there was still no news of Elle.

Clair did not think of herself as a devout Catholic, but every night she prayed for the courage to survive capture without betraying her friends or her country. She had to survive, to find her sister.

Blend in. Avril's voice again, forcing her to move. Head down, she tied her bicycle to a plane tree and walked toward a group of secretaries, dressed like herself in narrow skirts and white blouses, who had gathered by the benches near Square Boucicaut.

A wave of German voices, commotion on the boulevard. A parade of black Peugeots slowly approached the hotel's front doors and came to a stop. The Abwehr officers near the doors stood to attention as several men alighted from the cars. One man in particular caught Clair's attention.

A billow of blue *Gauloises* smoke obscured the man's face, but – a flash of sunlight lanced off the rims of small, thick round glasses just before he stepped into the shadows.

Light and dark. Light and dark.

She felt her heart constrict. Oh Holy Mother. She knew that thin build, the stiff shoulders, the jacket, heavy with medals. The narrow fox-like face with its line of scars, the flat, staring eyes. It was *him*! The man from the night train to Paris…

The Nazi who had been seated across from her on the night train last November.

She turned to run, felt a heavy hand clamp on her shoulder.

"*Mademoiselle* Rousseau!" Oberst Schneider, his breath smelling of stale beer, towered over her. Her chief at the Metropole, Schneider was an overweight bully with pock-marked jowls who still had no idea that she could speak German.

Setting a heavy hand on her back, he propelled her forward across the busy street. "Come inside with me. You must meet our new Chief of the Abwehr, all the way from Berlin. Kommandant Kurt Jager."

Turn around! Get away! Avril's voice screamed in her ear.

At that moment the new Kommandant turned and saw her.

An endless walk through the Hôtel Lutetia lobby, across the Art Deco mosaic of the sailing ship emblazoned on the marble floor – the ancient symbol of the resilience and courage of the Parisian people. *Fluctuat Nec Mergitur*. She is rocked by waves but does not sink.

Surrounded by Abwehr officers, Clair closed her eyes at the terrible irony. Voices faded, faces blurred around her. She could feel the thunder of her heartbeat pulsing in her ears. Would he recognize her? *She is rocked by waves but does not sink*, she told herself. Just breathe.

As if from a distance she heard Oberst Schneider click his heels together as he introduced her. "*Kommandant* Kurt Jager, allow me to introduce *Mademoiselle* Clair Rousseau."

Dear God, now he knows my name. Don't let him know you understand German!

She raised her head slowly. Kommandant Jager's face was just inches from hers, the flat cold eyes holding hers like a snake's.

She offered a small smile, heard herself say, "*Bonjour*," in a tinny, unfamiliar voice.

He continued to stare at her, until she thought her shuddering knees would give away, and then suddenly he leaned in very close and gripped her upper arm painfully. Against her ear, so that only she could hear, he whispered in German, "You little French cunt, someday soon I will strip you naked and force you to your knees in front of me."

GodGodPlease don't let him know I understand.

Somehow, she managed not to stiffen, to jerk away. Somehow, she forced her body to stay soft, keep the muscles of her mouth in the shape of an innocent, questioning smile as she stepped back and turned to him. Somehow, by lowering her lashes, she gave herself a moment to will the hatred from her eyes. "*Je ne comprends pas, Monsieur?*"

He stepped away, his flat snake's eyes still on hers, narrowed blurs through the thick round lenses. Considering, assessing. Remembering?

"We will meet again, *Mademoiselle*," he said in stilted French, before turning away.

"Holy Mother, Avril, I've never been more frightened in my life."

The two women sat on the floor, leaning against the unmade bed in the cold room above the butcher shop on rue Mouffetard. All the lamps were off, the only light coming from the burning red arc of Avril's cigarette. Clair came several times each week to the small apartment now, ever since Avril had asked her to play her son's piano.

He loved that damn piano. It needs to be played.

Non. I haven't played since I lost my mother and my sister. The music has left me.

Bloody nonsense. It's still there, deep inside you. Let it out, Clair. You need it, maybe more than I do. Your mother would never have wanted you to stop playing, it will keep her and your sister with you always.

Avril had been right. Her mother had loved listening to her music. She would say, *No matter what happens, when you play the piano, I will always be with you.* Clair could picture her now, sitting in her favorite blue-cushioned chair, eyes closed, swaying to Tchaikovsky's beautiful piano concerto. And oh, she'd missed her music desperately after her mother and sister were taken away. It was the one safe place Clair could find in her life, where she could disappear, return to a time of love and joy. Be with her mother and her little sister once more…

Avril's rasp jolted her back to the present – and the voice of Edith Piaf singing *Les Trois Cloches* that trembled in the smoke-filled air.

"You are sure Jager remembered you, Beauty Queen?"

"What he whispered… it was so sick, so filthy. So personal. How could he not?"

Avril blew a steam of blue smoke toward the ceiling. "German pig," she muttered. "But you're sure he does not know what you really do?"

"No. I don't think he knew that I understood his words. But –"

Clair leaped to her feet, ran to the window, parted the curtain just half an inch to search the narrow street. It was raining steadily now, big drops clattering on rooftop tiles and cobblestones, misting the dark glass windows across the way. No umbrellas passing by, no one stood in the wet shadows, no one sat at the soaked outdoor tables at the bistro across the street.

And yet…

Clair turned back to Avril. "His surname, Jager. It means 'hunter.' What if he had me followed? What if he finds out about the network?"

"I told you when we met, Clair, it's only a matter of time. We can't let the fear stop us." Avril struggled to her bare feet, set her empty whiskey glass on the crowded table, tossed the burned-down *Gauloises* stub into the sink. "We cannot worry about what might happen. We must focus on what we *can* do. What we *must* do."

Avril turned, her hand on the whiskey bottle. "Is there any more news of your sister?"

For the first time since she'd been at the Hôtel Lutetia that afternoon, Clair was able to smile. "*Père* believes she is still alive." She rested a hand on Avril's bony shoulder. "You are right about one thing, you crazy old spy. We cannot let the fear stop us. I will focus on what I *can* do."

She stood, moved to the piano, set a score on the wooden music desk.

"I believe my sister is alive, Avril. I have a plan. I know how I am going to find Elle. Just listen, it's all in the music. The infinite beauty and grace. It's a slow dance, loving, full of tenderness and joy. Just like Elle. I know I am going to be with my beloved sister again."

Her fingers on the keys, the music now her only connection to vanished happiness. To the memories of Elle that floated through her mind. She closed her eyes and began to play Chopin's Prelude No. 7. Intricate patterns filled the shadowed room, fervent, nostalgic and wistful, as Clair poured her longing and hope for a reunion with Elle into the beautiful chords.

CHAPTER 25

CANCALE, BRITTANY. PRESENT DAY

Late morning sun scattered diamond sparks across the water. Maggie stood on the rocks above the narrow sweep of beach, watching the seabirds glide on the wind like a necklace of feathers and listening to the shush and sigh of low tide. White clouds scudded across an endless sky, casting shadows over quivering grasses.

Yes, she thought. My grandmother stood in this very spot, walked across these very stones, gazed at the restless sea. This wild, lonely place spoke to her the way it speaks to me. Whispering with echoes of the past on the wind.

Footsteps behind her broke the reverie.

"*Madame* O'Shea?"

She turned to smile at their neighbor. "*Bonjour, Monsieur* Jouvert. Please, you must call me Maggie."

"With pleasure. And I am Gerard to my friends."

"Gerard." She looked past him. "And where is our young pianist this morning?"

"I'm afraid your father has already swept her up."

" Ah. The Maestro is quite the life force when he wants to be."

"So I saw." He hesitated. "It is because of my Frankie that your great-aunt now lives at Saint-Méloir."

Maggie's eyes widened in shock. "I don't understand."

"At the end of the summer, Elle began to understand that something was wrong with her. Small things. She forgot that dinner was in the oven, she found her pills in the refrigerator, a book in the shower. *Alors*, the problems of aging, yes? But then one afternoon she went for a walk and got lost. A neighbor found her, very confused and frightened, and brought her to me.

The next day she seemed fine, but then she forgot to turn off the kettle, started a small fire in the kitchen. She came to me, said she knew it wasn't safe for Frankie to be in the cottage. Frankie showed up there every day, you see. Elle said she would never put our beautiful child in danger."

"Are you saying that my Aunt Elle has Alzheimer's?"

He shook his head. "*Non.* But the early stages of dementia, *bien sûr.* Memory loss, confusion, the struggle to find the right word. Mood changes. The symptoms can change from day to day, sometimes even on the same day. But your *Tante* is well cared for, and seems happy most of the time." He flashed a boyish grin. "Except for the 'no whiskey' rule, of course."

Maggie returned his smile. "My kind of woman."

"No doubt. So, I believe that seeing you will be very good for your great-aunt. Are you ready to meet her?"

Maggie gazed out over the bay, where Mont-Saint-Michel wavered like a fairy-tale castle in the fog-laced distance. "I will admit, I'm a bit anxious."

"Very normal. Elle is in her nineties, as you must know. The ballet was her whole life. She taught dance until well into her seventies, but now of course she is quite frail. A strong heart, *oui,* but the dementia comes and goes. Still early onset, so something to be thankful for. One minute she knows Frankie, myself. The next… well." A Gallic shrug of shoulders. "Sometimes she lives only in the past. Memories of the war years are especially terrifying for her."

"How could they not be?" Maggie's breath came out. "May I ask her questions about my grandmother, and my mother? The last thing I want to do is frighten her."

"It will depend entirely on Elle's state of mind today. I can stay with you, if you'd like."

"Very much. You are a kind man, Gerard."

"Just a smart one. I still need you to teach me how to braid Frankie's hair." He smiled. "Come, let's go to the cottage and see what those two crazy kids are up to."

"The violins are chasing the piano. Faster, faster! *Non*, how can this happen? We cannot let the piano get caught by those crazy violins, can we? What must the piano do? Show me, child!"

Frankie was seated at the baby grand, her toes barely touching the floor, gazing up at Finn Stewart. The Maestro towered over her, leaning against the piano as if to steady himself, while his arms waved back and forth.

Gerard Jouvert took a step toward his daughter, but Maggie stopped him with a hand on his arm and a look that said, *Wait, it will be okay.*

The room was quiet as a held breath. All of a sudden Frankie's small fingers began to move, faster and faster, until they were flying over the keys. Mozart's chords tumbled, spun, shattered the air. Then the girl stopped, lifted her head, and made a soft, whispery sound of pleasure.

"*Mon Dieu*," murmured her father, his shocked eyes locked on his glowing child.

"Yes!" cried Finn, leaning toward the girl. "Exactly right. You saved your piano from the dreaded violins, little sprite. Well done."

The child remained silent, her eyes wide and shining.

"I agree," said Finn softly. "Talking is overrated, isn't it? The more we talk, the less we listen. I'm like you. I like to listen to Mozart, I like to let Mozart speak for me."

Maggie had a flash of memory. She'd been five or six, seated at the piano, desperate to learn Bach's Prelude in C. *Her father's huge hands, covering her own, guiding her fingers to the right notes – over and over, until she finally was able to play it on her own. Well done, little sprite, he had said.*

Her father's sharp oath snapped her back to the present. Finn had turned too quickly. She saw him sway, lose his balance for a brief moment. Before she could move, he lurched for the piano, righted himself, took a heaving breath.

"Take a minute, dad. You have time to –"

"Time is just what I *don't* have!" Waving a trembling hand in the air, he muttered, "Water break," and shuffled off toward the kitchen.

The doctor watched him leave, then looked down at Maggie. "Your father appears to be unwell. Would you like me to examine him?"

"He'll refuse. He insists it's jet lag, but..." Her eyes followed her father's slowly retreating back.

"I see. Well, I am just a shout away. Perhaps he would accept a cane for balance?" Jouvert raised a questioning brow, then turned back to the piano. "This Ibach was your grandmother's. During the war, I'm told, several German officers were stationed here, in the cottage. What the Boches couldn't steal, they destroyed. Including pianos, can you believe it? Of course your grandmother's Ibach was too big for the neighbors to move, or hide. But luckily, one of the German officers had children at home in Berlin, children who played the piano. He stopped the others from smashing the Ibach to pieces."

"Plato said, 'Music gives a soul to the universe,'" murmured Maggie, running a hand over the beautiful old instrument.

"He knew what he was talking about, yes? Perhaps that is why your Ibach was saved. I hope you will play for us before you leave," said Jouvert from behind her. "Come, Frankie. It's time we take our new friend Maggie to meet her great-aunt Elle."

CHAPTER 26

LES JARDINS DE SAINT-MÉLOIR, BRITTANY

Beyond a tall, intricately wrought iron gate, Les Jardins de Saint-Méloir Nursing Home was set on a gentle slope of land overlooking the sea, just outside the town of Saint-Méloir-des-Ondes. Under a sloping slate roof, ivy twined around the rose-colored stone and elegant shuttered windows of the graceful French country house. Paths wound beneath bare-branched trees, through autumn gardens of chrysanthemums and grasses in shades of emerald and tarnished gold.

Maggie, Finn, Gerard and his daughter followed the nurse to a wooden bench with a view of windswept sea and sky. A woman draped in a heavy blue shawl sat very still, back straight, her eyes on the horizon. A folded wheelchair rested next to a young aide who sat close by, reading aloud.

"*Madame Elle?* You have visitors."

The aide raised her head, stood with a quick smile and moved off to join the nurse. Finn sank into the vacated metal chair with a sigh.

The woman on the bench raised her head slowly, turned. The shawl fell back, exposing a coronet of hair the color of pearls above a sharp-boned, withered face with hollowed cheeks. Faded blue eyes, once the color of aquamarines, still glinted with intelligence and beauty. But not recognition.

Frankie broke away from her father and ran to the older woman.

Maggie held her breath as Elle Rousseau stared at Frankie for a long moment. Then, the bright spark in the eyes, the sudden tilt of head. "*Bébé!* My sweet Frankie, is it you?"

Frankie gave a vigorous nod and threw her arms around the old woman. Elle's arms, thin as sticks, pulled the child against her.

"Still no words, my dear *bébé*?" said Elle in a low, feathery voice. "They will come back, I promise you."

Frankie reached into her pocket and held up a pink hair brush. Elle smiled and reached for it. "So, my lovey, you want a braid today?" She turned the girl around, pulled her between her knees, and began to brush the long dark curls with a gentle, quivering hand.

"It's these small, unfurling moments that keep us centered, keep our lives in place," whispered Maggie against Gerard Jouvert's jacket.

He flashed a grateful look at Maggie and moved to touch Elle's shoulder. "*Madame Elle*, it's good to see you. As you can see, Frankie has missed you very much. She brought some friends all the way from the United States to meet you today."

Elle offered a faint, vague smile, then turned toward Maggie as she continued to braid the child's hair.

The pale blue eyes widened. A stifled gasp. The hairbrush fell to the grass.

"Oh my dear sweet God. *Clair!* You've come back to me."

Panic welled in Maggie's chest. She had no idea how to respond to her great-aunt and she turned to Gerard Jouvert for guidance.

He nodded, bent to Elle. "*Madame Elle*, this is Magdalena O'Shea, an American classical pianist. She looks so much like your sister Clair for a very good reason. She is Clair's granddaughter." He took Maggie's arm, drew her forward. "This is your great niece, Maggie. Lily's daughter."

"Hello, *Tante Elle*," said Maggie softly.

The pale blue eyes clouded with confusion as Elle shook her head back and forth. Then she turned slowly toward Maggie and there was a sudden flash of recognition, like a sunburst, in her eyes. "Magdalena? Lily's daughter? Come closer, child." She held out a bony hand, grasped Maggie's. The skin was papery, thin as tissue, cold. But the grip was fierce. "Magdalena was Clair's middle name," she whispered. "You are little Maggie – Clair's granddaughter?"

Maggie felt the quick hot rush of tears on her cheeks. "Yes! I did not know you were alive, *Tante*, I would have come so much sooner. Oh, I am so happy to see you." She reached to envelop her great aunt in her arms.

"Sweet child. Did you bring your mother with you?"

Maggie froze. Then, with a confident glance from Jouvert, she continued. "Not this time. I brought my father, Finn. This is my mother Lily's husband, Maestro Finn Stewart. He's an orchestra conductor."

Finn rose and stepped forward, bowed, and kissed Elle's hand. "It is an honor to meet my Lily's beautiful aunt," he said.

"Ah, you are a charming one," murmured Elle. "And handsome! My niece had good taste." She looked away, seemed to lose focus. Then, as if from a different conversation, "Tchaikovsky's Swan Lake was so beautiful. Did you know that I danced the role of the Black Swan?"

"I love that music," said Maggie gently. "I wish I could have seen you dance."

"They made me dance for them in the camp!" cried Elle suddenly, in a louder voice. Frankie jolted toward her father, frightened. "They called me *La Ballerine*." Then, "No! I don't want to remember."

Gerard Jouvert stepped forward, setting a gentle hand on her shoulder. "We understand, *Madame Elle*. You do not have to think of that time. You are safe here at *Les Jardins*."

"After the war, the curtain came down on my memories," whispered Elle. "I wanted them to! And now, the images are fading with age, and time…" Her thought died away. She raised her eyes to Jouvert. "But I must talk about it, before the memories are forgotten forever. We cannot forget the music."

She turned to Maggie. "Baudelaire kept my sister company in the dark days. Now he keeps your Grandmother's music safe." She lifted her head, listening. "*So I sleep on high, near starry courses.* The dead won't stay quiet. Can you not hear the echo of their voices?"

A moment passed. She smiled vaguely at Maggie, leaned forward to stare. "Hello, dear, are you the new aide? Perhaps you could help me find my room. I seem to have gotten lost again." Then the clouds washed across her eyes, and Elle began, very softly, to sing.

CHAPTER 27

SUNRISE RANCH. HUME, VA

"The colonel's plane must be landing in Paris just about now," said Robbie Brennan. "We should be hearing from him any time."

In the wide stable hallway, the teenager Dov remained quiet, brushing the mare's scarred flanks in slow, easy strokes. The scars were long, white, and jagged as lightning bolts.

"There's an old English proverb," said the priest into the silence. "Show me your horse, and I will tell you what you are."

"Lady's a rescue," said the boy, his hand sweeping over Lady in Black's mane, brushing it from her single eye. "Aren't you, pretty girl?"

"Well, that does not surprise me. She surely is beautiful." The priest sat in his wheelchair, eyes on the boy and horse. Shiloh lay close by, dozing in a small patch of sunlight that filtered through a high window in the horse's stall.

"The colonel found her. Kinda like he found me."

"Kinda."

Dov shot a look at the priest. "You think he told Maggie he was coming to France?"

"Afraid not."

"Don't see how that can end well."

"Afraid so."

Dov grinned. "I don't need a baby sitter, Padre, but you're okay."

"Thank you. I think." Robbie leaned back in his chair. "We're just a boy, a priest, a horse, and a dog, together in a stable," he murmured. "There's got to be a joke in here somewhere."

"Or a Hallmark movie," quipped the boy.

Robbie chuckled, then suddenly wheeled backwards as Lady edged toward him. Shiloh opened his eyes, alert and protective.

"Easy, girl." The boy grasped the reigns. "You don't have to be afraid, Padre." He rubbed a gentle hand down the mare's flank. "The thing about horses is, you have to touch them, get to know them. *Listen* to them. The Vets here say riding is good for the soul."

"What about the soulless?"

The boy glanced at the wheelchair, then away. "Not that I think you couldn't ride."

"It's okay to talk about my injuries," said Robbie. "Maggie and the colonel still call it an accident, but I know it was God's punishment for hubris."

"Like Icarus," said Dov, stroking Lady's lightning bolt scars. "His pride was his undoing."

Robbie raised a pale eyebrow. "Studying the Greek Gods in school?"

"I wish. Nah. But I have a book about them. Gotta love Zeus."

Shiloh wobbled to his three legs with a sigh-like woof, clearly uninterested in the conversation. Man and boy smiled at each other.

"The Gods versus one God?" The priest smiled. "Truth is, I can face down mortal sin in either religion, but think I may be afraid of horses," said Robbie, his eyes on Lady.

"You sound just like the colonel."

"Is that such a bad thing?"

Dov scowled at him. "Sometimes. I'm not his kid but he's been acting like I am."

"Again. Is that such a bad thing?"

"I heard the Vets talking one night. He had a son. Kid died when he was little." A hitched breath. The boy looked away. "The colonel never told me."

"I didn't know either. As Tolstoy said, 'Every heart has its own skeletons.'" Robbie reached out, took the boy's arm. "Hard to judge someone, Dov, until you've walked a mile in their shoes."

Dov turned back, a brief grin lighting his face. "Maybe, Padre. But at least you'll be a mile away and have new shoes. Or boots, in this case."

Robbie laughed. "*Now* who's sounding like the colonel? All I'm saying is, I've made a scorched earth of my life. Learned far too late that we can burn bridges or mend fences."

"You sure you're a priest, Padre?"

One of the Vets who worked at the ranch appeared at the stable door. "Hey, Dov, got a package for you. Special delivery." He tossed a small brown box to the boy and disappeared.

Dov looked down at the package, covered with red, white and blue Airmail stamps. "Must be from Maggie," he murmured with an expectant smile, tearing at the wrapping. "She's been sending me photographs and – *Jesus!*"

He lunged backwards as if burned, flinging the package contents to the hay-covered floor. The mare gave an anxious whinny as Shiloh's sharp protective bark filled the stable.

"Dov? What is it?" Robbie wheeled closer, bent to retrieve the small black object that lay half hidden in the bits of hay. "Good Lord."

It was a beautifully carved chess piece. A knight. A black horse's head.

"It's from Belankov," said Dov in a strangled voice. "He's the man who shot Lady! It has to be from him."

"If that's true then our Russian friend just made a huge mistake," said the priest. "He sent the wrong chess piece. He should have sent a bishop."

Yuri Belankov walked slowly along the Place du Trocadéro toward the Eiffel Tower. Flurries of early snow spun around him, blurring the beautiful tower that rose so gracefully into a swirling opalescent sky. It was one of his favorite places in Paris to walk. To think.

A young, attractive Frenchwoman gave him an appreciative glance, and he smiled to himself. He was getting used to this new look of his. He'd lost weight, allowed his hair to grow once again, added the streaks of silver. His salt-and-pepper beard was clipped to hug his jaw, new tinted glasses disguised his eyes. Small lifts in his leather boots, less swagger in his walk. A new career as an art gallery buyer. Even a new name. It was hard to give up the heavy gold necklace and rings, but he would wear them again one day.

Yes, he missed his trademark, smooth bald head. Who wouldn't? But hair could be shaved, eh? In the meantime, Yuri Belankov no longer existed.

He stopped to stand directly beneath the tower and stare up at the exquisite and very aptly named Iron Lady of Paris. Almost one thousand feet high, she was a technical miracle of latticed metal girders, columns, beams and supports. Seven tons of iron, he'd read somewhere, and built in just two years.

He stood for a long time, gazing up through the open latticework, watching the snow drift down between the rafters. He had nowhere else to be. No chess today. The weather had scared off even the most diehard players.

But who would complain about a life in Paris, with art galleries and croissants and chess?

The thought of chess brought him full circle. Had the boy gotten the chess piece yet? How had he reacted?

Time for the next move.

Sometimes, thought Yuri, you become so focused on one chess piece that you totally miss the piece on the other side of the board, the one that is sitting there threatening the entire game.

Let them focus, he thought. I am no longer the man I was. They won't see me coming now.

CHAPTER 28

CANCALE HARBOR, BRITTANY

Inhale. Exhale. Inhale. Exhale.

Maggie's old Nikes pounded the coastal path along Cancale's picturesque harbor in the steady beat of a Bach minuet. She had begun running several years earlier, as a way not to feel or think, when her husband had disappeared after his sailboat exploded off the coast of France. Somehow, running had helped her deal with the overwhelming grief of losing her husband and her music. Now, she ran at least three miles whenever she could find the time, because she simply couldn't *not* run.

The small fishing port, known for its seafood and *crêpes*, charmed her with its seventeenth century Breton stone houses set against jagged seaside cliffs below the 'upper town.' Lighthouse, tiny beaches, coves dotted with colorful fishing boats. The *Marché aux Huîtres* by the long pier, offering Cancale's famous oysters and shellfish. And always, the wavering reflection of distant Mont-Saint-Michel in the deep blue bay.

Inhale. Exhale. Inhale. Exhale.

This morning the cool air smelled sharply of shells, salt and the sea. The sky was painted with ribbons of wispy clouds and the music of the seabirds.

Music fathoms the sky, she thought.

She grinned as Beckett's words floated into her head when he'd given her the tee shirt. *Hell, Maggie, I'm not sure even Baudelaire knew what it meant.*

Baudelaire... Her thoughts spun to her great-aunt's words. *Baudelaire is keeping your grandmother's music safe.*

I know what she meant, thought Maggie suddenly. The answers are at the cottage.

She slowed, then turned east to head home. In the nearby car park, a flash of light on polished black metal caught her attention. A ghostly, familiar profile, turning quickly away.

She narrowed her eyes. The sound of a powerful engine, turning over. The Mercedes shot forward, sped toward the exit.

"Not a fan of oysters?" she murmured. She shook her head, and ran faster.

Maggie stopped short in the cottage doorway, her eyes on the pair by the piano. The lesson was over. Now her father sat astride the bench, with Frankie perched next to him. The solemn little girl held a stuffed bear dressed in a tuxedo against her chest while Finn tried, unsuccessfully, to braid her hair. He was in the midst of a totally inappropriate story of a drunken composer who fell into the violinists during a performance of Wagner's Symphony in C. Dark silky strands of curls escaped his trembling hands to fall over Frankie's shoulders and about her heart-shaped face.

"I never liked Wagner anyway," muttered Finn, as he tried to tuck one final rogue curl in place. Then he sat back, shook his head, and began to laugh. Miraculously, Frankie turned her head and trilled with him.

Her laughter was high, musical, and Maggie was spun back in time to a moment in her childhood when her father was brushing her hair and telling her a story about a renegade drummer. *I'm so glad you're here with me, Finn*, she told her father silently.

As if he heard her, he turned. "Ah, here's Maggie, just in time! Little sprite and I have been invited for tea and cookies at her house. Would you care to join us? Frankie's new friend 'Sir Bear-thoven' is coming as well."

Maggie smiled at Frankie. "You look beautiful," she told the child, meaning every word. Then she bent to shake the bear's paw. "Thank you for the invitation, Sir Bear, but you three go ahead. There is some work I have to do here."

Finn raised a pewter brow but kept silent. He stood slowly, nonchalantly reaching for the wooden walking stick he'd found in the foyer, and took a moment to ensure his balance. "Okay. More cookies for us," he said, looking down at the child. "Let us tomato."

Frankie chuckled and reached trustingly for his left hand. Maggie stood, heart in her throat, watching her father and the quiet little girl find their coats, then wander haltingly out toward the house in the woods. The sun was just setting over the trees, turning their tips to fire, and outlining man and child in gold.

A sudden flash, light on black metal. There, out by the road, beyond the woods. Gerard's Mercedes? Ice skittered up her spine.

She narrowed her eyes, searched the distance. But the car was gone.

Perhaps it was just a trick of the light.

Uneasy, she kept watch until the man and child disappeared through the safety of Gerard Jouvert's blue door. Then she turned to the laden bookcase.

Hundreds of books, pottery, and a shelf of four silver-framed photographs. Of course she was drawn to the pictures first. Elle, on pointe, dressed in a costume of cascading black feathers. Odile, Tchaikovsky's Black Swan, in his haunting Swan Lake. Next to it, a touching photo of her grandmother Clair, standing in front of The House of Echoes, holding her daughter Lily's hand. It must have been taken just before her mother left for the States to study piano.

The last two photographs were of her grandmother as a young woman. Maggie felt her heart trip in her chest. How many times had she wished she knew more about the lives of her mother, her grandmother?

In the first frame, Clair stood on the rocks in her red coat, gazing out to sea, her hair a flowing black banner in the wind and her expression pensive. Yearning. *I've sensed her there,* thought Maggie. *I've heard the echo of her presence.*

The last photo showed a young girl, seated at the Ibach, her head thrown back, eyes closed, lost in her music.

What piece was her grandmother playing?

Baudelaire is keeping your grandmother's music safe. Her great-aunt's words swirled through the air. Find the book.

Fifteen minutes later, she found it.

An old, tattered book of Baudelaire's poetry, on a high shelf tucked against a book of constellations. *So I sleep on high, near starry courses,* her great-aunt Elle had said. She pulled the volume toward her. There was something else on the shelf. She reached, grasped a thick, folded sheaf of papers that had been hidden behind the book.

The cottage was darkening with shadows now. Maggie climbed carefully down from the stepstool, set the book and packet on the coffee table, and reached for the lamp switch.

The thin book was tattered, its pages frayed. Words in script were scrawled across the opening page. *Property of Clair Rousseau.* Yes. As she'd thought, the book belonged to her grandmother.

Then she turned to the packet of pages she'd found behind the book and held them to the light.

Music Scores.

She held her breath. Let them be...*yes!* More of Chopin's Preludes. Like the preludes she'd found in her grandmother's trunk, each one had a date written across the top of the page in her grandmother's hand. The scores were in order by date. Her *Grand-mère* was continuing to tell her story through Chopin's music.

Maggie smiled softly. Chopin had become her favorite composer and pianist even before she could talk. Had it been the same for her grandmother? Her father's voice spilled across time into her memory.

"Chopin composed twenty-four preludes in the 1830s, sprite, each set in one of the twenty-four keys. Very short pieces — really just vignettes, sketches, moods – but oh so profoundly rich with emotional complexity, not preludes so much as self-contained, deeply felt moments. Not all of them technically difficult, true. But the challenge for Chopin was the interpretation. He focused on the music itself. The overflowing emotions. Perfect for you, Maggie-girl."

Maggie looked through the scores in her hand. Many of the preludes were composed in the minor keys — the saddest, most aching keys of all.

Her grandmother Clair had held these pages in her hands, made notes on the scores, played the preludes on her Ibach. The sudden feeling of connection to her grandmother was intense. Moment by moment, here in the cottage, she was beginning to connect her grandmother's life to her own.

Tell me the rest of your story through your music, *Grand-mère.*

The first two scores were both dated March, 1944. Across the top of the first score, Chopin's Prelude No. 7, her grandmother had written, *Memories of Elle float like perfume through my mind.* The notes were fervent, nostalgic. Wistful. Of course her grandmother would have been missing her baby sister, remembering her.

The second score was Chopin's Prelude No. 1 in C Major — often called "The Feverish Anticipation of a Loved One" or "Reunion." Also dated March, 1944, her grandmother had written, *My hope flares, burns with anticipation for our reunion.*

Had Clair finally gotten news that her sister was alive?

Maggie rose, moved to the Ibach, set the music on the piano desk. Only thirty-four measures in length, the Prelude No. 1 would be played in under one minute. *Agitato* — restless, agitated — building speed from the opening arpeggios to the coda.

Feverish Anticipation, she told herself, as she began to play. The intense, intimate opening chords soared as she fell into the music, the notes spilling like drops of hot silver mercury from her fingertips. She could feel the fevered longing, the depth of yearning. For… something. Someone?

"Help me tell her story, Chopin," she murmured. "I know you spoke to my grandmother. Now I am listening."

The notes flowed around her, embraced her, pulled her in, until she *became* the piano, fell *inside* the notes. Too soon, the final notes echoed in the now-darkened room.

Maggie sat very still, feeling as if her grandmother's history was suddenly coming alive through the music. She was certain that the beautiful, emotional piece conveyed Clair's hopes to reunite with her sister Elle. Of course her grandmother must have searched for her sister. Hopefully Elle could tell her the story of their reunion when they were together.

Suddenly aware of the tears coursing down her cheeks, Maggie realized with a shock that for the first time in months, she had felt the fierce emotion her grandmother had felt, found the heart of the music, made it come alive. Overwhelmed by her feelings and exhaustion, Maggie dropped her head into her hands.

At that moment she heard the stealthy rattle of the knob at the front door.

CHAPTER 29

Someone was trying to get into the cottage.

Maggie spun around, scattering sheets of music to the floor. There! A hooded figure, outlined against the dark glass. Had she locked the door? God, God, where was her cell phone?

In the bedroom.

Another rattle, the sound of glass breaking. A black shape, darker than the shadows. Panic swelled.

Tap, drag. Tap, drag.

He was in the cottage! Heart banging against her ribs, she ran down the dark hallway.

Forget the damned phone, just leave, get out! She twisted toward the back door. Saw a chilling silhouette of a dark figure beyond the rear window. No, no, a second man. Too late.

Slow footsteps crossing the living room. *Tap, drag. Tap, drag.* Turning toward the hallway.

No way out.

Fight back! She grasped a lamp from the hall table, flung it with all her might at the figure coming toward her.

A crashing sound, a grunt.

She ran to her bedroom, slammed the door, hit the lock, dragged a chair against it.

Her phone was on the bedspread. She punched futilely at the numbers. Dead. Ran to the window. Frozen closed.

Don't panic.

Tap, drag. Tap, drag.

Silence.

A sound at the door. She watched the bedroom knob turn slowly.

She could hear her heart thudding in her ears.

Please please no.

Should she scream? Just break the damned window.

A voice, silky and sinister, against the wooden door. "Magdalena."

Dane's voice.

"Magdalena," came the intimate whisper once more. "Open the door. I know you are in there."

Find a weapon. She ran into the small bathroom, wrenched open drawers, the cabinet. Metal nail file. Room spray. Scissors!

"I listened to your music, Magdalena. Exquisite. It would be such a terrible loss to the world if something happened to you."

The intimate voice fell silent. Something slammed against the wooden door.

She was shaking so hard she could barely hold the scissors. But she pointed them in front of her like a knife and faced the door.

"I have a gun," she shouted to the faceless voice. "I won't hesitate to use it on you. Get the hell out of here, now! I've called the *gendarmes.*"

Another sharp blow to the door. The wood shuddered. A splintering sound.

A shout. Sudden running footsteps.

Sounds of a violent struggle beyond the door.

A heavy thud.

Then, silence.

What had happened? Was Dane still there? She listened, counted to sixty. Counted to sixty again. Moved slowly to the door.

Scissors ready, she took a deep shuddering breath and quietly slid open the lock.

Inched the door open.

Boots, legs, torso… a body near the door. So still.

"Oh good God."

Michael Beckett lay unconscious and bleeding on the floor.

CHAPTER 30

CANCALE, BRITTANY

"Damned colonel took me by surprise, Firas. Lucky for me you were there."

The two men were in a sleek black Mercedes speeding down the dark coast road toward Saint-Malo.

"He surprised me, too, sir. He was not supposed to be in France." The man called Firas turned to Dane. "You are sure you're not hurt?"

A low chuckle, a swipe of linen at the thin stream of blood still dripping from a pale, lined forehead. "Nothing I can't handle. You did well. I would have been no match for the colonel. But I sent the message I wanted to send. Magdalena knows I am near. Waiting in the wings. That is enough." A harsh breath. "For now."

"Do we return to Greece?"

"Not yet, Firas. We need to spend one more night close by. There is one final message I want to send. Magdalena needs to know that I can always reach her. This time, I am giving you the honor of delivering my message. You will need to wait for just the right moment." Another chuckle, a rasping rattle. "And after that, I have a new plan. Something bigger, better. Much bigger. And this time the surprise will be all mine."

The Mercedes slowed to pass through the ramparts of the old town.

Dane gazed out into the moonless dark. "Time shall enfold what plighted cunning hides." He turned to Firas. "I hope you killed that damned colonel."

"Michael. Wake up. Talk to me, damn you."

They were in a small examination room in Gerard Jouvert's clinic. The doctor's dark head was bent over test results. Her father was shuffling restlessly from window to chair, chair to window, mumbling softly. Frankie, thank God, was down the hall, safe in a pediatric room playing games with a nurse.

She gazed down at Michael. He was very pale and very still, with a fresh bandage over his left eye.

Perched on the edge of his bed, Maggie bent to touch her lips to his. Hard, cold. No reaction. Her heart shifted in her chest.

Jouvert appeared next to her. "Breathe, Maggie, it's good news. No concussion. He's going to be fine. Just the stitches, and a nasty bruise coming. He must have turned away just in time. Your colonel was very lucky."

"Thank God. And thank *you*, Gerard. We're both lucky." She gazed at Michael's face. "When will he wake up, when can I take him home?"

"He should regain consciousness any moment now. But I'd like to keep him here overnight, just for observation." He hesitated. "Maggie, the local *gendarmes* are here to ask you both some questions."

"Of course. But I'm not leaving until Michael wakes up."

"Go home, darlin'. Get some rest. I'm fine, I'll see you in the morning."

"Michael!" His eyes were open, clear and locked on hers. Relief poured like water through her body. "I...you...when...how...?"

With a groan, Beckett turned slowly toward the doctor and forced a grin. "She's never handled surprises very well."

"I *hate* surprises," grumbled Maggie. Her head came up. "You have a lot of explaining to do, tough guy. Are Dov and Shiloh with you?"

"Back home at the ranch with Robbie."

"Ah. You've all ganged up on me. So much for your Plan A."

"Plan A was working just fine until I got whacked on the head."

"At least no one got shot. This time."

Beckett grinned at the doctor once more. "That's just code for *I'm so glad you're here, darling.*"

"Well, I, for one, am happy you're here," said Finn from across the room. "Welcome back, Mike. Glad you're okay. I'll go check on Frankie now." He sent a shaky mock salute and shuffled slowly, head bent, from the room.

Maggie watched her father leave, saw the concerned look on the doctor's face. *One thing at a time.*

Beckett's hand, gripping her arm, pulled her back. "What exactly happened back at the cottage?" His voice was low, confused. Angry.

"Apparently someone slugged you. Again."

"Ouch. Okay, true. Seemed like a bag of hammers this time. But could you work on your bedside manner? I was hoping for more of a 'my hero' moment." He turned painfully toward the doctor. "We take turns," he said, "saving each other."

"Got it," said Jouvert. "She's no damsel in distress."

"I like this guy," murmured Beckett, his eyes fluttering closed.

Maggie relented. "It was Dane, Michael. You were right, all along. He broke into the cottage. He had a cane." *Tap, drag.* The fear rushed back, took her breath. "I tried to stop him, but he –"

"Let me take a wild guess. You're the one who threw the lamp." His eyes found the doctor. "Leaps before she looks."

"I couldn't just give up without a fight."

"Maggie McFierce," muttered Beckett reaching out to clasp her hand. "Dane's no match for us, darlin'. I had him in my sights. But someone else was there. Took me from behind." He winced, with pain or chagrin, she wasn't sure. Probably both.

"Yes, someone was at the back door. You didn't see who it was?"

"No. I was focused on Dane." He drew a ragged breath. "I heard your voice, beyond the door. Dare I hope you really had a gun?"

"I lied."

"Thought so." His voice wavered, fell away.

She turned to Gerard. "I'm spending the night."

"No!" Both men spoke at the same time. Gerard smiled, took her arm. "Doctor's orders, Maggie. Your colonel needs to rest. So do you. Come back in the morning and take him off my hands."

Seeing the anxiety in her eyes, he added, "I'll be here all night. There's a room for Frankie as well. And a *gendarme* will be posted outside your cottage."

Maggie opened her mouth to argue, but caught the stormy look on Michael's face. "Okay," she said finally, "first thing tomorrow." She looked down at Michael. "Don't get shot while I'm gone."

Beckett looked at the doctor. "She always says that."

"Have you two considered counseling?" grinned Jouvert.

Back in her grandmother's cottage, Maggie sank into the soft sofa with a full glass of Pinot. Her father had lit the fire before retiring, and now, finally, she was beginning to relax, surrounded by the warmth and crackle of pine-scented wood. The gendarme was outside the front door, her father was snoring, and Yo Yo Ma was playing a cello suite on the radio. She had talked with both Robbie and Dov, knew all was well in Virginia. And Gerard had just told her Michael was safe and sound asleep at the clinic.

Okay, then. Good to go.

But she was too wired to sleep. Kicking off her shoes, she took a breath and reached for her grandmother's preludes.

She'd been playing the three Prelude scores she'd found in her grandmother's trunk in the Vineyard—the No. 13, *Loss*; the No. 15, *Death in the Shadows*; and the No. 22, *Révolte*. And last night, she had played Chopin's Prelude No. 1, the *Feverish Anticipation of a Loved One*. Maggie knew her *Grand-mère* had been mourning the loss of her family early in the war, knew from the ticket she'd found in the trunk that her grandmother had taken the night train to Paris in the winter of 1943. Now, from the preludes, she was certain that Clair had joined the Resistance when she returned to Paris, certain that Clair had believed her sister Elle was alive. So many questions she wanted to ask Elle when they met again.

Maggie closed her eyes. Each prelude described key moments and choices in her grandmother's life. Her grandmother had chosen and dated these preludes for a reason. Her father always said, *Music tells our stories.*

What had happened to Clair after she returned to Paris? How had she found her sister? Tell me the rest of your story through your music, *Grand-mère*.

She lifted the next score, Chopin's Prelude in B Minor. The bleak, despondent No. 6. *Lento Assai*—to be played very, very slowly. It was dated April, 1944. Just one month later...

This prelude, Maggie knew, was often called *Tolling Bells* because it was played at Chopin's funeral. It began with the full, sonorous tones of church bells. The left hand carried the melody, the right hand adding the deep echo of the bells.

The bells tolled, my world changed, Clair had written. What had happened in that war-torn April when bells tolled so many decades ago? Maggie set Chopin's beautiful, haunting B Minor score on the Ibach. She touched the keys and, picturing her grandmother once more, began to play.

Less than three minutes later Maggie's fingers stilled. She had held the final notes as long as she could, and she lifted her head, listening, as the room continued to echo with the last notes of the prelude like the fading vibrations of a distant bell. Suddenly, as if conjured by her thoughts and the music, the bells of Cancale's village church began to toll – flowing up over the cottage rooftop to echo out over the rocks and dark moonless sea.

Five, six, seven, eight…

Clair

"Tolling Bells"

CHAPTER 31

PARIS. APRIL, 1944

Five, six, seven, eight.

The bells of Saint-Séverin tolled, just beyond the curtains, echoing out above the dark chimneypots and rooftops of Paris.

Clair Rousseau stopped playing the Chopin, her fingers still, her eyes full of tears.

A hand clamped down on her shoulder.

"Enough, Beauty Queen! The music is too sad, it breaks my heart, fills me with longing. I feel as if it's warning us of impending doom." Avril set down her glass, tugged at Clair's wrist. "Come. It's almost time to go to the meeting." She handed Clair the worn copy of Baudelaire's poetry. "Don't forget your book."

Clair swiped at the tears that streaked her cheeks. "I feel it, too," she said, gazing into the shadows. "We cannot go on like this much longer."

"We'll go on as long as we bloody well have to! *Père* is certain the Allies will land any day. Any *hour*. We just have to hold on until the invasion. Then we will go find your sister."

Clair stood, reached for the tattered book, nodded at the fierce, haunted woman who had, against all odds, become her friend. "Your lips to God's ears, you crazy old spy."

The nave of Saint-Séverin was in deep shadow. Several members of the network hovered in the darkness, near the stairs to the crypt, talking quietly.

Quick footsteps echoed down the aisle.

Clair froze, then slipped behind a tall marble statue of a robed saint. Had she been followed? Where was Avril? Her friend had disappeared into the night on the way to the church. Like smoke. Like her code name.

Suddenly, the terrifying, two-note sound of the dreaded *Milice* sirens pierced the stillness. Coming closer!

The great doors flew open, Avril burst through. "*Se Cacher!*" she cried. *Hide.* "*Père* is dead! They are coming for us!"

Not *Père*... Clair felt her bones turn to ice. She turned, began to run toward Avril.

Beyond the great wooden doors, the screech of brakes. Shouts in German. Boots pounding up ancient stone steps.

Oh God, oh God.

The network members scattered, disappearing into the shadows.

Her eyes locked with Avril's. The older woman's hand shot out, a command for Clair to stay back. "*That* way," she hissed, pointing toward the confessionals on the far side of the nave.

Flashlights. Spearing like swords through the darkness. Sweeping over the pews, the altar, the columns, the statues. Crawling like bright snakes cross the stained glass, the vaulted ceilings.

With one final, desperate look at Clair, Avril turned and ran down the center aisle toward the altar. Leading the soldiers away from them. From her.

There! Achtung! Halt!

A shot, then a volley of shots, echoing against the stone. A high cry, cut off. A sickening thud.

Avril. No...

Clair crouched behind a towering marble statue of Joan d'Arc, certain the Germans could hear her thundering heartbeat. How, how had this happened?

She pushed her fists against her mouth, trying to stifle the sobs that welled from deep within her. Oh, please, not Avril…

GodGodplease. She said it over and over, like a prayer.

More shouts, in German. The echo of heavy boots striking stone.

Coming back! Coming toward her. She looked around wildly.

A hard hand gripping her shoulder. She spun with a sharp cry of terror.

"Shhhhh. Come with me."

Night.

He grasped her hand, pulled her beyond the confessionals, deeper into the darkness. Through a narrow door, hidden behind wide, medieval columns. The soft click of the lock closing behind them.

Very narrow, spiraling stone stairs. So dark. Up up up. *Don't fall.* She lost track of how many steps there were. Gasping for breath, she held on tightly and followed him up into the blackness.

Past the entrance to the organ chamber. Keep climbing.

Finally, minutes later, a tiny landing. An ancient door.

She followed him into a cold, black room. Wind. Stars. Night sky beyond the huge open arches. She glanced out, was hit by a wave of vertigo. Holy Mother. They were at least seven stories above Paris.

"Up this ladder, quickly!"

The ladder was thin, iron. Old. She emerged into a shadowed room with a wooden floor, the air above her crisscrossed by heavy, jutting oak beams. There was a huge square opening in the center of the floor.

Her rescuer turned to her. "You will be safe here."

"I'm afraid of heights."

"Better heights than the SS."

She turned, struck something hard, metal.

"Oh my God," she whispered.

They were in the belfry. The bell tower of Saint-Séverin.

"That bell is named *Macée*. Derived from Matthew. He is the oldest bell in Paris, first hung here around 1412. That huge hole in the floor is how they lifted the bells up here."

Clair sat with her back pressed to the outer stone wall, her knees clasped to her chest, shivering. She gazed at the four-hundred-pound, green-toned bell – cast in bronze, at least three feet high – then at the others. Silent now. Waiting.

"What time is it?" she asked suddenly.

Soft laughter. Night moved to sit next to her, slipped his jacket over her shuddering shoulders.

"We have some fifteen minutes before we go deaf."

"Holy *Mother!*"

He smiled at her expression of horror. *"Non,"* he relented. "Hearing loss in bell ringers is small, according to the studies, because even with the great intensity of sound, the bells ring only for a short time."

"Not helping," she muttered. "I play the piano. I cannot afford to go deaf. Avril counts on me to –"

At that moment, the reality of everything that had happened came crashing down on her. "Avril is gone..." she whispered. "And *Pére*. Oh, dear God, *why?*"

He slipped an arm around her, pulled her closer.

"What happened?" she said against his shoulder. "She would never betray us. She led them away from us, she *saved* us!"

"I think the informer was the butcher who lives below her apartment."

"Bastard." She looked up at him. "Do you think she...?"

"Is dead? I hope so, for her sake. She couldn't survive the torture. No one does. She will give up all the names she knows. Mine. Even yours." His eyes held hers. "The network is compromised for good. You can't go home tonight. If we are lucky she will hold out for a few more hours, give us time to get away. We have to get out of Paris as soon as possible."

She stared at him. "How?"

"You know *Pére's* brother has a network in Saint-Malo. I will get word to him, he will arrange a Lysander flight, or a boat, to England. The SOE and Uncle Bradley will take care of us there. We just have to get to Brittany."

"I lived near Saint-Malo for years, in a cottage in Cancale."

"You are full of surprises, Buttercup. A pianist from Saint-Malo…"

"And you," she whispered. "Surely not just a charming café manager."

"I paint," he said softly.

"Houses?"

"Canvases."

She smiled, gazed up at him, grasped his shirt. "My name is Clair Rousseau," she said. "Tell me yours."

Once more intense green eyes locked on hers. He was about to speak when a soft whirring sound filled the room. The mechanism of the bells engaging.

"Oh no, no," she murmured.

The first bell chimed, the sound deep, thunderous and resonating like giant drums in the tiny room.

The man with the burning green eyes and silvered temples placed both his palms along the sides of her face, covering her ears as he pulled her toward him. Then he leaned in, crushed his mouth on hers and began to kiss her.

CHAPTER 32

The journey from Paris to the walled town of Saint-Malo in Brittany – a trip that would normally take five hours in peacetime – took Clair and Night four full days.

They travelled mostly in the waning dark just before dawn, from shadow to shadow, when pale gray light blurred edges and offered cover. Partisans hid them in milk trucks and vegetable carts and laundry vans. Each day they biked or walked for miles, always trying to skirt around the villages and German roadblocks and patrols. Each night they slept in barns, burned-out cottages, or pine-scented woods beneath the stars.

On the first night, they found an abandoned stable on a farm some eighty miles west of Paris.

"Stay with me," she'd whispered. "Sleep with me."

"You are so young, Clair."

"I am almost eighteen, old enough to fight in a war. I have never been with a man. I do not want to die without knowing love."

And so that night, on a thick bed of hay and wrapped in an old horse blanket, they made love for the first time. It was fierce and passionate, erotic and wild and unrestrained – an elemental need to affirm their survival in the face of so much horror. For the first time in so many months, Clair felt alive. And, taking her by surprise, she felt the first faint stirrings of love.

Afterward, their faces touching, they told each other of their lives, their childhoods, their secrets. Their pain and loss.

Night spoke of his love of art, his hopes and dreams for a family one day, children. Of his mother, a beautiful French Jew, who was swept up in the mass arrests of Jewish families in Paris in July of 1942. Of her internment in Drancy, and then the unbearable pain of her deportation by boxcar to Auschwitz. Of the unexpected kindness of *Père*, hiding him in a small rear room in the church, and arranging a new identity. Of his hatred of the Nazis, and his rage-filled need to join the Resistance.

Of the nightmares that so often invaded his dreams. *I was not able to save my mother, Clair.* A voice raw, but not broken.

Clair spoke of her music – her love of the piano and Chopin – her childhood in Paris, her life as a teenager in Brittany. The murder of her father, the disappearance of her mother and sister. She described her beautiful younger sister Elle, who danced like an angel. Of her determination to find her. *I see her still, everywhere I look. She has to be alive.*

And, finally, she spoke of the chilling, sadistic German officer on the night train to Paris, and her fears that he was not gone from her life.

They shared their stories until the first pink blush of dawn bloomed above the trees beyond the old stable doors. Then they gathered their rucksacks and, holding hands, stepped into the waning shadows of morning and turned west.

On the third day, the Germans found them.

They were some seventy miles east of Saint-Malo, skirting a small village on ancient bicycles sold to them by an aging farmer's widow. No birdsong, no sounds of life. Only the lone, hungry barking of a wild dog. The smell of smoke was sharp in the thick gray air.

As they drew closer, sensing the carnage, they slowed. Fires still smoldered in the small church and cottages. Gardens were trampled, clothing and broken pottery littered the narrow lanes.

"Where is everyone?" murmured Clair in confusion. "No villagers, no farm animals. What has happened?"

"It looks as if the Germans took everyone in the town away."

Clair looked around at the empty lanes, the abandoned cottages, their doors hanging open. "Dear God. The women, too? The *children?*" She turned anguished eyes on him. "But how is that possible?"

"I've heard of such reprisals. There have been rumors of whole villages destroyed. Punishment, suffering, death, they don't care. We cannot imagine it, but–"

Footsteps. The crunch of heavy boots beyond the square. Words in German. *Two men.*

Night pulled her into a doorway and pushed her down into the shadows. She held her breath, felt him reach for the pistol in his waistband. *Holy Mother, please please.*

Sudden silence.

The door creaked, opened very slowly. Sunlight fell in a bright rectangle onto the floor. A tall German soldier stepped into the narrow bar of light. Night raised his gun and shot him in the back.

The second soldier shouted, smashed the door aside, and tackled Night. She saw his head hit the floor as his pistol flew across the floor. *No time to think!* Clair crawled toward the gun, clutched it in her hand, turned. The German lunged toward her. Clair closed her eyes and pulled the trigger.

Could you kill a man, Beauty Queen?

Avril's prophetic words tumbled and speared through Clair's head. Who have I become, she asked herself over and over as, shaking uncontrollably, she tore up the sheet she'd found to bandage the deep gash in Night's forehead.

Somehow she'd managed to drag the two bodies to a closet and hide them beneath a mound of rubble.

Finally, Night regained consciousness. He spoke only one sentence – "For the children they took."

Then they mounted their bicycles and rode away from the too-silent, ghost-haunted village into the setting sun.

On the fourth day, filthy and exhausted, they stood together after sunset on a rocky, wind-swept promontory just beyond the village of Cancale.

The cottage before them was in total darkness.

"*La Maison des Échos*," said Clair above the low sigh of the wind.

"It looks abandoned," said Night against her wildly blowing hair. "But it could be a trap."

Very cautiously, they moved through the black shadows, up the path, to peer through grimed windows. No sign of life. Wind echoed through the rotting wooden rafters and cracked panes with a hollow, moaning cry.

Clair climbed the two front steps, reached up, fingers searching the warped lintel over the door for the old iron key. There. Very slowly, she twisted the lock. Then she took his hand, and led him into the place that had been her home.

The cottage was very cold, smelling sharply of salt air and mildew. No electricity, no furniture left, except for the old scarred piano, a broken chair, and the huge, empty bookcase near the door. Windows were broken, the walls were bare. The kitchen table was scattered with used dishes and half-filled cups, as if the German officers who had been billeted there had left in a hurry. The refrigerator was empty.

"It's over. They all know it," whispered Night. "The invasion is coming, very soon."

They ate the bread partisans had shared with them, and took a photo of each other with the tiny Minox camera Clair had kept.

They found a torn quilt forgotten in a closet, set it on the floor, and wrapped their arms around each other to keep warm. They did not speak of the village they had found, the dead Germans they had left behind. There were no words.

Through the broken window, the moon was a narrow crescent in the dark night sky. Faint light streamed over them in angled bars, turning their skin to gold. Needing words, she read him the poems of Baudelaire.

Il est doux, a travers les brumes, de voir naitre,
L'etoile dans l'azur, La lame a la fenetre...

How sweet to watch the night open its eyes. First lamp, first star born in the azure deep.

They made love as if it were the last time, each touch profoundly, deeply tender.

Later, holding her close, he began to talk. "We meet the network in Saint-Malo tomorrow. An air rescue will be impossible with no full moon. So *Père's* brother has planned a sea rescue for us at dusk, in a harbor just beyond Saint-Brieuc."

"How will we know where to go?"

"A local partisan will lead us through the minefields to the beach."

"The others from the network will be there?"

"Those who have made it this far."

She closed her eyes, trying not to think of Avril. "And then what?"

"You know I will be working at the SOE in London with Uncle Bradley. The invasion is imminent. His last radio message said –" He stopped abruptly, looked away.

Her eyes flew open and she sat up. "You *know!*" she gasped. "You know when the invasion is coming? *Where* it will be?"

He nodded, finally, his deep jade eyes shining with secrets. "Yes, I know. But *you* know I can't tell you, Clair. It's the greatest secret of the war, knowing it could mean your death."

"And yours," she whispered. She rested her head on his shoulder, ran a hand along his too-thin, carved face. "I don't want to know," she said honestly. "I could never withstand the torture. Avril always warned me…" *Everyone talks, Beauty Queen.* A scalding tear ran down her cheek and she scraped it away.

He pulled her closer. "My beautiful Clair. You don't know how strong you are."

"I know one thing—we don't know how much time we have left."

But she knew, of course she knew, what was going to happen in Saint-Brieuc. What she was going to do.

Her eyes locked with his. "Tell me your name," she whispered once more, as she did every night, just before they drifted off to sleep.

"It's too dangerous for you to know," he repeated, as he did every night, against the pale skin of her shoulder.

"I promise, my love, it will be our secret forever," she whispered.

Just before sleep took her, he murmured his name into her mouth.

Charles.

CHAPTER 33

THE HOUSE OF ECHOES, BRITTANY. PRESENT DAY

He murmured his name against her mouth.

Maggie jolted from sleep. The bedroom was pitch black. Michael?

She reached out a hand, but the sheet next to her was empty, cold. Memory spun back. He was still at the clinic. She was alone. But she had felt his lips on hers...

Hadn't she? She sat up, breathing deeply to still her pounding heart. The small clock said it was after three a.m.

She had been dreaming. Of Michael? No. She closed her eyes, gazed into her dreams. A small, candlelit room. A quilt on the floor. A sliver of moonlight beyond the curtained window. A woman lifting her face. It was her grandmother's face she had seen. She'd felt her emotion. Her fear. Her love.

The last thing Maggie remembered was playing her grandmother's preludes, listening to the music, hearing the echoes of her grandmother's life across the decades.

And then...

Maggie rose, wrapped her robe around her, and went into the hallway. All quiet. Stopping outside her father's door, she could hear his soft snoring. Okay. She passed into the kitchen, gazed out the window toward the woods. Dark, but now touched by starlight. The police cruiser was still there, parked in the drive.

The wind rattled the windowpanes and echoed like whispers in the shadowed room. Maggie made her way to the Ibach piano, sat down on the bench, lifted the next piece of music. The prelude was dated April, 1944. It was Chopin's Prelude No. 4 in E Minor.

Across the top of the page her grandmother had written, *I cannot breathe.*

Dear God. Something horrible, unspeakable, must have happened to her *Grand-mère* in that long-ago spring.

She began to play. Overflowing with emotion, the chords were at once beautiful, nuanced, and filled with sorrow, despair and torment. Maggie remembered that Chopin had asked for this prelude to be played at his funeral. Von Bülow had called the Prelude *Suffocation.* Cortot's title was *Sur une tombe.* Above a grave.

The sorrowful phrases and chords spilled from Maggie's fingers, the music suffocating. She couldn't catch her breath, and her fingers stilled. Her breathing ragged, Maggie closed her eyes, listening to the echoes.

I cannot breathe.

Clair
"Suffocation"

CHAPTER 34

NEAR SAINT-BRIEUC, COAST OF BRITTANY. APRIL, 1944

The man who led them through the marshes, to avoid the mines, was short and quick, his cap pulled low to cover half his face. He disappeared into the mist as soon as they reached the sand.

Now, finally, they stood side by side in the shelter of the sea pines, staring at the narrow curve of beach. Shadows lay long and blue across the sand. On the far side of the beach, a lone building stood – a boathouse – now dark and abandoned. The silence was broken only by the high cry of the gulls and the murmur of the surf as it rolled and foamed cross the rocks.

Clair looked up at the man she now knew as Charles. The perfect name, she thought, for this tall, brave man with the startling jade eyes and silvered temples. She closed her eyes. He'd had another nightmare, just before dawn. If only she could forget the words he had shouted. Because now, she, too, knew the location of the Allied invasion.

If they catch you they will torture you until you tell everything you know. Avril's voice, relentless in her head. *Please God I don't want to know. Help me forget what Charles said.*

Clair shook her head, as if she could somehow banish the fear – the knowledge – and turned once more to search the beach. Some twenty feet away, a small knot of their fellow network members huddled in the dusk. Only nine others had made it this far. Clair hardly recognized them. They all had lost so much weight these past months. They were pale and gaunt, hollow eyed, stiff with fear. Like she was.

Even more so, now that she knew the greatest secret of the war.

Movement. She saw the beautiful, familiar face in a narrow flash of light. The radio operator known as Snapdragon, the only agent who still knew the taste of whipped cream and chocolates. Clair felt a moment of relief. They had to keep her away from the Germans.

The moon was behind the clouds, the horizon dark and empty. "The boat will be here soon," Charles said against her ear. And then, "Clair..."

She turned to him, knowing what was coming, her heart full of agony.

"If we get separated, if anything happens," he began. A harsh breath. "When the war is over, go to the cottage in Cancale. Wait for me there. I will come to you."

She stared at him, wanting to tell him the truth, but she could not bear to see the hurt in his eyes.

"I will," she promised.

He took her cold hand, raised it to his lips. "We will be together again, when all this madness is over."

She knew it would never happen. Knew what she was going to have to do in the next few moments. Knew how it would devastate him. How do I say goodbye? But still she spoke the lie. "I will wait for you, *mon cher.*"

A gray smudge appeared on the horizon, moving toward them. The boat! A low murmur of an engine trembled on the air.

The boat was coming in fast. The small group of French partisans moved as one toward the breaking line of surf. Seabirds rose in a flock of white feathers and headed out over the waves.

Clair looked around, suddenly anxious. The birds... Something wasn't right.

What was it?

Her eyes swept the beach. The boat, almost close enough now to board. The agents, stumbling into the surf. Waves, sand, rocks, pines, the old boathouse.

There. A glint of light on glass, in the broken boathouse window.

"Run!" she shouted. "It's a trap!"

A moment frozen in time. Then movement and sound everywhere, all at once. The Ghost Network's members flung themselves into the waves, toward the boat. A dozen German soldiers burst from the boathouse, guns blazing, the bullets bright streaks in the dusk. With a muttered curse, Charles grasped her arm and began to pull her toward the water.

For just a moment, she moved with him. Then with one last desperate glance, begging him with her eyes to understand the impossible, she pulled away from him and turned to run toward the shelter of the sea pines.

She heard him shout her name. Stumbled at the sound, sure her heart was breaking. "Charles," she whispered.

Volleys of gunfire, the sound deafening. Screams. The smell of cordite sharp in the air.

She couldn't help it. She stopped, just for a second, whirled around, breathless. Two bodies on sand that was red with blood. Another body in the water. *GodGod*, where was Charles? There!

In the waves, close to the boat, one of the female agents in his arms. Snapdragon. He lifted her, flung her up onto the deck. Reached for the ladder. Streaks of light above the water. He froze, his head suddenly arching back. Falling. Disappearing beneath the dark waves. *No!*

She couldn't let him die.

She began to run back toward the water.

A sudden hammer punch in her right shoulder, knocking her to her knees. The sharp, sickening spear of pain.

The last thing she saw was the twisted face of the German captain, bending over her.

CHAPTER 35

PARIS, THE HÔTEL LUTETIA. APRIL, 1944

Ice cold water shocked her to consciousness. Clair blinked her eyes, dizzy, nauseous, confused. Darkness. Pain. So cold. Shivering, she tried to raise her arm, but something rough held her down.

Rope?

Her eyes flew open.

She was tied to a chair. Vomit rose in her throat as she struggled against the tight, numbing cords. Oh, Holy Mother, please help me. Where was she?

The heavy dark closed in on her.

Don't panic. Don't panic.

Her lungs closed, she struggled to breathe. The scent of something sweet and metallic hit her. Blood. Her shoulder was throbbing as if she'd been stabbed by a spike. No. A bullet. It was her own blood she smelled.

Memory rushed back.

The beach, the water, the bullets flying through the air. Charles!

Charles, Charles, what happened to you?

The door opened.

A man stepped into the chamber, shined a bright, painful light in her face. Leaning toward her, he spoke in low, guttural German.

"Welcome back to the Hôtel Lutetia, *Mademoiselle* Rousseau. I told you we would meet again."

It was the voice that invaded her nightmares. The Abwehr officer from the night train to Paris...

Fear uncoiled like a snake in her chest.

He set the heavy flashlight on a small table, leaned forward. Light glinted off the thick round glasses, hiding his eyes. He smiled at her.

"You never should have trusted the man who led you through the mines," he said conversationally. "Led you all straight to us, as it happens."

She clamped her lips together and stared at him. *Don't show any weakness. Pretend you don't understand him. Do not cry.* Tears welled.

"No need to pretend," he said softly. "I know you understand me. You speak many languages, do you not? Little cunt liar." He reached out, prodded her injured shoulder with a sharp finger.

She screamed.

"Yes, that must hurt. And I'm afraid it is only the beginning for you." He stood, moved to a small table against the wall. He spoke over his shoulder. "I admit, I am curious about one thing. I'm told you didn't run for the boat with the others. You chose to stay behind. Why is that, *Mademoiselle* Rousseau? What could possibly be so important that a woman like you would choose torture and death over freedom?"

Elle, her mind cried out. *I could not leave my sister behind.*

"You will tell me," he said softly. "But first – the man you were with on the beach. Night, is it? Ah, you see that I know his name. I know he led your network. *Les Fantômes*. He had intelligence about the invasion, information that could change the course of the war. You were lovers, yes? I think he told you what I need to know. So now you are going to tell me what he told you, *Mademoiselle* Rousseau. And I am not a patient man."

No, no, you cannot say the words. Think of Charles. Think of Elle...

"I don't know," she whispered. "Please. He told me nothing. Not even his name."

The Abwehr officer stepped into the light, set a tray down on a small round table.

Clair turned her head, felt her spine turn to ice.

Only two instruments were on the tray. Pliers, and a hammer.

Her throat closed. Fear suffocated her.

I cannot breathe!

"I'm told you play the piano quite beautifully," he said in a low, silky voice, lifting the hammer and holding it to the light. The metal glinted in the shadows.

With a lightning-fast movement he spun around and smashed the hammer down onto her right hand.

The pain was excruciating, unimaginable. Crushing. The last thing she heard was her own agonized scream before the blessed blackness took her.

The pain woke her.

The world was spinning. She tried to sit up and vomited on the cold stone floor where she lay. It was pitch black in the cell. Her right shoulder was useless. She used her left arm to cradle her right hand against her chest, felt the hot, wet blood and sharp splinters of bone, and vomited once more before the blackness took her.

When she awakened again, her whole body was shuddering and throbbing with pain. What now? She did not think she could survive another hammer blow. She would say anything. Anything.

A moan, in the darkness to her left.

"Who's there?" The words, barely a croak, scraped through her swollen lips.

Somehow, she managed to shift her body toward the sound. Her eyes blinked, adjusting to the black shadows.

A body, crumpled against the wall. A woman?

"Where are you hurt?" she whispered.

A stirring, a head of shorn pale hair, streaked with blood. "Is that you, Beauty Queen?"

"Avril! Oh, sweet Holy Mother, Avril! What have they done to you?"

A hand lifted, the faintest touch on her cheek. "I'm sorry, Clair. I told them fucking everything. About Night. About you…"

"Hush, my dear friend, it's okay." The tears were hot streaks on her cheeks. She bit her lip against the pain as she tried to shift her body, to gather her friend against her with her still-good left arm.

"The piano…" whispered Avril. Her skin was hot, so hot.

The door opened.

The man from the night train to Paris stood over them in a rectangle of sudden light. Once more the fear closed Clair's throat. *I am suffocating*, she thought. *I am going to die.* And then – No. Breathe. Fight. You know what you have to do.

"I am done waiting, *Mademoiselle* Rousseau. You had your chance. Tell me when and where the invasion is to take place. Now!"

She raised her eyes to his. "I told you. I. Do. Not. Know."

"Liar!" He slapped her face so hard that she fell back against the stones.

"All right, *Mademoiselle*. We will see if your friend's life can loosen your memory." He grabbed Avril by the hair, pulled her toward him. A long, sharp knife glinted in this hand.

You will talk, Beauty Queen. They will threaten your lover, your mother, your friend, your dog. Avril's warning, when they'd met, echoed in Clair's head.

Somehow Avril managed to rasp, "Don't tell this bloody fucking butcher anything, Beau–" Her scream of agony swallowed her words as he sliced her cheek open.

He turned to Clair. "Next time it will be her tongue. Or her eye? Save her more suffering, *Mademoiselle*."

Sobbing, Clair reached toward Avril. The women locked eyes, saying with a look what words could no longer say.

"You win," whispered Clair. Her voice rasped, unrecognizable. "Just promise me death will be quick. Do not send me to Ravensbrück. My sister died there. Please. I beg you..."

Something leaped like a fire in the blank eyes, like a snake about to strike. He nodded slowly, smiled. "Done. Tell me."

"*Pas de Calais!*" Clair shouted Night's secret into the dark pulsing silence. "*Pas de Calais*, you filthy rotten bastard. Now let Avril go!"

A look of shock passed across Avril's eyes, just before they closed.

"*Gut*. You have earned your reward, *Mademoiselle*."

She stared at him, forced the words she knew he wanted to hear. The words that would give her what she wanted. "Have mercy, please."

The knife danced in front of her face and she closed her eyes. "Mercy? But I think after all that you deserve something less merciful than death. You will be on the train to Ravensbrück within the hour. I trust you will regret every moment I did not take your life, *Mademoiselle* Rousseau."

With one last kick at Avril's still body, he disappeared into the darkness.

Welcoming the dark, Clair crawled to Avril, rested her head on her friend's chest. The breaths were shallow, rasping. *Inhale, hold, exhale. Inhale, hold, exhale.*

"Oh, God, Avril, I'm so sorry. Don't leave me."

Avril's eyes fluttered open. "It was... a lie... Beauty Queen."

Clair bent her head to her friend's lips. "What? *What* was a lie, Avril?"

"*Pas de Calais*. Charles…"

Inhale, hold, exhale. Inhale, hold, exhale. Inhale, hold… hold…

Hold.

Silence.

"Please no, Avril." *Avril.*

And then, spinning into the dark, terrible silence, the echo of a single, soul-crushing word.

Ravensbrück.

But it wasn't fear that gripped her.

It was defiance.

I did it, Elle. I'm coming for you. Just hold on.

PART 3

"Echo is the voice of our reflection in a mirror."

Nathaniel Hawthorne

CHAPTER 36

THE HOUSE OF ECHOES. CANCALE, BRITTANY

Michael Beckett showed up at the cottage just after dawn, wearing his faded Rolling Stones tee shirt, in need of real coffee.

The sky was streaked with trails of amber and deep rose. They stood without speaking, watching the sun spill over the sea, and then she took his hand and drew him to the bedroom.

"Last night, when I saw you lying in the hallway," she said against his chest. "The thought of losing you..."

"Not gonna happen, darlin'. We're going to spend the rest of our lives together."

"Don't dare the universe, Michael."

He looked down at her. "I know you didn't expect me to show up here, darlin', I know we have to talk. But for right now – remember that last line from *Now, Voyager*, Maggie? *'Don't let's ask for the moon, we have the stars.'*"

"Talking can wait," she whispered against his mouth. "Right now, we have the stars." Closing her eyes, she pressed her body against him.

He circled her with both arms and the room began to swim.

He tossed his shirt aside. She locked her hands behind his head, kissing hard shoulders, taut throat, bristly cheek, and finally muscled mouth, as she pulled him deeper inside her.

We have the stars...

After their shower, Maggie stood at the cottage kitchen window, watching Beckett as he made his way slowly over the rocks, his dark silhouette outlined in silver by the morning light. His hair, longer now, lifted in the wind. Every few moments he stopped and raised his face to squint up at the deep bowl of sky, as if listening. To the echoes?

Her heart twisted in her chest and she smiled, sensing this wild land spoke to him the way it spoke to her.

A shuffling sound behind her. She turned. "Good morning, Finn. Sleep well?"

Finn Stewart scowled up at the copper pots, shook his head. "Nothing that coffee won't cure," was all he said, clasping his hands together on the table in a white-knuckle grip.

She stared at his trembling hands. Surely he hadn't been drinking? God help her, she just wasn't sure. Too many bad memories down that particular road.

She poured steaming coffee into a white pottery mug, set it on the table in front of him, and dropped a light kiss on the top of his head.

Surprise touched his eyes and he smiled wanly up at her, reaching for the coffee as she turned back to the window.

"God DAMN it to bloody hell!"

Maggie spun around. Her father's hand was shaking badly, spilling the hot coffee over his fingers and across the tabletop. He set the mug down with a sharp crack.

"Dad!" She grasped a towel, doused it with cold water and held the cotton to his hand. She could feel the shuddering of his fingers beneath the thin cloth. She bent down to lock eyes with his. "What is it, Finn? What's wrong? When are you going to tell me?"

"Dammit, sprite, it's nothing! Just leave me be."

"It's *not* nothing! You –"

Her father lurched up from the table, clutched his walking stick and, head held high, staggered from the room.

A sound at the back door. She turned, expecting to see Michael, but it was Gerard Jouvert who stood in the doorway.

"Sorry. Bad time?" he murmured.

"No, no. It's just..." She sighed. "My father spilled coffee on his hand."

The doctor's steady gaze held no surprise. "I'll take a look, if he'll let me."

"Good luck with that!"

"What was I thinking?" He flashed a brief smile of understanding. "Normally I wouldn't bother you so early, Maggie, but the nursing home called. Elle is having a good day, she's asked to see you."

"Oh! Of course." Maggie's eyes strayed toward the hallway. "Just give me a moment. I want to check on my father."

Gerard Jouvert set a hand on her arm. "Maggie. At some point your father is going to have to admit the truth to you. I think he has Parkinson's."

"Gerard is going to help me talk with my father," said Maggie.

She was standing on the sloping lawn of Saint-Méloir with Michael, watching Frankie and Elle play a game of cards called Bezique on a small table. Jouvert had disappeared into the château to consult with Elle's doctors.

"So the mustard is finally off the hot dog," said Michael. "Just let me know what I can do to help. Your father and I have an armed truce." He grinned. "Of sorts."

She grasped his arm, pulled him closer. "I'm glad you're here," she whispered against his chest. Then, grinning, "Just wondering what took you so long?"

"Had to give you some time to miss me." He flashed his lopsided grin. "And I'm even more handsome now than the last time you saw me, right?"

"Don't press your luck," she murmured. "Now come meet my great-aunt."

Today Elle's eyes, as she smiled up at Michael and offered a ringed hand, were bright with awareness. She gestured them to a pair of wicker garden chairs and turned to Frankie. "Here are colored pencils and a book on herbs for you, *bébé*. Why don't you take it over there, to the herb garden, and see how many you can identify? Just stay where we can see you, *ma chère*."

Elle turned to Maggie. "The memories I have to tell you are not for a child's ears."

Maggie grasped paper-thin, withered fingers. "Dear *Tante*. I found your sister's music, just where you said it would be. I've been playing the Chopin preludes, really listening to what the music says. I know that somehow you found each other. Can you tell me how that happened? But I don't want to cause you more pain. I don't want you to feel that you have to remember those terrible years."

"*Merde*," whispered Elle, staring up at the sky. "I would sell my soul right now for a double Vicomte whiskey. You are right, child, I don't want to talk about the past. I spent almost eighty years trying to *forget* it. *C'est compliqué, oui?* Both my sister and I had to get past the horror, the flashbacks, the survivor's guilt. We had to let the curtain fall on the war years, so that we could go on."

"I don't know how you both found the strength."

A gallic shrug of sharp-boned shoulders. "But you are Clair's granddaughter. I want you to know how brave your grandmother was, how strong and loving. She always said, 'Others did so much more, I was just one small stone.' But that wasn't true.

Your grandmother was a true hero, Maggie. She saved so many lives, including mine."

Elle leaned in, held Maggie's gaze with her bright blue eyes.

"I believe Clair would have wanted you to know her story. You come from a line of strong women, *ma chère*. History matters, Maggie. It's important that you understand what happened to us. Why we made the choices we made. What happened to make my sister so terrified of small spaces. And so agoraphobic." She looked up at the sky. "Clair's courage…"

"I still cannot imagine the courage it took for both of you to survive the concentration camp."

Elle's eyes flared. "Even more than you know, Maggie. I am talking about the courage it took for a young woman to fight her way *into* Ravensbrück. Clair *chose* to stay behind when she could have escaped France, she did whatever she had to do to be sent to the camp – all to find me. One fateful decision that changed everything."

"She *chose* Ravensbrück?" Maggie stiffened with shock. "My God, I had no idea. My mother only told me that my grandmother refused to travel because of what happened to her in the war."

"It was many years before my sister was finally able to tell your mother of those days in the camp. But only once."

"Because it was too hard for my mother to hear?"

"No, child. Because it was too hard to tell. Clair would only say, '*On ne peut pas nommer.*'"

One cannot speak of the unspeakable. Maggie gripped Michael's hand, unable to respond, her eyes on her great aunt.

Elle's eyes gazed into the distance. Into the past.

"For you to understand, I need to begin with my own story. Perhaps you know that I loved dance before I could walk? I had a small cloth doll in a pink tutu, I never let her out of my sight. Until…" She shook her head back and forth. "Until they came for us, and I never saw her again."

Maggie leaned forward. "I have your doll, *Tante.* I found it with your sister's things."

Elle blinked, looked away. "Ballet kept me alive until Clair found me. One night…" The words were slow, halting. She stopped, suddenly unable to go on.

Huge tears appeared, streaked down her sunken cheeks. She began to sob.

Maggie wrapped her arms around her great aunt. "Oh, *Tante.* My grandmother's story can wait for another day," she whispered. "Come, let me take you to your room."

Elle clung to Maggie. *"Non!* You deserve to know. I *want* you to know. But the memories are so harrowing. I cannot get past the wall." Her eyes clouded, as if the curtains once more were coming down on her past. A shuddering breath. *"No! I won't dance for you!"* she cried out.

CHAPTER 37

LES JARDINS DE SAINT-MÉLOIR, BRITTANY

An hour later, Elle sat wrapped in a woolen blanket, a mug of hot tea in her hands, her face turned toward the sea.

Gerard Jouvert had ordered the tea and talked softly to her until she calmed. Now, Elle smiled, grasped Maggie's hand. "I feel much better," she said softly. "Thank you for staying with me."

"I want to be with you," Maggie said simply. As she leaned in to kiss the dry, withered cheek, her grandmother's gold locket swung against her breast. Slipping it from over her head, she snapped it open and held it out to her aunt. "I have something beautiful to show you. I found this hidden in *Grand-mère's* trunk."

"Clair's trunk?" A soft fog swirled across Elle's eyes. She was very still, trying to capture a memory. With a start, she turned to Maggie. "*Oui!* I remember. After the war, the American captain who rescued us bought two small steamer trunks with our initials on the lid." She smiled. "He was so smitten by Clair."

Maggie leaned forward. "My grandmother sent her trunk to my mother, Lily. It's where she kept your doll dressed in the pink tutu. I found this locket, and some of her Chopin Preludes, there as well. Do you still have your trunk, *Tante*?"

Elle closed her eyes, searching her memory. Then a slow smile, a graceful gesture toward the château. "My room upstairs. In the back of the closet, I think. I had forgotten."

Maggie's breath caught in her chest. "Could you look in your trunk and let me know if you saved any memories that would help me know my grandmother?"

"Of course, child. I will do it tonight." She grinned. "If I can remember." Elle held out her hand. "Now. May I see the locket?"

Elle stared down at the tiny sepia faces. "Yes, of course that is my dear Clair. So young, such a beauty. But the man? *Tres bon, bien sûr. Mais l'etranger.* Not her husband." Elle shook her head slowly. "Perhaps they met while I was still in the hospital in Paris, *n'est pas?*" She became still. "There was one night…" She shook her head. "It was after the war, when I finally was well enough to return to Cancale. Clair and I slept in the same room for months. We both were afraid to be alone, you understand. Clair was so restless, dreaming. She cried out in her sleep."

"What did she say, *Tante?*"

"She whispered two words. *Charles.* And *Nuit.*" Night.

Elle closed her eyes, handing the locket back to Maggie with a shake of her head. "I'm sorry, child, that is all I can remember."

"One more mystery," murmured Maggie, as she slipped the locket around her neck and turned to Elle. "I brought you a gift, *Tante.* There is a photograph of you in the cottage, in a Black Swan costume. I thought you would enjoy this music." She reached into her purse and removed a small recorder. With the press of a button, the first slow, beautiful chords of Tchaikovsky's Swan Lake filled the air.

Elle's head came up, her expression rapt. "The Black Swan. How I loved dancing that role."

Very slowly, she began to lift her arms in time with the music. Eyes closed, face tilted, her thin veined hands fluttering like wings, she seemed to become a swan right before Maggie's eyes.

The body remembers, thought Maggie.

After several moments, Elle executed one last graceful dip, then raised her regal head. "Ballet kept me alive until my sister found me," whispered Elle. "The SS guards called me *Der Kleine Tänzerin.* The Little Dancer. The prisoners called me *La Ballerine.*

Elle gazed blindly toward the water and began to speak in a slow, halting voice.

"I was just fourteen when my father was murdered in the square. Not long after, the Germans woke my mother and me from sleep, took us to the local prison in Saint-Malo. Then the boxcar east. Dear God, you've read the stories, but you cannot imagine what it was like. Hundreds of us smashed in there together like animals, no food or water for days."

Elle put a hand up to her eyes, took a shuddering breath. "My mother and I were sent to a camp called Auschwitz first. In Poland. When we arrived, we stood in a line with all the others. My mother was told to go to the left. I turned to follow her, but suddenly a heavy hand clamped down on my shoulder. 'You! To the right,' said a German medical officer. I was crying, screaming for my mother. She was screaming, too, trying to reach me. The German dragged me away from her. 'Your mother is just going to have a shower,' he told me."

Elle shook her head as if to banish the memory, and fell silent.

"Oh, *Tante*," whispered Maggie, wiping the tears gently from her aunt's cheek, "this has to be unbearable for you. Please, don't try to remember any more."

"I thought it would be impossible to remember," said Elle in a quivering voice, "but now the dam has opened, and it is impossible to stop." She looked blindly out over the distant sea. "I never saw my mother again. But I was strong, and it was not long before I was sent with a work detail on a train back to Germany – to the women's prison at Ravensbrück."

Ravensbrück. Just hearing the name sent a ripple of sick fear down Maggie's spine.

Elle touched Maggie's hand. "You missed the simplest of things in the camps," she murmured. "A toothbrush, soap, warm water. A blanket, a book. A paper and pencil. Warm socks, hot soup. In our barracks, we shared bunks or straw mattresses.

Each so crowded, we had to sleep on our sides. If one rolled over we all rolled over. The older women talked about food, recipes, children, sex. Even politics and religion. We told stories and jokes. I formed a special friendship with several of the women – there were five of us. We called ourselves *Les Gloires*. The Glories."

Her beautiful face paled with memory. "Several of the women were artists, musicians. They sang opera, wrote poetry, drew pictures on tiny scraps of paper with charred bits of wood. One winter night, after a horrible ration of cold, thin soup, I began to teach the women simple ballet exercises. We needed to keep up our strength, you understand. To stay warm, to stay healthy. We needed to survive."

Elle stopped, pressed her lips together, was silent for several heartbeats.

"The senior officers began to search the barracks for talented prisoners to entertain them. One night, they came to our barracks. *'Wo ist der kleine tänzerin?'* one demanded. 'Where is the little dancer?' My friend Lilianna put a warning hand on my back. I was terrified, but I knew that if I did not speak up, everyone would be punished. So I stepped forward."

A small sob escaped her lips. "A soldier marched me outside. It was snowing. I can still see the snow on the ground so clearly, feel its cold touch on my eyelids, freezing my lashes. It was the night before my fifteenth birthday. I stopped. I refused to move. Better they shoot me right there, I thought. But they did not insist I dance for them, *oh no*. Instead, because I resisted, they doused me with water and made me stand for hours, barefoot, in the snow."

"Dear God, *Tante*," whispered Maggie. "Where did you find the courage?"

"It wasn't about courage, child. That night, with my feet frozen in the snow, it became about survival. I dreamed of having a future, dancing. Reuniting with my sister someday. I vowed that I would survive."

Elle's eyes shined at Maggie with a fierce, remembered fire.

"The next night, of course, the SS came again. I could barely walk, but this time I went with them. I was taken to an officer's home on the edge of the camp, commanded to dance. I was wearing just a thin, shapeless dress. No shoes. My toes were blue."

Elle's head came up, as if listening.

"I can still see that officer's face, with its rolls of fat and small cruel eyes. There was a Victrola, playing Wagner. But I imagined myself listening to Swan Lake, my favorite ballet. The Black Swan's dance was my solo. And so I began to dance. '*Tanz, kleine Tänzerin, tanz für mich*,' the officer demanded. 'Dance, little Dancer, dance for me.'" She turned to Maggie. "I was dancing for the devil himself."

Elle closed her eyes. "The Black Swan gave me her strength. When it was finally over, the devil rewarded me with a round cake covered in white icing. I brought it back and shared it with my Glories in the barracks. The irony, of course, is that it was my fifteenth birthday cake."

She turned to Maggie. "And that is how it was when my sister finally found me."

CHAPTER 38

THE HOUSE OF ECHOES. CANCALE

The notes spilled into the night-shadowed room. Haunted, tormented. Desperate.

Maggie stopped in the middle of a passage, bowed her head. Raising a shaky hand, she found hot tears streaking her cheeks.

Earlier in the day, listening to her great-aunt, she had learned what happened in Ravensbrück. Dear God. "How did you survive, *Grand-mère?*" she whispered into the darkness.

She gazed at her grandmother's writing across the top of the Chopin score. It was the Prelude No. 16 in B-flat Minor. Her grandmother had written, *May 1944. I descend into the black abyss of Ravensbrück.* Maggie closed her eyes. Descending into an abyss.

Her fingers touched the notes. The piece, despite its brevity, was terrifyingly difficult, the chords dazzling, complex, soaring. To Maggie, it was perhaps the most difficult of all twenty-four of the preludes. But it wasn't the treacherous, chaotic runs of the right hand that caused the difficulty. It was the thundering, heartbreaking passion of the left hand. The exploding, enormous leaps, stunning in intensity and torment. Maggie felt the pain and defiance in her fingertips. The darkness.

She held up her left hand, still throbbing with the technical challenges of that fierce progression of octaves. *The impassioned left hand.* Once more the sickening feeling hit her, sharp and jolting.

Earlier, in the peaceful gardens of Saint-Méloir, Elle had talked for more than an hour, lost in tears and memory, gripping Maggie's hand. Now, she knew what had happened to her grandmother's right hand. And the horror of what had happened in Ravensbrück.

A low voice behind her.

Maggie opened her eyes, suddenly aware of Beckett's hand on her shoulder, his voice a comfort in the darkness. "Come to bed, darlin'."

She turned her anguished gaze on him. "My grandmother lost her ability to play music when her right hand was crushed, just as I lost my music when my husband disappeared. For me it was a soul-crushing loss, but even more so for her. Her *hand*, Michael! She must have felt even more desperate, more lonely, than I did..."

Michael Beckett pulled her close. "But she found a way to go on, darlin', just like you did."

"I need to know more, Michael. I need to know *how*."

"You will, Maggie. Your grandmother will tell you, through the music."

"Even if she could no longer play?"

"She left you the preludes, Maggie. She left you her story."

Maggie stood slowly and gathered Chopin's prelude to her chest. The other scores rested on the table next to the piano – just over a dozen in all. *Her grandmother's story.*

She stood and took Michael's hand. As she turned, she caught her reflection in the mirror above the piano. The mirror was old and silvered, the image wavering. Maggie froze.

In the mirror, a shadowed figure quivered, appeared. A young woman, bending over. She staggered. A whisper of pain, her low voice like an echo in the darkness.

Clair

"Descent into the Abyss"

CHAPTER 39

RAVENSBRÜCK, GERMANY. MAY 31, 1944

Clair staggered, desperate not to fall.

Today's work detail was hauling rocks from the quarry for the nearby airfield. One rock, another. So heavy she could barely lift them. Especially with her throbbing, crushed right hand. A whisper of pain escaped her lips. The uncharacteristic weakness of her body frightened her more than the whips, the dogs. No cough yet, thank God. No TB. If you couldn't work, if you were sent to the infirmary – the women she'd met said that was the end of you.

But it was impossible to stay healthy. Last night, only thin soup. One of the guards had kicked the pot, spilling the soup across the earth, and laughed as several women fought over the scraps.

She no longer knew what day it was, but she thought she had been in Ravensbrück for almost two weeks, arriving sometime in mid-May. It was called *Straflage* – the punishment camp for woman from all the occupied nations, some fifty miles north of Berlin. Humiliating images spun in her head. The naked medical exam, the blue-and-white striped prison clothes, the red triangle on her sleeve that told the guards she was a political deportee. Standing for hours in the cold predawn roll call.

Life for prisoners in the camp was horrific. During her first week, she had been whipped, tortured, starved, and sexually abused by a filthy, foul-smelling guard. Witnessed dehumanizing cruelty and countless horrors. Seen dozens of dead women every day, their bodies twisted on the hard ground. And most unspeakable of all – the rumors of experiments on children. Yet she kept going. She had to.

She had to find her sister.

Every morning the Nazis used huge loudspeakers to broadcast military marches and war songs at maximum volume. For Clair, it was pure torture. But the blasting clamor proved to be an unexpected blessing, as it concealed whispered conversations. Clair learned to use the time to ask the women about her sister.

But finding one small young woman now seemed impossible. The camp was huge, with some twenty-five barracks, each one crammed with one thousand or more prisoners from all over Eastern and Western Europe. Everywhere she went, if she was able to speak the language, she asked, *"Do you know of a young Frenchwoman called La Ballerine? Have you seen her?"*

Rien. Nothing.

Another rock lifted onto the flatbed truck. Another. Clair bit her lip, determined not to cry. *Ravensbrück.* Holy Mother, it was a desperate place. Many of the women were barely alive, eyes dead, their starved bodies nothing but bones. Beaten, terrorized, with unhealed wounds and TB plundering caved-in chests. Whispers of unthinkable medical experiments… After the first days, she had realized that once you were caught, you didn't think about what you were fighting for anymore. She was incapable of thinking of the future. She thought of only one thing. Survival.

Every day, there were new rumors of the Allied invasion. Stories that they had landed. They were coming. There was hope. Every night, she clung to the memory of Charles and prayed for his bravery, his strength. She just had to survive. So she could find her sister. Take her home.

Another rock. Another. She stopped to catch her breath.

"Continuez à travailler! Le garder vous regarde!"

Hissed words from behind her, telling her to keep working, the guard was looking at her…*in French!* Without turning around,

Clair tilted her face away from the guard and whispered, "You are French?"

"*Oui.* I am Lilianna."

"Clair, from Paris. I'm looking for my sister, Elle. I'm told they call her *La Ballerine.* Can you help me?"

"*Mon Dieu!* You are Elle's sister, Clair?" The disembodied voice floated over her shoulder, filling her with joy. "Yes, *bien sûr,* I know her. Many Frenchwomen are in our Barracks, Number 22. Elle taught us dance exercises for months, she raised our spirits, gave us hope. But… lately she has not been well."

Fear clutched her heart. "I need to be with my sister, Lilianna. Can you help me get to her?"

"I will do anything for Elle. We all will. There are five of us, women who met on the train, who help each other. Elle shared her birthday cake with us many months ago, when we all were starving. Oh, I know she –" Her voice rose with hope.

"*Nicht Sprechen!*" The guard strode toward them, the German Shepherd by his side growling with menace. He grabbed the woman behind Clair, spun her to the ground. The snarling dog lunged. The woman shrieked as sharp fangs sank into her upper arm.

"No!" screamed Clair, hurling the rock in her hands at the SS guard. "You filthy pig, she has done nothing to you or your dog!" The guard shouted a command as he pulled the dog away from the woman, now bleeding and unconscious on the ground. Then he turned very slowly toward Clair, his face contorted in pain and fury as he reached for her. "*Du wagst es, mir die Stirn zu bieten, Schlampe?*"

You dare to defy me, bitch?

Someone was screaming.

Clair opened her eyes. Pitch black. Pain. Cold, so cold. Her mouth was so dry, her clothing soaked. She couldn't straighten her legs, couldn't stop shivering.

The box! OhGodOhGodOhGod…

The memories rushed back in a horrific rockslide. The furious SS guard had dragged her back to the camp, thrown her into a small wooden box outside the infirmary and slammed the door. The last sound she'd heard before she began to scream was the grating of the metal key.

How long had she been alone in the dark? An hour? A day? A *month?*

Am I dead?

No. But her mad gesture of defiance was going to kill her. Her skin was burning up, she was having fevered hallucinations now. They spun, jumbled and confusing, in her head.

There was her mother, making dinner in their Paris apartment, the tantalizing smell of coq au vin in the air. Elle, in her blue coat the color of hyacinths, dancing in mist that turned her golden hair to silver. Clair saw herself in the cottage in Brittany, playing Chopin, the notes trembling on a beautiful old Ibach piano…

And then – the low whistle of a night train, speeding through the darkness. Avril's profile, wreathed in cigarette smoke in a shadowed room. A man with flat snake eyes, raising a hammer that glinted in the light. The low voice of a prisoner named Lilianna, whispering Elle's name. The great bells of Saint-Séverin tolling and echoing around them as Charles kissed her.

Charles. His bloodied body spinning, disappearing beneath the freezing Channel waters. Had her sister's friend Lilianna suffered the same fate?

Clair's stomach clutched. I will never know, she thought. I am going to die in this filthy box. *I'm so sorry, Elle. Sorry I could not find you.*

A sound. The scrape of a key. Sudden, blinding light. She tumbled forward, onto the hard earth. Voices.

And then a voice she knew in her bones.

She twisted her head.

A cluster of women, gathered like scarecrows around the box. One of them was Lilianna, her upper arm wrapped in bloodied rags. And the woman weeping next to her – a profile she knew like her own.

She tried to speak, but her throat refused to make a sound.

Elle! Her brain screamed. *Elle…*

She felt herself falling into darkness.

CHAPTER 40

RAVENSBRÜCK, GERMANY. JUNE 6, 1944

Clair opened her eyes to a crack of blinding sunlight through splintered wood. A rough hand stroked her fevered forehead. Sharp pain, blurred vision, then a flash of dark hair.

"Am I dead?

"Non."

"Dreaming?"

"I'm afraid not. Do you remember me? I am Lilianna. You saved my life."

Memory flooded back. Clair's eyes widened. "Elle? Oh, sweet Holy Mother, I saw *Elle!*" She flung out her arm, searching. "Please, where is my sister?"

"She is safe. Lay back, try to stay quiet. I will tell you everything." Lilianna rose, settled Clair on a scrap of blanket, held out a small cup of water.

"Where am I?"

"Hidden in the back of our barracks. We dared not take you to the infirmary, then you truly would be dead."

"How…?" It was the only sound Clair could make.

"Ernst – the guard who hurt us – went on a wild bender with his cronies. I stole his keys when he was passed out drunk. We freed you, carried you here." She grinned, her teeth broken and yellow. "The stupid pig has no idea what happened."

"The box… I was in a box."

"Oui."

"How long have I been here?"

"Since yesterday. We could only protect you for one night. Without a prison number, you would have no access to food or shelter. But my friend Catherine died early this morning, God rest her soul. We hid her body, took her ID number and gave it to you. Now you must answer to Catherine until we figure out what to do next."

Clair's head was spinning. "And Elle?"

"She sat with you through the night. You were feverish, distraught. She calmed you. But now she is on a work detail."

"Not with Ernst!"

"*Non*, at the Siemens factory."

"Thank God she is well enough to work."

A quick catch of breath. "I'm sorry, *non*. Your sister is ill, but she forces herself to go. It is the TB, I think. Otherwise..." Lilianna looked away. "We all do what we can to protect each other. We must keep fighting, holding on is now more important than ever. We think the guards were drunk because" – her voice changed – "*because the invasion has finally begun.*"

Clair's eyes widened. "*Alors*, you are sure?" Charles' voice spun into her head. *The Allies will land at Pas de Calais.*

The shame rushed at her. Swamped her. *I told the Kommandant the Allies' secret.*

"The Americans and Brits have landed in *Pas de Calais?*" she whispered.

Lilianna flashed a surprised look. "*Non*. Normandy. The beaches."

Clair closed her eyes, shook her head back and forth. No, that was wrong. Charles had been told the invasion would begin at *Pas de Calais*. Nothing made sense.

"Perhaps it is only a matter of days now until they find us," whispered Lilianna. "Our survival is better if people know we are here, we are alive. Last night we gathered 400 more names, including yours. We wrote them on tiny bits of paper, passed them through the barbed wire to the French POWs in the next yard. They will try to get our names to the Red Cross."

"When will I see Elle?"

"After dark, when the buses return. I must go. Remember, you are Catherine."

Clair closed her eyes, listening to the sudden silence. Light burned through her eyelids.

Wait until dark.

Light and dark. Light and dark.

Clair fell in and out of restless sleep, plagued by haunting images and nightmares.

There was Elle, dancing, and then... The hammer! Elle collapsing to the floor.

A whisper. "Clair. Wake up, my darling sister."

That voice! Chopin's music flew into her head, the notes bright, like the singing of a stream. His exceptionally beautiful prelude, the No. 3 in G Major. *Finally, after all the hope, joy. The happiness of being with a loved one.* Could it be? Clair forced her eyes open.

Her sister's gaunt face floated before her in the shadows. "Elle? *Ma choupette?* Sweet Holy Mother, is it really you?"

"*Oui, c'est moi.*" Hot tears splashed onto Clair's cheek.

"Come closer, *ma chère.* Let me touch you. I have dreamed of this moment for so long." She looked into her sister's eyes. "*Maman?*" Elle just shook her head, eyes filled with sorrow.

"But we will be okay, Clair. You kept your promise to *Maman.* You came for me."

"You're my baby sister," whispered Clair, wrapping her arms around the too thin, brittle body. Then tighter, to still the shuddering of Elle's wracking cough. "Of course I did. I've come to take you home."

CHAPTER 41

CANCALE, BRITTANY. THE PRESENT

"Of all the cemeteries, in all the world…"

Maggie raised her head, saw Michael Beckett standing beside her, the afternoon sky a silvery mist behind him.

Concerned about her aunt, she had called Saint-Méloir earlier this morning. Elle was peaceful, all was well. And so Maggie had sought out the small, walled cemetery beyond the village, set on a rise overlooking the sea. Now she was on her knees in front of her grandmother's headstone. The bouquet of chrysanthemums she'd brought rested like bright white stars against the silver stone.

She smiled softly, reached out, her fingers brushing the engraved words.

Clair Rousseau Claymore
1926 – 1986
She loved her family, her music, and her country.

"I thought I'd find you here," said Beckett. "Yesterday was rough. Can you talk to me?"

"I've been telling my grandmother about you. How we met in a cemetery in Paris." She felt Michael's hand on her arm, and rose to stand beside him. "I feel so close to her here," she said softly. "Whether or not my Aunt Elle is able to share any more of her memories, it won't change what I feel. And I've been playing my grandmother's music, Michael. It's as if Chopin and my grandmother are telling me the story of what happened to her, chord by chord, phrase by phrase."

"I imagine you feel closer to your mother here as well," said Beckett against her hair.

She turned to gaze up at him. "Yes. I didn't expect to, when I decided to come here. It was all about my grandmother. But now, I also see my mother as a girl, everywhere I look." She leaned back against his solid chest. "I know you were concerned about my coming to Brittany. But it feels as if I'm finally closing a circle. Finding a piece of myself that was missing. That I needed to find."

Maggie's gaze swept the ancient cemetery. "I sense my grandmother everywhere. I hear the echoes of her music, of her life—in the cottage, in the garden, on the rocks by the sea. I can't imagine what it was like for her. What the occupation meant to French citizens like my grandmother. The country you love, invaded and at war."

"I visited the beaches of Normandy after my last tour in Afghanistan," Beckett said quietly. "All the graves face west. Toward home." His granite eyes softened. "French families have adopted all the graves there. The Europeans tend to the graves of our fallen in cemeteries all across western Europe." He raised her hand, held it against his chest. "And even in our sleep, pain that cannot forget falls drop by drop upon the heart."

"My God, I love you," said Maggie into the silence.

"I love you back, darlin', it's why I'm here." Beckett squinted up at the clouds racing across the sky. "It's a funny thing, Maggie. You can disappear into your music, and I know you are exactly where you belong. Music is who you *are*, not what you do. But disappearing from my side, physically—well, that's a whole different thing. Christ, I missed you *hard*. The way your hair smells like wildflowers, the way your voice turns fluid in the night. The way you become the music you are playing."

His breath came out. "The way I feel when we stand together in the quiet dark and look out at the mountains. I didn't think I could miss anyone that much. Worry that much."

She touched his cheek. "I should have known you would come. You are someone who shows up. But–"

"You're doing that thing you do with your eyes. But *what?*"

"Sometimes fixing is not the answer."

"We're together now, Maggie. I'm just trying to do the right thing, for both of us. I love you, I don't want to lose you. So of course I want to protect you."

"I know your heart is in the right place, Michael. And I love you for it, I love that you want me to be safe. But when you try to protect me, it takes me back to a time in my life when I felt powerless. I don't want to go back there, I don't need a hero now. I need to be strong on my own."

"I know you don't need me that way, darlin', I know how strong you are. Hell, I've seen you in action." The lopsided grin flashed. "I respect that you don't need a savior. But maybe we can face this together."

She took his hand, held it against her heart. "I need you more than I *want* to need you. I feel safe when I'm with you, I can breathe. And that scares me."

He gazed down at her. "I hear you, darlin'. You need me to trust you to handle your own life. Make your own decisions."

She smiled. "Maybe I just need a wingman."

He touched his forehead to hers. "One wingman, at your service, ma'am."

Dane's whispering voice flew into her head, calling her name, sending a shiver up her spine. "Your concern was right, Michael. Dane followed me here." She looked over her shoulder. "Do you think he is still here, still a threat to us?"

Beckett gazed toward the dark woods as if he expected Dane to appear from the shadowed pines. "Let's just say I'm not letting my guard down. At least there are no damn roses scattered about. Let me worry about him, and you concentrate on your grandmother and great-aunt. I'm your wingman, remember?"

She touched his cheek. "When I'm with you, I feel as if everything will be okay. But…"

"Talk to me, Maggie. I know everything's not okay. But I feel as if something *else* is going on with you." He looked down at her. "As if you are pulling away from me."

She couldn't meet his eyes, remained silent.

"If you want me to leave, go back to the States, I will."

"*No!* No, Michael, I want you to stay. It's just – Dane coming back into my life has frightened me more than I want to admit. I've been so happy these last months. With *you*. But Dane doesn't want me to be happy. He is sick and unstable and a tormentor. He didn't want to kill me in the cottage, he just wanted me to *suffer*. To know fear. He validates his life by using terror." She shook her head, at a loss. "I just don't want him to take away our happiness."

"Neither do I. But he is the most dangerous man you will ever know, Maggie. It's why I'm here."

She spun around. "And he knows we're getting married, Michael! I'm so afraid that our wedding – the future I want with you – might not happen. Dane would hurt both of us in a heartbeat. Oh, God, I *hate* that Dane has made me feel this way."

Beckett was very still. "He knows we're getting married?"

"I told you he sent me a book. Shakespeare's *Hamlet*. I didn't tell you that he wrote an inscription. '*For the Bride, With mirth in funeral and with dirge in marriage.*' A dirge is a song of lamentation and grief, Michael."

Beckett nodded slowly. "Okay. I hear you. But he can't break you if you won't *let* him break you, darlin'. We're not going to let him win. You and I are getting married, Maggie. Count on it."

"What do you –"

He held up a hand. "All will be revealed. For now, just know that I believe your grandmother's strength, her courage, runs in your blood, too. Your grandmother chose love over fear. You can, too. Trust me, darlin'." He slipped off his jacket, draped it across her shoulders. "But right now, it's late, getting cold. How about we go back and see what your father is up to? Tomorrow could be another tough day. I could surely use a bourbon. And I want to check in with Robbie and Dov."

She smiled. "It's only noon in Virginia. But my guess is that Dov is driving Robbie to drink the sacramental wine right about now."

"Don't be too sure, darlin'. I think our defiant young teen may just have met his match in Father Handsome."

"Score!"

"No way, Father!"

The whoosh of wheels across the gym floor as Robbie and several of the Vets and local high school boys fought for control of the basketball. Everyone was in a wheelchair, to even the playing field. But the kids were complaining loudly about the unfair advantage held by the experience of chair-bound Robbie and the disabled Vets on his team.

"You guys work your chairs better than we do," shouted Dov as Robbie deftly wheeled in to steal the ball. Shiloh barked his agreement from the sidelines.

"And we have God on our side, too," Robbie called back, laughter rumbling. He took the shot. "Swish!" The Vets erupted with cheers. "That's game!"

In the end it was close, the final score Rockstars 42, Jesuits 46. Afterward they all gathered in a haphazard circle, swilling water and trading good-natured insults.

Dov dropped down to the floor, next to Robbie's chair. "Not bad for an old guy. You've got some moves, Padre."

"Lucky shots." Robbie grinned as he ran a hand through his sweat-streaked hair.

"You won't be so lucky next time. I'm on to you now, you're a ringer!"

"You got me, kid. Played at Georgetown, when I still had legs." Robbie chuckled and wagged his fingers in the air. "It's all in the fingertips. And knowing when to pass the ball. So much to teach you, Grasshopper." Robbie cocked his chin toward a tall, good-looking boy with thick shoulders and watchful dark eyes, engrossed in a cell phone conversation. "Who's the new guy? Haven't seen him around."

Dov searched the crowd of high-schoolers milling by the bleachers. "Who? Oh, you mean Cady? He's in my Advanced Lit class. Moved here from New York a few days ago. Why the interest?"

"Just looks familiar, is all," murmured Robbie. "And older than the rest of you. A senior?"

Dov gave a "what-do-I-know" shrug and rose to join his friends. "He knows B-ball. See you for dinner," he called over his shoulder. "Winner buys."

"Chicken on the grill, Shiloh's favorite. Don't be late," said Robbie to Dov's back. But his eyes were on the boy with the dark watchful eyes, head still bent over his cell phone.

It was close to midnight in Paris, the sky above Notre Dame black with rainclouds. Yuri Belankov pulled his hood over his head, and moved quickly across the footbridge toward the lights of his favorite bistro on rue Saint Benoît.

He passed through the heavy wooden revolving door and shook the rain from his shoulders with a sigh. The old-fashioned bistro, with its framed photographs depicting the history of Paris, was still busy at this hour, warm and smelling of *confit de canard*. Yuri ordered the rough *vin rouge*, his thoughts turning to the message he'd just received. The flash drive, the information that would have sent him to prison, had disappeared from the evidence room in D.C., destroyed in a fire.

Finally, he thought. Let the Americans continue to search for me. They have nothing on me now. Nothing but the word of a vengeful teenaged boy.

He raised his glass, toasting his recent chess move. An unexpected gambit, eh? And now he had a decision to make. Stay in Europe, or go back to the States? His art collection, hidden where no one would find it, was waiting for him there.

And so was Dov Davidov.

CHAPTER 42

THE HOUSE OF ECHOES, CANCALE

"*Peter and the Wolf* is a musical fairy tale for children," Finn was saying to a silent, rapt Frankie. "All the characters have their own music, their own musical instrument. Peter lives with his grandfather, deep in the Russian forest. Peter's music is the string instruments – violin, viola. Listen." He pressed a button on his computer, and the lilting high notes filled the room. "Whenever you hear this music, it's Peter. Would you like to know the music for the other characters?"

Maggie and Beckett stood in the cottage doorway, watching the changing expressions fly across Frankie's face, her eyes round as bright coins. Beckett squeezed her shoulder.

"Peter's grandfather is the deep bassoon. The duck is an oboe, the bird a flute. And the cat, well, of course the cat is the regal clarinet. Like your Angus." Again, with the press of a button, each musical sound filled the room. "Do you want to try to make one of those sounds, Frankie?"

Frankie pursed her lips, and suddenly the softest flute-like whistle spilled into the air.

"Yes!" cried Finn. "Brava, little sprite! Just like a flute, I think you have made our bird sound." He leaned down until his face was close to hers. The slightest smile appeared on her face. "But this is a fairy tale, after all. There is always a wolf. Can you think what sound the wolf would make, little one?"

The child screwed up her delicate freckled face in a fearful scowl. Maggie felt Beckett begin to shake with silent laughter and flashed him a warning look.

"Yes, you're right, he would be scary," said Finn. "That's why Prokofiev, the composer who wrote the music, gave the wolf a frightening sound – three French horns. The perfect choice for a wolf." He threw Maggie a look as he pressed the computer button. The sound of the horns erupted, dark and menacing. Frankie jerked back, dark eyes wide.

Finn set a comforting hand on her shoulder. "It's okay, little sprite, don't be afraid. Peter will take care of that mean old wolf. You and I will make sure of that."

Beckett bent to whisper in Maggie's ear. "Doesn't the wolf swallow the duck?"

"Didn't you say something about pouring yourself a drink?" she whispered back, giving him an elbow in the ribs and a push toward the kitchen.

Shaking with laughter, Maggie stepped into the room. "Hello Frankie, hi Finn." She glanced toward the window, where sheet lightning flashed against the glass. "It's getting late, and starting to rain. Frankie needs to get home for her dinner." She bent to the child. "I'll walk you home, sweetheart. Do you think you can wait to find out what happens to the wolf until tomorrow?"

Frankie shook her head back and forth, curls flying, and Finn laughed at the child's clear disappointment. "It's okay, little sprite. I might have a surprise for you in the morning. But Maggie's right, it's time for you to head home, your father is waiting. Go get your coat and wait for Maggie. She'll be along in a minute."

He watched the child disappear into the kitchen, then turned to Maggie with a pleased expression.

"She has a spring in her step," murmured Maggie. "And the whistle – it's all thanks to you."

"I'm glad you noticed. Gerard says I'm really good for her." Finn stepped closer, his blue eyes intense. "And she's good for me, Maggie. So, I've decided to…"

"You're staying."

The bird-wing brows swooped upward with surprise. "Yes! For awhile, at least. Gerard and I had a long talk this morning. He's a good doctor, a good man. He said he told you about my Parkinson's and I –"

"Dad," she interrupted, "Why couldn't you tell me yourself?"

Finn Stewart shook his head. "Wasn't ready. Still not. I haven't known that long, Maggie. I was going to tell you in Boston, when we were at Symphony Hall. But, well, just got cold feet. I don't want you to worry. Parkinson's isn't usually hereditary, the risks are low."

"I'm not worried about myself, Finn, only you. Is this why you've been thinking of moving closer to family?"

He stared out the window, filled with clouds racing across the stormy sky. "One of the reasons. There's so much uncertainty with Parkinson's."

She put a gentle hand on his arm, felt the juddering tremors. "What does Gerard think? Will it get much worse?"

Finn smiled grimly. "It moves as slowly or as fast as it wants to. Truth is, sprite, I'm just a scared old man. Making music is the best thing in the world. Hard to face not having music in my life anymore, Maggie-girl."

"You will always have music, Finn. It's who you are."

"Maybe. Gerard's going to get me started on a new cocktail of meds, and an aggressive course of physical therapy. I want to keep working with Frankie. She's close, Maggie, so close to speaking again. I can *feel* it. You heard her today. I'd like to be here when she does. I could stay here, in the cottage, if it's okay. Work with Frankie on her music. She's so damned talented."

"Of course you should stay. I haven't seen you this happy, this engaged, in a very long time."

"Frankie is good for me, Maggie. She's giving me much more than I'm giving her. It's almost like having another chance with you. But this time I'll get it right. No running away." His breath came out as he looked away.

"That's all behind us, Dad."

"I hope so. I want it to be. We'll talk more, Maggie, I promise. About everything. I'll be home for the wedding. Frankie will be chattering like a magpie by then. In the meantime – I need to be here, where I can do some good. And where I can feel close to your mother again."

Unexpectedly, he leaned in, kissed her cheek. Then he turned and called out, "Okay, Frankie, time to head home. Will you tell your father about Peter and the wolf? Maybe you can make your bird sounds for him."

With a wink at Maggie, he grasped the walking stick and headed toward the kitchen.

Maggie touched her cheek, shook her head. *What just happened?*

She followed her father, reaching for the old hooded raincoat that always hung on a hook by the rear door.

"Wait," said Finn, taking the raincoat from her arms. "Let me take Frankie home. I want to talk to Gerard."

She hesitated. "You're sure? It's raining, the ground is probably soft and slippery."

"I'll be *fine*, sprite." He smiled down at the child, took her small hand in his. "It's fun to take a walk in the rain, isn't it? Rain makes its own music." They disappeared through the door.

Maggie moved to the window. Distant sheet lightning lit her father and Frankie, two moving shadows disappearing into the dark mist. Finn was bent toward the child, the gleam of his flashlight spearing the ground, faint and blurred by rain.

She did not see the man called Firas step from the woods.

CHAPTER 43

The man lunged out of the wet darkness.

Frankie saw him first, and screamed. Finn spun around, the raincoat hood falling from his face.

A sudden flash of lightning caught the man as he raised his arm. Something long and thin glinted in his hand. A knife?

Frankie! No time to react. Finn shouted and dropped the flashlight, thrusting the child behind him as he swung the heavy walking stick at the attacker.

The man's arm arced down. Finn twisted sideways. "Run, Frankie," he cried. A sharp prick, glancing off his shoulder. Not a knife, he registered. A needle. He felt himself falling. A sudden, jarring thud. The earth was wet, cold on his cheek. *A damned syringe?*

Frankie…

Her high, frightened voice, coming to him through water. "Help, *Papa!*"

The child's voice was the last thing he heard before the darkness swallowed him.

Maggie, standing by the window, froze as she heard the child's scream. The earth tilted beneath her.

"Michael! It's Frankie. Something's happened."

He was beside her in an instant. They bolted out the door and ran into the rain-filled darkness.

The flashlight was on the grass, its beam a faint path against the shadows, leading the way. Michael and Maggie reached Finn just as Gerard appeared, running toward them. She fell to her knees, sobbing. "Finn! Dad. Wake up, please." She turned toward the woods, shouted, "Why in God's name would you hurt a sick old man, damn you?"

"*Merde!* What happened? Finn, can you hear me?" Gerard bent over Finn's inert body. "Okay, his pulse is strong. We need to –" He froze, looked up. "Where is Frankie?"

For one horrified moment the three of them stared at each other. Then Gerard leaped to his feet. "Frankie!" he shouted, his anguished voice trembling with panic. "Where are you, *bébé?*"

Beckett put a hand on his arm, signaling silence. They all lifted their heads to listen. Only the rain answered.

"Stay with your father," Beckett commanded. "Call for an ambulance." Maggie lifted her head, saw Michael turn to Gerard Jouvert. "Go and search your house. Call the neighbors. He went toward the woods. I'm going after him." He punched his phone, dialing the local *gendarmes* as he ran into the darkness.

Beckett moved silently into the trees, keeping to the rain-filled shadows. He stopped, chin lifted, listening, eyes searching the shifting blackness.

Where was he?

He pushed the fierce rage to the back of his mind. Maggie's words echoed in his head. An old man. A child. Why?

No more. *Enough.* It had to end. *No matter what he had to do.*

A sound.

The figure leaped from behind a huge pine.

Beckett's arm shot out. Both men fell to the ground.

They rolled into the bushes, punching, grabbing, jabbing, kicking. The man was younger, stronger. Beckett had no weapon.

But Beckett had a soldier's memory – and a fierce, burning anger driving him.

Breaths rasped, pain spiked. Then, suddenly, the glint of metal, raised above his head. *No way, you bastard!* He twisted sideways, grasped a thick branch, swung with all his remaining strength. A sharp, satisfying crack, wood against bone. A strangled cry.

Beckett rolled free, struggled to his knees. Black eyes, covered by blood, gazed up at him.

Beckett felt the familiar darkness enveloping him. It has to end, he thought, and raised the wooden club once more.

Finally, Finn moaned, regaining consciousness. "What the hell?"

Maggie bent close, touched his cheek. "Thank God. Can you stand, Dad?"

"Dammit, forget about me. Where is Frankie?"

"Gerard and Michael are looking for her."

"*Looking for her?* Oh God *damn* it, Maggie!" He struggled to sit up.

"Come on, try to stand. We can look for her together. She needs us. She needs you."

Maggie helped her father to his feet and they made their way slowly to the Jouvert house as sirens sounded in the distance.

Gerard was standing at the door, wild-eyed.

Maggie's heart tightened in her chest. "You haven't found her."

"*Non.*"

"She's terrified," said Finn. "She's hiding, just like Maggie did when she was young. I know where to look." He pushed past them, staggered, then righted himself and headed into the main room.

Red lights flashed through the window as the ambulance approached.

"Frankie," he called softly, moving toward the grand piano. "It's Finn. You're safe now, little sprite."

An endless moment of silence. Then, a tiny rustle in the shadows. A whimper. The child was curled up beneath the piano, pressed against the back wall behind a large box of sheet music.

Finn bent, held out a trembling hand.

Very slowly, the little girl emerged. He gathered her into his arms, whispering something against her hair.

"Finn okay," she sighed. Then she turned and ran to her father.

Leaning against the doorframe, Finn watched as Frankie pounded on the Ibach keys. The thundering notes were discordant, jarring. God, he would kill for a double scotch tonight. Everything hurt, now including his head. Just a useless, shuffling old man. Where the hell was Gerard?

Still in the kitchen with the gendarmes. Okay, it was up to him.

"Whoa, little sprite," he said as eased down on the bench next to her. "What did this sweet piano ever do to you?"

The child ignored him, striking at the keys like a hammer.

Finn leaned in to whisper against the child's dark curls. "You and I have something else in common besides our love of the piano, you know."

Frankie slammed the keys once more, then stared up at him silently, her dark eyes shining with pain.

"When I was about your age," said Finn, "I didn't speak for months. Just like you. I was just terrified of talking, because I had a secret. I felt really scared, deep inside," he pointed to his heart, "and I didn't want people to know. I thought that if I spoke, people would hear how afraid I was. So I stayed silent."

With a soft sound of distress, Frankie took his trembling hand and held on tightly. Anxious eyes found his, huge and full of questions.

"Okay, Frankie, I will trust you with my secret," said Finn softly. "My father had just died. I didn't know what was going to happen to us. I was deathly afraid I would lose my mother, too. I could only speak through the piano." He hesitated. "Like you. The piano kept my secret."

The child sat frozen. Finn reached out to touch a shaking finger to Frankie's lips. "But you spoke tonight, sweetheart. You said, 'Finn okay.' They were the sweetest words I've heard in a very long time. Because I was wrong all those years ago. My mom helped me understand that talking about your feelings is the best way to heal. Do you think you can try to do that? For me? For *you?*"

For a long time, the child stared at him, conflict warring in her liquid eyes. Finally she whispered, so softly he had to bend close to hear, "I miss my mama."

Finn slipped an arm around her, hugged her close. "I know you do, little sprite. Your daddy misses her, too. Now, how about we go find your papa, and maybe you can tell him how you feel? There's no reason to be scared. The people you care about – Elle, me, your dad – we are here for you. Just tell your father what you told me. He will listen, and understand. And the hurting inside you will finally start to go away, I promise you."

Frankie lifted his hand, held it against her tearstained cheek. Then she leapt up and ran toward the kitchen. Toward her father.

Watching Gerard's face as he held his daughter, Finn Stewart felt the faint, unfamiliar stirring of hope. Somehow, he'd found his better angels tonight, lost for too long. He shook his head. *Maybe there's still a bit of gas left in the old tank after all,* he thought.

"It was the coat," said Beckett.

Maggie, her father, and a very pale Gerard sat around the Jouvert kitchen table, mugs of steaming coffee in hand. Frankie was sound asleep in her room.

Beckett paced back and forth. "He wasn't after Finn, or Frankie. He was after Maggie. She's worn that coat before. Finn was bent over, the hood covered his face. The attacker thought Finn was Maggie."

"Of course..." whispered Maggie. "It's me Dane wants to hurt." She looked at Gerard. "I'm so sorry. I never dreamed Frankie would be in danger because of me."

"No longer," said Beckett, staring at his phone. "Sugar just texted. There is security video of Dane at a small airport outside Saint-Malo, in the private jet terminal. His team is on top of it."

"Too damned late for that," said Maggie. She put a hand on Beckett's chest. "And the man who attacked us? You're sure he's no longer a danger?"

Beckett was silent for a moment, considering his words. "The *gendarmes* took him into custody. They say his name is Firas. Greek. There are two guards outside his hospital room. He's expected to make it." His breath came out. "There was a moment, Maggie... I made a choice. I hope to hell it was the right one."

"I trust you," was all she said.

Then she turned, her gaze taking in both her father and Gerard Jouvert. "With Dane and his man Firas gone, there shouldn't be any more threat to you now. But we can leave tomorrow if you will feel safer."

"We all want you to stay, Maggie," said Gerard. "For us. And for Elle."

Finn reached out and grasped her hand. "Thank God it was me and not you, sprite," he said into the silence. "Dane is no match for your old man."

CHAPTER 44

EMBRAER PRIVATE JET, EN ROUTE TO GREECE

The small private jet flew toward Mykonos through a starless night sky.

Dane sat back in the wide leather seat, absorbed in *Frankenstein* by Mary Bysshe Shelley. The last pages came too soon, and he closed the book with reverence, still caught up in the story. The monster is magnificent, he thought.

The nameless creature reminded him of himself at a young age. Sorrows yes, many unspeakable, far more than his share. But still – before his mother left, before his father's death – he had had a similar elegance of mind, a gentle temperament, a boy's love of the theater. Like the creature in the book who read Goethe's *The Sorrows of Young Werther*, a story of a young man's innocent longing for love.

Dane closed his eyes. So many comparisons to his own life. It had felt, at times, as if Mary Shelley somehow was writing his own story. In Shelley's book, the monster's creator, Victor Frankenstein, succeeds in giving life to a being. But not the perfect specimen he imagines that it will be, rather a hideous creature who is rejected by Victor and mankind in general. Abandoned by his creator, who refuses him a mate to calm his loneliness, the embittered creature seeks revenge on his creator and the world.

Dane's father had created him, but never understood or accepted his quiet, withdrawn son. Dane would never forget the beatings, the random cruelties, the terror. The loneliness. The tiny, windowless closet where he would be locked in for hours, listening to his mother's cries for help.

He turned, caught his reflection in the night-black glass and flinched at his distorted face. Since the unfinished surgery in Italy, he, too, was a monster. A monster seeking its revenge through murder and terror.

Once more Dane thought of Frankenstein's creature, who could find no one who did not recoil in fear and disgust from his stitched-together appearance, his yellow skin and eyes, his blackened lips.

Dane took a long swallow of his single malt Glenlivet Scotch and thought about the monster's heartbreaking lament. "Everywhere I see bliss, from which I alone am irrevocably excluded," he'd said. "I was benevolent and good; misery made me a fiend."

Dane shook his head. He had loved two women in his life, and he believed they had loved him back. But it hadn't been enough. His malignant nature had won.

Lights above his seat blinked. They were approaching the Greek Islands. It was time to plan his final move. Firas could no longer help him. But he had someone else, someone just as capable and now stirred by his own need for vengeance, already in place and setting his final plan in motion.

There was no turning back now.

"Failure is not an option," he said into the silence.

Beckett stood in the shadows by the cottage bedroom window, gazing up at the starless night. Simon Sugarman had called moments earlier. Finally, he had a real lead on Yuri Belankov. Now, just maybe, they could track down Belankov, end the threat to Dov once and for all. But something was off. Beckett frowned, shook his head. Sugar had been cryptic, refusing to give details, saying only that he had a plan, but that Dov was not going to be happy. Sugar's last words before he disconnected were, "You do what you gotta do."

What the hell?

He pictured Dov and Shiloh back at the cabin, best buds now, and realized how much he missed them. He would do anything to protect them. Anything.

He would find a way to deal with Sugar.

Turning from the window, Beckett gazed at Maggie. God, he loved her. One slender arm was flung toward his pillow, tangled hair a midnight curtain over her face. So beautiful in sleep. So vulnerable.

We have the stars, he'd told her.

But stars or not, the old nightmares had torn him from sleep. The village women walking toward him, smiling. The moment he realized they were hiding guns and grenades under their burkas – just before his helmet was shot off his head. Running through heavy fire to get to a wounded kid – the kid who, just hours earlier, had shown him a creased photo of his girlfriend back home. So much blood. Staggering toward the Huey, with the kid on his back. All for nothing.

A kid dies and you live. Fate? Random? A reason?

Christ. If you get to keep your life, what do you do with it? The jury was still out on that one.

Tonight, finding Firas in the woods, he'd come close, too close, to falling back into the darkness. He could still see the knowledge, the fear, in Firas' eyes. He'd known Beckett wanted him gone forever from their lives. *So close.*

Okay, so he'd done the right thing. This time.

But Dane was another matter all together. If their paths crossed again...

Failure will not be an option, thought Beckett.

Maggie could not sleep, could not still her spinning thoughts. So much had happened in the last few days, moments both beautiful and heart-wrenching. She lay still, trying to find a quiet place in her mind, but she was very aware that Michael stood by the bedroom window, talking on the phone. She'd been listening to his murmured conversation, knew he was talking with Simon Sugarman. Heard the frustration in his voice. And something more.

She wanted to get up and go to him, but for once she was determined to listen to her inner voice. Give him space. Let him be.

She closed her eyes, hoping to conjure the soothing, romantic chords of Rachmaninoff's Vocalize. But she was too unsettled for comfort. What she heard instead was Elle's trembling voice as she described their final days at Ravensbrück.

Earlier in the evening, Maggie had played Chopin's Prelude No. 8 in F-sharp Minor. *Desperation.* Across the top of the score, Clair had written, *We grew more desperate with every passing day. And then one fatal choice changed everything…*

Maggie ached for her grandmother, felt as if Clair were in the room with her. Chopin's notes swirled in her head, relentless and whirling. Dark, impassioned, tormented. She closed her eyes, trying to imagine how Clair felt as she and her sister tried to survive as they waited for the Allies.

Every moment leading up to that one fateful choice.

Clair

"Desperation"

CHAPTER 45

RAVENSBRÜCK, GERMANY. April, 1945

The Allies had landed, but freedom was as elusive as ever. Ten months went by, and still the Allies did not come.

Every morning, the prisoners continued to line up, exhausted and starving – but still somehow hopeful that this, finally, would be the day of their release. *Les Gloires* lost two more women, but Elle, Clair, and Lilianna held on together. Sometimes literally, with their arms around each other so one would not fall.

Clair knew that their network of strong women friendships was the key not only to their physical survival, but their emotional survival as well. Every night, at Clair's suggestion, Lilianna would pass around a bowl and each woman in the bunk would put in a spoonful of her soup. Then they gave it to the woman who needed it the most that day. The hunger was horrific but the women bonded over recipes of tartines and escargot, onion soup and cassoulet. One night Clair and Elle shared their mother's recipe for *coq au vin*, which was a tender and healing memory for both of them.

In January, 1945, there were over 45,000 female prisoners in Ravensbrück. But over the next several months, many died and many more were transported to the death camps. TB, diphtheria, pneumonia, broken bones and blood infections, starvation. The suffering was endless.

Now, as the first days of Spring approached, each of the three remaining *Les Gloires* – Lilianna, Elle, and Clair – weighed less than eighty pounds. But every night, when the lights were out, the three friends somehow found the strength to whisper and laugh together, and to plan their escape. They would hide in a laundry truck, the trunk of a car, a horse cart; crawl through a pipe, or a tunnel dug by spoons; sleep with an SS guard who had the necessary keys they needed; steal a guard's uniform, kill him with a sharp scrap of wood. Nothing was off limits. But each plan seemed impossible.

And then one cold morning in April they were told about The March.

"They are going to evacuate us!" whispered Lilianna. "All five thousand of us! I heard the guards talking this morning outside the latrine. Finally, the Russians are closing in."

"I'm afraid," whispered Elle. "A march is not an evacuation. We will be forced to walk miles, who knows how many, to God knows where. In the cold, with no shoes, bleeding feet and no warm clothing. How will we survive?"

"I know exactly how," said Clair. "Don't you see? Finally, this is the chance we've been waiting for."

"*Non*. Elle is right," argued Lili. "A march like that... it's far too dangerous. We cannot survive it. No one will."

"We don't have a choice," hissed Clair. "We either try to escape or we'll be killed or die starving." Her voice was fierce. "We call ourselves *Les Gloires* for a reason!"

A moment of silence as the three women stared at each other.

"Well?" said Clair. "Are you with me?"

Elle put her arms around her sister, smiled wanly at Lili. "Family stays together. Tell us your plan."

"Come closer," whispered Clair, "I'll tell you everything. We will escape this hell, my beautiful *Gloires*, I promise you. We are going home."

Two hours later, the plan was set. Clair stepped outside and took a deep, exhausted breath. The cold air burned her lungs. Nothing will stop us now, she thought.

The sound of an impatient horn in the distance. Clair raised her head, saw the sleek black sedan drive through the gates. Her heart tightened. Inexplicably frightened, she moved closer, staying out of sight behind a parked truck.

A heartbeat. Then a man in uniform appeared from the rear of the car, turned, lifted his face. A stream of gray cigarette smoke spiraled into the purple air. Twilight glinted on a pair of thick round eyeglasses. *Holy Mother, no, please.* She knew that face. The scarred, fox-like face that haunted her dreams. Kurt Jager, the Chief of the Abwehr, the man who had crushed her right hand so cruelly, stood in the fading light.

CHAPTER 46

RAVENSBRÜCK, GERMANY. LATE APRIL, 1945

For forty-eight hours, *Les Gloires* were able to hide Clair from the Kommandant. But she knew it was only a matter of time. She knew he was looking for her.

"The guards are packing up," whispered Elle in the barracks late that evening, her sunken blue eyes shining. "The March is imminent. They say tomorrow, or the next day for sure. You just have to stay hidden from Jager for a little while longer, Clair."

Clair reached out to touch her sister's hand. "Dear Elle. What would I do without you? Please, you need to take care of yourself, not worry about me. I won't let that monster stop us."

She closed her eyes, tried to breathe. It was inevitable that Jager would find her. He would hurt her, yes. But worse, she knew that this time, he would threaten her sister. She could not let that happen. She knew exactly what she had to do.

Please, please let me be brave enough, she prayed.

The guards came for her at midnight.

The room was dark, lit only by flickering firelight.

She sat on a hard chair, her hands tied behind her. She focused on breathing, on memorizing the room. Chairs, a table covered in books and files. Three doors – the entrance, a door to a closet or bedroom, and a door cracked open to a bathroom. To her right, a small stove, embers glowing red, the hiss of a cast-iron kettle. Would he burn her this time? Brand her?

Just past the stove, a bed in the far corner.

Her eyes searched the shadows. There, a desk. Metal lamp, more files. A letter opener? A paperweight! Her throbbing right shoulder and hand were useless. But if she could just get to the desk…

You can do this. You have to.

Across the room, a narrow mirror. A glimpse of a stranger, trapped in the wavering glass – tied to a chair, her face nothing but sharp bones and eyes huge and shining with fear.

"Help me," she whispered.

The woman in the mirror raised her head, lifted her chin, began to hum the notes of a fraught, despairing Chopin prelude. The No. 8 in F-sharp Minor. The screaming wind, the raging storm —*Desperation*. Clair lifted her head, listening to the voice of the reflection in the mirror, until the notes echoed in the silence.

The scrape of a boot shattered the stillness. A low voice, beyond the door. "*Verlasse uns.*" Leave us. More words. *Do not come back until morning.*

Dear God.

The door opened. He came slowly into the room.

Be strong. Be brave.

He took off his jacket, hung it carefully over the back of a chair. Then he turned to look at her. The reptilian eyes were huge and dead through the thick glasses.

"A long time, whore." The silken voice sent shudders down her spine.

"Not long enough. Why am I here? Haven't you already taken everything from me?"

"Not everything. You've stayed with me, Clair Rousseau, in my head. I should have known…You *wanted* to go to Ravensbrück, didn't you?" He shook his head. "I know why, now. I know about your sister. *La Ballerine*. She will be next. Your hand. Her legs."

Never. "She means nothing to you. It's me you want, I know it and so do you. I've seen the way you look at me. Take me instead."

His hand whipped out like a snake, tearing her shirt from her chest. He stared at her naked breasts, now nothing more than small, withered gray sacks. Reached out to squeeze a shrunken nipple.

She clamped her lips together, closed her eyes against the shock of pain. Vibrating with fear, she forced herself to meet his eyes. "Untie me, Kurt. I know how to make you forget about my sister."

He stared at her. She saw the beads of sweat on his forehead.

Do it. Do it NOW, you filthy bastard.

He untied her hands.

She stood up slowly, shoulders back, daring him to look at her.

In one swift movement he looped the rope around her neck, like an animal on a leash.

She froze.

He tugged the rope, degrading her, pulling her against him. His fingers dug into her breasts, her back. His thick tongue violated her mouth.

"Easy," she whispered in German against his lips. "It's been so long. I want it slow." She feathered her good left hand against his bulging crotch. Over his shoulder, her eyes found the heavy paperweight.

He grasped her arm and tightened the rope, turning her toward the bed.

No, a voice screamed in her head. *The desk, walk past the desk!*

But instead he dragged her past the tiny kitchen. Two steps. Four. The stove just ahead.

God, God, be brave.

She flung out her left arm, somehow gripped the iron kettle's handle in the claw of her hand.

She swung the heavy pot toward his head with all the strength she could find. Heard the sickening crunch of bone. The low moan as he collapsed to the floor.

Holy Mother help me.

She bent to his still body. Behind the shattered glasses, his eyes were open. Blood pooling beneath his head. Was he breathing? She wasn't sure.

Hurry!

She grabbed his ankles, pulled his leaden body with all her strength toward the bathroom. No time to worry about the trail of blood. She dragged off his boots, socks, shirt, pants, underwear. Left the bloody clothing in a pile on the floor, covered by a bath towel.

Now she was shuddering so hard she could hardly stand. But she slipped her arms under his, lifted him with an adrenalin strength she didn't know she possessed, somehow toppled him into the bathtub.

She turned on the faucet, let the cold water cascade over him while his dead eyes stared up at her. She watched the bright red blood swirl, circle the drain. Disappear. Vomit rose in her throat. She gagged, turned off the tap, left just a trickle of water.

Would they think he had slipped in the tub, fallen, hit his head? They would find the trail of blood, of course.

Just one day, she prayed. *That's all I need.*

She pulled the curtain across the bathtub, hiding his body. Back into the main room, tossing a small rug over the pool of blood on the floorboards where he'd fallen.

Then she pushed open a rear window, climbed over the sill, and disappeared into the night.

CHAPTER 47

RAVENSBRÜCK, GERMANY. Late April, 1945

"Jesus Jesus Jesus." Lilianna muttered the words over and over. In three days of forced marching across the German countryside, the women were starving, bleeding, staggering – just as Elle had feared – and becoming more desperate with every kilometer. By now Lili and Clair were supporting Elle, holding her up. One step, another.

"Soon," whispered Clair, pulling Elle closer. "Just hold on for a bit longer."

She had deliberately kept them in the rear of the column. Almost five thousand women were ahead of them, fighting their way through the trees.

"We've left the camp, that's what counts." Elle lifted her head, somehow found the strength to smile. "Do you think they found Jager yet?"

Clair shrugged. "There are good places to hide a body – and bad places. I did the best I could. At least the shower was better than a rolled-up rug."

Elle slapped a hand over her mouth to cover the laughter that bubbled out. "Or behind a window curtain..."

Unable to feel the humor, Clair turned away, shaking her head to dispel the nightmare image of red blood circling a drain, dead eyes staring into hers. *I did what I had to do*, she thought. *The camp is behind us now.*

One step, another.

It was almost dark when Clair saw what she had been looking for. The bodies of the women who were unable to continue marching, tossed like unwanted ragdolls into a ravine along the side of the road. "There!" she whispered. "This is it. One last gift from our beautiful brave sisters."

Their eyes on the guard who stalked behind them, the three women slowed, moved one by one oh-so-slowly to the edge of the ravine. When they were in place, Clair gripped a handful of the stones she had been gathering, held her breath, and waited for the guard to look away.

Now!

Clair threw the rocks away from the ravine with all her strength. The guard spun toward the sound, his rifle aimed. Several women cried out, broke from the lines in fear. Shots. In the chaos, Lili, Elle and Clair silently dropped into the ravine, on top of the dead, and lay still.

Not a word, not a breath. Their bodies touching, waiting.

Pleasepleaseplease.

Clair lay face down, eyes tightly closed, trying not to breathe, gripped by an unspeakable horror as her cheek pressed against the cold hard corpse of a woman who just yesterday had been marching with her.

The pounding of boots, shouts in German, growing more distant. A woman's scream, shattering the silence. Three minutes, five.

They were the worst moments of Clair's life.

I won't forget your sacrifice, she told the woman so still and cold beneath her. *Your life mattered. I promise you, I will find a way to honor your courage, your sacrifice, your life. I promise.*

Finally, it was quiet.

Still they kept to the plan, waiting thirty minutes more, barely breathing, before slowly climbing from the ravine. Now the air was purple in the last of the light. For a moment they joined hands, said a prayer for the women who had sheltered and protected them.

And then, still holding hands, they disappeared into the silence of the shadows.

"I don't think I can go on," gasped Elle.

They had walked west through the night, and now, beneath a wash of golden dawn in the sky, a tiny village appeared beyond the wood.

Lili pointed toward the cluster of houses. "We need rest," she murmured.

"It's too dangerous," said Clair. "We are still in Germany, the villagers are Germans. We could be walking into a trap." She put a hand on Lili's arm to stop her. "I think we must be in Saxony now. The front lines cannot be far. Please, just a bit farther..."

"*Non*," said Lili, determined. "You speak German, you will find a way to talk to the villagers. Tell them we are no threat, just hungry refugees. God knows there has to be some kindness left in the world. We need food, rest. Ah. Look, there."

A barn. A vegetable garden.

Lili and Clair crossed and locked arms, making a human chair to carry Elle. They stumbled forward.

Food. Sleep.

The next morning, they left before dawn.

Three days later, just before dark, they came to the river.

The three women stood together on the shore of the Mulde River, hidden in the shadows of ancient oaks. Not far beyond the trees, a small encampment of Germans was dug in, machine guns pointed toward the river.

Below them, dark water spun and frothed beneath a fragile, makeshift bridge that glinted in the last of the light. On the far bank, an American jeep. A GI stood on the hood, his binoculars trained across the river.

"Jesus Jesus Jesus," whispered Lili, her eyes narrowed in horror. "It's so exposed. *C'est impossible.*"

Clair shook her head fiercely. "It's *freedom!* We've come this far. We have no choice." Elle, no longer able to speak, turned huge, sunken eyes on her sister. Clair bent to touch her sister's burning cheek. Elle nodded slowly. *Yes.*

The sun disappeared beyond the woods. Overhead, the sudden whir of an engine broke the night's silence. In the new darkness, pinpricks of lights. A small plane flew down the river, dipped its wings. *American.*

The final struggle had come. Heart racing, Clair closed her eyes, played the first notes of Chopin's Prelude No. 24 in her mind for courage. The very last of the 24 preludes, the D Minor, its thundering left hand faster and faster toward the finale. The conclusion, a rain of booming unaccompanied notes.

In the end, she thought, *we have no choice.*

"It's time," said Clair, reaching toward her sister. "We go."

Lili and Clair helped Elle to stand. Very slowly, from shadow to shadow, they made their way down the sloping riverbank. One agonizing step at a time. Holding on to her sister for dear life, with the bridge so close, Clair knew that the next harrowing moments would change their lives forever.

"Easy, easy." Clair and Elle stepped onto the quivering, swaying bridge. Lilianna steadied Elle from behind. Water swirled against their feet, dark and cold. The boards trembled, rocked below them.

Twenty steps. Thirty. Halfway…

So close.

A sudden shout in German, a spotlight searching across the water, moving inexorably toward them. The terrifying rattle of bullets, spraying and pinging into the water. Smashing into the bridge.

Lilianna shoved Elle into Clair's arms. "*Courant, mes Gloires!*" she screamed. "Run!"

Clair clutched Elle against her body and stumbled forward with every ounce of strength she had left. Turning, she saw Lili facing the Germans, standing tall, waving her arms. "Take me, you fucking bastards!" she shouted. The searchlight found her, lit her like a fierce flame against the dark night. A horrific hail of bullets. An agonized scream. A splash. Sudden silence.

Lilianna...

Somehow, Clair held on to Elle and kept going. One final step – *from death to life*, thought Clair, half delirious, *the final struggle* – and she collapsed to the riverbank, with Elle gasping and retching in the mud beside her.

A Jeep roared toward them from the darkness. An American captain leaped out, reached for Elle, gathered her against his chest. "Medic!" he shouted, "Here!" Then, "You've found the 104th Timberwolf Division, ma'am," he said, his shocked eyes on Clair. "I'm Captain Henry Claymore. Welcome to freedom."

"Contact the Resistance in Paris..." whispered Clair. "Tell them we are alive!"

Stunned brown eyes stared down at her, and she realized the captain was seeing two women scarecrows who weighed less than eighty pounds each.

"Let's not get their hopes up just yet," said the American, reaching for her hand.

CHAPTER 48

THE HOUSE OF ECHOES. PRESENT DAY

"All set, Maggie?" Beckett glanced back at her as he loaded their luggage into the rental car.

"I cannot believe this is our last day in Cancale." Maggie stood in the cottage doorway, gazing out at a sea lit by morning light, the rocks a soft rose color in the rising sun.

Becket came to stand behind her, solid as granite, and set his hands on her shoulders.

"It's so hard to say goodbye," she whispered. "This cottage, this wild land, speaks to me so strongly."

"You hear the echoes of your past," said Beckett against her blowing hair, "the voices that are no longer here. You've met your grandmother. Found the child that was your mother."

"Yes. I feel as if somehow I've been living in the past and the present at the same time."

"I get it. So we're not going to say goodbye, darlin'. I was thinking... we could come back in the spring for a second honeymoon."

She turned to him. "You would do that for me?"

"For us. In case you haven't noticed, darlin', this place speaks to me, too. Solitary, rough. Heroic. Ancient, and dark with history. Like me." His mouth quirked. "Can't you just see Shiloh sitting on those rocks, gazing out to sea?"

"Oh, Michael."

They stood for several moments while the new sun warmed them, casting their connected shadows across the grass in long, slanting shapes.

Maggie thought about the prelude she had played the night before. *I descend into the abyss.* The sense of her grandmother's story. Her bravery. Choosing to go to Ravensbrück to save her sister. Her courage in the face of the unspeakable.

On ne peut pas nommer.

Now, in the music, her grandmother's acts of courage echoed through time. You are my hero, *Grand-mère,* she thought, gazing at the shining cottage. Would she ever know how the story ended?

What choices would I have made? she asked herself. I can only hope I would have been as brave.

Beckett's low voice brought her back.

"The red eye doesn't leave Paris for hours, the day is still young. And I have a surprise for you, Maggie."

She gave him a searching, suspicious look. "Do you know me, Michael?"

"You will like this surprise, I promise. But first, you need to see this." Beckett drew her close, led her toward the far end of the cottage, where her father and Frankie were hunched over a small plot of earth.

"Winter is coming," Finn was saying in his soft bass voice, "so the garden is sleeping. But in a few months, when the sun is warmer, we'll plant this garden for your mama. Did she have a favorite flower? Maybe violets? I think she would have wanted you to understand that to plant a garden is to believe in tomorrow."

Frankie lifted her small face to his, glowing like a rose unfurling to sunlight.

Oh, Dad, thought Maggie. She turned to Beckett. "Not only have I found my grandmother and my mother here. I've finally found my father."

Beckett tightened his grip on her shoulders. "Yes, you have," he said against her temple. "And your dad's found something, too, Maggie. Every child can change the world. Who knows what wonderful things Frankie will do when she grows up? She's a creator, like you. A reminder that humans are still capable of finding beauty and love in this crazy world. Young people like Frankie and Dov are our future, darlin'. They'll bring music and art and beauty into the world, not more wars. Make the world a better place some day."

"Michael. I love you with everything inside me."

At that moment Finn exclaimed in pain, his spade falling to the earth. His right hand was trembling uncontrollably. Before Maggie could react, Frankie had reached for his cramping hand with both of hers, holding it tightly against her cheek until the spasms stopped and Finn's expression eased.

Maggie felt her heart twist in her chest. She dropped down beside her father and the little girl and wrapped them both in her arms. "I see I'm leaving you in good hands, Dad. Literally. But you know I would stay in a heartbeat if you need me."

Finn Stewart shook his head, flashing her the old "I've got this" look she remembered.

Maggie smiled down at the child, smoothed her tumbling curls, and turned to her father. "Okay then. I'll call every day, and we'll see you next month in Virginia. Someone has to walk me down the aisle."

His arms tightened around her. She looked down at Frankie, touched a freckled cheek gently. "I also happen to need a flower girl for my wedding. What do you think, sweetheart? I'll talk to your father. Until then, you take good care of my father for me, little sprite."

Finn and Frankie exchanged a guilty, secretive look, and Maggie raised a brow. "Just what is going on, you two?"

"Patience, darlin', all will be revealed," said Beckett. Taking her hand, he winked at Frankie and pulled Maggie toward the sea.

"Keep your eyes closed, Maggie-girl."

The hours had passed quickly, and now Maggie found herself standing with her eyes shut in front of The House of Echoes in the early afternoon light. Her father's hand was on her elbow, guiding her. "What's going on, Finn?"

"So much for trust. Okay, fine, it's time you see for yourself."

Maggie opened her eyes and caught her breath. Some ten yards away, Michael stood on the rocks at the edge of the sea, cloaked in a silvery mist. Gathered around him were Elle, seated in her wheelchair, Gerard and Frankie, and a small bald man wearing the long white robes of a village priest.

Her shocked eyes found Michael's. "You planned this for me?" He responded with a flash of his crooked grin.

"Welcome to your wedding, sprite," Finn whispered in her ear. "Frankie has something old for you, from your great-aunt."

The smiling child, dressed in a short dress the color of the sky, skipped forward. Her dark hair fell over her shoulder in a perfect French braid, and Maggie flashed a secret smile at Gerard Jouvert. Then Frankie held out a spill of delicate ivory lace.

"A veil," murmured Maggie. "*Oh, Tante,* is this *Grand-mère's* wedding veil?"

Elle smiled serenely as Maggie set the beautiful lace over her hair.

Gerard pressed a button on his phone, and the joyful notes of Chopin's Prelude No. 19 – *O My Beloved* – spun into the air. The gorgeous virtuosic chords and spinning eighth notes were saturated with happiness and love.

Frankie tossed white rose petals toward Maggie, grinning as they caught the breeze and flew like tiny doves out across the water.

Maggie gazed at Michael, his tall dark shape outlined against sky and water that shimmered blue in the gauzy light, waiting for her in this beautiful wild place she had so quickly come to love. Her grandmother's image floated into her mind, her face framed by the lace veil Maggie now wore, walking across these very stones toward the dark figure of a waiting man.

Maggie's fingers brushed the lace that covered her hair. At that moment, surrounded by Chopin's jubilant prelude, she felt so close to her grandmother, so certain of the past. *You finally found joy, Grand-mère. Did you marry your love here in this beautiful place, overlooking the sea? Did you wear this veil? Hear this glorious music in the wind?* The heartfelt notes of Chopin's joy echoed over her, as if in answer.

Turning toward her father, she took his arm. And walked slowly across the stones toward Michael Beckett.

Unable to wait, he met her halfway, taking her hands in his and pulling her close. "The stars are enough, darlin'. Our love doesn't need a fancy celebration. Will you marry me right now, Maggie O'Shea, right here under the sky in this wild land your grandmother loved? Will you choose love over fear, the way she did?"

"You are complicated and challenging and impossibly noble," she whispered. "I've never met anyone like you. You love so *hard*. The way you look at me, like you are looking at me right now, you make me dizzy with love. When I'm with you, everything else falls away. How could I not want to marry you?"

"Right answer, ma'am. Because I am madly, deeply, totally in love with you. You know more about me than anyone else, you shine a light into the darkest places of my life. For the first time in my life I know what it's like to wake up next to a woman and be truly happy. I love you with everything inside me, darlin'."

"As I love you, Colonel Michael Jefferson Beckett. I choose love." She turned to the priest. "*I do*," she said, as Chopin's jubilant chords trembled and echoed out over the sea.

"One thing I know I will never forget is how much I love good French champagne." Elle sighed softly as she clinked her flute against Maggie's. "I'm so glad we've found each other, *ma chère*. You have given me so much. I feel connected to life again. I needed to face the memories, to remember. You have given me back my beloved sister. And now I have *you*." She smiled. "At this age, I never expected to find someone else in my life to love. Someone to love *me*. Yet here you are." She smiled gently, reached to touch Maggie's heart. "Whatever the future holds for me, we have each other now."

"Oh, *Tante*, I feel exactly the same. I am the lucky one to have found *you*, and I love you with all my heart. I only wish..."

"Don't fret, child. Gerard says I'm doing well, that you are the best medicine I could have had. I am content."

"You make me so happy."

Elle squeezed Maggie's hand. "Always remember, *ma chère*. Even if there comes a day when I cannot recognize you, I will *always* recognize your love."

Maggie leaned forward to kiss the withered cheek. "Thank you for helping me find my grandmother," she whispered.

"Ah, speaking of Clair..." Elle reached for two packages wrapped in white paper that were tucked inside her wheelchair's basket. "I found these in my trunk, Maggie darling. Clair's last messages. They were for you."

Maggie gazed at the packages. "For me? What are they?"

"Answers," whispered Elle. "The last pages of your grandmother's story."

"But we know what happened after the war."

Elle gazed toward the water, shook her head. "Not everything, *chère*. I was in the hospital in Paris for months just after we escaped, Maggie. Clair returned to Cancale alone. She never spoke of that time. I never knew what happened to her there."

"Did you read these letters, *Tante*? Do you know now?"

Elle smiled gently, touched a gnarled hand to Maggie's cheek. "It is Clair's story to tell, *ma chère*, not mine. Take her memories home, keep them safe. You will know when it is time to learn what happened to your *Grand-mère*."

"You are the most beautiful bride I have ever seen, Mrs. Beckett."

They stood on the rocks overlooking the sea, his arm around her, holding her close. Behind them, the cottage glowed silver in the billowing mist.

She looked up at him. "Sweet talker."

"I could drink a case of you, and I would still be on my feet."

She grinned. "Did not know you were a Joni Mitchell fan."

"Joni and I go way back. But you're still my best girl."

She pressed a palm against his chest. "I cannot believe you did all this for me, Michael."

"I will do anything for you, Maggie."

Anything. Maggie's heart twisted, suddenly fearful, but she forced the thought away. *Choose love over fear.*

"Time to leave, darlin'." He lifted her hand to his lips, kissed her fingertips. "Here's lookin' at you, kid."

Maggie took his hand, turned, and headed toward the waiting car.

At that moment she felt... something. Or someone? As if a hand, gossamer as mist, had just brushed her cheek. Maggie stopped and turned to gaze back at the cottage on the edge of the sea.

There. A glimmer of shadow, a flash of red, a reflection in the window's wavering glass. A voice, soft as a caress. Piano music...

The House of Echoes.

Our story is not done, Grand-mère.

The last notes of Chopin's joy-filled Prelude No. 19 echoed around her as the cottage disappeared into the opalescent fog.

PART 4

"No sound, once made, is ever truly lost.
In electric clouds, all are safely trapped, and with a
touch, if we find them, we can recapture those echoes
of sad, forgotten wars, long summers,
and sweet autumns."

Ray Bradbury, *Now and Forever*

CHAPTER 49

SUNRISE RANCH. HUME, VA

Father Robbie Brennan sat in his Dodge Caravan mobility car, drumming his fingers on the wheel and staring thoughtfully across the stable yard. The white van was a gift to himself, outfitted with every accessible feature he could afford. Usually just sitting in it – his running legs, he called it – filled him with pleasure and an intense sense of freedom. But today, his mind was on the scene unfolding in front of him.

More than a dozen teens were scattered around the outdoor basketball court just past the stables. On the court, five boys in red tee shirts, five in black, shouting, passing, fighting for the ball and the next basket. His eyes softened as he watched Dov Davidov take a leap and...*score!* A huge grin and a high five with a teammate, his skin sheened with sweat, redtops flashing across the court. Early afternoon sunlight fell in slanted bars through the overhead pines, turning the boy's too-long, wheat-colored hair to gold.

Pain and loss always shimmering behind the blue eyes. And yet – a really good, thoughtful kid. Funny, in a dry, old soul sort of way. Robbie sighed, not for the first time wondering what it would have been like to have a son of his own. A kid like Dov...

Why do you always ask me to choose, God?

But this was no time for wandering off the priestly path, dreaming about the roads not taken. No time to be questioning passion, free will, reason, doubt. *Faith.*

He glanced at his watch. The Colonel and Maggie would be landing in just hours. His thoughts shifted to the call he'd had moments before, from Agent Simon Sugarman, looking for Beckett. There was something in his voice. Robbie shook his head to dispel his misgivings. Sugarman was coming tomorrow, after he landed at Dulles, to see the Colonel.

The feeling of unease remained, and the priest's eyes returned to the basketball court. He knew all the boys by now, friends of Dov's from the local high school. His eyes settled on Cady, the newcomer from New York with his dark shiny hair and black eyes. Why did he still have suspicions about this teen? There was just something about the boy, something that didn't ring true. And he had counseled enough troubled teens to know. His trouble radar was on DEFCON.

Simon Sugarman. Dane. Yuri Belankov. Robbie shook his head. This boy was connected to one of these men. He was sure of it. *But which one?*

"Inform me when you know more."

Some eighteen hundred miles to the northwest, in his Paris apartment on rue Palatine, Yuri Belankov disconnected his cell phone and set it on the small side table.

His best source had confirmed what he had just read in the International New York Times. Hidden among the newest Black Hole theory, a massacre in Iran, Florida Real Estate and a recipe for Spicy Pasta with Lentils, one brief, surprising paragraph. International Classical Pianist Magdalena O'Shea was getting married. To that damned relentless Colonel Beckett.

Yuri leaned back against the blue velvet banquet, closed his eyes.

Magdalena was getting married.

Earlier in the year, in Washington, she had betrayed his friendship. And yet, not long after, he had saved her life. Let her live, when he so easily could have ended her life. Why? Well, surely the way she played Rachmaninoff's Piano Concerto No. 2. The gorgeous Rach Two, eh? Still his favorite. But that wasn't the whole truth. He had gotten to know her, months before, in Boston and London. When there was still trust between them. Over dinner, they had talked about art and music, his past in Russia. Her dreams.

He'd thought at one time that they might be friends. Until she betrayed him.

And yet...

Da, there was something about her. A goodness. Something that made him feel the way his oil paintings made him feel. Intelligence, honesty, integrity. Making him, in the deepest part of himself, want to be better.

She was a creator of beauty. Taking her from the world would be a sin against humanity.

And, well, to be honest, she was not wrong about him. Two women were dead, because of him. He had turned a gun on a boy and his horse, then on a nun and a beautiful young violinist. Threatened to shoot them all. He closed his eyes. All to protect himself. Well, he thought, there is a dark streak of self-destruction in every Russian, eh?

But now the flash drive, with evidence that could have sent him to prison, was nothing but ashes. Was it possible he could finally return to his old life? He shook his head. There were still too many acts of violence in his past. His sins came to him every night, now, in his dreams. He saw their faces – the women, the boy. The mare. And he felt something he could not name.

There are at least two sides to every story, he thought. There is always more. And—right or wrong, good or bad—there are reasons for what we do. For the choices we make.

Good and evil can both be born from the same fears, the same wanting, the same dreams.

A sharp rap on the door broke the stillness.

Yuri's head came up. Who was outside his door at this time of night? He knew no one in the building.

Another knock, louder.

He stood, reached for his pistol and tucked it against his back. Then he walked slowly to the door. "Who's there?"

"Open up, pal, I know you're in there."

What the hell?

He unlocked the bolt, slid the door open. Stared into the dark eyes of DOJ Agent Simon Sugarman.

"Surprise. Been too long, Yuri. Invite a pal in? You won't need your pistol, I just want to talk. Got an offer you can't refuse." Sugarman flashed a wide grin. "Gimme a ten letter word that means 'the act of being saved from your sins.'"

CHAPTER 50

BECKETT'S CABIN

"They should be here any minute," said Robbie Brennan.

Beyond the cabin, shadows cast by the pines lay sharp and long across the old road. Inside, in the warmth of the firelight, U2 sang "It's a Beautiful Day" and the scent of roasted chicken filled the air.

Dov stood at the window, gazing out toward the empty road that wound like a ribbon up the mountain. Shiloh sat, alert with expectancy and something more, pressed against the boy's leg. The Golden recognized a troubled soul, understood what was needed. Watching them together, Robbie felt his chest tighten. The boy was too quiet, kept everything inside. If only they had a few more days together. But that was Beckett's job.

The priest turned away with a sigh. Maybe it had been a mistake to come. Being here, spending time at the ranch with the boy and his dog, had unearthed feelings and longings deeply suppressed. Long forgotten dreams of family. Of belonging. Of love.

Robbie shook his head to banish the forbidden images. Tomorrow he would head back to his ivory tower world in Georgetown, a world of black vestments and scholarly research and prayer. Of being alone.

He looked down at his jean-clad legs, so still and thin in the titanium chair. Really, God? Haven't you tested me enough? What more do I have to do to prove my loyalty? *What are you asking of me?*

"Padre? Father? You okay?" Dov's low voice broke into his thoughts, scattering the questions for another day. *Father.* Robbie opened his eyes. Shiloh was loping toward the door.

"Their car is coming up the road," said Dov. "Maggie and the colonel are home."

Maggie and Dov stood alone on the deck, watching the sky dissolve from blue to gold to purple as the sun disappeared behind the mountains. The air around them smelled of woodsmoke, the lake glinted with soft violet light. Shiloh lay curled close to the fire pit, his eyes on the dancing flames.

"Don't you wonder what he's thinking?" said Maggie. And then, "It's so good to be home. We missed all this. We missed you." Beside her, Dov remained silent. She turned, looked up into the Paul-Newman-blue eyes. "I have so much to tell you. You would love Brittany, Dov. The House of Echoes, my great-aunt Elle. Everywhere you look it's so beautiful and wild, a photograph just waiting to be taken."

"I have some good photos of Shiloh and Lady to show you," said Dov finally. "And an epic one of the Padre on the basketball court."

Maggie smiled. "Can't wait. No one takes a photograph like you, you tell a story. I'm hoping you'll take some photos at the wedding for us." She gazed up at him. "How are you doing, Dov? Everything okay while we were gone?"

He gave her a look. "Just the usual. Night terrors, bad decisions and reaping the consequences, still disappointing the colonel. Oh, and Belankov sent me a chess piece of a black horse head."

"Good grief. You're wrong about disappointing Michael, Dov. But he needs to know about the chess piece." She hesitated. "We were talking on the plane. We want to go back to Brittany in the spring. If we make our plans for spring break, you could come with us, one more birthday celebration. You – what?" She stopped. His face had gone stony and distant. "I thought it would make you happy."

"Maybe. If I'm still here."

"Still here? What on earth do you mean?"

Dov turned away, bony shoulders raised in a shrug, his eyes gazing through the sliding glass doors into the cabin. Beckett and Robbie Brennan were clearly having a disagreement. No voices could be heard, but Beckett was pacing back and forth and the priest's face was stony.

"That's got to be about me, Maggie. What's going on?"

She stepped closer, reached up to set a gentle hand on his too-sharp shoulder. "I'm not sure. But you need to talk to Michael, Dov. Just talk to him."

It was after midnight. The fire was now flickering embers, shadows lay deep across the room. Robbie Brennan had returned to his room at the ranch, Maggie was upstairs. Beckett and Dov sat on opposite ends of the old sofa facing the fireplace, with Shiloh dozing between them.

Beckett's hand was on Shiloh's neck, rubbing the soft fur back and forth. "I missed this," he murmured. "Brittany is beautiful and I'm glad I went. But this – the mountains, Shiloh, *you* – this is home."

Dov's eyes were locked on the glowing embers. "But something's wrong. I saw you and the Padre arguing."

Christ. Beckett stiffened. No way he was going to talk about Yuri Belankov until he talked to Sugar. "Let's just say the good Father is not a fan of my pal Sugar right now."

"The Padre also told me that Dane showed up at the cottage in Brittany, threatened Maggie. That you took him on, ended up in the hospital."

There was something in the kid's voice. "Can't keep an old guy down, right, Shiloh?" Shiloh simply yawned while Dov waited.

"Okay, I should have told you. I'm sorry." His eyes found Dov's. "I knew you, Shiloh and Father Handsome were doing okay here. I didn't want you to worry. Now that I'm a father, I–"

"Again."

Beckett's hand stilled on Shiloh's fur and he turned slowly to the boy. "What the devil are you talking about?" Shiloh lifted his head, aware of the sudden sparks of conflict in the darkness.

"What's not to understand? You're a damned father *again*."

"We signed the papers. I thought you knew that."

"What I *know* is that you had a kid years ago. A son. I'm not your child. I'm just some kid you took in that you felt sorry for. A fucking consolation prize for the real thing." He held up his wrist, circled by the thick leather bracelet he'd worn since his first foster care experience. "No way I'm ever taking this off!"

Beckett's eyes widened in shock. "Christ, Dov, is that what you think? Why you've been so angry and distant, shutting me out these last weeks?"

"I heard the Vets talking at the stables. About you having a kid who died, a long time ago."

"I did. His name was Sam. I loved him like crazy. But he died of leukemia, another lifetime ago." Beckett lifted a hand to his burning eyes.

"Why didn't you *tell* me?"

"It was never a secret, Dov. Just a loss so deep, it hurts too much to talk about. But you are no damned replacement! You are *you*, a quiet kid whose life was shattered but is somehow brave enough to keep going, a kid who loves books and music and photography, Shiloh and Lady in Black. Smart, better than me. I'm so damn proud of you it hurts. You are my son in every way that counts, Dov."

"But –"

"No buts. Shiloh and Maggie have taught me that the heart is boundless when it comes to love."

Dov looked away. "I didn't know if you were coming home." The words were a broken whisper. "You took your gun with you."

Sweet Christ. "I had to protect Maggie, just like I would protect you. I didn't think you…" Beckett stopped as understanding flooded through him. "You thought I'd be killed. You were afraid of losing someone else in your life."

"You're not my therapist, Colonel."

Beckett reached out, set his hand on Dov's thin chest. "I am sorry I frightened you. But don't you get it, Dov? You're afraid of losing me because you love me. Just like I couldn't bear to lose you. And I promise you, that is not gonna happen."

The boy raised rain-filled eyes to his. "For the record, Colonel, I would protect Maggie from that monster Dane in a heartbeat, just like you did. Like I protected Lady."

"I know you would, son. It's who you are." Beckett swiped at his eyes. "What say you, me and Shiloh go find some cold pizza?"

Shiloh gave a relieved bark and hopped off toward the kitchen, with Dov just steps behind.

Beckett stood very still, watching them go, stunned by the depth of his emotion. "Didn't see that one coming," he muttered, blinking back the threatening tears. Dov's parting words still echoed in the dark room. *I would protect Maggie from that monster Dane, just like you did.*

No way I'll let that happen, son. I will protect Maggie, and you, from Dane with my life.

CHAPTER 51

MYKONOS, GREECE

On the terrace high above the sea, the woman stood before him, dressed in a long white gown, her face hidden by a gossamer veil. She dipped her head toward him.

Dane reached up, clasped her neck, pulled her down. Her long hair spilled from the lace, falling over him like a dark curtain.

"Shylock," she whispered against his withered cheek.

Then a thunderous, shattering sound as the terrace burst into crimson flames, bits of explosives and metal raining down on them like burning confetti.

Dane's eyes flew open. The air was silent, the morning sun already hot, the flat blue stones of the terrace unbroken.

The bride had called him Shylock, like Iago whispering in Othello's ear.

Shylock. How many years had it been since he had swept across the dusty stage of that small London theater, wrapped in Shylock's black cloak? Shylock, the most villainous character in Shakespeare's *The Merchant of Venice*. Revenge had spurred Shylock's steep and stunning fall. Undone by a need for vengeance, thought Dane. As I will be.

But not yet. Not until he had his final revenge. The plan was already in motion. He had the boy in place to help him now – the younger brother of Firas. He was in Virginia, gaining Dov's trust. He already had access to Beckett's ranch. Soon, he would gain access to the cabin. Learn the layout. Then, he would be ready to act, to follow Dane's instructions. The stage would be set for revenge. Just like Shylock.

"There is no power in the tongue of men to alter me," said Dane into the sunlit silence.

I will toss explosives like birdseed at her wedding.

In the apartment on rue Palatine, Yuri Belankov paced back and forth across the living area, while Simon Sugarman's offer played over and over in his head. *Help us find Dane, stop him, and all sins will be forgiven.*

That ten-letter word, burning like a flame in his head. *Redemption.*

Back and forth. Back and forth.

Da, he had the incriminating flash drive now. But he was wanted for other crimes too, eh? Other secrets, other sins. He still needed Sugarman's offer if it meant he could return to the States a free man. So. He knew he could find Dane, help to save Magdalena. If he chose to. If he *wanted* to.

Back and forth. Back and forth.

Look at my life now, he thought. An aging man, alone except for his chess partners. What if I could go back? he asked himself. What if I could change the past. Would I? Can a man be ruthless and still have a soul? What if, what if...

His bleak Russian soul demanded an answer. It surprised him, how much the answer mattered. But sometimes there were no answers.

Back and forth. Back and forth.

He pictured the boy, Dov Davidov, throwing himself in front of his horse, risking his own death to save the animal. It had happened months ago, but the image still burned in his mind. Who loves like that?

Not I. But could I have, given the chance? He might never know. Unless...

During that dinner with Magdalena in London so many months earlier, before everything went wrong, she had asked him what would make him happy.

He had answered that Russians do not know happiness, only tragedy.

And yet… What do you want now, he asked himself. *What would give you peace?*

He blinked, suddenly, astonishingly aware that vengeance, hurting the boy, was no longer driving him. He gazed down at his novel, *The Brothers Karamazov*, left open and face down on the chair. Dostoevsky had lost his own son, Alyosha. For so many years, Yuri had believed he had a missing daughter – and experienced unbearable grief upon learning that the young woman he found was not his child. You've been reading too many Russian novels, he told himself with a shake of his head.

He tried to imagine a different life for himself. One without sorrow, without death. *Without revenge.*

He pictured the house he'd bought, deep in the Maryland countryside, before he'd been forced to leave the States. The emerald glint of oak trees through tall windows, high blank walls waiting for his art.

Living in the country was my dream, he thought suddenly. Mountains and trees, in an old house on a narrow road with a fireplace and a porch, surrounded by beautiful art. I would have fallen in love with a woman in a bookstore, on a cold winter's night – a woman with hair like dark rain and a soft, soulful gaze. And we would have made love to Rachmaninoff, and had the daughter I always longed for…

Given the choice, he wondered, would I choose my art, my home in the mountains, a second chance at love, over revenge on an innocent boy?

Revenge has cost me, he thought.

He shook his head, amused. *Perhaps I am less Dostoevsky than I thought.*

Back and forth. Back and forth.

So. He had a decision to make. He'd spent the past several hours thinking, reading about Magdalena and Dane – their twisted, dangerous past. A Shakespearian tragedy in the making. The past is prologue, he thought. Dane is obsessed with hurting Magdalena. He is not done.

Yuri stopped to gaze out the window at Saint-Sulpice, a black shadow against the too-bright blue sky. He and Dane were more alike than he cared to admit. Both hurt, both wanting vengeance. What would I do if I were Dane, he asked himself.

The old Russian ways of cunning, persistence and patience would not work. Dane would not wait. There was no time to waste.

Back and forth. Back and forth.

Yuri came to his chessboard, stopped pacing. Stared down at the pieces frozen in mid-play. Like his fellow countryman Kasparov, his strength in chess was seeing the big picture. He could look at the position of the pieces and see how things connected from one side to the other.

I've been paying too much attention to the queen, he thought. It's the "move-behind-the-move-behind-the-move" that I have got to see. He closed his eyes, pictured the chessboard. What move would Dane make?

I know, he thought suddenly. I know what he is planning.

He could stop him. Call his contacts in Greece. Find the villa. Begin there. He reached for his cell phone, stopped. If he accepted Sugarman's offer, there would be no turning back. His life would forever be changed.

I am so tired, he thought. I have done enough damage to last a lifetime. And I am still alone.

Redemption. Was it even possible?

Is it worth it, he asked himself, to hurt the boy once more? *Will saving Magdalena save my Russian soul?*

CHAPTER 52

BECKETT'S CABIN

The morning was cold and windy, with snowflakes swirling in the air. Robbie Brennan sat in the Dodge Caravan, warming the engine, while Dov leaned against the open driver's window.

"Safe journey, Padre," said Dov. "Shiloh and I will miss those epic philosophical musings of yours."

"And I never even got to Thomas Aquinas. But I'll be back in ten days for the wedding. And I was hoping you might come to Georgetown one day soon. I'll give you an insider's tour of the university."

Dov grew still. "Why?"

"Ah. Socrates believed that all answers could be discovered by asking questions." Robbie smiled. "So. Why do you think, Grasshopper?"

"You think I'd be a good fit there?"

"I know you would."

Before Dov could respond a Jeep roared up the drive, screeched to a halt. Six of his friends tumbled out, slinging huge backpacks over their shoulders.

"Looks like the clown car has arrived," grinned Robbie.

"Study group. The colonel made chili."

Robbie saw Cady in the group of boys and frowned. Breaching the inner sanctum, he thought. He turned to Dov. "Just be careful of –"

A black SUV pulled up the drive, parked next to the jeep. "Sheesh," murmured Dov, "it's Grand Central Station around here today." Then he froze. "That's Simon Sugarman. Maybe there's news about Yuri Belankov."

Robbie reached out a hand to touch the boy's arm. "Whatever he says, just listen, take time to think about it. Talk to Beckett. And remember, I'm only a phone call away."

"I just want justice for my mom. For Lady in Black."

"My old friend Thomas Aquinas said, 'Justice without mercy is cruelty.' There are many sides to every choice, Dov."

"Yeah, well, maybe your old friend Tommy didn't watch his mom die."

"What fresh hell is this, Sugar?"

Beckett and Simon Sugarman were on the cabin deck, side by side, leaning against the railing. Sugar had been talking for several minutes. Beckett shook his head in disbelief, trying to dispel the burning anger in his chest.

Inside the cabin, everything was normal. The teens were gathered on the floor around the fireplace, surrounded by books, sodas and bowls of popcorn while Ariana Grande blasted *One Last Time*. Shiloh was in his usual place by Dov's side, easily catching the popcorn tossed his way and basking in all the attention. Even Maggie had joined them, perched on the arm of the sofa, laughing and looking like a teenager herself in narrow jeans and an oversized school sweatshirt that said GO BLUE.

But Simon's news was anything but normal. Beckett could feel both Maggie's and Dov's eyes on them. What the devil was he supposed to tell Dov?

"You heard me, pal. I offered Yuri Belankov a deal, and he accepted."

"*JesuseffingChrist*, Sugar, what were you thinking?"

"Stop clutching your pearls, grandma. He's got powerful underworld contacts on every continent. I need him for a big new case I'll be running at Justice. But right now, bottom line, he's the best way I know to find Dane, stop him, and protect Maggie. Tick tock, pal. Time's running out. You do what you gotta do."

"You work for the *Justice* Department, Sugar. *Justice*. Do you see the irony here?"

"Look, I know the kid wants justice for his mother. But we both know Lady Justice is too often nuanced, not clear. I had a long talk with Belankov in Paris. He's agreed to help protect Maggie, so maybe he has a conscience after all. Deeply hidden, but still... Hell, I'm choosing the best of two bad options, Mike."

"Fine words can excuse the worst crimes, Sugar. Belankov is guilty of more than one criminal act, he needs to be held accountable. That kid sitting inside saw his mother's violent death!"

"He didn't *see* her die, Mike, he *found* her. Big difference. And there's no longer any proof, ashes won't stand up in court. Yuri will be free as a bird, no matter what. At least this way he has a chance to do some *good*. It's a done deal, pal. As I said, I'm doing what I gotta do, to protect Maggie. C'mon, Mike, you know Yuri's the best chance we've got."

Beckett stared at him through narrowed eyes. "Maybe. But Dov won't see it that way."

"About Dov..." said Sugarman. "There's one more part to this deal. Yuri walks away from the kid. No more threats."

Beckett was very still. "How in hell did you get him to agree to that?"

Sugarman's smile was enigmatic. "It was all his idea, Mike. Go figure."

The clock was chiming nine p.m. when the boys' Jeep pulled out of the driveway with an arc of headlights and the roar of spinning wheels.

Beckett stood at the door, watching the blink of red taillights. Christ, he was too old for this. But Dov had assured him there was no alcohol smuggled in the backpacks. Trust, Beckett reminded himself. The kids all appeared sober, just teenagers having a good time. Except for Cady.

Robbie Brennan had called just after Sugarman left, asked him to keep an eye on the newcomer from New York. No reason, just a feeling. But after decades in the military, Beckett had learned to trust his feelings. JDFR. Just didn't feel right. It was a real gut reaction he trusted. And he'd just trusted Robbie Brennan for several days with Dov's life.

The boys had stayed together in the main room most of the time, but, face it, they'd had the run of the main floor – kitchen, bathroom, Dov's bedroom, the deck. An hour earlier, he'd found Cady alone on the deck, peering over the railing.

Looking for something, Cady?

Spinning around, startled. Shoving his lit cell phone into his jeans pocket. Guilty?

Uh, no, sir. Just getting some air. You know, the fireplace smoke and all.

Beckett shook his head. Just the new kid trying to fit in? Or casing the cabin… I'm seeing bad guys everywhere, he thought. That's on me, not Cady.

And yet.

First, he needed to talk to Dov. But Dov had headed to bed. Just as well. He needed time to think about what he was going to say. *Sorry, kid, the man who killed your mom is not going to pay for his crimes.*

All Beckett wanted to do was climb the stairs, find comfort in Maggie's arms. His eyes found Shiloh, still awake by the fire. "Feels like I seized the wrong day," he muttered. The Golden returned his stare as if he understood the irony.

"Okay, I'll let the kid have one more night of peace," said Beckett. "I'll talk to him in the morning."

He turned toward the stairs. Damned coward, he thought. This father thing was harder than he'd ever imagined.

"Michael? What's wrong?"

Suddenly wide awake, Maggie sat up in the bed. He was across the room, a figure darker than the shadows, slipping a key into a locked metal box. The box he kept on the top shelf of the closet. The box that held his M18 service pistol.

He removed the pistol, hefted it in his hand. "Hello, old friend," he said into the silence. "Long time no see."

"Michael!"

"Go back to sleep, darlin'."

Maggie tossed the covers back, swung her feet to the floor and stood to face him. "Like hell I will. Why do you need your gun? Tell me what's going on. You're scaring me."

Beckett blew out his breath in a long sigh. Then he secured the M18 back in its case and turned to her.

"Don't be afraid, darlin'. I'm sorry I scared you. The pistol will stay in the closet. For now." His low voice vibrated with anger. "Sugar made a deal with Belankov. All charges against him are dropped if he helps Sugar find Dane, take him down."

"No! Can he do that?"

"Says he can. Says he did. It's a done deal, Maggie."

"Oh, God. Dov…"

"Yeah. He doesn't know yet. It's going to hit him hard. Boulder hard. I don't know what he'll do."

"It's never easy watching a child suffer. Do you want to talk to him together?"

His eyes found hers in the darkness. "Maggie McFierce. I wish. But he can't feel blindsided by both of us. I need to be the bad guy, Maggie, the fork in his roomful of balloons. Not you. Better for him if you show up after, to wrap him in your arms."

"You're not the bad guy, Michael. But I'll be there for both of you. Now please, come to bed."

With one last glance at the closet, Beckett climbed into the bed and into her waiting arms.

Within moments, his slowed breath against her breast told her he was asleep. But she was wide awake, holding Beckett close against her body as she stared into the shadows.

Realization pierced the darkness like a knife and her stomach clutched. *Sugar made that deal because of me,* she thought. I will be the cause of Dov's pain – this troubled child I have come to love. Her eyes drifted to the closet, then to Beckett's key chain, glinting in a shaft of moonlight on the bedside table.

The chain where he kept the key to the locked box.

The key…

CHAPTER 53

MYKONOS, GREECE

Just before dawn on the island of Mykonos, the Hellenic police SWAT team quietly surrounded Dane's villa. At the captain's signal, guns were drawn. Shouts of warning were followed almost simultaneously by the shattering of the tall, white front doors. The team surged into the main room, spread out, began the search.

Ten minutes later, they gathered once more on the terrace. The villa was empty. Dane was gone.

Beckett and Dov stood together on the shore of the lake, watching Shiloh chase Kamikaze, the neighbor's cat. Ice crystals glittered on the surface of the water, the air was heavy with the threat of snow.

"He'll never catch her," murmured Beckett, watching Shiloh's slow, hopping lope. "It's a cat's world."

Under the knitted ski cap, Dov's blue eyes found Beckett's. "Stop dancing around and just say it, Colonel. Get it over with. Something is wrong. I know it's bad news."

"Yeah, kid, the worst. Brace yourself. Sugarman tracked down Yuri Belankov, cut a deal with him."

Dov became very still. "He found Yuri? Where? But that's good, right?" A breath. "Wait. What kind of deal?"

"Yuri's been hiding in Paris. He goes free it he helps Sugar find Dane and stop him, once and for all. All charges against Yuri will be dropped."

"What the fuck, Colonel? Oh, God *damn* it to hell!"

The deep sound of hurt in the boy's voice tore through the air. Shiloh lifted his head, soft eyes full of concern, and found his way to Dov's side just as Beckett reached out to grip Dov's shoulder. "You have every right to feel betrayed, Dov. But we'll get through this together."

"Betrayed? This is an epic fail, Colonel." Dov's breath was jagged as icy tears seeped down his cheeks. "It's a fucking Get-Out-of-Jail-Free card! *Why?* What about my mother? This is so wrong."

"Sugar says he made the best of two bad choices."

"Then I'll just have to go after that monster myself," growled the boy. "It would be a just murder for sure."

"Hold on, son. We've talked about this. It's the *last* thing any of us wants for you. Surely not what your mom would have wanted." Beckett hesitated. "What do you think your Grandfather Yev would have said to you?"

Dov looked away. Finally he said, "That we all have our own battlefields."

Beckett nodded. "And this one's yours. I think Yev would have told you that nothing can bring your mom back. We can't go back and change the bad. But we all have the capacity to love, or to hate. *The choice is yours.* And you love Maggie, right? If we stop Dane, we can still protect Maggie. We can do something *good*, something to make your mom proud."

Dov turned eyes filled with blue rain on him. "I remember what we talked about at Gettysburg, Colonel. But part of me still wants justice for my mom. And the truth is, part of me wants something more."

"Vengeance won't give you closure, son. Violence ruins *two* lives, not one."

"I don't give a flying fuck about closure!" shouted Dov, shaking his head wildly. "I don't know what to feel. What to do."

"Sugar believes that the end justifies the means. Do you?"

"If the end is saving Maggie?"

"Yeah. Saving Maggie."

Beckett watched the thoughts race like clouds across Dov's pale face. "Your Padre gave me a book by an American theologian named Frederick Buechner. He wrote, 'Here is the world. Beautiful and terrible things will happen. Don't be afraid.'"

"Hard not to be."

"Agree. But we can protect the beautiful, make it matter." Beckett looked into the distance. "When a life is saved, who else will be saved because of this person? Like an echo, over generations. Maggie's heart, her music, make the world a better place. She will echo into the future."

Dov stared at him. "You agree with Sugar. You think it's the best choice, too." The words seem to strangle in his throat.

Beckett locked eyes on Dov, bent closer. "I do. It would be different if we had proof that Yuri killed your mom. But there's *nothing*. No DNA, no eye witness. Now no flash drive."

"I was fucking *there* in that alley, Colonel!"

"But there's no proof that *Yuri* was there. And it was after your mother was already gone, Dov. You never saw what happened. It's your word against his. All circumstantial. No way the DA would prosecute, no way a jury would vote for conviction."

"So he just fucking gets away with murdering my mother?"

"Do you remember me telling you that sometimes we do the wrong thing for the right reasons?"

"We let him walk so he can help us save Maggie…"

"I'm counting on it, kid."

Dov bent to Shiloh, buried his head against the silken fur of the Golden's neck. "I know you're trying to help," he said, his words muffled. "But–that quote you told me? I have to find a way to deal with the terrible." He stood. "Come on, Brigadier."

The boy and Golden turned away, disappearing into the ice-coated woods. Watching them go, Beckett felt one more crack in his soul.

Give him what he needs, the dark voice in his head whispered. *Beautiful and terrible things will happen. Take away his terrible.*

Standing by the piano, Maggie pulled her sweater more tightly around her. She'd been planning to practice a Chopin Étude but there was no way she could focus. Beyond the window, she'd watched Beckett and Dov down by the lake. It was like watching a tragic silent movie, their pain and anger throbbing in the air. Her heart twisted for them. Two men she loved.

She saw Dov and Shiloh turn toward the cabin, leaving Beckett alone. Moments passed, then the slam of a door, footsteps running toward her. She stood, turned, held her breath. Dov came crashing into the room, froze when he saw her.

"Maggie."

She held out her arms, overwhelmed by guilt. "Oh, Dov, this is all my fault."

The boy ran to her, flung his arms around her. She felt his tears, hot against her cheek, and held his trembling body against her. "It will be okay, darling. We will get through this together."

He lifted his head. "Together? How, Maggie? You already have a son, the colonel had a son once. I don't belong, I won't take their place."

"We have chosen to be a family, darling. You, the colonel, me and Shiloh. We're not separate individuals anymore, we're together. This wedding isn't just about the two of us, it's about *all* of us. Trust in us, Dov. Trust the love."

She held him close, Shiloh whining softly beside her, until the trembling stopped.

Later, alone once more in the great room, Maggie turned to the piano, her solace in the bad times. Dov had disappeared into his room, Michael had taken his boat out on the lake – his way, she knew, of dealing with his demons.

All of her grandmother Clair's preludes were set on the old upright, in order by their dates. Maggie had played almost all of them, beginning with No. 13, *Loss*, when she was in Brittany. There were only two left. By now she knew her grandmother had survived the war, had found her way home to the House of Echoes. Eventually she had married the American captain, Henry Claymore. And after that? There was still so much Maggie didn't know. Might never know.

But her great-aunt had said that many of the answers were in the envelope she had found in her trunk and given to Maggie just before she left Brittany. That envelope, still unopened, was upstairs by the bed. She had decided to wait until all of her grandmother's preludes had been played, until she had listened to her *Grand-mère*'s story.

Okay, then. She lifted the score of Chopin's Prelude No. 2 in A Minor. Across the top, her grandmother had written: *June 1945. Finally, I return to La Maison des Échos alone, aching with the Guilt of Surviving. Painful Meditation by the Deserted Sea.*

Maggie set her fingers on the keys. The left hand began this piece alone, in a minor chord throbbing with sorrow. She thought of her grandmother's shattered right hand, felt the pain rip through her like a knife. How had she survived all the loss? Where did such bravery come from?

The deserted sea…Maggie closed her eyes, saw in her mind the lonely outcrop of rocks where she had stood above the wild water, listening to the voices on the wind. She pictured a young Clair, returning home after unimaginable pain and loss, standing alone on those rocks, staring out to sea. What must she have been feeling?

She took a deep, hurting breath, lifted her left hand, and began to play.

Clair
"The Distant, Deserted Sea…"

CHAPTER 54

THE HOUSE OF ECHOES, CANCALE. JUNE, 1945

The sun was falling into the sea as Clair Rousseau walked slowly over the stones, her legs still unsteady. Late spring flowers spilled from the rock crevices, vines and petals of lavender and rose and pale gold. She stopped on the very edge of the shore, standing still, gazing out over the water. The wind, whispering with memories, whipped her shawl back like a banner. No birds, no boats. The sea was deserted, the color of liquid mercury in the dying light.

"I've missed you," she whispered to the undulating waves. "I never thought I would see you again. I was so far away, I never thought I would come home." *I thought I was going to die.*

Had it been only a year since she'd stood here on this very spot with Charles? April, 1944, just after they'd fled Paris for the Breton coast. Before she'd seen him on the beach near Saint-Brieuc for the last heartrending time...

Charles.

One year – but one lifetime. Clair sighed deeply and pulled the shawl more closely around her razor-blade shoulders. The June evening was soft, lit by warm pink light, but she was always cold now. In the months since she'd been convalescing in Paris, she had slowly regained some of the weight and strength she'd lost. But she still had a long way to go. Her hair was just growing back, a soft gray halo around her sharp-boned face. Impossible to believe she was just nineteen. Holy Mother, she looked and felt like an old woman.

So much had happened in the two years since she'd taken the night train to Paris...

A war, and the end of a war. A sister lost, a sister found. Two men dead by her hand – two mortal sins on her soul. A German soldier in a lifeless French village. And Kurt Jurgen. Clair held up her right hand, now a broken, grotesque claw. The pain, still excruciating, would always remind her of Jurgen's cruelty. The inhumanity of the Nazis. The agonizing deaths of her friends. The guilt of surviving. The loss of her beloved music. *The loss of Charles.*

She turned from the sea, gazed toward the small white cottage perched on the edge of the rocks. What would she find inside? Nothing, the small voice in her head warned her. The Nazis had taken everything from her.

I am finally free, yes, she thought. *But with a broken hand and a broken spirit.* What do I do now?

A wave of loneliness washed over her. A longing for her sister Elle, still recuperating in Paris. The separation, after their too-brief reunion, was a searing ache. But necessary. She had to get the cottage ready for Elle's homecoming. Build a ramp, add railings in the bath. Henry Claymore had promised he would drive over from Paris to help her as soon as he had a few days leave.

Henry. Clair smiled, thinking of the kind, sweetly funny American captain who was so smitten by her. Who walked with her in the gardens of the hospital, her hand tucked safely in the crook of his elbow. Who brought her chocolate croissants from the local patisserie, told her charming stories of his family in a far-away place called Maine. Someday he would take her there, he'd promised her on the day she left Paris.

But that was a dream for another day. Today, she was here in Cancale. And the empty cottage, with all its memories, was waiting for her. You're home, she told herself. You are safe here. You are alive.

Now, you go on.

Clair lifted her chin, took a deep breath, and began to make her way across the rocks toward the cottage.

The oil lamps cast wavering shadows across the bare floor and empty walls.

Clair stood in the center of the room, her eyes on the old Ibach grand piano, willing herself not to weep. The piano was one of the few pieces still there, abandoned by the Nazis in the sudden rush to escape after the tide of the war turned. So much had been looted, destroyed.

But she'd been prepared. The cottage was the same as the last day she'd been here, with Charles, after their escape from Paris a year earlier. *Night.* They'd slept right there on the floor, wrapped in an old, forgotten quilt. The night he'd told her his name.

She shook her head to dispel the memories as she gazed around the room. No electricity, no water. A broken chair, the huge empty bookcase, too heavy to steal. The frayed quilt, on the floor in the corner where they'd left it.

Now, just like all her countrymen, it was time to rebuild. To go forward. To put the past behind her. She would sweep and clean tomorrow, find the village market, search for a bed, a chair. A hammer and nails. But right now…

She moved slowly across the floor toward the piano. Jurgen had taken away her right hand, but not her left. He had not been able to take her dignity. Her heart. *Her soul.* Even in death, she would not let him win. She found the music she'd bought in Paris in the bottom of her frayed carpet bag, beneath the new book of Baudelaire's poetry Henry had given her. She chose a prelude, set the score on the piano, and settled on the scarred piano bench.

During those first weeks in the hospital in Paris, agonizing weeks when she thought she was going to die, she'd made a vow. If she lived, she would tell her story through Chopin's music. Chopin had been with her in the darkest moments. His music had given her courage. Now, his preludes would help her find a way to heal. To have hope once again.

And when I die, she thought, *I will have left a story – a legacy – for those who come after, so they will never forget. Music would be the link, across the generations. An echo of my life.*

She would begin at the beginning, in 1943, when she lost her family. The loss that had shattered her spirit until, on that fateful evening in November, she'd met *Père* on the night train to Paris. Yes. She would tell her story by beginning with Chopin's Prelude No. 13, *Loss*.

But tonight, finally home once more in her beloved *La Maison des Échos* on the edge of the sea, she needed to play what she was feeling in her heart right this moment. The discordance of her survival and guilt, the aching for all those she had lost, the loneliness. All the painful thoughts that swirled in the wind above the restless sea. Curling her trembling right hand in her lap, she raised her left hand to the keys. A breath, a wish. Help me find the words, my dear Chopin. Come back to me. Show me how to tell my story.

Across the top of the page, with her left hand, she wrote: *June 1945. Finally, I return to La Maison des Échos, aching with the guilt of surviving. Painful Meditation by the Deserted Sea.*

She sat, very still, chin lifted. Listening. Outside the sea wind sighed, shaking the windows. And then she began to play Chopin's Prelude No. 2 in A Minor, letting herself fall into the music, while her frozen right hand throbbed with want and remembrance. The prelude was bleak, dissonant, dark, poignant – opened by the left hand alone in an aching minor key. It said everything she was feeling, deep in her broken heart.

For over an hour she played, her left hand finding the notes she could reach, while the memories and questions tumbled through her mind.

Why did I say yes to *Père?* Why did Avril and Lilli have to die? Why did I stay in France when I could have escaped, why did I risk my life by going to Ravensbrück?

You know why, the throbbing chords whispered. For Elle. *For love.*

She had never thought of herself as brave. Where does such courage come from, she asked the music. What if I had made different choices?

It wasn't a choice, the music answered. It was simply what you did. You could not have done anything else.

A sharp knock on the door shattered her thoughts, scattering the notes into the empty darkness.

Clair's head came up as the prelude's last chords echoed in the empty cottage. Who would come at this hour? Captain Claymore?

She rose slowly, clutching her throbbing right hand against her chest. Across the room, hesitating at the door.

Another rap, softer this time.

Clair cracked open the old door and found herself gazing into impossibly green eyes.

Her heart stopped. *Holy Mother.*

That slow, enigmatic smile. "*Bon soir, ma belle Buttercup.*"

"Night..." she whispered. "It can't be. I saw you die."

CHAPTER 55

They spent the night wrapped in each other's arms.

He told her what had happened on the beach, after he'd been shot. Showed her the scars on this back, from the bullet wounds.

Somehow, he had managed to swim underwater to the side of the boat. They'd dragged him onboard, just before roaring away. Only seven of them made it to England. Six men and Snapdragon.

In London, he'd finally met their Resistance contact, Uncle Bradley.

"He lied to you," she whispered in the darkness. "Lied about the Allies plan for the invasion."

"*Oui*. He was convinced I would be captured. He knew I would be tortured, eventually tell what I believed to be the truth."

"It was unconscionable," she murmured.

"It was war," he said against her bare shoulder.

When she stayed silent, he said, "I stayed in London, working with Uncle Bradley and the SOE – the Special Operations Executive – until it was disbanded. Then I moved to MI5, Military Intelligence. I'm still working for them, Clair, traveling between London and Paris. For too many of us, the war has not yet ended."

"But the Yalta conference met," she murmured. "They've committed to rebuild our war-torn continent, find a new order for post-war Europe."

"*D'accord*. But Stalin continues to demand a Soviet sphere of influence. He cannot be trusted, Clair. Already there is conflict in

Poland, talk of a Cold War coming. I may be needed in Eastern Europe."

"No, Charles! It's too dangerous."

He tilted her chin up, gazed into her brimming green eyes. "You joined the Resistance, you risked your life for others every single day. I know you understand. Would you have done anything differently?"

She looked down at her curled, shattered right hand, then raised her eyes to his.

"*Non.*"

"I cannot either. So much you and I fought for is gone. Our cities and towns are destroyed, bridges and railroads bombed, the countryside is scorched earth. An unimaginable loss of lives." He swiped at eyes shining with deep green tears. "Too many of us did nothing. I have to help rebuild, Clair. There is no choice."

"I know..." she whispered.

He took her hand, lifted it to his lips. "It took me a long time to get over the hurt – the anger – when you chose to stay behind that day on the beach," he murmured. "I thought we loved each other."

"We did." She smiled faintly. "We do."

Into the sudden silence, she whispered, "I've cost us so much. Will you be able to forgive me for leaving you?"

"There is nothing to forgive, Clair, I finally understood that. You were suffering just as much as I. I remembered your sister Elle, and I realized that you had no choice. It's an amazing thing, to be willing to die for someone you love. You stayed behind, you risked dying at Ravensbrück, for love."

"But I loved you, too! Staying behind on that beach, watching you leave, broke my heart," she whispered. "All I could think about was that last day we were in the cottage together. When we promised to return, to find each other here, after the war. And then I saw you shot. Oh, God!"

"One of the men on the boat told me he'd seen you taken prisoner. I had to come back. I had to know if you were still alive."

She touched his face. "I thought I would never see you again."

He held her crushed fingers against his heart. "I know you have suffered, Clair. I cannot imagine how much."

You don't want to know, Charles. I watched women tortured, watched them die. I murdered two men in cold blood.

But she only whispered, "*On ne peut pas nommer.*"

One cannot speak of the unspeakable.

"Then I will not ask you to," said Charles softly. "No more talk, *ma chère.* I join Snapdragon and our team in Paris two days from now. We have tonight, and tomorrow, before I have to leave you. We will live every moment we have together, and make new memories to hold us. Memories of joy and love. And hope."

He pulled her against him, began to kiss her. Tenderly at first, then deeper, deeper, until she did not know where his body ended and hers began.

Clair awakened at dawn. She reached out, touched only the cold sheet, felt the panic stir. "Charles?"

He was not in the cottage. She found him outside, standing on the rocks with the sea behind him, backlit by morning light. A large canvas was propped against a mound of stones, the white cottage taking shape against a sky the color of old coins.

"Oh," she breathed. "How beautiful."

He smiled, not taking his eyes off the painting. "I wanted you to have a memory of our time together in *La Maison des Échos* before I go."

Moving to stand behind him, she slipped her arms around his waist. "I don't want you to leave," she whispered. "I don't want tomorrow to come. I'm afraid I'll never see you again."

Paintbrush in mid-air, he stopped and turned to her. "Afraid? *Mais non*, not you, Buttercup! You have survived what most humans could not. I've never known anyone as brave as you."

An image of Kurt Jurgen speared into her mind. "I just did what I had to do," she murmured.

"And now it is my turn," he said against her hair. He set the paintbrush down, set a hand on the small of her back and turned her toward the beach. "We will not talk of my leaving. Come, I have another surprise for you."

When they stood together on the rocks, facing the sea, he bent to one knee and held out a small box.

Clair took a shocked step back, her hand on her heart. "What's this?"

"Do you remember that tiny Minox I gave you in Paris, to photograph Nazi files?"

"How could I forget?"

"The first time we were here at the cottage, we used it to take pictures of each other. I don't have a ring, *ma chère*, but I think this will have even more meaning. I had it made for you in London. I had to believe I would find you alive."

Her hands shook as she opened the small box, gasped as she lifted the gold locket and held it to the light. It spun from a fine chain, sparking as it caught the morning sun. "Oh, Charles."

He put his hands over hers, took the locket and pressed a small catch. She gazed down at the images. Charles' face on the left, herself in the small disc next to him.

"We look so young," she murmured. "It was before we were separated. Before the camps…a lifetime ago."

"We *were* young," he said softly, turning the locket over. "I added an inscription on the back. *Toujours se Rappeler, 1943*. Always remember. It was the year our eyes first met."

He slipped the locket around her neck, so that it fell between her breasts.

"Marry me, Clair. Right here, today, by the sea. We will pledge our love to each other in the sight of God. A love that will last forever, no matter where we may be."

Toujours se Rappeler.

They walked hand in hand into the village. Many of the shops along the quai were still abandoned, destroyed by fire or bombs. But house by house, stone by stone, the town was rebuilding. Fine sawdust, and the sound of hammers on wood, filled the air.

They found a small flower cart with pails full of white roses. And in a twisting alley above the sea, they found an antique shop, its windows still boarded up. There, in a back room lit by lanterns, they discovered a shoulder-length veil the color of old pearls, made of French lace.

Later, as the sun was setting, they stood together on the rocks above the sea and pledged their love for each other. Her veil caught the breeze, and floated like a cloak of white mist about her shoulders. Just for a moment, overcome by joy, she heard the echo of Chopin's Prelude No. 19 – *O My Beloved* – on the wind.

She gazed into Charles' deep green eyes, then looked out over the rocks, at the sea beneath a blue vault of sky. Her soul place. It's been so long since I felt free of danger, she thought, free of pain. And she opened her heart to the unfamiliar feeling of peace.

Later, he made love to her on a bed of white rose petals. The only thing she wore was the locket, as warm and alive as his lips against her breasts.

Toujours se Rappeler.

He left her at dawn the next morning.

Three days later, Captain Henry Claymore showed up at the cottage door and asked her to marry him.

PART 5

"There is no love that is not an echo."
Theodor Adorno

CHAPTER 56

THE BLUE RIDGE MOUNTAINS.
ONE WEEK UNTIL THE WEDDING

Inhale. Exhale. Inhale. Exhale.

Maggie's feet pounded the rubbery high school track with the steady beat of a metronome. On this thirty-degree Sunday after Thanksgiving, Dov's school was dark and quiet. Snow flurries spun around her, stinging her cheeks. Only a few crazy souls, wrapped in layers against the cold, were running the track with her on this late, blustery afternoon. She would have preferred the silence and beauty of the forest paths, but she had promised Michael she would only run in public places until it was safer.

Safer. Don't think about Dane. Only good thoughts today.

Inhale. Exhale. Inhale. Exhale.

The days were flying by. Hard to believe it was only three weeks since she'd discovered her grandmother Clair's music and locket in the trunk at the Vineyard – and then flown to Brittany. Falling in love with The House of Echoes. Meeting Elle, Gerard and Frankie. Learning about her grandmother through Chopin's preludes, listening to the echoes of the past. Taking vows with Michael on a windy bluff overlooking the sea.

And now, she was back in Virginia. Thanksgiving had come and gone in a blurred, happy whirlwind. Michael, Dov and Shiloh had wisely banished her from the kitchen and cooked the dinner, which they'd shared with Robbie and two of Michael's close Vet friends in front of the fire. Then they'd all gone to the ranch to bring a special treat to Dov's mare, Lady in Black, and pies for all the Vets.

And suddenly, only seven days remained until next Saturday's wedding. Everything was set, thanks to the help of Luze, the manager of her Boston music shop and dear close friend since college. Maggie grinned as the recent conversation she'd had with Luze spun into her head.

"What? Only twenty guests, Maggs? That's it? *Twenty?*" The jangle of silver bracelets was loud with disappointment in the background. "I had more guests than that for Thanksgiving dinner!"

"Michael and I just want our family and closest friends, Luze."

"On a deck perched over a mountainside in East-Bumble-Fuck-Virginia? In *December!* What's happened to you, Maggie?"

Maggie had to laugh. "I hardly recognize myself these days. But the mountains are so beautiful, Luze. Intimate is what I want. What I *need*."

"If you want intimate, fine. I think I can still get us that small rooftop room here at the Four Seasons, overlooking the gardens."

"Say goodnight, Luze."

A huge sigh, another frustrated jangle of silver. "Okay, okay. I know that voice." A hesitation and then, softer, "It's going to be beautiful, Maggs. *You* are going to be beautiful. I just want you to be happy."

"I *am* happy, Luze. See you next week."

"I'll be the one in ten pounds of ski clothes. Not my best look, Maggs."

Dial tone.

Inhale. Exhale. Inhale. Exhale.

Smiling, Maggie shook her head. Luze had seen her through the good times, and the bad. Thank God for her friendship and quirky sense of humor. Thanks to Luze, the simple ivory long-sleeved wedding dress was hanging in the cabin's hall closet. Dov and his friend Cady were going to take photos, the catering was all set, her dear friend Hannah was going to play the cello during the ceremony. Frankie could not wait to be her Flower Girl. Her son Brian would be her "Person of Honor." Dark suits were ready and waiting for Michael, Dov, and her father. And sweetest of all, Shiloh preening before the mirror in his new black bow tie.

Michael had surprised her with two very special gifts. He'd invited Robbie to officiate the ceremony, and he'd planned her bouquet – white lilacs, the flowers he'd given her ever since she'd told him that a secret fan always left white lilacs for Rachmaninoff.

I am blessed, she thought. I am loved.

She thought once more of the emotional ceremony she and Michael had shared at The House of Echoes. *In the eyes of God,* the village priest had said. Since Brittany, she'd felt different. She *felt* married.

Please, she prayed. Let us have this life together.

Inhale. Exhale. Inhale. Exhale.

Okay. It was getting dark. One more turn around the track and she would head for home. *Home.* Suddenly anxious to get home to Michael, she ran faster, passing another runner with a grin and a wave.

Toward the end of the final loop, Maggie began to slow her speed and headed toward the exit to the parking lot.

Running steps behind her, coming fast. Too fast.

What the hell? She spun around. A tall figure all in black, closing in.

Maggie gripped her car keys, metal tips pointed out between clenched fingers the way the Colonel had taught her.

The man sprinted by in a blur, without a glance at her.

Maggie watched him disappear into the rapidly fading light.

I won't do this anymore, she thought. I can't. No more hiding in the shadows. I want to be as brave as my grandmother Clair.

Her aunt Elle had told her, in broken shards of memory, about her grandmother's final days in the camp before their escape. Clair had taken the life of the Nazi who tortured her.

My God, thought Maggie. The now-familiar questions spun into her head. What would I have done? *Could I be that brave?*

She pictured Michael's service pistol, locked in the closet. *If I have to be.*

Then she turned and jogged toward her car.

Inhale. Exhale. Inhale. Exhale.

CHAPTER 57

BECKETT'S CABIN. FIVE DAYS BEFORE THE WEDDING

Christ, it was cold.

Michael Beckett stood on the redwood deck above the lake, hunched in his scarred leather jacket, his eyes locked on the battered night vision field glasses he had used in Afghanistan. He scanned slowly to the left, slowly to the right. Down towards the lake, then up toward the distant mountains.

There, up on the ridge, a movement. A shape darker than the shadows.

Eyes on the figure, he reached one hand behind his back. His SIG M18 was tucked into the back waistband of his jeans. Just in case.

More movement. His breath came out. Okay. Not human. A deer, maybe. He shook his head.

His fingers brushed the smooth handle of the pistol. *You are out there*, he said to Dane, his eyes on the shadows. *Somewhere. I know it. I smell it. You are close. Come on. I'm ready for you.*

A soft scrape behind him. He spun around, bending at the knees, reaching for his gun.

Froze just in time as Shiloh slow-hopped toward him across the deck. Christ! Get a grip. It could have been Dov. Or Maggie. Ignoring the sudden burning pain in his knees, Beckett eased the pistol back into his waistband and said, "Hey, big guy. Couldn't sleep either? Remember when we used to walk the perimeters at base camp at midnight? I'm feeling that way tonight. On guard. Expecting trouble. You sense it, too?"

Shiloh set his watchful gaze on the darkened woods, ears back, fur bristling.

"Yeah. Glad you're here. You've always had my six. And it's kinda nice to have some time with my Best Dog."

Shiloh gave a soft woof of agreement as he settled close by Beckett's favorite chair.

"Good idea, think I'll join you." Beckett dropped into the chair with a tired sigh and reached to stroke the silky ears. "No bourbon or guitar tonight, gotta keep watch. Maggie's asleep. Only five days 'til the I do's."

Shiloh gazed up at him, his liquid eyes wistful. Beckett nodded in agreement. "Yeah, I remember when it was just the two of us guys, too. Pizza every night, right? BBQ. And donuts. Then along came Maggie. And kale. And sushi."

A soft rumble in the Golden's throat. Beckett grinned. "Thank Christ Dov showed up to save us. At least we got our pizza back." He glanced back toward the darkened cabin. "He's sleeping, right? No night terrors?"

At the mention of Dov's name, Shiloh's eyes glinted with concern. And conflict.

"It's okay, you know," said Beckett. "Okay to be there for him. You and me, we'll always be a team, nothing can come between us. But it's okay to love more than one person. Maggie taught me that." He nodded slowly. "And Dov needs you. More than he needs me right now. You're on his team, too."

They sat together in easy silence, until Beckett murmured, "Not the first time you and I have pulled an all-nighter, right? Waiting, watching. We both know he's coming."

They turned as one to search the shadowed woods.

"It will be okay," he murmured to the Golden. "Dane started it, but I'm gonna finish it. Whatever he's planning, we won't let Dane hurt Maggie. She just has to stay out of the way."

Shiloh kept his opinion to himself, his watchful eyes on the black mountains.

The theater lights were blinking. Only moments remained before the curtain lifted for the final act of *King Lear*. Dane sat forward in his seat, his eyes on the curtain. Waiting. Remembering.

'Mr. William Lear' had arrived in D.C. from Canada the prior evening. Checked into his room at the Hay-Adams with its unparalleled view of the White House, ordered a very rare filet mignon with truffle sauce and a bottle of 2012 Moet & Chandon, and slept off his jet lag – for once, without dreaming.

Dane had come to Washington many times over the years, but always with dark intent. Today, for the first time, he had been a tourist, donning his mirrored aviator blue Ray-Bans and leaning heavily on his cane to visit the places he'd never had time to explore.

The highlight was spending the afternoon at the Folger Shakespeare Library on Capitol Hill, an Elizabethan monument of white marble with the largest collection of printed works by Shakespeare in the world. The First Folios and letters were astonishing, as was the art, but his favorite collections were Playbills and Costumes. He'd been certain he had worn that exquisite embroidered-velvet tunic in a London production of *King Richard III*, the night several of the arrows they'd shot went into the audience...

Dane grimaced at the memory. Total chaos, ambulance sirens, several audience members hospitalized. Their own fault, he thought. *Richard III* was always a risk.

The *pièce de résistance* of his visit, of course, was attending tonight's Shakespeare Theatre Company's production of *King Lear* here at the Lansburgh Theatre. It was beautiful and intimate, with red velvet seats curving like arms toward the small stage, reminding him of the theaters in London.

The lights dimmed, the curtain began to rise. In moments, Lear would lose all three of his daughters – the wicked Goneril and Regan, and gentle Cordelia, their upcoming fate sealed since Act I.

A king. A father. One more Shakespearian character with a steep and stunning downfall. Lear, undone by his pride, ambition and greed, bringing the royal roof caving in.

Quite the tragedy, thought Dane. A man wants to be King, chooses power over family, goes mad in a storm, then everyone dies. He smiled in the darkness. His own storm was about to hit. The royal roof was about to cave in, literally. Just five more days.

Everyone dies, he thought.

CHAPTER 58

BECKETT'S CABIN

They were standing on the deck of the cabin, surrounded by family and friends. Maggie, draped in her grandmother's veil, smiling up into Michael's eyes. The sun dropped toward the mountains behind him, outlining his face with gold.

Suddenly the wind picked up, whipping the veil across her eyes. She couldn't see! She heard a shout, then a gunshot. Michael's gun? Everything was black. Someone pushed her to the redwood deck. What is happening? Why can't I see?

Another volley of gunshots, louder now. Closer. Someone was screaming.

No, please…

Maggie's eyes flew open. It was pitch black.

"Michael? What's happened, where are you?" Panic stabbed her chest.

Silence. Shadows taking shape. She took a shuddering breath, her heartbeat slowing as she realized she was in the cabin bedroom. A dream. No, a nightmare. Five days until the wedding. Of course she was anxious.

The bedside clock read 9:45. Not late at all. She must have fallen asleep while reading.

Maggie reached out her left hand. The sheet was cold. Empty. Where was Michael?

He'd been so restless, so quiet lately. His eyes on a distant place. She was afraid he was going to what he called his dark place. But this time it wasn't because of Afghanistan. It was because of her. His love, his need to protect her.

Her eyes moved to the closet. Had he taken his gun?

Maggie stood by the window, gazing down at the man and his dog together on the deck. Below them, the icy lake glimmered with starlight, the mountains sleeping black shapes against the night sky.

God, she loved those two. No way she was going to go back to sleep now, knowing they were out in the cold because of her. She would be waiting for Michael when he finally came inside.

Until then... tea and the piano, she thought. Music always calmed her. Her grandmother's Chopin preludes were still on the piano bench where she'd left them. She'd been playing a prelude each day, in order by her grandmother's dates. Chopin was a composer of many moods, and each prelude was a brief, nuanced sketch of an emotion, a mood, a moment. Personal, and so intimate. Like tiny shooting stars, flaring into music.

Thinking about her grandmother, Maggie slipped on her robe. Turning toward the stairs, she stopped. Yesterday she had finished playing all the preludes her grandmother had left for her, learning – and feeling – her grandmother's story through the music. But Clair's story wasn't done. Maggie still had no idea how her story ended. Tonight was the perfect time to finally open the envelope *Tante* Elle had given her just before she'd left Brittany. The last message from her grandmother Clair, so long forgotten in Elle's trunk.

She'd set the thick manila envelope in the drawer of her bedside table for safe-keeping. Retrieving it now, the last conversation with her great-aunt spun into her head.

"What is in this envelope, Tante Elle?"

"Answers," whispered Elle. "The last pages of your grandmother's story."

"But we know what happened after the war."

"*Not everything, chère. I was in the hospital in Paris for months just after we escaped, Maggie. Clair returned to Cancale alone. She never spoke of that time. I never knew what happened to her.*"

"*Did you read these pages, Tante? Do you know now?*"

"*It is Clair's story to tell, ma chère, not mine. Take her memories home, keep them safe. You will know when it is time to learn what happened to your Grand-mère.*"

Maggie descended the stairs, holding the envelope against her heart. A glance toward the deck, her eyes resting for a moment on Michael and his Golden, sitting so close together. Then she sat down in front of the still-smoldering fire.

For Maggie was written across the center of the envelope in a spidery hand. Rubbing her fingers gently over the script, Maggie closed her eyes. Clair had known she had a granddaughter, living in the States, and written something just for her. *Tell me the rest of your story, Grand-mère. I will honor your memories and keep them safe.*

A log snapped with a shower of sparks. Taking a deep breath, Maggie tore open the envelope, and withdrew a sheaf of yellowed papers.

"Oh," she breathed. On top, several pages of a letter that began *Ma Chère Maggie.* Beneath the letter, a musical score. Tilting the pages toward the firelight, she saw that it was a penciled score for a piano concerto. The name Clair Rousseau was scribbled across the top, just below the title – *Des Échos dans le Vent.* Echoes on the Wind. And then the words, *For all the beautiful and brave women who gave their lives for us all. We will never forget you.*

Maggie hummed the opening chords. Beautiful, haunting. She had never heard this music before. Had her grandmother composed this piece?

She would play the music after she read the letter. Setting the score gently aside, she lifted her grandmother's hand-written pages. The words were in French – awkward, slanting, surely written by her un-injured left hand. The parchment, old and yellowed, crackled beneath her fingers. Was there just the faintest hint of flowers?

Ma Chère Maggie,

Je suis ta Grand-mère. Je voudrais vous dire le passe.

I am your grandmother. I want to tell you about the past.

Clair

"Our echoes roll from soul to soul,
And grow for ever and for ever."
Alfred, Lord Tennyson

CHAPTER 59

LA MAISON DES ÈCHOS, CANCALE.
NOVEMBER 11, 1986

My dearest Maggie,

I am your grandmother. I want to tell you about the past. I want you to know me and my sister Elle – your family.

It was Clair's sixty-first birthday. Overcome by emotion, she sat at the old cherry desk she had purchased just after the war in the Cancale market. There was so much she wanted to say. Her granddaughter Maggie needed to know how much she was loved. She needed to know the rest of the story. She needed to know the truth.

Her heart fluttered painfully in her chest. Beyond the window, the sea wind whispered like voices against the glass. Clair closed her eyes for a moment, seeking courage, and then began to write.

Tu es ma seule petit-fille. You are my only grandchild. We have never met, but your mother Lily has told me so much about you, and sent so many photographs, I feel as if I know you. Now, it is time for you to know me. I have so much to tell you.

Your mother loved you very much. We were planning a special visit to Cancale for your thirteenth birthday when she died.

Désolée.

I have not been able to travel for a very long time, or I would have come to you then. Thankfully your father called to say that you were in his mother's care, so I knew you would be loved. And yet...

I felt so close to you then, and I still do. I know you look just like your beautiful mother. Dare I say, just like me? I know you are kind, and brave. I know you play the piano with great emotion and passion, as I did once. We both love Chopin. Do you talk to him the way I do? If not, ma chère, time to start talking!

I feel as if we are especially connected through our music. Do you feel it? It is why I chose to send you the preludes. There are things that happen to us that are unspeakable. On ne peut pas nommer. After the war, so many Frenchmen felt ashamed. They didn't want to know the truth, to talk about all the suffering and loss. Even our heroes wanted to forget.

But still, it is important that you know the past. The truth. To understand the choices I made. The choices I didn't make.

Alors. Somehow I knew I could tell my story, without words, through art and music. I chose Chopin's Preludes right after the war, when I returned to my beloved La Maison des Échos in Brittany. Some years after you were born, I shipped two gifts to your mother. First, an exquisite oil painting of the cottage. Then I slipped a locket, and the first few prelude scores I had chosen, into an old trunk, sending it all to your mother. My story was for my daughter Lily, and her children and grandchildren. We lost your Maman too soon, my love, but I hope that when you read this letter, you will have seen the painting, found my locket and those preludes I hid in the trunk (and the other scores I left for you in the cottage). Then you will have begun to understand my story, and what happened to our family – your family – during the war.

Maggie my dear, the past is like the ripples of a stone thrown into water. The decisions we make ripple over generations, across time and space. Echoes that roll from soul to soul. It is why I left La Maison des Échos to my beautiful Lily in my will so long ago. And now, in a full circle, the echoes of the past will come to you.

But there is one thing, ma chère, that I cannot say through music. It is a secret I have kept for far too long. I was going to tell your mother when you both came to Cancale to visit for your birthday. But fate had other plans.

And so I write this letter, and will give it to my sister Elle for safekeeping. You are still so young. It's impossible to believe that I was just your age when the war changed my life forever.

My heart, I feel myself slipping away, like the light fading at the end of the day. I don't think I will see another Christmas. Now, I can no longer keep my secret. Those months I returned to Brittany, in the summer of 1945, are still as clear to me as if they happened yesterday.

I was finally back home at La Maison des Èchos. The healing was painfully slow, all the loss still unbearable. The war took so much from me. War makes us into people we don't know.

And then, the miracle. Even Elle does not know that I had fallen deeply in love for the first time in Paris during the war – the one tender mercy during an unspeakable time. His name was Charles, but his code name in the network was Night. Oh, he was handsome, with his too-long dark hair silvered at the temples and the most intense, startling green eyes I had ever seen. For too short a time, we were happy. And then I saw him die, shot down in the sea the night that I was taken prisoner on the beach during our escape.

But somehow Charles lived, and found me at the cottage in Cancale. We pledged our love – body and mind, heart and soul – and married each other in the eyes of God on the rocks overlooking the sea. But my joy was short-lived. Charles was *still fighting the war, and had to leave for Eastern Europe. He promised to return for me.*

As for what happened next, soon only God will be my judge.

CHAPTER 60

"Marry me, Clair Rousseau. Come home to Boston with me, and be my wife."

The American Army Captain, Henry Claymore, was down on one knee, gazing up at her. Stunned by his words, Clair looked into his soft gray eyes and raised a hand to clutch the gold locket around her neck. "Oh, my dear Henry." She took his outstretched hands in hers. "Please, stand up. I... don't know what to say."

Henry Claymore stood slowly, his eyes locked on hers. "I think you just gave me my answer, Clair."

She felt the tears threaten. "It's so good to see you, Henry. I've missed you. Walk with me." She led him across the rocks, until they stood together in the wind on the edge of the sea.

He touched a finger to her cheek. "I think I fell in love with you that first time I saw you, in the mud on the edge of the Mulde River, with your sister cradled in your arms. By God, I've never seen a woman so brave, so strong. So beautiful."

She smiled faintly, ran a hand over her spikes of silvered hair. "Americans are such sweet liars. But I remember that moment, too. You were my hero that day, Henry. You still are."

"A friend, a hero... but not the man you love."

"I do feel love for you, Henry, you did not misunderstand that. But–"

His eyes glinted with sudden understanding. "But there is someone else?"

She could not bear to hurt him, but she cared too much to lie to him. "Yes. A man I met in Paris, in the Resistance, when the war began. We pledged our love for each other, planned a future together. And then our network was betrayed. I thought he died on the coast, during an escape attempt, just moments before I was captured. But somehow, he survived. He came here, to see me, not long ago."

"And then?"

"He left for Eastern Europe. Still fighting, still at war. I know his work is dangerous. I've heard nothing, not a word." She closed her eyes, overwhelmed by a building sense of dread.

Claymore looked out over the sea, white-capped and turbulent. Finally, he turned to her. "If it would ease your heart, Clair, I could try to find out if he is okay."

She stared at him. "You would do that for me?"

"I would do anything for you."

"Thank you," she whispered, struck by his kindness.

He gave her a wistful smile, then shrugged broad shoulders. "So how about we take those measurements for your sister's wheelchair ramp before it gets too dark?"

He took her hand, and they walked together in silence toward the cottage.

Toward the end of July, a knock on the cottage door woke Clair from a sound sleep.

"*Un moment*," she called, dragging herself to the door.

Henry Claymore was waiting for her. "Elle is coming home to you in two weeks," he announced with a broad grin. "I've brought bread, cheese, wine to celebrate. And, as promised, the new safety bars for the bathroom." He frowned, leaned down toward her. "What's the matter, Clair, you're pale as a ghost."

"No wine," she gasped. Then she turned her back on him and fell into the nearest chair.

Dropping his packages to the floor, he knelt beside her, touching her forehead with concern. "Are you sick, sweetheart?"

"No, but... Charles..."

"Good God. Have you finally heard from him? I've been trying to get news of him for weeks with no luck. He must be deep undercover."

"No, there's been no word," she whispered. She turned huge, swimming green eyes to his. "I'm pregnant, Henry. I'm going to have Charles' child."

Five weeks later, Clair and Elle sat in the small garden, drinking tea and talking softly. The heat of late August shimmered on the waving seagrass bent toward them by the stiff ocean breeze.

Clair rested a gentle hand on her growing abdomen as she gazed fondly at her sister. In her new silver wheelchair, Elle was growing stronger every day. They did not talk about the past, by mutual agreement, but they were enjoying being together again in the cottage and sharing a simple life in Cancale. Finally, they were able to smile again.

"Is Henry coming today?" asked Elle. "He always brings my favorite chocolate croissants, from the shop on rue du Mars." She grinned, poking a thin finger at her sister fondly. "If only he would look at me the way he looks at you."

"Yes, he's coming in time for an early dinner. You shall have your special dessert tonight." Clair shook her head. "And hush, *ma choupette*, he looks at us both in exactly the same way."

"You never were a good liar, Clair! It's why I always beat you at poker. I remember one time in Paris when you –"

Both women turned at the sudden crunch of tires on gravel. A low black sedan slowly came to a stop.

"That can't be Henry," murmured Clair. "It's too early."

The car door opened slowly.

Hit by a sudden, inexplicable wave of dread, Clair touched the locket against her heart.

A tall, too-thin woman emerged from the car. Her face was hidden by a curtain of long dark hair, but Clair saw the familiar flash of bright red lipstick. A sudden faint whiff of Evening in Paris on the air.

As if in a dream, Clair rose slowly from her chair, holding out a hand as if to stop what she knew was coming.

"No... Please, no."

The woman raised her head and locked hollow eyes with Clair. Tears ran down her cheeks in trails of black mascara.

Snapdragon.

Clair's body folded and she fell to her knees.

In the flickering quiet of Beckett's cabin, a single, low sob escaped Maggie's lips as she came to the end of her grandmother's letter, forgotten in Elle's trunk for decades.

Months after the death of the man she loved, her grandmother had agreed to marry the American captain, Henry Claymore. Henry had promised to raise, and love, her child as his own. Maggie thought of the old wedding photograph in her mother's Vineyard cottage. There had been something wistful in her grandmother's expression.

My biological grandfather was named Charles, thought Maggie. *Charles*, the signature on the gorgeous oil painting of The House of Echoes in the Vineyard bedroom. She opened the gold locket around her neck, gazed down at the dark-haired, handsome face. He was the great love of my grandmother's life. He was a hero who gave his life for the people hurt by war. He was an artist, a creator. He gave my mother and me his startling bright green eyes.

Clair had described their marriage on the rocks overlooking the sea – "In the eyes of God," her grandmother had written – just the way she had married Michael. Clair had worn the same lace veil she'd left for Maggie. No wonder I sensed her presence so strongly that day, thought Maggie. Somehow, Clair was there, in the echo of the music on the wind.

Maggie gazed down at the final paragraphs of her grandmother's letter.

There are times you think the world has ended. But you go on, you learn to live again. My claustrophobia was too severe for travel, so Henry and I built a good life in Cancale. Lily Avril gave us such joy. Henry was a loving husband and a good father who adored Lily like she was his own. Oh, how we missed her when she left to study in New York. But she was happy studying her music. All those years, we never told her, or Elle, the truth.

I composed this concerto for you, Maggie, just after your mother died, in honor of all the remarkable and courageous women who fought beside us. Some of us survived, too many did not. I wanted you to know that we all fought and sacrificed to make the world a better place for you and the generations to come. As your grandfather said, it is an amazing thing, to be willing to die for the people we love.

"Oh, *Grand-mère*," whispered Maggie, overwhelmed. She reached for the gold locket, clicked open the small heart, gazed down once more at the face of her grandfather. Charles. His eyes as deeply green as her own. The secret was a gift, both painful and beautiful. "I wish I had known you," she said softly. "I wish you had known me."

Her gaze moved to her grandmother's face, marveling at her incredible strength. "You endured so much, *Grand-mère*," she said into the silence, "but somehow you found a way to survive. To embrace life. I feel so close to you tonight. Thank you for telling me your story. I understand, now. I promise I will honor the past. I'm so glad you were my grandmother."

Our echoes roll from soul to soul, her grandmother had written. My grandmother's acts of courage have echoed through time, thought Maggie. Her eyes settled on the piano. Now, finally, she could play the concerto her grandmother had composed after the war.

But not tonight.

She stood, turned toward the doors that led to the redwood deck.

Tonight, she needed to be in Michael's arms.

CHAPTER 61

SUNRISE RANCH. FOUR DAYS BEFORE THE WEDDING

The next afternoon, Father Robbie Brennan rolled his wheelchair into the stables at Sunrise Ranch. Surprisingly, during his stay, he'd come to enjoy the mingled scents of horses, leather and hay, the sounds of jingling bridles, restless hooves, a soft whinny on the air.

"Anyone here needing a priest?" he called. "Half price sale for weddings this week."

"Hey, Padre!" Dov's head appeared over the top half of the door to Lady in Black's stall. "Welcome back. Thank God you're here." The wooden door creaked open and Dov stepped from the stall, followed by a hopping, tail-wagging Shiloh.

"God says you're welcome," grinned Robbie, reaching to scratch the Golden's silken ears. "Where else would I be, four days before the wedding? I'm guessing Colonel White Hat needs to be talked off the roof right about now."

Dov laughed. "Worse. He's fishing."

"Is he? Well, have you considered that perhaps fishing is not an escape from life for the colonel, but a deeper immersion *into* it."

An eye-rolling look passed between Shiloh and the boy. "Aaaannnd, we're off," murmured Dov under his breath. "Whatever, Padre."

"Ouch, not exactly the response I was hoping for," said Robbie. "But – whatever."

Dov had the grace to smile. Shiloh yawned loudly.

Robbie held out his hands. "I've missed you two. I hear you are Beckett's 'Best Men.' Tell me how you're doing."

"Haven't caused any trouble in the last twenty minutes or so, right, Brigadier? Haven't exploded in rage, punched anyone, or disappointed anyone either, far as I know."

Shiloh appeared to be less certain.

"But it's still only afternoon," added Dov, and the Golden seemed to agree.

Robbie shook his head. "You've never disappointed me, Dov. But I want to know how you are doing, *really*."

"This 'we'll-be-a-family' thing is new to me. But Maggie is so happy, so easy. So loving. And it's worked okay for Shiloh, so, worth a try, right?

"Very worth it." Robbie waited. "And?"

Dov looked away. "Okay, yeah, maybe there's more. You know Yuri Belankov cut a deal, right? They're no longer charging him with my mother's death. He can come back to the States." A bright flash of pain and anger in the depths of blue eyes.

"Beckett told me. I can only imagine how betrayed you feel. Do you want to talk about it?"

"Already did, with the colonel."

"Ah. Good. How'd that go?"

"How do you think? We argued about vengeance versus justice. Choices and consequences."

"Not on the same side, I suspect."

"Hardly. But he got me to thinking. About doing the wrong thing for the right reasons. About doing what's right, even if your heart wants something else. Protecting what is good and beautiful. The colonel says there are three kinds of people in the world. The Creators, the Maintainers, and the Destroyers. Maggie is a Creator. We have to protect the Creators from the Destroyers."

"Yes. Very similar to the 'Three Beings Worthy of Respect' – the priest, the soldier, and the poet. To know. To kill. To create."

The boy stared at him. "I have to think about the killing part, Padre. The colonel says I have to decide who I am, who I want to be. He said we don't always see things as they are, sometimes we see things as *we* are."

Robbie's brows went up. "Beckett said that?"

Dov grinned. "Yeah, surprised me, too. But the words make me want to know more. I need to understand what I feel, and why. Beckett says no one can take away what you've put in your mind." A slight shrug of shoulders, a scuff of boot. "So I've been thinking about that tour of Georgetown University you offered me."

"Still stands, Dov. Any time." Robbie waited a moment. "Dare I hope you might be interested in studying philosophy?"

Dov shot the Golden a look. "Okay, we can check off disappointing someone." He grinned at the priest. "I'm thinking, maybe, law school? Criminal law."

Robbie raised surprised brows. "A jurist! Like Thomas Aquinas. Yes, I can see it. Have you told Beckett?"

"Nah, I'll keep him on the hook for awhile."

Robbie Brennan leaned forward, his eyes locked on the boy. "What Beckett told you, Dov... It's what a father would say to his son."

Dov stood very still, surprise etched on his face. He gazed down at the leather cord around his wrist, indecision and recognition warring in the blue eyes.

"Padre, I think I finally –"

The sound of tires on gravel beyond the open stable doors.

Man and boy turned, saw the black SUV pull slowly to a stop, its windows dark.

Shiloh came to his feet, golden fur bristling, a growl low in his throat.

"Hide in Lady's stall," said the priest. "*Now!* Stay there and *do not come out, no matter what!*"

"No, Padre. No way I'm leaving you."

"Then do it for Maggie and Beckett. *Trust me*, Dov."

The door of the SUV began to open.

A frozen moment. Then Dov whispered, "Protect the Padre, Shiloh." With one final look, Dov slipped into the mare's stall and closed the door.

Robbie turned his chair, and, closely followed by Shiloh, rolled toward the entrance.

Yuri Belankov stepped from the car and walked toward them.

CHAPTER 62

SUNRISE RANCH

"Father Brennan," said Yuri Belankov in his low rumbling voice. "We cross paths again. I did not expect to see you here."

"What do you want, Belankov?" Robbie hardly recognized the man standing in front of him. Thinner, and no longer bald. Now, the long hair of a poet brushed a frayed collar. Shiloh snarled beside him, baring sharp teeth. Setting a calming hand on the Golden's back, the priest kept his eyes on the Russian. "You're not welcome here."

"Casting stones does not become you. Your halo is still tarnished, I see."

"At least it's not broken."

"*Touché.* But I am unarmed." Belankov held out his hands, palms up. "I'm not here to cause trouble. I came here to meet with Agent Sugarman and the colonel. But first I wanted to see the boy."

"But he doesn't want to see you. You've done enough harm to him for a lifetime. You need to leave. Now."

"Not until I talk to him. He doesn't know the whole story. No one does."

"You killed his mother. Just months ago you shot his horse, tried to kill him. You threatened two women and held a gun on Maggie, a woman Dov has come to love. More *story* won't change that."

"It's true, all of it. I am a man with a soul half empty."

Robbie watched him coldly, waiting. He could feel Shiloh trembling beside him. Finally he said, "If you are looking for absolution, it's too late. You've come to the wrong priest."

"There is no absolution for me, I know that. Redemption is not the reason I accepted Agent Sugarman's offer. For once, I will do the right thing. I just want to tell the boy the truth. Then I will leave. He will never see me again."

Robbie closed his eyes, fighting decades of religious training to forgive the sinner. A soft whinny sounded from Lady's stable. Don't look at that door, he commanded himself. *Just stay where you are, Dov. Listen.*

Taking a harsh breath, he said, "Perhaps a man with a soul half empty still has a fragment of a soul left to fill."

Belankov's black eyes bore into his. "A moral dilemma, eh? Very Russian."

Restless movement from Lady in Black's stall. Robbie froze.

Then a low, breathy nicker. Both men turned as Lady's sleek, scarred black head appeared over the half door.

"I am glad she is okay," said the Russian, gazing into the mare's single eye. "My shot went wild that day when your dog attacked me. I did not deliberately aim at her."

"Not nearly enough," said the priest.

Belankov stared into the shadows. "The truth? I loved Dov's mother for years. She was beautiful, smart. Lonely. She understood my Russian soul. I trusted her, and eventually told her all my secrets, professional and personal. The boy never knew."

Belankov began to pace, caught up in memory. "When she betrayed me, I was blindsided. The pain was shattering, the rage overwhelming. I could not understand *why*. I called her, demanding answers. We arranged to meet in the alley by the Tatiana Nightclub. All I wanted was to understand. By God, as if I would ever dream of hurting her."

He stopped pacing, turned to Robbie, his voice stark and haunted. "When I got to the alley, it was too quiet. Then I saw her, collapsed on the stones. Piano wire around her neck, the old Russian way. I don't know how long I stood there, staring down at her, knowing she was gone. Then I heard a sound. I looked up. Her son was standing at the end of the alley, looking at me in horror." Belankov stopped, his dark eyes blind with pain. "I was a coward. I disappeared into the shadows, left him standing there."

Robbie shook his head. "I don't know if I believe you." Beside him, Shiloh growled his agreement.

"There is no reason you should, eh? If you force the pieces in chess, you can miss the truth. It was my fault his mother died, I don't deny it. I was a powerful man with many enemies in the Red Mafia – men who wanted me out of the way. But I never meant to hurt Irina. Still, I blame myself for her death, *da*, and I committed many more sins in the months to come. No, I am not here to ask for forgiveness. It's true that I blamed the boy for his accusations, I wanted to hurt him the way his mother hurt me. I wanted to protect my freedom. But I no longer want that. Months of hiding, of reading Dostoevsky, of thinking, of asking the impossible questions, have finally taught me what I want. Life is too short to be consumed by vengeance. There are more valuable things to chase in the years I have left. I am not *all* bad, Father. I am not like Dane."

"No. Finally, something I believe."

"It seems I care about Maggie O'Shea as well. It's the first rule of chess. *Protect the Queen.* And if I can help stop Dane from hurting Maggie, well, that is best for the boy, too, eh? He is brave and fierce, like his mother. He needs to have love in his life. I owe him, maybe I can give him that. Balance the scales. And keep beautiful music in the world. For once, I want someone to see the good in me, not the bad."

A sudden loud creak broke the silence as the door to Lady in Black's stall swung open. Dov Davidov stepped from the shadows, his eyes like twin blue flames. Shiloh immediately moved in front of the boy. "Easy, Shiloh," said Dov.

Yuri spoke into the silence. "*Malen'kiy chelovek.* You heard?"

"Every word. But I am not your 'little man.'"

"No, you are not. I just meant –"

In one swift stride Dov was in front of the Russian. Fast as a bolt of lightning, with all the strength he possessed, his fist slammed into Belankov's jaw.

Belankov toppled like an oak tree to the stable floor.

"For my mother, and for Lady," said Dov. He looked down at the Golden. "Guess now we can check off 'Exploded in Rage, and Punched Someone' today, too," he murmured.

Then the boy and his dog walked slowly from the stable without looking back.

CHAPTER 63

BECKETT'S CABIN

They sat on the bedroom floor in front of the fire, facing each other, bare toes touching. Wintry late afternoon light flowed through the French doors. The fire's embers threw flickering red patterns across their skin.

Reaching to pull her face closer, Beckett leaned forward and kissed her lips slowly.

Maggie smiled into his eyes. "What was that for?"

"Don't need a reason to kiss a beautiful woman."

"True. But I know that look. You're keeping something from me."

He held her eyes. "If you don't ask, then I won't have to lie to you."

"You're protecting someone, then. Dov? Robbie? No. Sugarman."

"How do you do that? Make me feel like I'm driving a fast car without a steering wheel."

She rubbed her toes against his. "It's a gift."

"You're not going to like it."

"Do you?"

"Hard no. Sugar thinks we should use our wedding as a trap for Dane."

Maggie nodded slowly. "It sounds like him. We all know Dane is not finished with me. He will try again. And Sugar is an 'end justifies the means' kind of agent. Using the wedding to trap Dane would be a good plan if –"

"If there weren't family, friends and kids at risk. Especially the kids – your grandson, Dov, Frankie. Just for the record, I told him that you and I would never put a child in danger. For any reason."

"For any reason," she echoed. "But that doesn't mean Sugar's idea wouldn't work. We just have to look at it another way. I wonder…"

Beckett grinned, reached out to grasp her behind the knees, and pulled her toward him. "I like the way you think," he murmured against her neck. "What say we take this conversation to the bed?"

She wrapped her knees around his waist, pressed closer. Skin to skin. "What say we keep this conversation right here on the floor?" she said, her voice a whisper in the half-dark.

That night, in the dusk-filled hour before dinner, Dov, Finn, Robbie, Beckett and Shiloh gathered in front of the fire.

"Feels good to be here," said Maggie's father, gazing at the circle of men. "Where's my daughter? Cooking dinner?" He grinned as laughter filled the room. "Well, the apple didn't fall far from the tree," he chuckled. "Take-out it is. Better than kale salad any day. So, what have I missed since Brittany?"

"How much time do you have?" smiled Robbie.

"I hear Dov decked Belankov today," said Beckett, leaning toward Dov with a grin. "Guess those boxing lessons paid off."

"It was a good day," said Dov simply. Shiloh, half asleep on the floor, gave a low woof of agreement.

"You're not my Best Men for nothing," said Beckett.

"Your Best Men want to know what Belankov told you," said Dov.

"That makes four of us," said Robbie, including the Golden with a glance. "How did your meeting with Sugar and Belankov go?"

Beckett lifted his shoulders. "Belankov is still convinced Dane is planning something. Something *big*. No news there, we all agree. The question is, *what is he planning?* Sugar wants to have all his security in place by tomorrow night. For him it's all about protecting Maggie. The trouble is, she doesn't see it quite that way and I –" Beckett stopped speaking as Maggie entered the room.

Looking at their faces, she arched an eyebrow. "Something's going on. Anything I should know?"

"No." All four men responded at the same time. Shiloh turned away to gaze innocently into the fire.

"I'm going to ignore those sheepish, guilty looks," said Maggie, "because we all have to talk. Michael and I have made a decision, and we hope you will agree."

Maggie gazed at the quiet, stunned faces staring at her. "I take it the vote is a unanimous *yes*," she said. "I knew we could count on you, so I've already made the calls. My son and his family have canceled their flight, Gerard and Frankie will stay out of harm's way in Cancale. Everyone understands that this is a *postponement*, for everyone's safety. I just couldn't take a chance that the people we love the most could be hurt because of me."

"So, there will be no wedding four days from now," said Finn into the sudden silence. "But we all continue to act as if the celebration will take place. And Sugar will be waiting when Dane shows up."

"That's the plan," said Beckett. "Sugar will be here, but we won't." His eyes found Dov and the Golden. "But right now, it's a beautiful November night. And since you all are here… well, it would be a shame not to celebrate with our officiant and my Best Men. I just happen to have two gold rings in my pocket."

Smiling, Maggie stepped forward and held out black bow ties to Dov and Shiloh. "Meet on the deck in ten minutes," she whispered.

Maggie stood just inside the French doors, her hand on her father's arm. Outside, across the deck, Beckett waited with Robbie and his Best Men against the backdrop of the mountains he loved. Candles flickered, the small firepit glowed with warmth, stars pierced the high dark sky.

She glimpsed her reflection in the door's wavering glass, saw the new confidence in the eyes that gazed back at her. You are taking control of your life again, she told herself.

It was a good plan. They couldn't stop Dane from heading to Virginia, but now there would be no risk of danger to the people they loved. They would celebrate all together when it was safe.

Her father pressed her hand and reached for the doorknob. It was time.

She saw Michael turn, his stony eyes glinting only for her.

She gazed one last time at the woman in the shimmering glass, her face framed by grandmother's veil. "I feel you with me tonight, *Grand-mère*," she murmured. "I am going to walk through that door and into a new family, a new life."

Smiling at Beckett, she stepped into her future.

CHAPTER 64

BECKETT'S CABIN

The clock on the cabin wall chimed ten p.m. Robbie, Fin and Dov sat around the fire, talking softly, enjoying a final coffee, and watching the embers glow deep red in the shadows. Shiloh dreamed against Dov's crossed boots.

Maggie, curled on the sofa against Beckett, stood slowly. "It's been a night to remember," she said, "and I know you all are tired. But I have one more surprise. Something beautiful and meaningful to share with you."

She moved to the piano. "My grandmother Clair sent me a wedding gift," she said with a smile soft with memory. "She could no longer play the piano, but she could still compose." Maggie held up a score of music. "She composed a piano concerto, telling the story of her life. The story of all the women who stood up against the horrors of war. I'd like to play it for you tonight."

She sat down at the piano, set her grandmother's score on the frame, and closed her eyes. In the men's sudden silence, she heard the expectancy – the sound of listening. Then she began to play.

The concerto's first movement was in A Minor, that most sorrowful of keys, chosen to describe the emotions of war. In a very personal musical challenge, Clair had written most of the technical difficulty for the left hand.

The opening six bold chords began with the fateful, ominous tolling of bells, then cascaded dramatically down into the confusion and fear, the conflict and determination of the Resistance. The inhumanity of the camps. Treacherously difficult runs soared up and down the keyboard, creating a haunting, heartbreaking lament of anguish, suffering and loss. Complex and astonishing, Clair ended the movement with fading dissonant chords that trembled with chaos and despair.

The much slower second movement, an Adagio in D-flat Major, was poignant and tender, introspective, and stirringly beautiful. Clair told the story of her love for Charles and The House of Echoes in music that was lyrical and joy giving, sensual and passionate. The underlying heart of the melody, like a thread woven through the music, was the whisper of the sea and the long sigh of the wind.

Finally, in the valiant notes of the third movement, Maggie's grandmother celebrated survival with bravura, life-affirming chords. The piece began with an explosion of impassioned notes, with leaping right -hand runs and fierce, thundering left-hand chords. A virtuosic cadenza spiraled with courage, honor and invincibility. The final notes were heroic, as freedom and hope for the future echoed into the darkness.

Maggie fought for breath as her hands stilled on the keyboard. The room was silent. When she raised her head, she saw that all four men had tears on their cheeks.

Her father stood up slowly, gripping the chair for balance. "Your mother would have been so touched and proud, Maggie-girl," Finn whispered into the silence. "Your grandmother's music tells not only her own story, but the story of war – of cruelty and sacrifice, courage and survival. Her concerto will go out into the world and move humanity with its passion and hope."

"Thank you, Dad," said Maggie, touched beyond measure. "You all just had the great honor of hearing the premiere of *Des Échos dans le Vent*, Echoes on the Wind, composed by Clair Rousseau Claymore. My grandmother. It's the story of her life."

CHAPTER 65

Saturday, the original day of the wedding, came and went with no sign of Dane. Beckett's cabin remained dark and empty. Sunday was quiet as well. On Monday, Agent Simon Sugarman and his team packed up and headed back to D.C., leaving only one agent behind. Beckett and Maggie returned to the cabin the following day, after a brief but romantic honeymoon at the beautiful Goodstone Inn in Virginia.

It was still dark the next morning when Beckett and Shiloh stepped cautiously out onto the snow-covered deck. Huge flakes swirled from the black sky, obliterating the lake and mountains in a blowing curtain of white.

"Glad you woke me, big guy," said Beckett in a low voice. "I trust your instincts, I feel it, too." He lifted his chin to listen. The moan of the wind, eerie in the pine branches. The warning whisper of the snow. Then, the heavy silence. The sense of waiting. "Yeah, something just doesn't feel right."

Shiloh moved closer to Beckett, head lifted, senses alert. "Should have brought the M18," muttered Beckett, gripping the small service revolver he'd taken instead from its locked box hidden in a kitchen cabinet.

Beckett stopped. "There," he whispered, gesturing toward footprints near the stairs, rapidly disappearing in the snow. Shiloh sniffed the air, bristling, but stayed quiet. They moved together through the blinding flakes toward the edge of the deck.

A body, under a light dust of snow. Sugar's one remaining guard. *Sweet Christ.* Beckett bent, searched for a pulse. None. The man was cold, had been dead for some time.

"Okay," said Beckett. "Dane's made his move. We've got to find him before he–"

The Golden was the first to sense the danger, lunging to his left with a snarl. Beckett, his immediate instinct to protect, spun toward his dog. A flash of light in the trees, a muffled *pop. Damn!* Beckett twisted away, felt a searing pain on his left side, as if he'd been punched. *Christ that hurt. If the bullet didn't kill him, Maggie would.*

"Shiloh," he whispered. He tried to say *Get to Maggie, protect her* but the words would not come.

His last thought was, *He wanted me out of the house.*

The white air went darker and darker and he felt himself falling to the snow.

Just after dawn, Maggie stood at the window, gazing at mountains clothed in swirling white snow.

I love being married, she thought.

Behind her, the bed was empty. She blushed, remembering Michael's hands on her body in the darkness just hours earlier. His mouth tasting like bourbon and music. An early riser since they'd met, he was probably downstairs making coffee.

For his wife.

Maggie held out her left hand, the thick gold wedding band catching the lamplight. She smiled, remembering their small ceremony on the deck just days earlier. We pulled it off, she told her reflection in the window. And, oh, it was beautiful.

Maggie gazed at her grandmother's lace veil, still draping the bedside chair, and smiled as all the tender moments unfurled once more in her head. People she loved, gathered together on the intimate, candlelit deck with its breath-taking view of the mountains at sunset. Her father, holding her arm tightly as they walked across the deck. Robbie, so elegant and eloquent, giving his blessing. The Best Men, Dov so handsome and Shiloh proudly sporting his new black tie. And Michael, with all the love she could hope for in those deep, fathomless silver eyes.

You come at me from all directions, Maggie. You remind me of everything that's bright and good in this world. You've taught me to let another person into my heart. To lead with my heart once in awhile. Like now. These words are coming from deep in my blood, darlin'. I love you with everything inside me. I want nothing more than to live with you, Dov, and Shiloh here in the shadow of the mountains for the rest of my life."

I am married, she thought. To the man I love. To his son. To his dog. To this world of green mountains and star-filled skies and lakes the color of silver. Not one big thing but a million little things…

She turned, reached for her robe. God, she needed coffee. What was keeping Michael?

And then, somewhere downstairs, she heard the shattering of glass.

CHAPTER 66

In his suite at the historic Willard Hotel on Pennsylvania Avenue, Yuri Belankov awakened from a sound sleep.

"What the hell?" he murmured into the darkness.

The digital clock said 5:22. Too early to get up. Too much vodka the night before.

But something had jolted him awake. A dream? A nightmare? A sound? The TV flickered on the desk, it's volume off. He sat up, rubbed his eyes, his jaw throbbing painfully. The kid packed quite a punch.

Think. Something important, hovering just on the edge of his consciousness. *Think!*

It had to be about Dane. Somehow, stopping him had become personal. A Russian would not be bested by a psychopath, eh?

He knew that Maggie's canceled wedding day had come and gone without incident. He'd had his own men at the cabin, working side by side with Sugarman's security team.

Dane was nowhere to be seen. Somehow, he'd known the wedding was off.

But that was days ago. Why did he feel so uneasy this morning?

He closed his eyes. So. Dane's grand plan to disrupt the wedding, whatever it was, had been thwarted. Ruined. What would I do if I were Dane? Yuri asked himself.

Think chess, he thought. When one piece cannot be moved, move another. Chess is ruthless. You've got to be prepared to kill people.

And then it came to him. *I know what woke me,* he thought. *I know what I would do if I were Dane. If I'd been tricked.*

Patience. Wait for another move to present itself.

But how would Dane do it? He would need help. Firas was no longer an option.

A blur of white against the windows. The predicted snowstorm. Yuri blinked. *Predicted.* The perfect cover.

He leaped from the bed, reached for his pants.

He had to get to the ranch. Dov should be there by now, with the horses. Somehow he sensed the boy would have the answers.

He was dialing Michael Beckett as he ran to the elevators.

Father Robbie Brennan awakened at dawn in his quiet Georgetown bedroom. He usually slept well, but now he missed the sounds of the ranch. Horses, therapy dogs, the Vets. Much more sound and movement than he was used to.

It was still dark beyond the window but the glass was fogged with white crystals. In the distance, the low roar of a plow. It must have snowed in the night.

Okay, he would give himself ten more minutes to fall back to sleep. He closed his eyes, intent on morning prayers, but his thoughts drifted to the ceremony several nights ago. Everything had been beautiful for Maggie. Maybe he'd had too much wine, but it had felt so good to be among friends. Now, if only –

Church bells broke the silence. Six a.m. Dov was probably already at the ranch, in the stables with Lady and the other mares for the early chores. Robbie missed the easy way they'd fallen in to having breakfast together.

He was just maneuvering his legs to the edge of the bed and reaching for his wheels when his cell phone rang.

Yuri and Robbie found Dov in the barn. The boy stared at them, suddenly motionless with the realization that something was wrong.

"Thank God you're all right," said Robbie into the silence.

Blue eyes locked on the priest. "Padre?" whispered Dov. "What's happened?"

"Nothing yet," said Yuri, his hand on his purple, throbbing jaw. "But I have a bad feeling that something is *going* to happen. Today."

"Did you call the colonel?"

"Straight to voicemail."

The three men looked at each other. Not good. "Tell Dov what you're thinking," said Robbie.

Yuri stepped closer. "We all agreed that Dane would choose the wedding to make his grand statement. Show up with a curse like the Wicked Queen in Sleeping Beauty, eh? I asked myself what I would do, if the wedding didn't happen. If I'd been tricked, humiliated, after all my planning. If I didn't have the chance for my very public revenge."

"Dane had to be enraged," said Robbie. "And more determined than ever to cause violence."

Dov's body jolted. "Jesus, he's been waiting for Beckett and Maggie to return to the cabin? We have to get to them! Shiloh is there, too. What if –"

"Hold on, Dov. Not without a plan." Robbie gestured at Yuri.

"Somehow, Dane knew the wedding was canceled. We've been assuming he was working alone. But Dane has had serious injuries, we know he's needed help in the past. When he threatened Maggie in the Vineyard, and later in Brittany, it was with the help of a Greek thug named Firas."

"But Beckett told me Firas is in France awaiting trial," said Dov.

Yuri nodded. *"Da.* So Dane had to find someone else, after Brittany. Someone who could come here well before the wedding, gain your trust, do Dane's work from the inside. Like the missing piece on a chessboard, eh?" Yuri turned to Dov. "The ranch is the perfect cover. Who started working here in the last few weeks? With the animals, or maybe in the kitchen, office, gym? Physical therapy, Infirmary?"

Dov shook his head. "No one. I know all the men and women now. They would never hurt the colonel."

"What about a disabled Vet new to your program? Training with the dogs, learning skills?"

"I don't know many of the clients," said Dov.

"Wait." Robbie eased his chair forward. "The kids! Your friends, the boys who come to play basketball after school."

Dov froze. "There is one guy who just moved here. Cady. Seems okay, but..."

"But what?"

Dov blinked. "Well, Cady's the only guy Shiloh growls at."

Yuri stepped closer to the boy. "Has this Cady been to the cabin?"

"Yeah, study group. He likes photography, like me. Offered to help me take photos at the wedding, but I—*Jesus!"*

"What is Cady's full name?" asked Yuri in an odd voice.

"Cady? Short for Cadmus, I think. He has one of those unpronounceable last names."

"Cadmus was a Greek hero who slayed monsters in mythology," said Robbie. "Cady is Greek. Like Firas."

"Oh, fuck me, I told him we didn't need him for photos, the wedding was cancelled," whispered Dov. "And yesterday I told him Maggie and Beckett were headed back to the cabin..."

"That's it," said Yuri, turning toward the exit. "Crazy bastard has been lying in wait. And whatever he's planning, he's got help to make it happen. I'm going to the cabin. Call Sugarman, and keep calling Beckett, tell him–"

"Like hell," shouted Dov. "The Padre can get to Beckett, I'm going with you!"

The Russian stared at him. "No time to argue, *khrabryy chelovek*. Come if you are coming."

They ran together toward the SUV.

CHAPTER 67

BECKETT'S CABIN

Maggie locked the bedroom door, ran to the window. The glass was a thick wall of white. Was that the howl of a dog, over the wind? Heart pounding, she dialed Beckett's cell. Dead.

God, Michael, where are you? She took a deep, hurting breath and dialed 911. The blizzard was bad, they told her. Lock the door and stay put, they would get up the mountain as soon as they could.

Okay, she was on her own. But *stay put?* No way in hell. Just don't panic. You can do this. Dov was at the ranch, thank God. She and Beckett had been alone at the cabin with Shiloh.

The wind flung ice crystals against the window. Frantic, she pulled on heavy pants, a sweater, boots. Down jacket, scarf, hat. Slipped her phone deep into her pants pocket.

There were back stairs to the kitchen. If she could just get outside she could –

Another sound! A footstep. On the stairs?

God, God.

Find a weapon. *The closet!*

She ran to the closet, pulled the metal gun box down from the top shelf. Locked. Keys! Please, please let Michael's keys be on the bureau. She spun around. *Yes!*

Somehow her shaking hands managed to fit the key into the lock.

She'd only fired a gun once in her life, two years earlier in the South of France just after she'd met Michael. The pistol was cold, heavy, unfamiliar in her hands. *Hands made for music,* her brain hammered wildly. Not violence.

No hope for it. She had to get to Michael and Shiloh. She'd seen Michael load the pistol some months earlier. Locking the slide, she inserted the magazine.

Like her grandmother Clair, she would do what she had to do to protect those she loved. Nothing changes you so much as loving someone, she thought. *Who am I now?* There was no answer in the trembling silence.

She turned and ran toward the back stairway.

Maggie stood on the snow-covered deck, crystal flakes swirling like a white shroud around her. Suddenly disoriented, she peered into shifting shadows, trying to get her bearings. "Michael?" she whispered. No movement, no answer. Listen, she told herself, lifting her head.

The wind sighed around her, trees crackled with ice. And then she heard it, the soft whine of the Golden. There! To the left.

She fought her way through the snow, following Shiloh's call. Where, where?

Moments later she saw the Golden pressed against a low, snow-covered body. Her heart shot to her throat. *Oh, God, please.*

She stumbled forward, fell to her knees, brushed the snow from Beckett's pale frozen face. "Michael!" She shook him, felt for a pulse. *Thank you God.*

Shiloh, refusing to leave his colonel, had lain on top of him for warmth. "Good boy," whispered Maggie, shaking off her down jacket and draping it over Beckett. "Thank you thank you, you are my hero." Desperate, she rubbed Beckett's face, his arms. Something wet, still warm, a coppery smell, on his left side. She looked down at her fingers. Dark red. He'd been shot.

Somehow she remembered the phone in her pants pocket, turned on the light, tried to turn his body. Where was the blood coming from? There. Between his arm and his chest. She bent closer. His arm. Thank God. Tearing off her wool hat, she pressed it hard against the wound. Scarf next, tying it in a tight tourniquet just above the pulsing wound. The flow of blood eased.

"Good, Michael. Just hang on."

Once more, fingers shaking and slippery with blood, she dialed 911. "*Yes*, I called earlier from Colonel Michael Beckett's cabin up on the ridge. There is an armed intruder here, the colonel has been shot. We need an ambulance *now*, and police. Please hurry, the colonel is on the back deck."

She was turning off the phone light for safety when Beckett gave a low groan.

"I'm here, Michael," she whispered. "Shiloh, too. The ambulance is on its way. Just hold on."

Clutching her phone again, she texted Robbie. *Dane at cabin, send Yuri. NOT Dov, danger!*

A siren pierced the distance. Then she heard the voice, over the siren and the moan of the wind. The low, sinister whisper that still broke into her dreams.

"Magdalena… Where are you, my Magdalena?"

Oh God. She gazed down at Michael's still face. *What should I do?* How can I leave him? Maggie closed her eyes, knowing in the depths of her heart what her grandmother would have done for those she loved.

Dane would come back for Michael, if only to make her suffering greater. No. She had to get Dane away from her husband.

She eased Shiloh's single front paw onto the scarf, pressed it down. "Keep your paw there, darling boy. Yes, that's it. Don't leave him, Shiloh. *Stay*."

The Golden settled closer, never taking his mournful eyes off Beckett's face.

Maggie bent to her husband and kissed his cold lips. You never know, she thought suddenly, when something is happening for the last time. Tucking her coat close around his head and body to keep him warm, she kissed him once more and whispered, "I will always love you, Michael."

Then, with one final nod at the Golden, she ran off toward the woods.

At the tree line she stopped. "You'll never find me, you sadistic bastard," she shouted into the swirling storm, daring Dane to come after her.

Then she turned and disappeared into a forest of white.

Yuri skidded the SUV around the last turn and the cabin came into view.

"Oh sweet Jesus," murmured Dov, staring at the flashing lights of an ambulance.

"We will find your family," said Yuri, driving the SUV as close to the cabin as possible and parking next to the ambulance. Before he turned off the engine, Dov jumped out and ran toward the door.

Loud, frantic barking erupted from behind the cabin. "Dov!" shouted Yuri. "I see them, they are on the deck out back. You go there, I will search the cabin."

Dov turned and ran through the snow toward the lights.

"Colonel!" he cried, pushing past an EMT to get to the man on the stretcher. "Colonel, I'm here, what's happened to you?" Shiloh appeared at his side, pressed his face against Dov's hip. Dov spun to the EMT. "How is he? How's my dad?"

"GSW to his left arm," said the medic. "Grazed his chest. Six inches to the left and he'd be gone. But your dad will be fine.

Someone stopped the blood loss. With a hat. The dog did the rest."

Dov closed his eyes, touched Shiloh's head gratefully. And then, "*Someone* helped him?" His eyes fell on a silken patch of blue at the foot of the stretcher. "That's Maggie's jacket! Where _"

At that moment Yuri Belankov ran from the shadows. "No one is in the cabin now," he told Dov, "but someone broke in. Colonel Beckett! Where is Magdalena?"

"Maggie," whispered Beckett, eyelids fluttering. "Need to find..." His eyes closed.

Suddenly, behind them, a deep, muffled blast shook the earth. Crimson flames flared in the cabin as the downstairs windows shattered and a cloud of black smoke blocked out the snow.

A stunned moment of silence.

"Fire!" shouted Yuri. He spun toward the boy. The cabin or the woman?

Dov locked eyes with Yuri. No question. "There's a well and hoses by the garage," he shouted to the emergency team. Then he bent to the Golden. "Find Maggie!" he commanded.

With one final look at the colonel, Shiloh turned and loped off toward the woods, Yuri and Dov close behind as the sky above them turned to scarlet.

CHAPTER 68

THE BLUE RIDGE MOUNTAINS

Inhale. Exhale. Inhale. Exhale.

She was running through a world of white. Where was Dane? *Follow me, you bastard.*

He had injuries, he could not move quickly. She could outrun him so easily. But she wouldn't. It was time to end this nightmare. I need to be done with him forever, she thought. Once and for all.

She came to a clearing, moved behind a tangle of thick pines, their branches cloaked in snow. Slipping Beckett's pistol from her waistband, she waited.

Scanning the forest, she saw a red glow in the sky beyond the treetops. Dear God. *What had Dane done?*

Maggie looked down at the gun in her hand. He has to be stopped, she told herself. *It has to be me. The one who's lost so much because of him.*

One minute. Two. Three.

The whisper of the wind, the hush of falling snow. Then, the sharp crack of a twig. To the left. She held her breath.

Dane stepped slowly from the trees into the clearing. He was limping, breathing heavily. He stopped, dropped a bulky backpack to the snow and bent to unzip it.

Clutching the pistol in both hands, Maggie stepped from behind the pines. "Don't move! Do not take anything from your backpack. I know you have a gun. I won't hesitate to shoot you." She pointed the M18 toward him.

"Ah, Magdalena, you know me so well by now." Dane gave a rictus smile. "As I know you." Ignoring her words, he held up a handgun, then tossed it theatrically to the snow. "Because of you, I only have sight in one eye now. My aim is off, the gun no use to me. I was aiming for your colonel's heart, but... I should have used my knife."

She stared at him, sickened. Was he unarmed now? *Just pull the damn trigger.*

"This will work much better." Dane pulled a heavy-looking object from the canvas and set it down on the snow. It was the size and shape of a child's football, black and metallic. Malevolent.

Maggie felt a cold sense of dread wash over her.

"Yes, you realize what this is, of course. A specially built bomb, state of the art. A grenade, if you will, only much more powerful. A touch of the code on my phone will set it off. *Boom!* I left one in the cabin for you, too, one final wedding gift. The bombs were meant for your wedding day, Magdalena, everything was planned. I had help, someone on the inside. The bomb was to be hidden on the deck. But you disappointed me. Again. So, here we are."

A bomb at the cabin? *Michael.* But he was outside on the deck, he had to be okay.

The wail of a siren sounded in the distance and Dane raised his head, an animal scenting the air. "That ominous and fearful owl of death," he quoted softly.

Stark fear flooded through her. *I am going to die.*

She gripped the pistol with both hands, but was shuddering so hard that she could not aim. Just keep him talking, she told herself. Help is on the way.

Maggie stared into Dane's disfigured face.

He stared back at her and smiled.

Horror-stuck, she closed her eyes. "I've always tried to find the good in people," she said into the silence. "But after everything you have done to me and the people I love...My God, what you have done to the people *you've* cared for! There would have been *children* at my wedding, Dane. I cannot find the good in you."

"Because there is none to find, Magdalena," he rasped. "I was a good person once, I think. But he disappeared a very long time ago."

She clutched the gun more tightly. "We have to take responsibility for who we are *now*, Dane, for who we've become. We are adults, no longer children. You have chosen your path, and the consequences. The guilt is yours alone."

"Enough! I am finally done with this life. 'Tired with all these, for restful death I cry.'"

He raised his phone in front of him, waved it toward her, threatening.

Time stood still.

"*Boom!*" he whispered once more.

She aimed at his heart and pulled the trigger.

Everything happened at once, in terrifying slow motion.

Shiloh burst into the clearing, followed by Yuri, and leaped at Dane with fangs bared. Dov ran straight to Maggie.

"The wheel has come full circle! " shouted Dane, pressing the ignition button.

A bright flash of hot searing light, an explosion like thunder. A scarlet ball of fire. The clearing shattered into a thousand burning crystals. Maggie screamed, wrapping her body around Dov to shield him just as he reached for her. They were flung backwards, falling together to the snow. Protecting each other.

Something hard and sharp slammed into her head. Above them the sky surged with red, roaring like a hurricane. The air swirled with smoke and ash and flaming embers as shards of metal fell like black snow around them.

Gripped by swelling panic, Maggie clutched Dov against her chest and whispered, "Help me, *Grand-mère*. Help me to be brave."

For a moment she thought she heard her grandmother's voice, from a great distance, like an echo in the flame-stirred air.

Don't be afraid, I'm with you.

The world became a kaleidoscope of color. Then the burning sky swooped down. Everything disappeared.

CHAPTER 69

THE BLUE RIDGE MOUNTAINS

Maggie tried to open her eyes. Blinded by blood, and the flash of the explosion, she swiped at her face. "Dov!" she called, frantic. "Shiloh!"

Silence.

The air smelled like smoke and blood, sickening her. Oh, God, please. "Dov, where are you?"

A movement next to her. Dov sat up slowly, reached for her shoulder. "Maggie?"

Thank you, God. "Tell me you're okay," she whispered, touching his face.

"Just disoriented," he breathed. "Maggie, the Colonel is okay! The EMTs are with him, he's going to be fine. But there was a fire in the cabin, I don't know if – " He stopped. "Your head is bleeding."

Michael was okay. She sat up slowly, trembling, her ears ringing like cymbals. Nauseous and dizzy, she closed her eyes against the hammering pain in her right temple. "Just find Shiloh. Help is coming, I'll be fine."

"Shiloh and Yuri tried to stop Dane," said Dov, his voice a jagged whisper. "But the bomb…"

A sharp, familiar bark to their right. "Shiloh!" Hope leaped in the blue eyes.

"You heard him. Shiloh is alive, his bark is strong. But he needs to know you are okay. Go to him, darling."

Shrugging off his jacket, Dov slipped it around her shuddering shoulders. "I'll be back as soon as I can." Then he staggered to his feet and disappeared into a flickering curtain of white.

Michael was okay. That was all she'd needed to know. She turned to search the scorched clearing for Dane.

A low moan. There. He was only ten feet from her, lying face up. Ignoring the pulsing pain in her head, she crawled toward him, sat near his shoulder. His one good eye was open, the strange gold iris blurred and staring at her. Bright red blood dripped from the side of his head, staining the snow.

"I thought I saw you die in New York last year," she said, her voice low and scraping. "But I was wrong. This time death is *your* choice. This time I am going to wait. I am going to be sure. I *need* to be sure. It's just you and me now. I can't forgive all the suffering you caused, I don't know if you will ever find the peace you need. But no one should die alone."

He blinked at her, understanding. Then he smiled.

"You will spy my shadow in the sun," he whispered.

They waited together without speaking.

A breath. A breath. A breath.

A long sigh.

Silence.

Maggie felt Dane's neck for a pulse.

For a long moment she sat in the snow, alone, gazing up at the swirling sky.

Then she stood slowly, needing to find Michael. She took a step, another. Staggered. The ringing sirens in her ears rose to a crescendo. The world began to whirl. Then the sky swooped down once more and she felt herself falling into a cloud of white.

Somewhere, a Chopin Prelude was playing.

Maggie opened her eyes and gazed around her. Everything was white. Where was she? Fear brushed her. But then Chopin's notes became colors that spun and fell around her like jewels – crimson, sapphire, a yellow as bright as the sun. Emerald as green as her mother's eyes.

She was surrounded by beautiful, fifty-foot-tall stained glass windows. How had she gotten here? Where was everyone?

"Hello?" she whispered. "Is anyone here? Where am I?"

"I'm here, *ma chère*. You are not alone."

Her grandmother's voice.

"You are in the Chapel of Saint-Chapelle in Paris, my darling. I first came here when I was thirteen. We still lived in Paris then, the war was just starting." Clair's voice was soft with memory. "All those beautiful pieces of stained glass...*Père* asked us – your *Tante* Elle and I, and so many of our neighbors – to help remove all the glass fragments and wrap them in paper, so the windows could be hidden and safe from the bombing."

Maggie felt the reassuring touch of her grandmother's hand on her brow.

"I was very frightened of the coming war. But *Père* told me to have faith, that I would return here one day to see the stained glass windows back in the chapel where they belonged. He said beauty and goodness could not be destroyed."

A close, warm breath on her cheek.

"Many years later, even though I could barely force myself to leave the cottage, my dear husband insisted that I take one last trip. He brought me and your mother Lily to Paris to see the stained glass windows that had finally been restored. It was so beautiful, Maggie. The colors made me think of music – the way I felt when I played the piano. There was still beauty and goodness in the world, *ma chère*. My life had come full circle."

Full circle. Maggie gazed around the chapel. Suddenly the music began to fade, the colors disappearing into great clouds of white silence. "*Grand-mère?*" she whispered. "I can't hear the music now. I'm so afraid."

"The music will not be gone forever, *ma chère*. It will give you a long life, rich with beauty, compassion, passion and love — for your children and grandchildren as well. Look for me in the music, my darling Maggie. For *there is no love without an echo.*"

Her grandmother's voice grew fainter, vanishing into the white cloud.

Somewhere a strange voice shouted, "We're losing her!"

Maggie felt herself following her grandmother, spinning, falling into the deep stillness.

Suddenly another voice, deep with love and need, broke through the vast silence.

"Dammit, Maggie, come back to me!"

CHAPTER 70

"Dammit, Maggie, come back to me! Open your eyes. Stay with me, darlin'. *Maggie!*"

The sound of his voice, saying her name, woke her. Maggie slowly opened her eyes. The world was spinning, her head was pounding. The taste of smoke on her lips. Flashing red lights, blinding her. Beckett was bent over her, his face inches from her, his silver eyes fierce with worry and love.

"Welcome back," he said.

Michael. He was here. Everything was going to be okay. She lifted her hand, touched his face. "I was dreaming,"she murmured. "Or – maybe it was a memory of a story my mother told me, long ago..."

He brushed the snowflakes from her forehead, smiled down at her.

Another memory, Michael lying in the snow. "You got shot, damn you. Again."

"Only my arm this time, darlin'." He shifted his left arm to show off the sling. "Thanks to you, my fierce Maggie. The cabin took a worse hit than me. But you have a head injury, darlin'. The EMTs are taking you to the hospital." The crooked grin. But there were tears on his face.

Head injury? Maggie tried to focus. She was on a stretcher. Snowflakes spiraled down from a splintered sky.

More memories rushed in. An explosion. A sharp stab of fear. She struggled to sit up, fell back. "Dov? Shiloh?"

"Easy, darlin'. Dov is fine, Shiloh too. They're together, Maggie, they're heroes. The bomb exploded away from Shiloh and Yuri. Toward you."

"Yuri was there?"

"He was hurt, don't know how bad, he's on his way to the hospital. I owe him."

His voice was coming from far away. She shook her head to clear it, felt the sudden sharp jackhammer of pain.

"Cabin?" she gasped. "Preludes?"

"Don't try to talk," said Beckett, bending closer. "Fire's out, downstairs a mess. I told them to save your grandmother's music first, darlin'. But the rest of it is just *stuff*. What matters is that you, Dov and Shiloh are okay. Shiloh has some cuts and bruises, but he's going to be fine." A hesitation. "Dane's body shielded him. Talk about irony."

"Dane is dead. It's finally over."

They locked eyes.

"Tell me you didn't try to kill him, Maggie."

She could barely hear his words. "I did what I had to do," she whispered. "I didn't want it to be you."

"Should have been. But Dane's bomb ended his life, Maggie. Not you. It's the way he wanted it."

"Is the nightmare finally over?" she whispered.

Beckett's lips moved in answer but the sound in her head became a discordant clang, a screeching hammer on metal, cutting off his words. "Can't hear you," she murmured, brushing at her right ear. *Was this how Beethoven had felt when he could no longer hear his music?*

Her lips tried to form the word she needed. "Scared," she breathed.

Beckett bent until his forehead touched hers. Against her ear, he said, "You don't have to be scared, darlin'. We can rebuild the cabin, we can get through anything together. We have each other.

We have the stars." His voice wavered, broke. "Dov called me his dad. His *dad!* He took that damned bracelet off, Maggie. We're a family now, we need you."

"I love you, Michael." Had she said the words out loud?

"And I've loved you since the first time I set eyes on you in that Paris cemetery. We didn't come this far to lose each other now. You're the best thing that's ever happened to me, Maggie." He blinked, swiped at his eyes. There was a look on his face she had never seen. "I've got you, this is not the end for us. I love you more than you can imagine, darlin'."

The ringing became the tolling of great bells filling her head. *I love you more than you can imagine.* They were the last words she'd heard him say. You never know, she told herself once again, when something has happened for the last time.

Michael slipped his arms around her, held her close. She felt his mouth, warm against her lips. His kiss tasted like forever.

Then the stretcher beneath her began to move. She felt herself lifted, saw the snow-filled sky tilt above her, then disappear. Saw Michael's lips moving, his eyes locked on hers.

Stabs of bright crushing pain in her head.

A sudden silence, deep as the snow, enveloped her. Dear God, how had Beethoven gone on when he could no longer hear his beloved music? "I'm so afraid, *Grand-mère*," she whispered. "I can't..."

Don't be afraid, I'm with you. Her grandmother's voice, like the low notes of a cello against her ear. *You can do this, Maggie. You are strong, you are a survivor, just like me. You will make your beautiful music again, I promise. Just choose love over fear.*

Maggie closed her eyes. You are your grandmother's granddaughter. She thought of Chopin, and her grandmother's music. Grasping the locket around her neck, she began to play Clair's concerto in her head. *Listen to the music in your heart,* she told herself. *Hear it.* You can do this. Beauty and goodness can never be destroyed. Hold on, don't let the music go…

Beneath her, the vibration of wheels, movement. But no siren, no sound.

Just the beauty of her grandmother's music in her head – fierce, brave, life-affirming. Invincible. She was falling, flying, diminuendo and crescendo, the notes a kaleidoscope of brilliant colors spinning through her mind.

Look for me in the music. Once more she felt her grandmother beside her. The music was like time and memory unfurling over the decades, echoing down through the years. On and on. She saw the cottage on the edge of the sea, felt the wind touch her cheek. She heard her mother's laughter. Saw her son, holding her blue-eyed grandson. There, her father, conducting Beethoven's *Eroica*. Her music shop in Boston, with its beautiful purple-paned bow window. She saw a darkened stage, where a grand piano waited for her. Dov and Shiloh, in the stables with Lady. Breathed the scent of the forest in the morning.

And then she saw Michael's face. *I love you more than you can imagine,* he'd said.

We can get through anything together, she thought. There is no love without an echo.

I will choose love over fear, Grand-mère. I will be okay, I promise you. Filled with new hope for the future, she smiled, falling into the music. Listening.

Very slowly, the last chords of the concerto dissolved one by one, until there was only the echo of Michael's words on the wind.

Love. Love. Love.

Love.

ACKNOWLEDGMENTS

I am most grateful to my seven early readers – the people whose thoughtful comments, insights, suggestions and support made Echoes on the Wind so much better: Susan Braun, Gail Crockett, Anne Isotta, Sue Kinsler, Deborah Schiff, Kaye Schmitz – and my husband, Ron Mario.

Once again, I want to acknowledge – and express my heartfelt appreciation for – our service men and women and their families, for their remarkable patriotism, bravery, strength and sacrifice. Colonel Beckett and Simon Sugarman could not have "come to life" without their stories and inspiration.

A special thank you, also, to Stella, the beautiful three-legged rescue dog I met in Sarasota, FL, who was the inspiration for Shiloh.

I am beyond grateful to my friend Madeira James of Xuni.com for designing the beautiful cover, just as I imagined it.

Finally, a very personal thank you to David Ivester and his team at Suncoast Publishing for their remarkable publishing and writing skills, and love of books. Thank you for believing in Maggie's story.

AUTHOR'S NOTES

Thank you for joining me in Maggie's world.

Once again, I wanted to create characters with depth, paint pictures with words, and draw readers in to Maggie's story. And, whenever possible, to make the reader feel.

Even after the publications of *The Lost Concerto, Dark Rhapsody,* and *Shadow Music,* I felt that Maggie's story was still not done. And so Echoes on the Wind was born. But as with any series, the main characters – and the author as well – must change and grow. In the writing of this book I gave myself two new challenges: Because of my interest in World War II, I wanted to create a Dual Timeline with strong Historical Genre chapters woven in with Maggie's present. And, because I always have said that '*Music tells our stories,*' I challenged myself to tell the story of Maggie's French Grandmother Clair through the music of Chopin.

In the World War II chapters, I made a decision to name my two main French women characters Clair and Elle. With apologies to my French-speaking readers, I know that the feminine Clair is spelled with an 'e' in France – Claire – and that Elle is not a woman's name but the pronoun for 'she' or 'her' in French. I chose my characters' names to honor my two beautiful granddaughters, Clair and Ellie.

I always have believed that the right setting can truly enrich a scene. There are some places that just speak to you – and the coast of Brittany in France is such a place. Echoes on the Wind was inspired by a beautiful painting in my home, an oil by the French artist M. Vezinet that depicts a small white cottage set on the edge of a wind-swept sea. Its title is *L'Automne en Bretagne* –Autumn in Brittany. I could see Maggie, and her grandmother, standing there.

The most important aspect of writing a Dual Timeline is authenticity, which requires countless hours of research. I owe a huge and heartfelt thank you to the stories, courage and inspiration of three remarkable women: Jeannie Rousseau, a young French woman who survived Ravensbrück and was 'one of the most effective, if unheralded, spies of World War II'; Edith Eger, a trained ballerina who survived Auschwitz; and Hélène Podliasky, a French woman who was forced to walk miles on a harrowing Nazi death march after her concentration camp was evacuated. I am grateful, as well, to the New York Times for their many pieces about the people, places and events of World War II France. Finally, I need to mention that one of Clair's scenes in Part 2 is based on the true story of Oradour-sur-Glane, a French village totally destroyed in June, 1944.

You may be interested to know that, like Firebird, The Lost Concerto, Dark Rhapsody, and Shadow Music, proceeds from sales of Echoes on the Wind will go to non-profit organizations that benefit our most vulnerable women, children and families, via the Helaine and Ronald Mario Fund. Royalties will support inner city food banks, education, health and shelter, with an emphasis on Reading, Art and Music programs for children. A list of these organizations is included on my website, HelaineMario. com

If you have enjoyed getting to know Colonel Beckett and Shiloh, and are interested in learning more about PTSD and animals helping veterans, here are several websites for more information:

https://www.ptsd.va.gov/public/ptsd-overview/basics/what-is-ptsd.asp

K9s for Warriors: www.k9sforwarriors.org

Paws for Veterans: www.pawsforveterans.com

And, of course, the music.

As many of my readers know, my son, Sean, was the inspiration for Maggie's vocation and her beloved classical music pieces. For those of you who love classical music or simply want to hear these pieces, I'm re-listing below several of "Maggie's favorites," including, now, the music that tells Clair's story in Echoes on the Wind.

Bach – Cello Suites (played by Yo Yo Ma)

Beethoven – Moonlight Sonata

Beethoven – Piano Concerto No. 1 in C Major

Beethoven – Piano Concerto No. 5 in E-flat (The Emperor)

Beethoven – Concerto in D Major for Violin

Beethoven – Symphony No. 3 in E-flat Major (The Eroica)

Chopin – Piano Concerto No. 2 in F Minor

Chopin – Ballades, Nos. 1 – 4

Chopin – Heroic Polonaise

Chopin – the 24 Preludes (Introduced in Echoes on the Wind)

Chopin – the 27 Études

Dvorak – Cello Concerto in B Minor

Grieg – Piano Concerto in A Minor

Khachaturian – Toccata in E-flat Minor

Liszt – Hungarian Rhapsody No. 2 in C-sharp Minor

Mozart – Piano Concerto No. 19 in F Major

Mozart – Piano Concerto No. 21 in C (associated with Elvira Madigan)

Prokofiev – Piano Concerto No. 2

Rachmaninoff – Rhapsody on a Theme of Paganini

Rachmaninoff – Piano Concerto No. 2 in C Minor

Tchaikovsky – Piano Concerto No. 1 in B-flat Minor

Tchaikovsky – Concerto in D Major for Violin

Vivaldi – The Four Seasons

And finally, a 'Spoiler,' so if you did not finish this book, please read no further. But for those of you who have read this far and are wondering, after reading the final chapters of Echoes on the Wind, if Maggie's story is truly finished – the good news is that there is one final Maggie book being written. My plan is to share Maggie's story with Alexandra Marik, the art curator and single mom introduced in my only stand-alone suspense novel, Firebird. Alexandra, too, needs to have her story resolved, and these beautiful, smart, brave women are the perfect match. The working title of Maggie #5 is Red Orchestra. Please check my website for updates – HelaineMario.com

A most heartfelt thank you to all my beautiful readers for loving Maggie all these years. Her stories are for all of you. I am grateful beyond measure.

Meet
HELAINE MARIO

Best-selling author Helaine Mario grew up in NYC and is a graduate of Boston University. Now living in Arlington, VA, this mother of two, grandmother of five, and passionate advocate for women's and children's issues came to writing later in life. Her first novel, *The Lost Concerto*, won the Benjamin Franklin Award Silver Medal. *Echoes on the Wind* is her fifth novel and the fourth in her Maggie O'Shea Classical Music Suspense Series. Royalties from her books go to children's music and reading programs. Helaine recently lost her husband, Ron, after 57 years together. Her new book echoes with loss, grief and, ultimately, the healing power of love.